Pulse

ALSO BY MICHAEL HARVEY

Brighton

The Governor's Wife

The Innocence Game

We All Fall Down

The Third Rail

The Fifth Floor

The Chicago Way

Pulse

A Novel

Michael Harvey

An Imprint of HarperCollinsPublishers

This book is a work of fiction. References to real people, events, establishments, organizations, or locales are intended only to provide a sense of authenticity, and are used fictitiously. All other characters, and all incidents and dialogue, are drawn from the author's imagination and are not to be construed as real.

HarperCollins books may be purchased for educational, business, or sales promotional use. For information please e-mail the Special Markets Department at SPsales@harpercollins.com.

FIRST HARPERLUXE EDITION

ISBN: 978-0-06-286119-1

HarperLuxe™ is a trademark of HarperCollins Publishers.

Library of Congress Cataloging-in-Publication Data is available upon request.

18 19 20 21 22   ID/LSC   10 9 8 7 6 5 4 3 2 1

Human madness is oftentimes a cunning and most feline thing. When you think it fled, it may have but become transfigured into some still subtler form.

MOBY-DICK
Herman Melville

Pulse

PART I
1970

1

Heavy hands pull him from a skim of sleep, a blind scramble for the door handle and the backseat of the car, vinyl rough on his face as he's dragged across it. He wriggles like bait on a hook, cold air pimpling bare skin, the mouth of the trunk grinning wide and deep. And then he's dropped inside, a blur of features flashing at the edge of the frame before the lid slams shut and the voices recede and he huddles against a spare tire, smelling the cold rubber and grease, retreating into the womb while the radio gets turned up and the voices rise and fall, bubbles of laughter giving way to a gentle rocking in the springs, low moans in rhythm, building.

He hears his mother's sigh, long and circling down, whispering her pleasure, whispering her sadness, whis-

pering her fear, whispering apologies to the son she'd never see again. A second voice breaks the surface, a man's, muscular and pulsing, calling Daniel's mother by her first name as he wraps his hands around her throat and claims her life.

"Easy now, Violet." The man speaks like he strangles, in smooth, velvet strokes. "Little more, little more. That's it. Now, down you go."

And then it grows still. A rattle of keys and the dry cough of an engine. The car begins to roll, picking up speed as it tumbles forward. Daniel pulls up his legs and kicks at the wall of the trunk with both feet. As the car goes airborne, the eight-year-old is birthed all over again, this time into the backseat of a '58 Buick.

Daniel Fitzsimmons opened his eyes and scanned the bumpy terrain of the schoolyard, the fall of the gulley that led to the street, faces in the windows of a bus as it toiled past. When you're different, really different, you know it. You wear it like a second skin, one you'd give anything to slip even if just for a moment. But you can't. You're inside the game and the game's inside you and it runs your head and messes with your mind and there's no way back, no way forward, no map to "normal." No matter what anyone tells you. At least not in this life.

He'd known all this before he was ever capable of knowing. It worked in his blood like a fever, surging and ebbing, keeping him off-balance, at odds, adrift in a sea of shifting depths. Then his mother died. And no one suspected the truth but him. No one ever would. And now he was ten.

He'd never been much of a talker. After the crash and the hospital and the rest of it, his world shrank to a single point—just him and his brother. Barely a word for well-meaning foster parents, cow-eyed teachers and counselors. Not a scrap for any of the kids in any of the schools. It wasn't a surprise then that he had no friends. And if you had no friends on a schoolyard in Dorchester, you sure as hell had enemies.

Joey Watts was older. Thirteen, fourteen. Big, dumb as a hog, hard in the chin and eyes. Suspicious, greedy, scared of the world, and pure bully. He came up behind Daniel as he sheltered against a wall, waiting for the bell that would take them into class. Daniel could feel the bully's approach, tracking it in his head in some way he didn't yet understand. Watts stopped a few feet away, measuring. Then he stepped forward and popped Daniel's cap off his head. Watts snickered. Three of his pals were watching and snickered as well.

"Freak," the bully said.

"Fitzsimmons the freak," his friends echoed.

Daniel bent for the black-and-gold Bruins cap. His hand found a rock, hard and smooth, shaped to a purpose. Daniel gripped it and felt its curve while something stirred in his chest, something ancient and evil, blessed and sublime. The young warrior in him wanted to strike out even as the old man within counseled patience. The enemy still lay hidden, not yet ready to be named.

Daniel let the rock slip from his fingers and picked up the cap. As he straightened, Watts lashed out again, catching Daniel in the ribs with a boot. He fell forward, pulping his face against the pavement and splitting his lip to the meat. He tasted blood rich in his mouth and heard his mind whisper as it whirred, spinning fast, stopping at the nexus of a certain time and a certain place. The pale sun shifted behind some clouds and the air grew bitter. Daniel wiped his face and raised his eyes to his tormentor, piercing him to his essence, fixing him to his fate.

"You drowned her. You didn't mean it. You were just being mean. But you did it."

In a stroke, Daniel had slipped inside Joey Watts, two now one. He saw the bully as a boy, in the summer of his eleventh year, standing nipple deep in the cold waters of the Quincy quarry, pushing down on the head of nine-year-old Jeannie Jameson. Daniel watched her mouth fill as she went under for the last time, felt the grim thrill that coursed through Watts's body as the little grub thrashed and kicked and her life streamed away in a string of tiny bubbles. And then everything blurred, a final fingernail scratching the back of Watts's wrist before her limbs went soft and sloppy and sank.

"You watched them try to revive her on the rocks," Daniel said. "And then you left with your pals."

He reached out to touch Watts, but the boy reared back, nostrils flaring, a wild look in his eyes. And then he ran, the others with him. No shame was so great they couldn't bear, anything to be distant from those eyes and the god-awful truth that lived therein.

Twenty years distant, Joey Watts would climb over a railing on the upper deck of the Tobin Bridge during rush hour, take one look at the pale-ribbed water below, and jump like a motherfucker. In his studio apartment, the cops would find a woman dead in a bathtub along with a note about Jeannie Jameson and that summer day at the quarry. They'd also find Daniel's initials scrawled all over the walls. No one would ever make heads or tails out of that part of it. No one ever could.

The playground in Dorchester was empty; the wind stilled. A bell tolled, calling Daniel to class. By the time he slipped into his seat, he'd chalked up the whole thing with Joey Watts to his imagination. The lead in his belly, however, told a different tale. Whatever had taken hold of him was still there, submerged in the blood, waiting.

Six years later, it would resurface.

2

1976

The apartment was above the Rathskeller, a Kenmore Square dive known to the locals as the Rat. If he'd been older, the name might have given him pause, but Daniel was all of sixteen and the price was right. So he pulled the index card off the window, tucked it in his gym bag, and trudged up a staircase decorated with trash that looked like it had blown in off the street. At the top of the stairs was a plain wooden door with no name, no mailbox, and no doorknob. Daniel banged on it with the heel of his hand only to hear an audible click as the door swung in.

The apartment was a surprise—old-school Victorian with waxed floors that smelled like cut lemons and heavy, double-pane windows framed in their original woodwork and finished with brass fittings. A clock ticked away the time on a wall, its hands reading ten o'clock even though it was well past two in the afternoon. Nearby a silvered cat with one eye of cobalt blue and the other glassy white stared out from a shelf. The cat flexed his long back and leaped through a ribbon of sunlight, landing noiselessly on a desk before winding his way through stacks of paper and disappearing behind a pile of books. An old-fashioned turf fire smoldered in a blackened fireplace. The reeky smell mingled with a hint of pipe smoke, giving the room the feel of Galway or Mayo circa 1880. A shabby couch and soft leather chair completed the picture, huddling for warmth around the hearth while a table to one side held the fixings for tea and coffee.

Daniel moved tentatively to the center of the room. He was as awkward as a teenager got, tall and scrawny with pale oversized features, a scattering of acne, and long brown hair curling at the ends and trailing out over a hooded gray sweatshirt that had BOSTON LATIN printed across the front in boxy purple letters. He turned once in a circle, taking in the layout before drifting over to the desk and picking a piece of paper off one of the many stacks.

"Can I help you?"

Daniel could have stood in the room until day gave way to night and never noticed the person who spoke. So perfectly had he painted himself into the contours of the wall he was leaning against that it wasn't until he moved before the boy could actually put form to voice. Or, rather, shadow to voice.

"The door was open." Daniel pulled out the index card with pieces of Scotch tape stuck on each corner. "I'm here for the room."

The shadow moved like, well, a shadow. The voice seemed to be everywhere. "Your name?"

"Daniel. Daniel Fitzsimmons."

"Irish?"

"Yes. Does that matter?"

"Course not. Take a seat." An open hand directed Daniel to a chair. He sat while his host moved behind the big desk and settled, steepling his fingers and holding the tips to his lips. By the muted light of the window, Daniel got his first good look at the man. If he'd been more self-aware, or not so self-aware, Daniel might have noticed the man's eyes, pulling energy from whatever they touched, or the skin around the edges of his face, like butter someone had smoothed over with a knife.

"My name is Simon Lane," the man said. "But you can call me Simon."

"Okay."

Simon gestured impatiently at the index card Daniel still held in his hand. He slid it across and watched two veins that crisscrossed in the man's forehead.

"You want the room?"

"If it's still available."

"I wouldn't have left the card up if it weren't. Hmmm, maybe you won't do."

"Do for what?"

"You go to Latin School."

It was more of a statement than question so Daniel didn't respond.

"Not as old as I'd like." Again more statement than question, but this time inviting a response.

"I'm eighteen."

Simon held up a finger, crooked at the middle knuckle. "Lie."

"Seventeen."

"Won't do. Won't do at all."

"I'm sixteen. I know, it's young."

"To a person who dies at fifteen, it's an eternity. Did you think I wouldn't give you the room because of your age?"

"I wasn't sure."

"Are you a runaway? No, of course not." Simon nodded at Daniel's sweatshirt. "Where is Latin School, by the way?"

Daniel pointed vaguely out the window. "In the Fens. Avenue Louis Pasteur."

"Yes. And what year was it founded?"

"Sixteen thirty-five."

"And what book must every sixie read? And when you answer, please preface by explaining to me what a sixie is."

"A sixie is a seventh grader at Latin. He's got six years to go before he graduates. And the book we all have to read is called *Breeder of Democracy*. It's the history of Latin School."

"Boring as sin, right?"

Daniel nodded.

"See, your bona fides is established. Not a runaway. Just a local seeking a place to sleep. The rent is fine?"

The room had been advertised at fifty dollars a month. Incredibly cheap.

"The rent's great."

"Yes, it would be. Any questions for me?"

"How old are you?"

"I thought you'd ask to see the room."

"That, too."

"I'm twenty-three years older than you, Daniel. Give or take." Simon opened a desk drawer, then another, mumbling to himself as he rummaged. Daniel half expected him to come out with a runny candlestick, holding it aloft like some moth-eaten character from a Dickens novel. Instead, it was a flashlight.

"Out here by the windows isn't bad, but once we get into the hallway, the lights are hit or miss. Come on." Simon led the way toward a kitchenette tucked into the back of the room. There was a sink, a stove, a refrigerator, and a butcher-block countertop with two stools. Daniel saw a couple of plates and mugs in an open cabinet.

"Do you cook?"

Daniel shook his head.

"The refrigerator's there if you want to use it. Just leave me some space."

They reached a door cut into the wall next to the sink. It opened to a long, narrow hallway that smelled of damp. Simon snapped a light switch up and down to no avail. "I'll fix that." He clicked on the flashlight and moved it along the passage. At the far end were two more doors.

"Those are my rooms. I work in one and sleep in the other." Simon pointed at each door with the light.

"You're at the other end. Bathroom's between us. This way."

For fifty bucks a month, Daniel didn't expect much, and he wasn't disappointed. Bed, dresser, mirror, and a tiny window that looked out onto the redbrick face of a building across the alley.

"All right?" Simon poked the light at Daniel, who held up his hand and squinted.

"Does the electricity work in here?"

Simon grunted and reached up to pull on a cord. A naked bulb dropped on a wire from the ceiling cast a wavering glow over the room.

"How's that?"

"Great."

"So you want it?"

Daniel shrugged. Of course he wanted it. They made their way back to the main room and took their seats again at the desk. Daniel noticed white threads running wild through Simon's dark head of hair.

"Where's your stuff?" he said.

"I don't have much. Maybe I can bring it over later?"

"Fine." Simon produced an envelope from the top drawer. "Two keys. The gold opens the door down-stairs. Usually you can just push it in, but sometimes the lock works. The silver opens the front door to the apartment."

"There's no doorknob."

"Just push that one in as well. Don't look so horrified. I've got a deadbolt on the thing."

"How do I leave?"

"There's a little handle on the inside. Works fine. You thinking of moving in tonight?"

"Probably. When do you need the rent?"

Simon waved at the notion. "Whenever. I'll get a bulb for the hall. You want tea? Good. Let's sit over here."

Simon directed Daniel to a seat on the couch next to the fireplace and walked back to the kitchenette, where he filled a kettle with water. The man was tall, big hands, knotted muscle for forearms. Not someone who worked out a lot, but possessing a natural strength that would serve him well should he ever need it. He put the kettle on a burner and returned to the main room, settling in the easy chair and once again studying Daniel over tented fingers.

"I work mostly at night in the rooms you saw at the end of the hall. That's my private area, just as your room is private. We'll share this common space. Fair enough?"

"Sure. If you don't mind me asking, what do you do? For work, I mean?"

"I'm a professor at Harvard. Well, I used to teach there. Theoretical physics."

"I'm taking physics now."

A dry smile flitted across Simon's lips. "You like science?"

"I guess. What's that?"

To one side of the fireplace was a small easel with a sketchpad on it and some pencils. Simon brought the pad over.

"I dabble. Chalk, pencil, the occasional acrylic. This is a beach at night. It's half finished."

The sky was the color of pitch, with a moon dipped in red and hanging low, casting pale bars of light across wet sand and sheening the hard, black water. A tarred road wound up from the beach, dotted with snarled trees and tufts of dark weeds. Vague white lumps grew out from the road here and there like soft tumors. The sketch still needed to be shaped and left Daniel uneasy. He was happy to hand it back to its owner.

"It's not very good," Simon said.

"I like it."

"Really?"

"Kind of creepy, but maybe that's what you're going for?"

"Maybe. If you want, I'll give you a look when it's done." Simon flipped the pad to a blank page and returned it to the easel. The kettle had begun to whistle. He went back to the kitchen and fixed them each a cup.

Daniel's was the way he liked it, strong with milk and three sugars. He took a sip and set the cup down on a low table next to a folded copy of the *Boston Globe*. Simon moved the *Globe* to one side and picked up a copy of the *Harvard Crimson* that was tucked underneath. The article he showed Daniel was from last summer, a preseason piece about the Crimson's All-Ivy running back, Harry Fitzsimmons.

"That your brother, Daniel?"

"How did you know?"

Simon blew on his tea and took a sip. "There's a resemblance."

"Really?"

"More than you think. I assume you don't play football?"

"Too skinny."

"Still, you're an athlete. I'd guess runner. Long distance, maybe? Mile in the spring, cross-country in the fall?"

"You haven't been reading about me in the papers."

"It's your shoes." Simon nodded at Daniel's running shoes, blue nylon with yellow laces and white racing stripes down the sides. "Tigers. Japanese racing flats. Bad sneakers, but great if you're a runner."

"You're not supposed to wear them as sneakers."

"Exactly. Then there's your body type. All legs and lungs. You're not as good at longer distances, but the strength will come. And then you'll be very good, if you want that."

Daniel returned the paper to the table. "I like to run."

"But not race? Compete?"

"I didn't say that."

"Hmm." Another sip of tea.

"Tell me about theoretical physics."

Outside, a spasm of rain drummed against the windows and was gone. Simon put down his cup and pulled a pipe from his pocket. "You mind?"

Daniel shook his head.

"Love a good pipe. This one's a Dunhill Bulldog. Here, you can see the markings on the bowl." Simon turned the pipe over. On the underside were stamped the words:

DUNHILL   MADE IN

SHELL BRIAR   ENGLAND4

"What does the '4' mean?" Daniel said.

"That's how Dunhill dates their pipes. The baseline for this series is 1960. Add on whatever number is stamped there and you have the year the pipe was made."

"So this one's from 1964?"

Simon winked as he packed the bowl and lit it with a wooden match. When he had it going to his satisfaction, he sat back again and took a couple of puffs. "Beautiful draw." His mumbles were lost in a layer of smoke and the scent of ripe berries. Daniel didn't mind a bit and allowed his mind to float. There was a banging on the stairs below and then it grew quiet again. Simon's voice cut through the fog.

"What were we talking about?"

"Theoretical physics."

"Of course."

"Do you have a specialty?"

"Most of my work's in the field of quantum mechanics."

"The study of subatomic particles."

Simon pulled the pipe from his mouth and pointed the stem at Daniel. "They teach you that at Latin School?"

"I read it somewhere."

"I study the quantum state. Specifically, I focus on a phenomenon known as entanglement. Ever heard of that?"

"No."

"Einstein first flagged it in the 1930s. Called it 'spooky.'"

"Is it? Spooky, I mean?"

"Hell, yes." Simon leaned forward so his long face was bathed in licks of red from the fire, except for the circles around his eyes, which were black with white at the very center. It should have been frightening, but Daniel felt entirely at home, as if he'd been in the room with the smell of tobacco and old books, the glow of the turf and windows closed to the weather outside for most, if not all, of his sixteen years. That was how Daniel felt as he took another sip of his tea and wriggled his toes in his Tigers and waited to hear about the professor's research.

"Imagine," Simon said, pausing to issue a stream of smoke from one side of his mouth, "that you have a charged electron isolated in this room, sitting on this very table between us, and another electron sitting on the edge of the Milky Way, a hundred thousand light-years away."

"Okay."

"Now, imagine that the two particles are entangled—that is, in an entangled state."

"What does that mean?"

"Hell of a question. Let's think of it this way. If I rotate the electron sitting on this table, say, a half turn to the left"—Simon used a thumb and forefinger to spin his imaginary electron—"its entangled companion will turn that exact same amount to the right." Simon sat back to gauge the effect of his words.

"So the two particles are communicating?"

"No. Well, yes and no. That's the spooky part. In our hypothetical, if the two electrons were actually communicating, even if they were communicating at the speed of light, it would still take a hundred thousand years for that signal to travel across the galaxy, correct?"

Daniel nodded.

"In an entangled state, however, the change between the particles happens instantaneously."

"So the signal is traveling faster than the speed of light?"

"It would appear that way. And your Latin School physics tells you what?"

"That's impossible."

"Precisely."

"Then what's happening?"

"No one's sure. What we do know is this—for the period of time that our two particles are entangled, they move in concert regardless of the distance between them, as if they were two parts of the same body. For all intents and purposes, they are."

"Are what?"

"One and the same."

"Even though they're on opposite sides of the galaxy?"

"You've studied Einstein's special theory of relativity."

"$E = mc2$."

"Mass converted into energy, the two being essentially interchangeable. I suspect, and I'm not alone, that entanglement is more of the same, except at a level and in a world we don't fully perceive or understand."

"A world? You mean some other world?"

"The universe isn't about the lumps of matter we can see, Daniel." Simon shook his head, trailing more smoke from his mouth and narrow, probing nose. "Stars, planets, animals, people, rocks. Abhorrent, obvious things. No, the universe is about everything we can't see—energy. Beams of the stuff running through everything that is, connecting all creation in an infinite number of impossible ways. Ways that violate what we know, or thought we knew, about the physical world. That's the piano one has to play if one wants to understand quantum mechanics. That's the piano I play, and entanglement is merely the opening chord in the symphony, the first glimmer of what lies underneath. And there's so much underneath. You take Latin?"

"Everyone at Latin School takes Latin."

"The word *conscire.* Translation?"

"'To know.'"

"Literal meaning?"

"'Scio' and 'con.' To know with."

"And it's where we get our word *consciousness*?"

"If you say so."

"Pull out your dictionary and look it up. *Conscire*, 'to know with,' provides the root concept for our idea of *consciousness*."

"I'm not sure where you're headed."

"It's right there in the word. The very act of human consciousness is a communal effort, a shared experience. To know *with* someone. In fact, I contend it would be entirely impossible for a human being to be 'conscious' as we understand the term without at least one other sentient being at the other end to record that fact."

"Because the signal would have no recipient?"

"The signal. That's exactly right. Human consciousness is nothing more or less than a signal, a pulse of energy, and entanglement describes the process by which that energy is transmitted, received, and sometimes manipulated."

"Manipulated how?"

"Einstein again. Energy cannot be destroyed. Either it is transformed into some other state or it gets passed along. You feel anger, you feel hatred, fear, envy. You must learn, we all must learn, to change it into something productive. If not, it will fester and spread, infecting everything and everyone it touches."

"Can you prove any of this?"

"You sound like you don't believe me."

Daniel shrugged. "I thought science was supposed to be all about proof."

"Have you ever heard of Einstein's thought experiments?"

"No."

"He was your age, sixteen, when he first started thinking about chasing a beam of light. He'd sit in his high school physics class and imagine riding up alongside it. If such a thing were possible, Einstein thought, surely the light would appear to be at rest, frozen in time. Later, he'd say it was his first insight into what would become the special theory of relativity."

"I'm no Einstein."

"The point is there was no blackboard in the beginning. No long strings of numbers. No concrete proof. Just a young man and his willingness to open himself up to the tension of the universe and everything it holds. The easy and the difficult. The light and the dark. The good and the evil that lies within it."

For the first time in a long time, Daniel thought about the playground in Dorchester and the feeling when he'd slipped inside Joey Watts's skin. And then Joey was there, sitting in the room along with Jeannie Jameson, dripping water and smelling of the quarry, staring at Daniel with her slack mouth and her fish eyes.

"What is it?" Simon was peering at him through a lazy circle of smoke. A smile sharpened the edges of his lips.

"Nothing."

Simon nodded and puffed, the mutter of Kenmore Square traffic distant in the street below. When the apartment buzzer rang, it was sharp and raw, scattering Daniel's soggy childhood pals and nearly knocking him off the couch. Simon padded over to the front window.

"Oh, hell." He slammed the window open and leaned out. "I told you tomorrow. Hang on." Simon went back behind his desk.

"Maybe I should go get my stuff," Daniel said.

Simon looked up. "Sorry, it's this student. He dropped out of Harvard and is heading back to California. Guy's nuts for computers. Stays up all night writing source code. You know anything about that? Never mind. I told him I'd give him something to play with. You say you'll be back tonight?"

"If that's okay?"

"Sure, sure. Listen, tell this guy to come up when you go downstairs. Name's Gates."

Daniel started to respond, but Simon was already deep in a notebook, making some calculations. From a bottom drawer, he'd pulled out a small black box with a blue *X* taped across the top. Simon looked up from his work and noticed Daniel staring at it.

"Prototype for a portable computer. I call it a laptop. You ever heard of internetworking?"

Daniel shook his head.

"Right now, it's just a few universities connecting on mainframes. But this thing"—Simon tapped the top of the black box—"this is the game changer. Of course, it's child's play compared to what we were talking about, but Gates asked if he could take a look. You got your keys?"

Daniel nodded, but Simon was gone again, popping open his prototype and typing on what looked like a keyboard. Daniel left the apartment, walking back down the stairs slowly. Gates's first name was Bill. He was grad-student thin with horn-rimmed glasses and a wild mop of ginger hair. He offered a friendly if curious smile and brushed past as Daniel told him to go up. Then Daniel was alone on the street.

He jogged across Commonwealth Avenue and cut through the Kenmore Square bus shelter. On the corner a man was grilling hot dogs at a stand painted mustard yellow. Business was good, the line five deep, customers with bills in hand, shifting back and forth in the cold, going up on their tiptoes to get a look at the dogs cooking shoulder to shoulder with thick links of Italian sausage and German bratwurst. Next to the stand sat a spaniel mix at full attention, back muscles aquiver, head tracking the cook's every move, a long drool of saliva swan diving off his lower jaw toward the pavement.

Daniel closed his eyes and thought about his new roomie, the slightly crazy, slightly scary professor from Harvard. Maybe they were all wack jobs in Cambridge. Or maybe it was just physics. No wonder Daniel liked the stuff. He smiled to himself and breathed through his nose, exhaling as a door in his mind swung open. He found himself untethered, adrift in a cream of fog, dark shapes zooming up and whispering past. Ahead a light flickered and grew, dissolving the fog to a thin mist. It was Albert Einstein, Albert the teenager, skimming his way toward Daniel across a surf of colors and numbers, grinning and waving as he rode his beam of light to his destiny. Daniel moved closer, looking up at young Einstein, who held out his hand. Daniel reached for it and fell, weightless, nameless, tipping head over heels into a space devoid of form. Einstein was gone, his beam of light transformed into a ripe, juicy sausage, dripping golden fat and oozing smoke and heat.

Hot dog.

Sausage.

No, hot dog.

No, sausage.

Daniel sat at the bottom of a well, a dog's-eye view, staring up at the man from the stand as the man stared down, something pinched between his fingers. It smelled like gristle and grease and meat. Glorious, wonderful, amazing meat. The prospect of it moved through Daniel like a current, wiggling his body from head to toe and back again. Then the man tossed the scrap into the air, and Daniel rose as it fell, jaws snapping, saliva streaming, belly in full growl.

He opened his eyes. To one side of the hot dog stand the spaniel's butt was up, tail waving as he feasted on leavings the cook had thrown his way. Otherwise, nothing had changed. Unless everything had. He circled closer, scratching the dog between the ears and running a hand across his flank. The dog paid no attention, but a woman in line did. She was staring at Daniel kind of funny, like maybe he'd been barking or howling or foaming at the mouth or something. He flashed a quick smile and hurried down the block.

On the next corner stood New England Music City.

Daniel stopped in front of the plateglass windows and stared at the Andy Warhol cover for *Sticky Fingers*. Next to the album was a pair of dice and the sheet music for "Brown Sugar." Beyond that, the most beautiful girl he'd ever seen in his life or any other. When she smiled, all thoughts of Einstein, Simon Lane, and a dog's life went right out the window. Daniel waved and hustled inside.

3

Like most things in the city, South Boston was all about geography. The place was surrounded on three sides by water and hermetically sealed on the fourth by six lanes of expressway. A virtual island in a city full of them, Southie was the cousin who drank all the beer at your wedding, threw up in the punch bowl, and tried to fuck your sister for good measure on the way out. No one wandered into the place by accident. You were there cuz you grew up there or you knew someone. And that someone you knew better know the guys you were talking to. And they better be on good terms. Sort of like hitting the trifecta at Suffolk Downs, except if your horse didn't come in, there was likely to be a pack of crazy fucks trying to cave your roof in with a piece of pipe or a hockey stick. And that was if you were white and Irish and looked the part. If you were black, well, black people didn't actually go into South Boston, not unless they were under federal order and sitting in the back of a yellow school bus. And wasn't that just fun as fuck.

William Barkley Jones hit his blinker and hung a left. He didn't give a good goddamn what anyone did or didn't do in South Boston, or anywhere else for that matter. He was a black man with a badge and a gun. He was also six-five and north of two and a half bills. If the I.R.A. wanted to go to war, so be it.

Barkley parked on D Street and watched as his partner came out of a corner grocery store. Tommy Dillon was five-nine and a buck sixty soaking wet. Still, he had the strut, the swagger, the *I'm from Southie and if you don't like it, fucking try me* attitude that defined his life and wrote the moment and manner of his death in windswept strokes of gray. But that was for another day. Today, Tommy was sipping coffee from a Styrofoam cup and carrying a paper plate wrapped in tinfoil. He climbed in the passenger's side along with the smell of breakfast.

"Cocksucker bookie had a stroke last week. Can't get outta bed."

"So you're taking him scrambled eggs?"

"And chopped-up bits of sausage. Prick's a hundred

and fucking six. Gums this shit down for dinner. Say a prayer he chokes."

Barkley chuckled and started up the car.

"You think it's funny?"

"More like humiliating." Barkley swept away from the curb. "How much you owe?"

"You sound like Katie."

"How much?"

"A hondo. Bet the Pats last week. Took it right up the ass."

Barkley grunted and tapped his fingers on the steering wheel.

"What?"

"You know you got the monkey, Tommy." Barkley's partner had spent six months in rehab a year back. Gambling, booze. The department didn't know about the coke. If they had, they probably would have shit-canned him, but Barkley covered. And Tommy's wife, Katie, nursed him through the rest. Tommy thought he was out the other side. Barkley wondered if it wasn't past time to look for a new partner.

"Jesus, B. It's a hundred bucks and a plate of eggs."

"If that's all it is . . ."

"That's all it is. Come on. He's in the South End."

They cruised a block that looked just like the last four—three-deckers, two families, all jammed up one against the other. Irish everywhere, mayonnaise faces playing hockey in the street, sitting on the front steps, hanging on the corner, big eyes, hard eyes, flat eyes, gypsy eyes, pointing at Barkley, one little fuck giving him the finger as the big-shouldered car cruised past.

"Assholes," Tommy said.

"Forget it." Barkley blew through a red light and turned onto Dorchester Street. The city was in its third year of forced busing; the protests that started outside high schools in Charlestown and South Boston had metastasized into a pitched battle between a federal judge determined to integrate Boston's public schools and the city's white working class, just as determined to protect their turf and not be told what to do with their kids by the government . . . or anyone else. Last spring Bostonians watched, some in horror, some in grim satisfaction, as a gang of white kids attacked a black man outside city hall, charging at him with the pointed end of an American flag. A photographer from the *Herald* caught the moment and splashed it across the front page. A couple of weeks later, some black kids in Roxbury pulled a white guy from his car and cracked his skull open with a paving stone. A crowd chanted "Let him die" while the cops arrived and EMTs loaded the guy into an ambulance. As the summer of 1976 ground on, the city burned in a blaze of its own making. Residents stuck to their block. Those who did wander into the wrong neighborhood kept their car doors locked and, if they were smart, didn't stop for nothing until they were back on safe ground. For Barkley and Tommy, it didn't really matter. They were homicide detectives and business was good—people killing other people for all kinds of fucked-up reasons. And a bunch of kids going to school in yellow buses didn't change one stroke of that.

"Check it out." Tommy pointed at a blue police bus packed with staties stitched up in their best riot gear. A second and third bus rolled right behind the first as kids began to pour into the streets, congregating in angry knots of muscle and moving in packs.

"What do you think?" Barkley said.

"Gotta be the high school."

"You wanna take a look?"

"Like I don't have enough fucking heartache? Let's go see my book."

Barkley shrugged and wheeled the car onto West Broadway. A mile later, they shot under the expressway and into the South End.

They found a spot on Albany Street, across from a Chinese restaurant called Hom's. A dirty rain slanted across the windshield and was gone as quick as it had arrived. Barkley nodded at a thick silver watch that hung loose on his partner's wrist.

"New?"

Tommy smiled and adjusted the bauble. "Nice, right? Check it out. The band is inlaid with turquoise."

"Katie give it to you?"

"Pawnshop. She likes it, though."

"How long you gonna be?"

"Ten minutes. Fifteen, tops."

"Don't forget your dinner." Barkley grinned and held out the paper plate of scrambled eggs, still covered in tinfoil. Tommy gave him the finger, grabbed the plate, and jogged across the street, disappearing into a fenced-off salvage yard jammed up next to a garage with a sign overhead that read STEVENS AUTO SUPPLY. Barkley switched on the radio and turned up the volume.

WRKO. DJ Mike Addams talking a mile a minute about the lowdown on the hoedown tonight at who the fuck knew where. Fifty-cent drink specials, except for the ladies. They drank free. Barkley switched off the noise and gazed out the window. The South End was a study in urban rot, gently putrefying from the inside out. Halfway down the block a flophouse advertised rooms for seven bucks a week. Next to it was a bar with a 'Gansett sign in the window and no name on the front. On the other side of the bar, a soup kitchen where the boozers could refuel for their next bender.

The door to Hom's swung open and an Asian woman popped out. She was carrying a bag of food in one hand and dragging a young girl with the other. The woman wore a cloth coat and black galoshes with metal buckles. The kid shuffled along in green boots with yellow heels.

Barkley watched as the pair picked their way around a string of trash cans and on down the block. He wasn't the only one. A whisper of a man hung in a doorway, smoking a cigarette and shivering in a jean jacket. He let the woman and child go past, then tossed his cigarette and followed. The woman ducked into a three-decker that looked like it was about to topple into the street. The man went right in after her. Barkley cursed his luck and got out of the car.

Someone had propped open the front door to the building with a chunk of cement. Barkley brushed his hand across his gun. Domestics, loud parties, dogs barking, cat up a fucking tree. It was always the most mundane, penny-ante, bullshit things that got cops shot. He shouldered open the door. To his left, a skylight striped a narrow staircase in prison bars of gray. Straight ahead, the girl with the green-and-yellow boots sat on a small bench, tongue curled between her teeth, working hard with crayons on a coloring book. Barkley squatted down so he was eye level and put a finger to his lips.

"Where's your mom?"

The girl widened her eyes and chewed on the end of a Crayola.

"She in there?" Barkley pointed at a door behind the girl, who nodded.

"That man take her in?"

Her face clouded. Barkley told the girl to stay put and sidled up to the door. He could hear a low bubble of sound that resolved into voices growing louder, more urgent. A man screamed something in what sounded like Chinese. Barkley glanced at the girl, pulled his gun, and pushed inside.

The room looked like it might have once been a garage. Cement floor, high roof with large overhead lights fixed to a double set of steel girders. On one side of the room six dingy Asian men were crowded around a table covered in pai gow tiles and cash, mostly fifties and hundreds. Five of the men were seated. The sixth, the one who had screamed, was standing up, still screaming in Chinese and shaking a golden metal cup over his head. With a final oath, he slammed the cup on the table just as Barkley came through the door.

Tiles and money went flying and some dice tumbled out of the cup. No one, however, was watching where they landed. Why bother with that shit when there was a massive black man sticking a gun in your face?

"Hey, what you want?"

The woman with the buckle boots was smoking a pink cigarette and chewing on an egg roll. The man in the jean jacket sat next to her at an angle. He had a fork full of what looked like chow mein raised to his mouth and a healthy length of noodle hanging from his lower lip. In front of them was a table packed with more cash and a pile of papers. The money was wrapped in rubber bands and organized into neat stacks. Barkley flashed his badge at the woman and lowered his piece.

"Is this your little girl?" Barkley nodded at the girl, who was standing wide-eyed on the threshold. The woman barked something and the girl scurried in, disappearing behind the woman so all Barkley could see were the child's eyes, peeking out from the crook of the woman's arm.

"Bark, what the fuck?" Tommy popped out of a back room, wiping his fingers with a paper towel. "That's Tian Chen." Tommy pointed to the man eating the chow mein. "And his wife."

"Yolanda." The woman offered a limp hand. Her smile looked like an empty pocket.

"Tell them not to leave the kid outside."

"Don't leave the kid outside. They don't speak much English, B."

Barkley holstered his gun and left. Tommy followed.

"Bark."

"Chen's your bookie?"

"I told you my book had a stroke. He's holed up in the back. Yolanda and Chen run the dice and card games. Actually, Yolanda runs them. Real fucking ball-breaker, too."

"So you go in through the salvage yard?"

"Cut down the alley and came in the back."

Barkley paused at the front door to the building. "Lot of cloak-and-dagger for a hundred-dollar bet, Tommy."

"I told you they run the pai gow games in here. Piles of cash lying around and these fuckers are paranoid as shit."

Barkley started to leave. Tommy grabbed him by the shoulder. "It's nothing, B. A hondo. Go back and check with Yolanda."

Barkley walked off. He was pissed at his partner and felt stupid about pulling the piece. More the latter than the former, but Tommy didn't need to know that. A pickup struggled down the street, grinding its gears and belching flourishes of black smoke. Barkley squinted at the machine smell of oil and turned his head just as a woman came out of the Chinese restaurant, her arms full of packages. Barkley veered to avoid her, but she dipped right into his path and the two bumped shoulders. He reached for the woman's elbow as she started to topple into the gutter. She was weightless, hollowed out in the way incredibly old people get even though she was no more than thirty. Barkley noted her hands, marbled in blue, and her fingers, one decorated with a silver ring enameled in red and encrusted with diamonds in the shape of a rose.

The woman slid her hand along Barkley's wrist and gripped it, sending a hot wire up his arm and pulling him in. Her face was Western, smooth and unlined, cheeks touched with powder that smelled like the notes spinning off an old jazz record on a phonograph in a picture hanging on a wall. Then she unhooded her eyes. And Barkley's world exploded.

The concussion was silent, short-circuiting the sparks of conscious thought that arced in his brain while snatching him clean off his feet. He fell through hanging mists of pink and white, bouncing off the plateglass window of the restaurant before landing face-first on the pavement. Except it wasn't pavement anymore. It was wood, old and buckled, rotting and warped, smelling of the sea and salt and hobbled with hard round nails that bit into his cheek. Barkley opened his eyes and recognized the long wobbly run of a pier on Boston's waterfront. Below he could see the harbor, slicked with circles of oil and mottled in lumps of gray and green. The water began to bubble and then something popped to the surface. Bloated, spread-eagled, and floating on its belly, the body sagged like a half-deflated balloon. A wave swept under the pier, banging the naked corpse off a piling and rolling it over and over. In the churn Barkley spotted bits and pieces of what had once been a person—elbow, ear-lobe, a flash of bleached thigh leading to an ankle rubbed raw where it had slipped its tether of chains and anchor of cinder blocks. A seagull blew in sideways, circling the corpse before perching on the meat part of the shoulder. The gull stared at Barkley with a fierce black eye as its claws worked the slack flesh in small, worried circles. The bird took flight again, pushing the corpse so it rolled once more in the wash and set-tled faceup, lolling and bobbing merrily in the lumpy water. Barkley watched as the corpse's blue lips curled into a perfect bow and its eyelids shot open.

"Hey, Bark, what the fuck you looking at?" Tommy Dillon winked as his arm stretched out of the harbor like a bleached rubber band, snaking up a piling and across the pier. Five mossy fingers wrapped around

Barkley's wrist and pulled him over the side, headfirst toward the broken sea where his partner lay in wait, jaws agape, tongue curled, eager to feed, eager to swallow him whole.

Barkley recoiled, head popping off the brick facade of the restaurant. He was back on the pavement in front of Hom's, sitting up while Tommy looked at him all kinds of funny.

"B, you all right?"

Barkley felt for a lump on the back of his head and let Tommy help him to his feet.

"Where's the woman?" Barkley scanned up and down the block.

"What woman?"

"There was a woman coming out of the restaurant." Barkley pointed toward a CLOSED sign in the window.

"They closed up twenty minutes ago, B. I seen you fall."

"Yeah?"

"Looked like you tripped or something. Hit your head pretty good off the side of the building."

"There was a woman."

Tommy shrugged. "What say we go grab a coffee or something?"

They made their way across the street to the car. Tommy wanted to drive. Barkley told him to go fuck himself and took a hard look at the street as he sat behind the wheel.

"We going?" Tommy said.

"You think I'm crazy."

"We're all crazy, B. It's just your day today. Come on. There's a place with good pie two blocks over."

Dispatch popped on the radio. Tommy took down the details as Barkley listened, a dead finger prickling the skin of his soul. Sure as fuck, someone had just pulled a body out of Boston Harbor. He started up the car and spun the wheel into traffic. But it was Fate who was driving. And they were all just along for the ride.

4

She was standing in the ROCK aisle. Albums from artists beginning A–M ran down one side, N–Z down the other. As he got closer Daniel could smell the soap on her skin, see the moisture on her cheek and lashes.

"You're wet," he said.

"Got caught in the rain." Grace Nguyen swung her long mane of hair, catching it with both hands and piling it atop her head. "I've got to get this mop cut."

"I like it."

"Short or long?"

"Just leave it the way it is."

"Easy for you to say. You don't have to brush it and wash it and deal with it." She let the hair drop past her shoulders and clasped his arm, pulling him over to the

"S" section, where she found the new Stevie Wonder, *Songs in the Key of Life*.

"They should have him in the 'W's,'" Daniel said. "Anyway, you like him more than I do."

"Seriously? Stevie Wonder?" Grace widened her eyes in mock horror.

"He's awesome, but I like Bruce. *Born to Run*. And the Stones."

"The Stones. Always the Stones."

"There's nothing purer in rock and roll than the first twenty seconds of 'Jumping Jack Flash.'"

"Oh my God. Let me guess, you saw *Sticky Fingers* in the window?"

"What else you gonna put in the window? We don't have the money to buy anything anyway."

"Yeah, but if we did . . . it'd be Stevie every time." Grace slid the album back in its slot and Daniel swore the minute he got the money scraped together he was gonna buy a bunch of Stevie Wonder albums, wrap them up, and watch her open them. Then they'd listen to the whole stack and he'd tell her Stevie was great but not the best and listen to her explain how he knew nothing about music and she hardly knew why she wasted her time.

"Did you stay for seventh period?" he said.

"Zzzzz." Grace closed her eyes and rested her cheek

on folded hands. "Total snore. We're supposed to finish 'Book 1' by the end of next week."

Like Daniel, Grace was a sophomore at Latin School. They had a lot of classes together, including Latin, where they were in the middle of translating Ovid's *Metamorphoses*.

"Did anyone notice I wasn't there?" Daniel said.

"No, but Hamilton said there's gonna be a test. You wanna get something to eat?"

"Can't. Gotta go for a run."

They spent most days together after school bumming around Kenmore Square. For Daniel, it didn't matter where they went or what they did. He was with her and whatever came next was more than enough. So they'd hit the record store, grab a cheeseburger at Charlie's, rummage through the bins at Supersocks, or just sit on the curb and people-watch. Kenmore Square was great for that—a lot of drifters and panhandlers, hippies and Hare Krishnas mixed in with students, wannabe musicians, and artists living in cheap apartments up and down Beacon Street.

In the summer the show moved to the other side of the Pike and Fenway Park. They'd walk down Lansdowne and sit against the wall outside Gate C. Sully was always there. The scalper from Charlestown wore jeans and a white T-shirt with a pack of cigarettes rolled up old-school in his sleeve. He'd hold his tickets low by his side, making no attempt to get the attention of fans as they floated past. Cool worked better than fine in Boston and the regulars went out of their way to find him, whisper in his ear, and shove money in his hands as if Sully's reserved grandstand were somehow better than the guy selling on the next corner. Daniel and Grace were never looking for tickets, but that didn't stop people from dropping extras in their laps. Sometimes they went in if it was a good game. Usually they just gave them to Sully.

One afternoon they met a kid from Somerville named Dapper. He worked on the grounds crew and asked if they wanted to get into a Yankees game the next night. Grace was on it in a blink. Two hours before game time, they met him outside a service gate Daniel had never noticed before. Dapper shoved a couple of dark green slickers at them and said to put them on, tugging the hood up over Grace's head and tightening the string under her chin. They followed him into the belly of the park, dipping beneath the grandstand, staying quiet and small as Dapper nodded and bullshitted with ushers and concession guys who were stocking up on peanuts and rolling in kegs. He led them down a set of stairs and along a cramped corridor, then up another set. They surfaced in a gangway that opened to a rectangle of light and the baseball cathedral that was a half-empty Fenway Park at twilight. Dapper stashed them in a corner behind some buckets and rakes while he and the rest of the grounds crew got the field ready. The crew knew who they were with and were fine with it. Dapper told them everyone got a turn sneaking in someone during the season and this was his night. Daniel wondered why Dapper would use his free pass on a couple of kids he barely knew, but then Sherm Feller came over the loudspeaker.

Ladies and gentlemen, boys and girls, welcome to Fenway Park . . .

After Sherm, everything spun into another dimension. Daniel felt the weight, the buzz, the Friday night jazz of thirty-thousand plus—first dates, last dates, fathers with sons, guys flashing eyes at girls, loners with their transistors and scorecards, kids like Daniel and Grace, except with tickets and parents and all the rest. They gathered like supplicants, row after row rising up into the night—field box, grandstand, bleachers, kids hanging off the Canadian Club sign in the outfield—welling until they filled the precious and finely cut chalice that was Fenway to overflow, their ferocity and their angst pouring out of the stands, bent toward the destruction and ruin of the hated and hateful Yankees.

Daniel turned his eyes toward the jeweled perfection of the diamond and found himself lost in it—the green of the outfield, bases blindingly white, the soft red skin of the infield. Daniel was sure he could curl up in the hollow of shortstop and never wake up. And then Tiant strolled out of the dugout. Luis grabbed the rosin off the slope of the mound, bouncing the bag across the back of his knuckles before pounding it back to the ground. He started in on his warm-ups, chewing on a cud of tobacco as he threw, kicking at the dirt in front of the mound like a Cuban *toro*. Yastrzemski lobbed grounders across the infield. Closest to Daniel, Rico Petrocelli stood by third, chatting casually with the ump as everything swirled in colors around them. A warm breeze pumped up the gangway, recirculating all the Fenway smells—cigar smoke soaked in draft beer, roasted peanuts in the shell, Fenway franks and Gulden's mustard. A wrapper floated on the slipstream, dancing past Daniel, brushing the edge of the tarp and tumbling toward the infield. The ump talking to Petrocelli saw it out of the corner of his eye and snagged it with his right hand, jamming it into his back pocket without ever breaking stride in the confab with Rico.

Tiant had finished warming up and the ball was tossed around the diamond. Mickey Rivers strode to the plate, Sherm Feller taking a good thirty seconds to announce Mick the Quick's arrival as the crowd rose to its feet. Petrocelli kicked the third-base bag and looked directly at Daniel, touching the brim of his cap and pointing a finger before grabbing a handful of dirt and turning back toward home. Daniel's heart jumped three sizes in his chest. He turned to Grace to ask if she'd seen Rico see him. No Grace. Tiant cut loose. Strike one. In the lee of the crowd's roar came the boom of an usher's voice. He was pointing at Grace, who'd wandered away and was leaning over a small gate that opened onto the field. Even worse, the hood had slipped off her head. Dapper looked back at Daniel as if he were responsible. Daniel had visions of them all being tossed into the deepest, darkest Fenway Park dungeon the Yawkey family could find. Then Grace smiled, a nuclear weapon for sure, and the old usher just melted, right there in the field box section. He waved her back and mimed for her to put the hood back on and tie it tight. She did, tucking beside Daniel and squeezing his hand, thrilling him, thrilling her, probably thrilling the heck out of the usher.

Later, after the Sox had won one-zip on a Tiant three-hitter, after they'd thanked Dapper a dozen times and said good-bye, they walked across Lansdowne to a warehouse that sometimes left a side door open when the janitors were cleaning at night. It was ajar and Daniel and Grace slipped in, running quiet as a couple of Fenway mice up seven flights to the roof and crawling into their usual spot between two huge AC units. Fenway's lights were mostly off, but the moon hung rich and buttery over the park, bathing them in a healing light that gave texture and movement to their postmortem. They went over every moment, laughing at Grace with the usher, talking four or five times about Rico and his nod to Daniel (Grace said she'd seen it—how could she miss it!), sitting quietly and sharing without ever having to say a word. They were two aliens in this world—Grace, a refugee from Vietnam, arriving on a boat five years ago, the only English speaker in her family and a picture-perfect one at that, warm, open, brilliant, and kept at arm's length by the blinding whiteness of the world around her; Daniel, a refugee of another kind, no parents, foster homes, and huge chunks of his life already gone AWOL. His brother had football, Harry's fluency with the game easing his passage. Daniel had no such passport. What he did have was his mind in all its strangeness. And Grace. They had each other and wasn't that a hell of a thing. He studied her in the moonlight that drenched the rooftop and suddenly saw what Dapper from Somerville had seen, why he'd given them the cook's tour of Fenway. Daniel's friend was more than a friend. She was on the cusp of becoming a beautiful young woman. And so the world shifted on its axis and, from that night on, things got a little more complicated, a little more sudden.

"You gonna tell me why you skipped out?" Grace said, snapping him from his reverie as she pulled out another Stevie Wonder album, took a look, and replaced it just as quickly.

"No reason. Just had to take care of something."

She raised her hands and wiggled her fingers on either side of her face. "Oooh, big mystery."

"Hilarious."

"Just kidding. If you don't want to tell me, that's cool."

Daniel's secret pushed him a little closer. "If I tell you, will you promise to keep quiet?"

"Really? You have to ask?"

Why was he hesitating? Of course he was gonna tell her. It was Grace.

"I just rented a room above the Rat."

"Across the street?"

"Second floor. Looks right out over the square."

"Wow. Does your brother know?"

"Gonna meet him after my run. He won't like it, but we've got no choice. If school finds out I'm living in Cambridge . . ."

"They won't find out."

"Still . . ."

"Hey, I think it's great."

"Yeah, it's pretty cool. The guy who lives there is a prof from Harvard. Giving me the room for fifty bucks a month."

Grace whistled.

"I know. Dirt cheap, right? And the place is actually not half bad."

"When can I come over?"

"Tomorrow, maybe. Once I get settled and stuff."

Grace sighed. "My life is soooo boring."

"What are you gonna do this afternoon?"

"I don't know. Go home and work on Ovid, I guess. Call me tonight if you can. We'll go over what you missed in class."

"I'm probably gonna be moving in."

"So jealous."

"Yeah, right." He reached for another album. *Station to Station* by David Bowie. Grace reached at the same time and their fingertips touched. He felt a tingle up his arm while a single star shot across the yawning chasm of his consciousness. He knew it was her. Not him thinking of her, not him pretending to be her, but her, Grace Nguyen, living inside his head. Entangled. She rubbed the edge of her finger against his and the star shivered before exploding into countless particles of spinning light that fell in lovely streams all around him.

"Daniel?"

"What?"

He dared a look into her eyes and saw a thousand different doors that opened to a thousand different rooms and he wanted to explore each in turn. Then she leaned in just the perfect amount, at the perfect angle, in the perfect moment, and kissed him. Perfectly. Right there in the aisle of Music City.

"Why did you do that?" His voice was hoarse and choked with he had no idea what. Grace giggled.

"I don't know. Felt like it, I guess. Why? Was it that bad?"

Daniel shook his head and she touched his arm, her fingers so much finer than his. "Has anyone ever kissed you, Daniel?"

A middle-aged woman saved him, shooting them a murderous look and a "Shhh" from the CLASSICAL aisle. Grace waved at the lady, who sniffed and went back to perusing Bach.

"Probably a cat lover," Daniel said, and they both laughed hysterically for no reason at all.

"I gotta go," Grace said, pulling back but not before pushing a lock of hair behind his ear. "You're very sweet, Daniel."

"Just what a guy wants to hear."

"Shut up and tell your brother about the apartment."

"I will."

"Good. And call me if you can." She walked toward the front of the store, stopping behind the Bach lady to swipe at her back and give her a mock meow. Daniel laughed as the woman turned to see what was going on. Grace booted it down the aisle and out the door.

He watched as she wound her way through the afternoon crowd, stopping once to look back and see if he was still there. Daniel waved. She waved back and disappeared into the subway. Daniel pulled the sheet music for "Brown Sugar" from the front window, then put it back and went over to a case where they kept stacks of sheet music and lyrics. He found Stevie Wonder's "Higher Ground" and took it to the register. Daniel had a quarter for the bus and another seventy-five cents for something to eat. The lyrics cost two dollars, but the kid who worked there knew Daniel and gave him a deal. He took his purchase into the men's room and locked the door. Carefully, he folded up the sheet and placed it at the bottom of his gym bag. Then he changed into a pair of running pants and a long-sleeved Bruins shirt made of lightweight mesh. He pulled on a hat and stuffed an extra pair of socks into his pocket. He'd use them as gloves while he ran. The clerk kept the gym bag with his clothes and the lyrics behind the counter. He'd done it before and had a face Daniel trusted.

Outside he shook his legs and arms loose. A clock on an insurance building across the street read 3:46. He began to run west toward BU's campus and the river. In the first half-dozen strides, all the awkwardness of adolescence disappeared, and the man Daniel would become emerged. Inside his head, however, he was still a teenager and for the first mile all he thought about was Grace Nguyen, his first "real" kiss, and whether or not he'd stacked the deck to get it.

5

The dead man lying on the pier looked nothing like Tommy Dillon. Thank fucking God.

The corpse was long, young, and well muscled. Hispanic, clad in white sweatpants and a long-sleeved BU sweatshirt. The fishermen who'd found him said he'd gotten hung up on a line from one of their lobster pots. They were huddled at the far end of the dock, a clump of yellow and orange slickers giving their statements to a couple of uniforms. Three forensics guys were working on the body. Barkley told them to take a break, leaving the scene to the two detectives. They circled like the jackals they'd become for longer than they'd known.

"How much time in the water?" Barkley said.

"Tech says not more than a couple of hours." Tommy

squatted by the head and stared into the corpse's ear for some godforsaken Tommy reason. "Hispanic, for sure. Maybe twenty-five."

"No pockets," Barkley said. "No ID."

Tommy grumbled and stood up, one knee popping with the effort.

"What's that?" Barkley pointed to a rip in the sweat-shirt.

"Pulled him in with a gaff." Tommy rolled the body onto one side with the toe of his boot. The corpse grinned, a trickle of seawater coming from the side of his mouth and a horseshoe crab crawling out from inside his shirt.

"Two in the head," Tommy said.

Barkley walked around and took a look. Two small-caliber holes drilled into the curve of the skull just above the spine. "Twenty-two?"

"Be my guess." Tommy let the body flop back onto the deck. The sun had sunk down into the harbor and light was going fast.

"What do you think?" Barkley said.

"I think he's a drug dealer, probably an illegal. We'll spend the better part of two weeks beating the bushes and get nowhere. Then we'll shove it into the cold pile with the rest of 'em."

"Love your job, don't you, Tommy?"

They'd been working crime scenes for eight years running. Barkley was the alpha. Did most of the interviews, handled the press, took the heat from the brass if there was any coming down. As for Tommy, he was good at two things. First, he knew the streets better than any cop in the city. His home turf, Dorchester, Mattapan, Charlestown, North End, South End, Allston-Brighton. Tommy had contacts everywhere. And he always came up with a name. Barkley never asked what Tommy promised, or to whom. Looking back, maybe he should have, but he never did. The other thing Tommy was good at was records. Turn him loose in a room full of files and he was a happy fucking camper. Worked fast and, again, did what he did best—sniffed out names, addresses, leads.

"I'll get going on an ID tomorrow. You want to talk to the guys from the boat?"

"Why not?"

Tommy started over to the uniforms. Barkley stopped him.

"About earlier. When I fell."

"I didn't see no woman, B. You just tripped is all."

"When I was out, I had a vision or a dream or some fucking thing."

"Oh, yeah?" Tommy seemed a little anxious and

a little amused. But that's how Tommy seemed with most things.

"I thought I was down here, on the docks. A body came up out of the water. Tied up in chains and shit."

"Fuck me. Look anything like our Juan Doe?"

Not really, Barkley thought. *As a matter of fact, it looked like you, Tommy, your scarier-than-shit face floating in a burp of seawater. How's that, partner? Pretty fucking funny, huh?*

"Bark, you hear me?"

"I didn't see the face, Tommy, but, no, I don't think it was our guy."

"I told you, B. It's the job. Every time I close my eyes at night, the creeping Jesus motherfuckers crawl all over me, up my ass, tickle the balls, right down my fucking throat."

"And you say you got no demons."

"Let's go the No Name. Get a bowl of chowder."

"We gotta talk to the fishermen."

"Chowder, B. Then the rest."

Barkley nodded for his partner to take the lead and watched him walk down the pier, stopping once to joke with one of the forensics guys. Barkley followed quietly in his wake.

6

Harry Fitzsimmons put his fist in the mud and leaned forward, weight perfectly balanced in a three-point stance. His lungs were on fire and his legs felt like lead. Push through. One more. Now. Harry shot forward, keeping low for the first few strides then letting his body rise as he accelerated. The wind pushed at his back, sweeping off the river, lifting as he went. He flew past ten yards, then twenty, floating now, breath and body one, moving in perfect sync. It wasn't until the last twenty that he started to tie up, thighs cramping a touch, lungs spent. The final ten yards were all about form. Lift the legs, pump the arms, lean through the finish. As he crossed the goal line, he popped the stopwatch wrapped in his fist.

"What are you doing them in?" Pat Costello was sitting a few rows up in the end zone seats at Harvard Stadium. Not that Harry had a problem hearing him. Costello coached Harvard's defensive backs. Like most football coaches, his normal tone of voice started at bellow and only deepened from there. Harry raised a hand and bent at the waist, sucking in air as Costello made his way down to the field. He took the watch from Harry and gave it a look.

"Not bad. How many did you do?"

"Two sets of ten at sixty. Before that, forty-yarders." Harry's words came in fits and starts, his breath steaming in the November chill.

"You lift?"

"Couple hours."

"Damn." Costello handed back the watch as Harry straightened, breathing nearly back to normal. He didn't know Costello all that well but had heard good things. The two men took their time, walking across the broken turf toward the players' tunnel. At six two with his buzz cut, brushed wire on top shaved down to bone on the sides, Harry towered over the former Syracuse corner.

"You know the season's over, Fitzsimmons. I mean, you got the memo."

The Crimson had played their final game last weekend, a win over Yale and a second-place finish in the

Ivy League. Harry was a shoo-in for All-Ivy. There was even talk of honorable mention All-American.

"Just don't want to lose the edge, Coach, especially with the cardio. Once you lose it, it's a bitch to get back."

"Yeah, well, it's good to unwind as well. You ready for exams?"

"I should be good." Harry was carrying a 3.8 average and everyone in the program knew it.

"All right, then. Why don't you call it a day? Grab a shower and go home."

"Actually, I told someone I'd meet them here."

Costello grinned. "Girl?"

"My brother, Daniel."

"Didn't know you had a brother."

"He's a sophomore at Latin. After my mom died, we stayed together."

Costello slackened his pace. "Must have been rough."

"We got through it okay."

"Where you living now?"

"I got a place off-campus with Prescott."

"Prescott?" The coach shook his head. Neil Prescott was a backup running back and full-time tool.

"He had a spare bedroom and didn't mind Daniel so it all worked out."

They came to the mouth of the tunnel and stopped.

Costello leaned back with his shoulders and jiggled a set of keys in his pocket. "What do the Fitzsimmons brothers got going for Thanksgiving?"

Harry shrugged. The truth was they had no plans. Prescott was supposed to be heading home, so the apartment would be empty. They'd probably get a pizza and watch football.

"Why don't you come out to the house? We do a big thing. Fifty, sixty people. Lots of food and beer. Tag football game. More of it on the tube. I got five kids, one of whom has your jersey, by the way, and would love to get it signed."

"Thanks, Coach, but we'll probably just bachelor it at the apartment. I don't get to see Danny much with practice and school and everything."

"You sure?"

"Yeah, but thanks. Bring that jersey in and I'll sign it for your son."

"I will. And let me know if you change your mind."

"Will do, Coach."

Harry watched Costello disappear up the tunnel, then took a seat in the stands, tipping his head back and soaking in the emptiness of the stadium. There wasn't anything about football Harry didn't love. Sweat in the summer. Snow and ice in the winter. Cut grass and mud. The snap of the chinstrap and taste of the mouthpiece. Feel of the pads when they got worked in just right. The thrill of hitting and being hit. But mostly Harry loved the locker room. He wasn't a big talker, preferring to lead by example. And he did lead, always first to accept the challenge, first to hold himself accountable whether he deserved it or not. For Harry it was about the team, something bigger than him, bigger than all of them. He'd never found anything else quite like it and knew he probably never would.

He got up from his seat and walked back across the field, pausing for a final look before heading up the tunnel and out of the stadium. Traffic from Soldiers Field Road swept by in a line to his left. Beyond that was the Charles River, slate gray with crests creaming white. Harry worked his way across a patchwork of practice fields. His limbs hung loose in their sockets and there was the pleasant tingling of fatigue settling in his bones. He found a spot in the grass and stretched his legs out in front of him, wind freezing the sweat in his hair and prickling his scalp. He bent forward slowly at the waist, feeling the pull in his hamstrings. All the while he kept an eye focused on a bend in the river.

Daniel appeared as a tiny black wedge. He looked like he was barely moving, but Harry knew that was a lie. He'd run with Daniel many times, but only once in a race—a three-miler in Watertown when Daniel was thirteen. They went out with the lead pack, college runners and older. Harry stayed with the group for the first mile then told Daniel he was going to dial it back. As he dropped off the pace, he stole a look at his kid brother. His face was a mask, no pain, no fatigue, no acknowledgment of Harry's imminent demise. Daniel came in third that day. The next week he started running for Latin as an eighth grader. His times were good enough to qualify for the state cross-country finals, but Daniel never seemed interested in any of that. He'd show up for some meets. Skip others. It drove his coach crazy.

He was closer now so Harry could make out some details. His little brother was wearing a Bruins jersey and a black watch cap with white socks covering his hands. He wore blue-and-white running shoes that flashed as he went, the only indication of how quickly he was moving. Daniel disappeared for a moment, then popped up again, slipping through an open gate and stopping just inside it. He pulled the socks off his hands as Harry approached.

"How far did you go?" Harry said.

"Five, six."

"Why don't you wear gloves?"

"Don't like 'em."

"They make them now for running. Superlight."

Daniel shrugged. His cheeks were stained red and his hair was sopping with sweat when he took off his hat. Otherwise, you'd never know he'd gone for a run. And a hard one at that.

"You work out?" Daniel said.

"Yeah. One of my coaches invited us for Thanksgiving." Harry waited but knew Daniel wouldn't entertain the notion of going. "I told him we were gonna hang at the apartment."

"You can go if you want."

"Hell, no. Besides, we got football games to watch." They began to walk. Harry had an old Saab he'd parked near Harvard's field house. They'd drive back to the apartment. Harry would take a shower first. By the time Daniel got done, Harry would be working on dinner.

"I found a place today," Daniel said.

"A place for what?"

"My own place."

Harry stopped walking. "That's not gonna happen, Daniel."

"Already done. Fifty a month in Kenmore Square."

"What is it? A cardboard box?"

"This guy lives above the Rat. He's got an extra room."

"You're serious?"

"I'm sick of being a mooch."

"You're not."

"I am. Sleeping on the floor of your bedroom. You're gonna have girls . . ."

"I don't have a girl. Besides, that doesn't matter."

"I know it doesn't matter to you, but what about me? I feel like a jerk."

"You're sixteen. You can't be living on your own."

"Yeah, right."

Of course he could live on his own. Daniel could do whatever he wanted. He already had. And they both knew it.

"Who is this guy?" Harry said.

"Actually, he's a professor right here."

"At Harvard? What's his name?"

"Lane. Simon Lane."

"Never heard of him."

"I think he's on sabbatical or something. Teaches physics. Anyway, it's all set. I'm moving my stuff tonight."

"Tonight?"

"Sooner the better. If school finds out I live in Cambridge, it's gonna be a problem."

Boston Latin School was part of the public school system and thus free—provided you lived in the city. Harry had gone to Latin before Daniel, but that didn't really matter. If the school discovered Daniel was living in Cambridge, they could charge him thousands of dollars in tuition. Or maybe just throw him out altogether.

"No one's gonna find out," Harry said.

"You don't know that. And don't tell me you don't get girls. If you're a football player at Harvard and you're breathing, you're gonna get girls. Even a guy who looks like you."

Harry feinted a left. Daniel ducked away, smirking. They walked some more.

"You hate all this, don't you?" Harry said.

"All what?"

Harry raised his eyes toward the stadium, a black bowl outlined against a sky of hard silver. "Harvard, football. All the stuff that goes with all that."

"You know I don't."

"No?"

"I couldn't be prouder of you, Harry. And I couldn't love anyone more than I love you." Daniel shrugged as if that was just as obvious as the breath that moved between them.

"But it's not for you?"

"What's not for me? Your life? Of course not. Your life's yours and my life's mine. But my brother's special. And it's not cuz he's smart or plays football for Harvard. He was special long before that."

"Yeah?"

"The rest of it's just stuff, Harry. Comes and goes, you know? So you're okay with the apartment?"

"I want to see it. And I still want to hear from you every day."

"Sure."

"How you gonna get over there?"

"Red Line. Green Line. Fifteen minutes."

"I'll drive you."

"No, you won't. I'm taking the T. Once I get moved in, you can come over and check it out. Okay?"

"Let's go home and eat."

They walked the rest of the way in silence, the older brother with his head down, younger watching the first, each frozen in the other's echo on the muddy stain of grass. And then they stepped onto the hardtop of the parking lot and the slack tightened, time spinning forward again as Harry found his car and Daniel walked around to the passenger's side. Inside, the windows fogged with their collected breath. Daniel wiped the glass with his sleeve while Harry worked the wipers and they both waited for the heater to kick in. At the apartment Harry made dinner—burgers and tater tots. In the other room his little brother packed his things.

7

It was past nine before they finished on the dock, almost ten when they turned down Tommy's block. There were still plenty of kids out. A handful leaned on their sticks and watched resentfully as the detectives cruised through the middle of their street hockey game. By the time they'd parked, the game had resumed. Pools of light illuminated the action, the frantic chatter of wood against blacktop filling the night.

"Pricks out here twenty-four fucking seven," Tommy said. "Think they're all Bobby Orr or something."

"You were probably the same way."

"My ass." Tommy lived on G Street, a block and a half from where he grew up. Southie bred and buttered. Like a lot of folks born here, the neighborhood was beginning and end. Cradle to coffin. Nothing better, nothing worse. And Tommy wouldn't have it any other way. Not that he ever really had a choice.

"I'll get rolling on Juan Doe first thing tomorrow, B."

"Where you thinking of starting?"

"Run Juan's prints. Make some calls to a few guys I know down at the waterfront."

"You think someone seen him down there?"

Tommy shrugged. "Could be."

Barkley watched a kid rip a wrist shot toward a goal marked out by a pair of Timberlands. The orange ball was blocked by the kid in the goal. There was a scramble for the rebound and someone scored, the ball scooting just inside one of the boots and halfway down the street. Cheers, yelling, one kid pushing another as a third chased the ball. The game rumbled on.

"Sorry again about today," Barkley said. "Must have been the knock on the head or something."

"Don't worry about it. I told you, I believe in all that vision shit."

"You're Irish. You got no choice."

Tommy skimmed him a look. "I ever tell you about the fairy rings they got over there? Don't say nothing."

"I didn't say shit."

"You were thinking it."

Barkley nodded toward Tommy's three-decker, slumping peacefully at the corner. "Is Katie waiting for you?"

"The fairy ring's a pack of mushrooms growing in a circle in a field. Back in the old country, they think it's enchanted."

"You're fucking enchanted."

"Listen to me, B. If you walk into one of these things, these rings, you can't ever get out. You're in there forever, running in circles while the demons chase you."

"Demons?"

"Your demons, the ones you make out of nothing, the ones that live inside your dreams, except now they're flesh and blood and bone. Turned loose to drive you shithouse crazy." Tommy's eyes shone with the telling and Barkley thought about the booze and the cocaine and the gambling and figured it was all lit by the same quenchless fire.

"Go on inside, Tommy. Katie's waiting."

"Come in for a pop. She'd love to see you."

On cue the door to the apartment opened, and Katie Dillon appeared on the stoop. Tommy's wife was tiny, maybe five three, and Southie tough. First team all-scholastic point guard in high school, she'd gotten a full ride to play hoops at B.C. The summer of her senior year she met Tommy and decided to defer for a year.

That Christmas they got married. Eight months later, the twins arrived. One dream dead, another begun. She still looked young and college fresh, a beauty who'd maybe lost her way, wandering through Southie in her hip-hugger jeans, Converse sneaks, and hooded B.C. sweatshirt. One of the hockey players yelled at her as she crossed the street and Katie waved. Then she was there, leaning through the window with her brown hair in messy curls and hard-as-diamond smile.

"Someone's gonna call the cops on you two. Hey, Bark."

She pressed her cheek against his, letting him feel the flutter of her eyelashes as he smelled her life—Ivory soap and hot water, kids scrubbed fresh, the makings of dinner, all the small, warm moments that bubbled and beat in her blood. Tommy leaned over and touched a hand to the steering wheel.

"Hey, babe. I was just trying to get him to come in."

"It's late," Barkley said. "And I'm beat."

Katie stepped back, cocking her hip and resting her eyes on her husband. "Let the man go home, Tommy. Besides, the girls just woke up and I need you to get them back down."

"How old are they now?" Barkley said.

"Nearly seven. I know, can you believe it? Molly's a terror. Maggie, of course, is an angel."

"Just a quick one, B," Tommy said. "You can stick your head in and see the girls."

"How about we figure out a night for dinner?" Katie said. "Bark can come over and I'll cook. Open up a bottle of wine and we can all catch up."

"Done," Barkley said.

"Awesome. And if you want to bring someone . . ." She smiled with her eyes and leaned in again to give him a quick kiss on the cheek. "Great seeing you, Bark."

"I'll be there in five," Tommy said.

Katie made her way back across the street. The two men watched until she disappeared inside.

"Best part of my life," Tommy said.

"You got that right. What about tomorrow? You driving?"

"Supposed to pick up the car in the morning."

"Call me if it's not ready. Now, go see your wife. And don't forget to hug your kids."

Tommy bumped Barkley's fist and climbed out of the car. Katie met him on the stoop, letting her husband go inside and then leaning against the doorframe, smiling at Barkley and lifting a lonely hand his way. He popped the horn and waited until she'd gone in before starting up the car. Fuck the Irish pricks with their hockey sticks and shaved heads, painter's pants and shamrock tats. The real danger in South Boston was right here. Flesh and blood. Katie fucking Dillon. Shit.

He pulled away from the curb, laying on the horn and watching all the wannabe Bobby Orrs scatter. It was too late for Carson so he'd sit up in his apartment and watch one of those detective movies. Hoped it was a Columbo. He wouldn't think about today. Fucking lie. Of course he would. Think about today, then think about the fire escape outside his window. His own private fairy ring, whispering with his own personal pack of demons. Barkley pressed down on the gas, sparks flying as old thoughts ran ahead and were lost in the night.

8

Daniel climbed out of the Kenmore T station at a little after ten. A trio of girls was huddled by the front door to the Rat. Wrapped in leather and jingling rings on every finger, they smoked their cigarettes and chattered brightly, shaking out spikes of hair dyed in pastel swirls of color and flashing pale smiles at one another in the steam and the hard light. A bouncer checked their IDs and collected the cover, adding the bills to a fold of money he kept under his jacket. The girls descended into the ragged mouth of the Rat while Daniel negotiated the front steps to his new place, a garbage bag with everything he owned thrown over his shoulder and his brother's sad smile floating just ahead. The good-byes had been hard, but Daniel would see Harry soon enough. He'd promised. And Harry always kept his promises.

Daniel's key turned easily in the outer lock. He walked up the interior set of stairs, thought about knocking, then let himself in. The apartment was dark and cold. Daniel dumped his bag by the door and fumbled along the wall until he found a light switch. He could have sworn the place was empty, but there was Simon, ghost again, sitting behind his desk, packing another pipe, this one small and flat with a perforated metal bowl.

"Sorry, I didn't see you," Daniel said.

Simon fired up the pipe and launched a gentle spiral of smoke. "I was watching you cross the street." He gestured to the bag of clothes. "Is this all you have?"

"Pretty much."

"Must be nice to be that free. You want to take it back to your room?"

"Sure." Daniel took a seat on the couch and placed the bag between his knees. "What kind of tobacco is that?"

"You trying to be funny?"

"Sort of."

"It's pot. If you're not all right with that, I can go up to the roof."

"It's fine."

"Good. It's cold on the roof."

"How do you know I don't smoke myself?"

Simon didn't bother to answer, reaching over with a long arm and cracking one of the windows. "Did you tell your brother you were moving out?"

"Yes."

"What did he say?"

"He didn't want me to go."

"And already you miss him."

"I know, sounds stupid."

"Not at all." Simon checked the bowl of his pipe and knocked the contents into an ashtray. He slipped the pipe into his desk along with a thick plastic bag that Daniel assumed held his weed.

"I tried what you talked about," Daniel said.

"What's that?"

"The entanglement thing."

"It's not a toy, you know."

Daniel thought about the hot-dog stand and the spaniel with the wagging tail. "Does it work with animals?"

Simon smirked. "Is that what you really want to talk about?"

"There's a girl."

"Always is."

"What does that mean?"

"You'll find out. Let me guess. You like her and tried to use what we spoke about to get her to like you back."

"I just wanted to see if there'd be any effect."

"But the effect you wanted was for her to like you back."

"I don't know."

"You don't know." Simon shook his head. "Fine. So what happened?"

"We talked. I concentrated like you talked about."

"Directed your thoughts. Focused them."

"Yes."

The cat appeared out of nowhere, a sliver blade flashing up onto a bookshelf as Simon's voice sharpened and tightened. "Tell me, what did it feel like?"

"I guess it felt like I was pushing something."

"And you felt resistance?"

"Resistance?"

"From the other side? Like you were actually pushing against a physical object?"

Daniel tried to summon up the moment when he touched Grace's mind. "Yes, I think so. For a second, anyway."

"And then what?"

"And then she kissed me."

Simon leaned back, brushing the side of his desk

with his fingers and magically producing another pipe, the Dunhill from this afternoon. Daniel watched as he packed it and lit a match, flames leaping across the pulled-down bones of his face. When he had it going, Simon plucked the pipe from between long, thin lips. "This is regular tobacco."

"I told you, it's fine with me."

"Go put your clothes away. I'll make some tea."

When Daniel returned, Simon was sitting in his chair by the fireplace. There was a fire in the grate and a pot set on a table.

"Help yourself."

Daniel poured himself a cup of green tea and sat on the couch. The overhead light had been extinguished and the glow from the fire cast shadows that reached across the floor. Daniel took a sip and felt the warmth on his feet.

"You're happy about the girl," Simon said.

"Are you asking or telling me?"

"It's a responsibility, you know."

"What's that?"

"Entanglement. I'm assuming you now believe what I told you?"

"Maybe."

"You felt something?"

"I told you I did."

"Why do you think I'm sharing all this with you?"

Daniel shrugged.

"You think I'm boasting?"

"I didn't say that."

"You didn't have to. Of course that would be the assumption. In this case, however, you're wrong. I told you about entanglement for a very specific reason. I know a little bit about you."

The tea went cold in Daniel's mouth, and he could feel the cup and saucer grow heavy in his hands.

"Relax, Daniel. Remember when I told you about internetworking."

Daniel nodded.

"Well, it allows me, among other things, to research people. There will be much more information available in the future, of course, but if you know what you're doing, it's a place to start."

Daniel put his cup down. Simon's face was cast in darkness, but he could see the smooth curve of his forearm in the flickering light as he held the bowl of his pipe and the soft glow as he puffed and the twist of his smoky exhale as it lifted and wreathed around them.

"How could you have researched me? I didn't even know I was going to come here until I saw the sign on your front door."

Simon's shadow nodded on the far wall, but the man said nothing. Daniel continued to think out loud.

"You knew I was going to come here?"

"In a way."

"Are you saying you pushed me here? Entangled me? Is that possible?"

Simon dipped his face into their shared light. "I read about your brother in the newspaper, but I knew about you before that. Hospital records. Letters. A couple of phone calls. Don't leave, Daniel. What happened to you makes you who you are. Makes you perfect for this. If you truly felt something today, you know that to be true."

Daniel was standing, staring down at the wooden floorboards, striped in ribbons of moonlight from the windows.

"Stay, Daniel. Find out about the rest."

Daniel found himself sitting again. Simon offered, and Daniel allowed him to refill his cup with the fragrant tea. Then they began.

"The first rule is this." Simon held up a finger. "I will never lie to you. And I'll do everything I can to keep you out of harm's way."

"Who would want to harm me?"

"You already know the answer to that. What time do you leave for school tomorrow?"

"It's a shorter commute from here. I'll probably leave about seven."

"You have your appointment."

He knew about that. How did he know about that?

"You think this is about pushing other people," Simon said. "Affecting their behavior. Control."

"Isn't it?"

"You think I can sit here and concentrate and get you to do whatever I want?"

"I'm in this apartment, aren't I?"

"Only because you wanted to be. Entanglement is a two-way street, Daniel. You won't be able to affect every person you meet. Others will be an open book. At times you might not even have a choice in the matter. The point is this. You'll be pushed even as you push someone else. Take on another's pain while you unearth your own. It's part of the price paid for opening up oneself. In fact, I suspect it's the whole point."

"I'm not following you."

"Once we get past the power trip, the ego trip that seduces with the idea we might be able to affect someone else's actions, it inevitably comes back to us. Who's willing to peel away the layers of himself and evolve? Who isn't? Who lives, who dies? Darwin, of course, had it right all along."

"So you're saying I can't make someone do something?"

"Probably not against their will, no. When you feel that push, it's just you bumping up against them, allowing them to feel what was already there, maybe learn a little about themselves. Maybe learn something they don't want to know."

"Is this thing dangerous?"

The room filled with a soft hiss as Simon drew on his pipe and the tobacco glowed and crackled and burned.

"Of course it's fucking dangerous. Now, go get some sleep."

Daniel crawled between a set of unfamiliar sheets, resigned to a night of staring at the ceiling and listening for strange sounds. Almost immediately, however, reality began to fray, his mind melting, body sloping down the slippery hallways of his dreams. Nurses came. Nurses went. Doctors stood at one end of an impossibly long bed, arguing over shadows on an x-ray before turning to stare at their patient. Words dripped down into his consciousness—

HEAD TRAUMA, COMA, DISASSOCIATION

Some wanted to stimulate his cerebral cortex. Others preferred to let him sleep. Let him heal. The others held sway and so Daniel lay in his coffin, in the absolute zero cold of his mind, watching as they fed him through clear tubes, emptied his bowels, and pored over their endless medical tests.

He was eight years old, buried alive in a coma, and entirely alone. Well, not entirely. Harry sat at the foot of his bed during the day. And then there was Daniel's special visitor. He came late at night, when the ward was dark and the only sounds were the drowsy beeps of machines that charted the pump and push of heart and lungs. Larry Rosen worked as an orderly at Boston City Hospital. Curly black hair, narrow-shouldered, crooked and skinny, with a protruding Adam's apple that was creased in the middle and teeth that crowded up into the front of his mouth. On the first night he dragged a chair close and studied Daniel as he slept. On the second night he played with Daniel's face, lifting an eyelid and opening his mouth, giggling furiously while Daniel sat up high in a corner of the room and watched. On the third night Rosen brought out the needle. The orderly took his time, toothy grin washed in moonlight, eyes hungry for any hint of pain as the steel sank into the pocket of Daniel's hip. Rosen got nothing for his trouble, not even a flicker as the needle pierced muscle, fascia, and bone. The next night he was back. And the night after. Different-size needles. Different parts of Daniel's body. Never a twitch along the expanse of skin. Never a murmur on Daniel's lips. Still, the eight-year-old watched everything Larry Rosen did. Watched and took notes.

Daniel felt his eyes flutter and open. He was back in the narrow bedroom above Kenmore Square, the fire inside his head dimmed to a scalpel's edge of light that reached across the wooden floor toward the foot of the bed. He'd closed the door before going to sleep, but now it stood ajar and something was crawling hot and funny on his skin, feeling here and there at the soft parts of his face. Daniel dared not move, dared not look directly at the door, and when he finally did there was nothing to see but an exhale of air stirring the golden fill from the corridor.

He stole out of bed and into the hall. Daniel was committed now and didn't think about it, lest he think better and jump back under the covers. At the end of the hallway the door to Simon's workroom was cracked an inch. Daniel made a pretense of knocking even as he pushed in. A cold slab of mirror hung on one wall and he jumped at his own startled reflection, mobile skin stretched over a rack of bones, brown hair wild

and tufted, fists clenched on either side, his attempt at
ferocity more likely to elicit sympathy than fear. Such
was the lot of a sixteen-year-old, or at least this sixteen-
year-old.

He moved around the cage of a room, dominated
by a large desk scraped clean of paper, book, and pen.
A window gazed out over Kenmore Square, empty
at three in the morning and shivering under twitching sheets of rain. A breeze, fresh and wet and full of
the night, drifted across his feet and up the legs of his
Latin School sweats. The draft was coming from beneath a door that connected this first room to Simon's
bedroom. Again, Daniel didn't pause. Simon's bed had
not been slept in and the only window was flung open,
the storm tugging at the shades and casting a fine spray
of mist across the floor. Daniel moved closer and saw a
boot print limned in wet drops of silver on the sill. He
climbed out onto the fire escape.

The weather was fiercer than he'd imagined, a rake
of wind pushing him to the iron railing where he stared
down at the roof of a green VW bus and a skull-cracking
expanse of sidewalk. The squall pivoted again, turning
his shoulders and pulling him back toward the building.
Simon was standing in the storm's blind spot, waiting.
He seized Daniel by the shirt, sucking him close and
lifting him clear so he dangled out over the city. Daniel

looked down at his legs, bicycling in midair, then back at Simon, who tossed him into the night.

I never seen you looking so bad my funky one
You tell me that your superfine mind has come undone

Daniel dropped headfirst, Steely Dan ribboning his brain as he split the roof of the VW and plunged through a translucent pool of water—layers of warm salty greens, fading to blues, fading to blacks. He fell until there was nowhere left to fall, and then he floated, unable to speak, unable to think, unable to see his hand in front of his face. He was in the place where thoughts got shredded and Plato went to die, the place where the unconscious found its shape and its form. Moon-skinned demons with eyes on stalks and heart-shaped tears. Snakes in circles, feeding on themselves as they fed on one another. Clocks running around and around like a Chuck Berry song gone mad. And Daniel. He felt his heartbeat in his tongue and wondered what it might be like to consider. To ponder. To choose. From somewhere below a watery lamp was lit. Daniel dove, the current fierce and cold, fighting him as something inside impelled, pushed him onward, willed him to be. The last ten feet were a mad, blind struggle. And then Daniel reached for the light, ripping the sheets off his face and sitting straight up in bed.

For a moment, he imagined he was alone in his bedroom, safe in his cocoon of darkness, listening to the black drumbeat of rain outside and tasting the intimacy of all that lived within it. Then he saw him. Simon was standing by the room's only window, long face bathed in wet blues and wetter whites.

"You were screaming."

"Sorry, just a bad dream."

"Do you dream a lot?" His voice lived on the end of a string, swinging free in the night, measured and even like a ticking watch.

"It was nothing."

"Dreams are windows, Daniel. Windows into streams of time."

"I'm not sure I know what you mean."

Outside the storm tightened, lashing against the cracked New England brick and rattling all around the apartment. Simon leaned forward, allowing a brushstroke of light to play across his face. "Have you ever heard of something called 'deep time'?"

"No. Should I?"

Simon shrugged. "Get some rest. We can talk later." And then he left, closing the door behind him so it clicked.

Daniel lay back in the darkness, trying to determine where his dreams ended and his bedroom began. It was all a woolly jumble, his brain sodden with sleep. Daniel's last thoughts were that the whole thing was a trick and the stuff he imagined at night would look far different in the skeptical light of day. He wanted above all to open his eyes, just to make doubly certain his door was still shut. Then he was gone, tumbling into the abyss, this time failing to stir until morning.

9

*F*airy rings.

Barkley cracked an eye, letting the fevered carousel of his dreams slow to a stop. His alarm clock showed five minutes to seven, which meant he'd gotten four and a half hours of sleep. Plenty.

The black-and-white TV was still on in the kitchen, but Columbo was long gone, cigars smoked, case solved, bad guy in cuffs. Barkley snapped off the set and filled a kettle with water. He liked his coffee hot and strong in the morning. Black with two sugars.

He drank that first cup like he always did, sitting at the kitchen table, eyes fastened on a pair of boots he kept by the stove. When he finished, he washed out the cup and put it on the sideboard to dry. Then he pulled on the boots, lacing them tight, and shrugged into an overcoat he kept on a hook sunk into the wall.

Next to the kitchen was a pantry with a window that let onto a fire escape. Barkley cranked open the window and stepped out. His apartment was on the sixth floor of a walk-up overlooking Sullivan Square in Charlestown. The building was old and tired and the fire escape creaked under his weight as he moved to the center of the grated floor and peered through the cold iron at the concrete below. Then he began to jump. Two hundred fifty pounds, cracking hard, cracking mean, cracking fast. The rods that anchored the fire escape shifted in their moorings, separating a good six inches from the brick face of the building as the fire escape bucked and swayed. Barkley planted his palms against the exterior wall and started to rock. The building groaned in its bones and scrapes of red rust floated in the air. Still, the goddamn thing held.

Barkley sat down on the windowsill and pulled out a pack of Marlboros, lighting up the one he allowed himself every morning and staring out at the dark buildings and bright sky. By his boot was a small container of potting soil. Barkley dug in a thumb, breaking through the frozen crust and turning up the bones of old ghosts. Twelve years ago they'd lived wrapped in a cloud on the top floor of a Roxbury tenement. He was just out of school. Unformed clay. She was everything anyone could ever be and never feared it ending. People like her never did. That's why they had people like him. He'd told her to stay off the fire escape. More than once. But he'd never nailed the window shut, had he? And Jess loved her flowers. She kept a half-dozen different kinds all around the apartment, potted plants stuck in every available chink of light. She told him the apartment was magic, how the sun flooded their space and the rain dripped off the roof in cold, clean streams, all of it conspiring to feed their life and their love, sanctifying, purifying, keeping them safe and whole. She told him morning sun was best. And nowhere was it better than in the east-facing window off their kitchen, the one that let onto the fire escape.

He'd even bought nails, long silver ones, and a hammer. They were sitting in a drawer on that Sunday morning in June while Barkley slept in. He smelled the flowers first, hints of them floating through the apartment. He recalled smiling in his sleep. He thought about that smile often, the luxury of it, the arrogance of it, and wondered if he hadn't been so lazy. So fucking lazy. The scent of the flowers lived on a breeze and the breeze came from the kitchen. She'd opened the window. And if the window was open, she was out on the fire escape. Feeling the magic. Living in its light.

Barkley jumped from their bed just as the first bolt sheared. Caught the tail end of her scream as he reached the window. He might have called her name as she fell, a carousel of bolts and broken steel, plants and clods of dirt and Jess in the middle, staring up at him, reaching for him, telling him with her eyes that it would be all right and don't be angry, don't withdraw, don't let it fester, don't let in the wolf. Don't, don't, don't. Then she turned to face the pavement, extending her hands as if they could somehow break the fall.

He ran down six flights and found her, fine traces of potting soil patterned on her cheek and throat, a scattering of blossoms all around, still fragrant, no longer magic. He covered her body with his and groaned into the earth, wanting nothing more than for it to swallow them whole, leave them to lie together and feel everything or molder. A couple of neighbors came out and stared, then the police and an ambulance. It wasn't until three days after the funeral that they told him about his unborn daughter, eight weeks along. Then his education was complete and the circle closed itself.

Barkley promised himself he'd never live in the ghetto again. White-people buildings only. They might not look him in the eye and cross to the other side of the street when they did see him, but white folks were also less likely to die for nothing. And he'd had enough of that.

Or so he thought—until he picked up the badge and gun and became a merchant of death, until he moved into the oldest building he could find in the white person's world, until he started playing Russian roulette with his ghosts on yet another creaky fire escape.

He took a pull on his cigarette and flicked the butt into the breeze. Then he stepped back through the window and hung up his coat. Boots back in their spot by the stove. He took a long shower, letting the water run as hot as he could stand, and got dressed— brown suit with a soft stripe, blue shirt, and mocha tie. Barkley shined his shoes slowly, nagged by a feeling that this day wouldn't be like every other. Today was a day to lay traps for one's demons. And see what the fuck was what.

10

Harry Fitzsimmons picked his way through the early morning bead sellers and bookshops, sidestepping a long-haired guy strumming a guitar in front of the Coop and a couple of girls in low-slung bell-bottoms buying postcards off a rack. The chunky smell of weed was already hanging thick over Harvard Square, mingling with a waft of cheap beer as the front door to the Wursthaus burped open and a Puerto Rican in a white apron popped out, lugging a crate full of empties. Next door every stool in the Tasty was taken, locals scarfing down two eggs, home fries, and white toast for a buck and a half. And that included coffee.

Harry jogged across the street and bought a *Rolling Stone* at the Out of Town newsstand. A fleet of commuters swept past, two or three breaking off like fighter planes to buy their papers before disappearing into the wooden shack that marked the open mouth of the Red Line. Harry rolled up his magazine and tucked it in his back pocket, dodging between a couple of cars stopped at a light and angling for a set of wrought-iron gates. Harry enjoyed Harvard Square, a collection of odds and ends that marched to its own beat, a talisman of what was hip and what was about to be, even if it never was. Harvard Square, however, was not Harvard. Maybe its schizophrenic stepchild, or some demented relation, but not the pristine, unsullied image most folks had of America's premier university. To get that, to feel that, to smell that, one needed to dip into the oldest part of the past, the adult drinking tea in the parlor—Harvard Yard.

He entered off Peabody Street, slipping inside Johnston Gate and past the freshman dorms—Mass Hall where the president of Harvard had his office, Weld where JFK once slept, Wigg in all its various and sundry forms, a handful of others, each with its own history and rites of passage for its wet-behind-the-ears, wide-eyed residents. Harry ventured a little deeper, doubling back through the Old Yard and into the beating heart of the place—also known as Tercentenary Theatre. For him, this would always be the best part of Harvard and the only place, besides the football field, where he felt at peace. Along one side of the quadrangle was University Hall, its white granite defiant among a forest of Georgian brick. Across from it crouched Sever, impossibly heavy with its round bay windows, hipped roof, and whispering archways. Closing off either end of Tercentenary were the twin idols of religion and reason. Memorial Church seemed almost quaint, like a poor relation invited to peal its bells in celebration of its soaring cousin, the Widener Library.

One of the world's great libraries, the Widener had never been accused of being subtle, boasting a sweeping run of unnaturally broad steps ending in a row of Corinthian columns fronting a building made of brick the color of blood. Inside, the library housed more than three million volumes spread out over fifty-seven miles of shelving. Even better, no one working there had a clue as to where anything might be shelved and the only obvious sign in the place was one that read EXIT over the front door. The thinking was, if you were smart enough (or lucky enough or connected enough or rich enough) to get into Harvard, you sure as hell should be able to find a book on your own. And if the book you were looking for happened to be a copy of the Gutenberg Bible? Well, you'd come to the right place. There were only forty-seven such copies in the world and, of course, the Widener had one of them. One night a would-be robber tried to steal Harvard's Gutenberg. He was found the next morning facedown and unconscious after he slipped trying to shimmy down a rope hung from one of the library's upper windows. The burglar got a cracked skull for his trouble. The two-volume, seventy-pound bible emerged without a scratch. The message for all those wannabe book thieves out there: Don't fuck with Harvard lest the gods themselves smite ye down.

Harry found a seat near the top of the library steps and looked out over the Yard, still dozing in the early morning chill. Thanksgiving break didn't start until next Tuesday, but a lot of students were already clearing out. Harry didn't mind a bit. He closed his eyes and dropped his head back, letting the winter sun warm his face. Most of the jock types at Harvard went for collared polos and khakis, topsiders in the spring and duck boots in the fall. Harry was wearing a beat-up leather jacket with ripped jeans tucked into a pair of paratroop boots he'd bought at an army surplus store.

"Who you waiting on?"

"Go away." Harry spoke without opening his eyes. Jesus Sanchez wasn't having it. Harry shaded his face and watched the man everyone called "Zeus" climb the final few steps, his massive stride one of the few things on campus that was a match for the Widener's staircase.

Zeus had barely taken a seat when a woman called out and waved. The woman's name was Suzanne and hell yes, she was going to be at the Oxford Ale House this afternoon for happy hour. Were Zeus and his pals going to be there? Good, she'd look for them. Zeus watched until she disappeared from sight.

"You know who that is?"

"I bet you're gonna tell me."

"Hot, that's who that is. Hot as hell." Zeus swung his keg of a head around. "Dude, she'd love someone like you."

"Yeah, right."

"Women love that rebel shit. By the way, I'd bleach the hair."

"No way."

"Why not? The season's over. Bleach it pure fucking white. You'd look like Bowie."

"Let Bowie look like Bowie. You been running?"

Zeus was wearing a maroon practice jersey and plain gray bottoms. His black hair was wrung with sweat and he had a towel wrapped around his neck. "Three miles along the river."

Harry held out his fist. Zeus touched it.

"Had to get rid of the poison. Too many beers at Wursthaus last night. Then we went over to Eliot."

"Eliot. What were you doing over there?"

Eliot House was "more Harvard than Harvard"—full of blue bloods who liked to drink G&Ts, talk about their families' money, and laugh up their sleeves at everyone who wasn't them. Of course they had the best parties with the best women and everyone secretly wanted to live there.

"That's what I was thinking," Zeus said. "What the fuck am I doing here? You know what, though? They're not bad guys. Told me I should think about transferring next year."

The backup offensive tackle should have been an afterthought at a place like Eliot, a poor Hispanic kid from Hyde Park who'd wheedled his way into Harvard cuz he had some heft and could play football, not spectacularly well but good enough for the Ivies. Still, there was something about Zeus, an oozing brand of charisma that was hard to nail down and even harder to resist. Whether he was hanging with the crew who cut the grass at the stadium or the Saltonstalls from Eliot, Zeus had a way of making people feel good about themselves, drawing them in even as he kept them at a distance. Harry figured Zeus was the first natural-born politician he'd ever met.

"Met a nice woman last night, Harry."

"At Eliot?"

"The Wursthaus, but then she came over with us. Premed at Tufts. Hot."

Harry snuck a glance. With his baker's belly, old man jowls, and receding hairline, Zeus didn't remind anyone of Paul Newman. Still, the women were as helpless against the man's powers of persuasion as anyone else.

"That's great, Zeus. I'd like to meet her."

"Really?"

"Sure. You gonna be okay for exams?"

Zeus was majoring in finance, with an eye toward Harvard's B-school. Long shot? Maybe. Then again, it was Zeus, so maybe not.

"Stats is a bitch," he said. "Otherwise, I'm good."

"Let me know if you need help."

"How about tonight?"

"I already told you."

"You need to go, Harry."

It was an unofficial tradition among the football players. Every year at the end of the season a handful of them piled into a car (sometimes cars) and headed down to Boston's Combat Zone. They'd park on Washington, crack the windows, and watch the action. The girls would come over and flirt, maybe drink a beer with the college kids, even do a little business in the alley if anyone had the cash.

"You know I work down there," Harry said. For the past year and a half, he'd been volunteering at Boston's Pine Street Inn. The first few months it was handing out coffee and sandwiches from the basement of a dark, damp building in Chinatown. Pretty soon he was tagging along with a couple of social workers as they ventured into the Zone, passing out pamphlets on venereal disease and strips of condoms. If the girls didn't know him by name, they'd probably know his face.

"Be an hour. Two, tops. Drink some beers, whistle at the girls, and we're out." Zeus cocked his head and gave Harry his best hangdog look. Harry knew he was being worked but didn't mind it. That was the genius of Zeus. Harry sometimes wondered what the guy was like when he wasn't onstage, when he wasn't working it.

"We don't get out of the car," Harry said.

"What do you think? I wanna get my dick sucked in an alley by some toothless grandma? We're tourists. Windows up, doors locked, enjoy the show. You wanna grab breakfast?"

"Tasty?"

"Let's go."

Zeus got up first and started down the Widener's front steps. Harry hung back. Maybe it was his little brother leaving the apartment, maybe it was something else, but a sudden melancholy had stolen over him, like it was all happening too fast and the best of it had already passed him by. He took a last look out over the Yard and inhaled, wanting nothing more than to put the morning in a bottle and take it with him. Then Zeus yelled and waved an arm. Harry exhaled and followed his best friend down the steps.

11

Daniel sat near the back of the bus and felt the two bottles in his pocket. One contained clear capsules, a tiny snowfall of white powder heaped up in each. The other was filled with multicolored tablets, reds and oranges and purples that always reminded him of Flintstone vitamins. Except they weren't. They were dream chasers.

Twice a month, Daniel visited the clinic where his doctor asked the same questions. How did he feel? Sad? Glad? Angry? Anxious? Describe, if he could, his color wheel of emotion. When he talked, which wasn't often, Daniel told the doctor he couldn't feel a thing. That was a lie. He felt everything. His feelings, hers, the people down the corridor sitting in the waiting room. Everyone's. And it weighed on him, rendered him numb.

He cracked the window and closed his eyes, letting the wind pucker his cheeks. The bus groaned to a stop and spit out a few passengers, then picked up speed as it slipped back into traffic. Daniel glanced around to see if anyone was watching. All he saw were the backs of newspapers. No one watched anyone on the Brookline Avenue bus at seven in the morning. It was a living, breathing hearse, rolling down the street in a velvet green fog.

Daniel pulled out the two bottles of pills and held them tight in his lap. He hadn't told the doc about his dreams from last night. She would have loved them. And why not? Dreams were the red meat of the mind. And these were prime cuts. A tumble of images so fast and so fresh and so real they threatened to break through the skin of sleep and burst into some unhinged mutation of reality.

Terrifying. Fascinating. And entirely his.

Daniel unscrewed the top of the Flintstone bottle and slowly tipped it upside down, watching Wilma and Fred and Barney bounce off the side of the bus and disappear under its spinning rubber wheels. Then he did the same with the capsules, laying a lovely trail of dream chasers down Brookline Avenue for anyone who might care to follow.

He got off at Longwood Avenue, walking the half mile or so to Avenue Louis Pasteur. There was a line of buses outside Latin School, belching smoke and burping out dozens of kids who streamed up the steps and through the front doors. Daniel made his way down the row, searching for the charter from Dorchester and not finding it. He sat on the curb to wait. Five minutes, ten. Finally, it hit the corner, driver fat and white, face lobster red with concentration, lips mouthing a string of silent curses while the yellow bus slammed to the bottom of a pothole and struggled to hold the turn. Daniel stood up as the charter slid to a stop, brakes grinding in protest, and the door opened. The driver studied Daniel with whiskey eyes that blinked once then disappeared behind a wall of kids, all elbows and fists, fighting to get off first like the bus was gonna blow up or something. The Dorchester charter ran through Dot and Roxbury, snaking through the South End and Chinatown at the tail end of its route. Most of the kids on the bus hailed from neighborhoods like Fields Corner, Savin Hill, and Dudley Square. Some had parents who gave a shit. Plenty didn't. Still, they were on the bus every morning. And that said something.

Grace was one of the last to get off. Ben Jacob was just ahead of her. Daniel had first met Ben on the charter two years ago when they were in the eighth grade. Ben lived in Milton and his parents were both doctors. Later, Daniel would discover Ben could have gotten a ride every day from his dad, but he wanted to take the charter. So his father dropped him off at a stop in the city and he rode in. That first day Ben was sitting in a seat across from Daniel when another kid, Billy Shine, got on. Shine was a fullback on the football team and a grade-A asshole. He took one look at Ben and ripped him out of his seat. The side of Ben's face hit a metal pole in the middle of the aisle, and he fell into the well for the back steps. A couple of kids snickered. Most just pushed past to grab whatever seats were left.

Ben was on his hands and knees gathering up books and papers when Daniel knelt down to help him. "Fuckin' hebe" rang down from somewhere behind them, a titter of nervous laughter following. Ben pinned a black yarmulke back on his mop of hair and settled himself on the top step. His glasses were broken, so he got out a roll of electric tape and began to mend them. Shine sat ten feet away, gazing out the window. Daniel joined Ben on the step, turning and staring as hard as he could at Shine, challenging, daring him to make eye contact. He knew Shine wouldn't mess with him because of Harry, who was still at Latin and a senior. If Shine did come after him, that was all right, too. Daniel had never been afraid of a beating. In the end, Shine did what bullies usually do when someone pushes back, even a little. He looked around for easier pickings. It would be another six months before Daniel actually talked to Ben, but Daniel always felt good about that first day. Ben would have, too, if he'd ever noticed. But that was Ben.

"Hey, Daniel." Ben gave up a high five, bumping a large brown briefcase against Daniel's legs and adjusting his glasses.

"Hey, Ben."

Grace crowded close by Ben's shoulder. "You didn't call."

"Sorry," Daniel said. "I got busy."

Grace wanted to hear about the apartment, but Daniel shook his head and the three of them started walking.

"You have all your lines translated?" Grace said.

Daniel hadn't done any of his homework and would just have to hope he didn't get called on.

"I can help," Ben said. He was in advanced Latin and Greek. Basically, Ben knew Virgil better than Virgil. He was also the kind of guy who'd help anyone who asked and never make a big deal out of it.

"Thanks," Daniel said, stopping about halfway up the front steps of the high school. "Where are you first period?"

"Study hall, but I'm working as a door monitor. One of the side doors near the gym. How about you?"

Daniel pointed at himself and Grace. "We got study hall, too. Working in the English Department."

"Let's go." Grace tugged at Daniel's sleeve. Most of the kids had already filtered into school. Ben was looking anxiously across the street.

"What is it?" Daniel said.

Ben poked his chin toward the hulking outline of Boston English. The second-oldest high school in the city, English dated back to 1821. Unlike Latin School, English was not an exam school and had a student population that was more than ninety percent black. Two weeks ago, a kid from English was beaten up outside a drugstore on Huntington Avenue. Three days later, two Latin School kids were mugged in the Fens. One of the Latin School kids got slashed in the side with a knife and showed off the wound to twenty or so students in the bathroom. Last week, more than a hundred English students massed on the street shared by the two schools. Daniel watched from the windows like everyone else as one of the kids from English climbed up on a car and the students started to chant. As quickly as it started, however, the thing lost its momentum, the crowd breaking up into smaller groups and drifting away. Pretty soon the block was quiet again. But the time bomb was ticking and everyone knew it.

"Nothing's gonna happen," Daniel said, while Grace continued to nudge.

"You don't sound like you believe it," Ben said.

"You worried about being on the door?"

"Heck no."

Ben weighed a hundred pounds on a good day and had never thrown a punch, or anything else, in anger in his life. As door monitor he'd be Latin School's first line of defense should something happen. Not the best of plans—in fact, probably the worst—but it was what they had. The three friends ran up the steps and ducked inside just as the bell for homeroom rang.

12

The Tasty's early morning rush had subsided for the moment, allowing them to spread out at one end of the counter. Harry took a sip of coffee and stared out the window at traffic, listening idly as Zeus ordered four eggs scrambled and a side of toast. The counterman asked Harry what he wanted. He got an English muffin just to be polite, then put down his mug and rubbed a hand over his scalp. The counterman must have thought that was some sort of signal because he hustled over with the pot and gave them both a refill.

"He thinks you're from fucking Mars," Zeus said.

"It's Harvard Square. The guy sees all kinds coming through the door."

"Yeah, but none of them made first team All-Ivy."

Harry laughed.

"You think he doesn't know who you are?"

"Save it."

"I'm serious. People know you, Harry. And that means something."

Zeus's mountain of eggs took less time to cook than they did to crack. Harry watched as the big tackle pulled across the salt and pepper shakers and began to season his food.

"What's bugging you?" Harry said.

"Nothing."

"Come on."

"You should be careful, that's all."

"Careful of what? I got a couple of mentions in the Globe. Big deal."

"Folks notice. That's all I'm saying."

"I don't get it. One minute you're telling me to be careful, then you're dragging me down to the Zone."

"Different."

"How so?"

"Cuz it's one night and I'll be there."

"And you're gonna look after me?"

"I'm always looking after you, bro. Always." Zeus shoveled a forkful of eggs onto a piece of toast and folded it into his mouth, washing it down with a mouthful of coffee. "Hey, look, it's your asshole roomie."

Harry followed Zeus's gaze out the front window.

Neil Prescott stood in the shadow of the Red Line stop, talking to a woman Harry didn't recognize, probably trying to get her number with an eye toward getting her drunk and into his bed.

"Guy's a tool," Harry said.

"Hence the moniker—asshole roomie. Fuck, he's coming over."

Most students at Harvard lived on campus. Prescott was a junior who couldn't. Harry wasn't privy to all the details, but there was a rumor of gambling during his freshman year. And something about a fifteen-year-old he'd knocked up. Prescott's dad and grandfather were both Harvard men, both football players, so it all got handled. Harry didn't really care. Prescott had an apartment near campus with an empty bedroom. And Harry had Daniel. So they struck their deal. Harry watched as Prescott made his way across the street and into the diner. He slid onto a stool next to Zeus but turned his attention immediately to Harry.

"What's up, Fitzsimmons?" Prescott called everyone by their last name.

"Just hangin'."

"You sleep in the apartment last night?"

Harry nodded. He knew Prescott had been out all night and was dying to share details of his latest conquest. Again, Harry wasn't interested.

"I left you a note back at the place," he said. "My brother moved out."

Prescott didn't give a shit. As long as the rent got paid Harry could do what he liked. Zeus was a different story.

"Moved out? Kid's in fucking high school." Zeus had only met Daniel once, but it didn't matter. Daniel was a Fitzsimmons, and that meant family.

"Technically, he's supposed to live in Boston to attend Latin School," Harry said. "So he found a room in Kenmore Square. Says he's renting from a Harvard prof. Simon Lane?"

"Never heard of him," Zeus said. Prescott shook his head.

"You working out?" Prescott nodded at Zeus's sweats.

"Little morning jog."

"How about you?" Prescott glanced at Harry. Prescott had been a hot-shit running back in high school, but the speed hadn't translated to college. Still, he was a jock in his head and that horse died hard, if at all.

"Lifted yesterday. Did some cardio."

Prescott nodded like he was the guy who kept track of that stuff.

"Just talking about tonight," Zeus said.

"You in, superstar?" It'd be like Prescott to make a big deal if Harry said no.

"Yeah, I'm in."

"Awesome. I'm driving. Sanchez, you're getting your dick sucked. Fitzsimmons, who the fuck knows?"

The door to the Tasty opened and two women walked in. Behind them was a tall, middle-aged man, tightly wound through the neck and shoulders, the tension releasing in a shock of curly hair. The man's eyes widened a touch when he saw the three of them sitting at the counter. Prescott raised his hand.

"Nick, over here. You guys know Nick Toney?"

Nick Toney was a photographer, one of those high-end guys with exhibitions at universities and places like the Museum of Fine Arts. For some reason Prescott loved photography and had all kinds of fancy-ass equipment lying around the apartment. Toney had come over one night to talk to him about some gear. Harry hadn't been there, but Prescott told him Toney's advice was simple. Stop buying cameras and start taking pictures. Harry liked that.

"How you guys doing?" Toney slid in next to Harry as Prescott made the introductions. Zeus grunted through a mouthful of eggs. Harry shook the man's hand.

"Nice to meet you, sir."

"Do me a favor and drop the 'sir.' You're Neil's roommate?"

"Yes, sir. I mean, Nick."

"I feel like I know you from somewhere?"

Harry shrugged. "I don't think so."

"No?" Toney cocked his head and offered up his best doorman's grin, teeth white and straight and strong.

"You probably seen him in the paper," Zeus said. "First team, All-Ivy."

"Whoa. Superstar."

"Hardly." Harry felt the burn at the back of his neck and in his cheeks.

"He's the modest type," Prescott said, buttering a piece of Zeus's toast and enjoying the hell out of Harry's discomfort.

"Nothing wrong with being modest," Toney said. "Still, that's a hell of a thing, Harry."

"Thanks."

"You guys headed home for Turkey Day?"

"Staying in town," Harry said. "Me and my brother are just gonna hang around the apartment."

Toney raised his chin and let his eyes drop over to Zeus.

"Probably head home."

"We were just talking about tonight," Prescott said. "Thinking about going down to the Zone." Prescott looked expectantly at Toney, who shifted his shoulders and grinned uneasily.

"Nick does a lot of shooting down there," Prescott said.

"Actually, I've got some studio space. I do portraits of the girls when they're not working. Try to document their lives."

"I volunteer in Chinatown," Harry said. "We do a lot of outreach in the Zone."

Toney shot a finger at Harry. "Maybe that's where I've seen you."

"Could be. You probably get a lot of college guys down there."

"College, high school. Businessmen, tourists. Perverts, priests, fuckers older than dirt. All kinds, my friend. All kinds." The counterman came by with a coffee for the photographer. Toney stirred in some sugar and took a measured sip. "Something I don't understand. Football players from Harvard, right? World by the balls. So why in the fuck would you wanna go down the Zone? I mean, to me, it makes no sense."

"It's sort of an end-of-the-season tradition," Harry said, feeling as stupid as he sounded and trying to figure out how and why he was explaining something he wanted no part of.

"Not a nice place, Harry, but you already know that."

"It's just a night."

"It's always just a night. I mean, what else can it be, right? Anyway, I'll give you a free piece of advice. Take it for what it's worth." Toney dropped his voice a notch as the three Harvard boys leaned in. "I know most of the girls who work down there. I know the guys who run the girls. No offense, but they live for a crew like you. Drunk, horny as shit." Toney rubbed a finger and thumb together. "Plenty of cashish. Girls will pick your pocket, pimps roll you in an alley. And that's just the start. So what you gotta do is play it smart. Stay together. In the bars, on the street. Together. Do that and you'll be fine. All right?"

They nodded. Toney made eye contact with each in turn, lingering on Harry, taking note of the ripped-up clothes and the rest of it. "It's always the crazy-looking fucks that wind up being the most responsible. Am I wrong?"

"I don't think we should be going if that's what you're asking."

"But you'll keep an eye out?"

"Yes, sir. Sorry, Nick."

"Good. I feel better. Come on, Neil. If you want me

to take a look at those lenses, we better get moving. Later, boys."

Toney threw down enough money to pay for everyone. Then he and Prescott left.

"Guy acts like he knows us," Zeus said.

"Probably just seen a lot of idiots like us."

Zeus shrugged.

"What is it?"

"Been thinking 'bout tonight. Maybe it's not such a great idea."

"Now you come around. Christ, what did Toney say that I didn't?"

"I don't know. Nothing."

"Well, we gotta go now. Otherwise, I'll have to listen to asshole roomie. Anyway, Toney's right. If we stay together, it's not a problem. You done?"

Zeus nodded and they both got up.

"What time we supposed to meet?" Harry said.

"Seven o'clock. Prescott wants to grab dinner first."

"Don't worry, Zeus. Like you said, an hour. Two, tops, and we're out of there." Harry patted the big tackle on the shoulder. "Besides, I got you watching my back."

13

Kids everywhere, sprinting up and down stairs, yelling at each other in the halls, slamming lockers, dropping books, everyone rushing to beat the bell. Grace led the way, tackling the main staircase two steps at a time. A door opened and they caught a glimpse of the school's auditorium. Benjamin Franklin, Samuel Adams, and Ralph Waldo Emerson were just a few of the names carved into the white frieze that ran around the room. Daniel remembered staring up at them the first time he sat in the auditorium. Their headmaster, William Keating, told the class of five hundred seventh graders to take a good look at the student to his left and his right. "Two of you won't be graduating with a Latin School diploma," Keating assured them with a grin that was more predator than educator. After all, *Sumus Primi* and all that. So let the games begin.

Grace had slipped just ahead, taking a corner at the top of the stairs. Daniel sprinted up the last flight, Ben sharp on his heels. They caught up to her just as she hit homeroom. One kid had his head on his desk and was dead asleep. Two others played football with a bus pass, sliding the plastic disk across the width of the table and trying to get it to hang over the edge without falling off. If one of them scored, he got to kick an extra point by flicking the disk with his fingers while the other kid held his hands together and made a goalpost.

"Haverly is out sick." One of the table football players spoke without ever taking his eyes off the game. "No homeroom today."

The three of them walked back into the hallway. Eddie Spaulding was chewing on a plastic straw and sitting in a chair, balanced on its two rear legs and tilted back against the wall.

"Bookworm." Eddie was a senior, starting running back and safety on the football team. The hype had him pegged as a star in college, but Daniel thought high school might be as good as it got. For some unfathomable reason, Eddie had opted to study ancient Greek and it quickly became his bane. In other words, Ben was his best friend.

"Hey, Eddie." Ben didn't seem to care about the nickname Eddie had given him. Maybe he was oblivious, or, again, maybe just Ben.

Eddie tipped forward so all four legs of his chair were on the floor. "Haverly's out today."

"They told us," Grace said. "What are you doing out here?"

Eddie's eyes moved from Grace to Daniel before settling again on Ben.

"Let me guess," Grace said. "You need help?"

"It's the fucking *Iliad*. I was up until three in the morning and got nowhere."

"We're in the middle of 'Book Six,'" Ben said. "Hector and Andromache." He plopped down on the floor and opened his briefcase. Eddie Spaulding began to pull books out of a canvas bag he'd stashed by his feet. First came a copy of the *Iliad* in the original Greek, then a Greek dictionary followed by a spiral notebook with a few lines of English translation scribbled in it. The fourth book was smaller, bound in red with its title written in tiny script on the spine.

"What's that?" Daniel said.

"It's a trot," Grace said. "Gives you Greek on one page and English on the other."

Daniel picked up the book and flipped it open. He'd heard of them but never actually seen one. "Wow."

"Don't get so excited," Eddie said. "DiCara can smell a trot a mile away."

"That's true," Ben said. "Most of the teachers here

can tell if you're using a translation aid. Besides, Eddie, you don't need it."

"Because I have you?" Eddie grinned as the bell rang, signaling two minutes until the start of first period.

"Because you're smart." Ben tapped his temple. "It's just a matter of sticking with it. Remember what DiCara said about the grain of sand trapped in an oyster."

"It doesn't become a pearl overnight."

"It takes time and diligence. Just like football."

"Yeah, yeah, that's pissa. Just help me with a couple of spots." Eddie pointed to a line in the Greek text. Ben took a look.

"ἐϋκνήμιδες Ἀχαιοί. It means 'strong-greaved Achaeans.'"

"That's what the trot says. Gimme another word."

"'Well-greaved.'"

"What the fuck are greaves?"

"They're like shin pads for hockey. The Greeks wore them during battle."

Eddie looked up from his scribbles. "You're kidding?"

"It's an epithet. Homer uses them throughout the poem. Most people think it was a mnemonic device as well as a way to keep the lines in meter."

"Can I say shin guards?"

"No, Eddie. Say 'greaved.' 'Well-greaved.' That will get you by."

Eddie scribbled some more and fretted. "Shit, I got a lot more."

"I'm on door duty by the gym for first period."

Grace shook her head. "Ben? Seriously?"

"Come by and we'll go over the rest of it."

"You'll give me the lines?" Eddie said.

"Only after we go over them."

The bell rang again. One minute to first period.

"Thanks, Bookworm. Sorry, I mean Ben. I'll come by." Spaulding stood up, giving Grace a longer glance than Daniel would have liked before drifting around the corner. Ben picked up his briefcase and took off running in the opposite direction, the words floating back over his shoulder.

"I like to help people, Grace. It's what I'm good at."

"Guess he told you." Daniel elbowed Grace in the ribs and followed Ben, the three of them skidding to a halt in the stairwell.

"You know they have asbestos in this place?" Ben pointed to an insulated pipe running across the ceiling and a burst of white filament feathering into fine strands. "I read an article that says it's toxic."

"Forget about the asbestos," Grace said, touching Ben's sleeve. "Just keep your door closed and locked."

"You think something's going to happen?"

"Better safe than sorry."

The bell rang a final time, this one longer and louder, indicating the beginning of first period. Grace and Daniel watched as Ben tumbled down the stairs. Then they hustled up a flight, slipping into the English Department just as Mr. Rozner stepped out of the teachers' lounge, reading the *New York Times* and sipping a cup of coffee.

Daniel and Grace buried themselves at the back of the department, the familiar smells of copying fluid and textbooks saturating the air around them. Grace got to work shelving copies of *David Copperfield*. Daniel reviewed a stencil of next month's schedule for the department and snapped it onto the ink-filled drum of the mimeograph machine. He'd just begun to turn out copies when Rozner came in. Usually the head of the English Department wandered back to their work area for a brief chat. Today, however, he went straight to his desk. Then Daniel heard something he'd never heard in his three months of working there—the sound of a television.

Mr. Rozner was tucked into his tiny desk, half-moon glasses pushed down his nose, riveted to a small black-and-white perched atop an annotated edition of William Shakespeare's complete works. Daniel cleared his throat and rustled up against a stack of books. Rozner half turned.

"You were late. Both of you were."

"Sorry, sir." Daniel felt Grace bump up behind him. "The buses were running slow today."

Rozner dumped a spoonful of Cremora into his coffee and took a sip. "Not surprising. Not surprising at all."

Daniel could feel Grace stiffen even though she wasn't actually touching him. Rozner was old-school and had that effect on everyone who worked for him. In class he was supposed to be even worse.

"Nguyen."

"Yes, sir."

"Go see Professor Lonergan in Room 311. He's got a book I need you to pick up."

Grace left without a word. Rozner went back to watching television. On the tiny screen, a fist of a woman stood at a microphone. The sound was too low for Daniel to make out the words, but he could see her pale face and red-lipped mouth opened wide to accommodate whatever was coming out of it. The camera panned back to reveal the crowd. They covered City Hall Plaza, filling the red-brick and concrete tiers all the way to the Government Center T stop. Handmade signs of varying designs and shapes waved up and down, back and forth. NO BUSING. RESIST. EAST BOSTON AGAINST FORCED BUSING. Rozner turned down the sound all the way. They listened in the quiet as footsteps passed in the hall. Sheets of dust drifted in yellow light falling from a cracked porcelain fixture that hung off the wall. The light was newly born but already seemed old beyond knowing. Daniel wondered if other students had labored beneath it, generation after generation, making their copies while mapping their futures in their heads.

"You're Harry Fitzsimmons's brother?"

Daniel jumped. Rozner was watching him closely. Daniel had no idea what he'd seen. "Yes, sir."

"How's he doing at Harvard?"

"Pretty well."

"I remember about that. Your mother and all."

"I was eight."

"Yes, well, I heard about it. Later, of course. What's Harry now?"

"A sophomore, sir."

"A sophomore?" Rozner pulled off his glasses and rubbed his hands over his face. His Shakespeare class was a rite of passage for juniors and seniors, his command of the material and attention to detail the stuff of Latin School legend. This morning, however, Rozner seemed far more man than myth, deep red lines creased down both sides of his nose, his white head of hair slightly mussed on top and at the sides.

"Do we have you working here for the whole year?"

"That's up to you, sir. I'd prefer the whole year."

Rozner gestured to the straight-backed chair beside his desk. "Sit down."

Daniel did.

"You know what Latin School does, Fitzsimmons?"

"Gives you a good education."

"It does a hell of a lot more than that."

"Yes, sir."

"It gives you a chance. Something you might not ever have otherwise. You realize how fragile that is?"

"Fragile?"

"Yes, fragile." Rozner nodded at the silent images flashing across his TV screen. "What you see there is the genie let out of the bottle. I thought it might tire itself out."

"But it's not?"

"I'm afraid not." Rozner straightened his shoulders and sat up. "Latin School provides the opportunity, but it's up to you to make something of it. Do you understand?"

"Yes, sir."

"Good. That's good." The head of Latin School's English Department ran his hands quietly over his hair as if to compose himself and replaced his glasses, the black edges of the frames fitting neatly into the grooves in his nose they'd carved there. Then he cleared his throat and began to shuffle through a stack of blue books piled up on his desk. "There's some notices that need to be copied and sent out. They're on the table beside the mimeograph."

Daniel found the stencils right where Rozner said he would. He clipped the first one to the large steel cylinder on the mimeograph and began to crank. Rozner sat at his desk and read, the veins in his cheeks threaded with color, thick fingers working as he cut and slashed his way through the blue books. They didn't exchange another word for the rest of the period. When the bell rang, Rozner came over and checked Daniel's copies. He made a couple of notations on a sheet, nodded, and moved to the door. Grace was standing there.

"I didn't tell you to get lost for the period," Rozner said.

"I'm sorry, sir. Mr. Lonergan couldn't find the book. And then the headmaster came in and wanted to talk. And then . . ."

There was a sudden rumbling from somewhere in the bowels of the building, followed by a boom like an explosion, then a second. Rozner rushed into the hall as teachers and students poked their heads from classrooms. Word spread quickly. Boston English had gone off again. And now they were coming across the street to liberate their Latin School brethren.

14

Daniel ran to a set of windows overlooking Avenue Louis Pasteur, wedging out a spot for himself and Grace among the chattering students and peering down into the street. A steady stream of bodies poured out of English, flowing down the block and up the steps of Latin School. The crowd cleared space around the front door while a steel pole was stripped of its stop sign and passed overhead. The first rank of kids, all twitch and itch, lined up the pole and started to ram it against the door. The crowd cheered with each blow, none of which seemed to have much effect on the door. Inside Latin School, however, it was a different story. Some of the students were scared. Some wanted to get out on the street and bust heads. A rock flew through the air, falling short of its mark. The second broke a first-floor window, sending the crowd on the street into hysterics. The kids on the pole redoubled their efforts. Grace punched Daniel in the shoulder and pointed. A section of the mob had broken off and was running down the far side of the building.

"They're headed to the gym," Grace said.

"Ben."

They flew down one flight, then a second. The sound of banging echoed up the stairwell. Grace and Daniel turned the corner together and found Ben hanging on to a set of push bars as the door he was supposed to protect bowed and buckled under the weight of the assault. Daniel could hear screams and swears through the door. "Jew boy. We gonna fuck you up."

Daniel grabbed on to the push bars. His friend's shirt was torn at the shoulder.

"Did they hurt you?" Daniel said.

"No, but I barely got the thing closed."

Someone outside was talking about liberating the white man. There was a lot of laughter and the doors bowed outward again. A hand reached through to grip the inside of the frame and a shoulder followed, wedging the doors open. Ben pointed to a Koho hockey stick by his feet. The shoulder had been joined by a head as Ben's door gave birth to a smiling teenager explaining to them how much he was looking forward to kicking some Latin School ass. Grace picked up the Koho and popped the butt end off the kid's forehead. Then she tomahawked down with a two-hander. The kid fell away and the doors slammed shut again. She slid the stick between the two inside handles, securing the doors for the moment.

"Holy shit." Ben's eyes goggled out of his head as he absorbed her handiwork.

"I know, right?" Grace held her hand over her mouth and started to giggle. Just then there was another massive boom and the hockey stick snapped like kindling.

"What do we do now?" Grace said.

Daniel pulled her back as the doors blew out, light shafting the dark gray of the stairwell. A hand yanked Ben outside, leaving behind nothing except his scream. Eddie Spaulding appeared at the top of the steps. He paused for a moment, then rushed down the stairs and plowed into the mob after Ben. Daniel followed him through the gap.

Daniel tripped over something and stumbled down a short flight of steps, scraping his chin and hitting his nose before winding up face-first in the dirt. He was on the edge of a rough field that ran down one side of Latin School. To his right was an empty parking lot, to his left thirty to forty kids enveloped in a rising din of fists and curses and shoves and elbows. At the very center of the mass was Eddie, an attacker on his back and a second hanging off his arm as Ben kicked and clawed to stay by the football player's side. Daniel pulled himself to his feet and dove in. His fist cracked off the side of a skull with no apparent effect. He swung again, this time connecting and hearing the crunch of what might have been bone or tooth or both. Someone screamed in his ear and pulled his hair as he fell to his knees. A blow glanced off his cheek and someone bit his shoulder. There was no pain in any of it, his blood spiked with adrenaline as a tangle of bodies threatened to crush him. He rolled to one side and watched the pile of arms and legs tumble past, windmilling across the field until it slammed into the side of a green Dumpster.

For a moment the space cleared and the action seemed to slow. Eddie Spaulding had Ben behind him, safe for now between the Dumpster and the building as a half-dozen kids circled. Eddie had blood and snot bubbling from one nostril. A swipe of fingernails had scraped his cheek. He caught Daniel's eye and raised his chin. Daniel turned just as a tree branch swung out of the sun. It clipped him on the shoulder, freezing one side of his body as he fell. The kid swinging the branch wasn't much bigger than Daniel, the weight of the limb carrying him ass over teakettle past Daniel and into the dirt. Daniel was about to get up and jump on the kid's back when he felt a second presence behind him. Another kid, more man than kid, stepped forward, stopping within arm's reach and looking down at Daniel. His forehead was heavy and thick; his eyes sunk deep in his skull. He was wrapped in a long leather coat with gray sweats and black winter boots and held his hands loose and quiet by his sides. The man-child wore a white do-rag with short dreads poking out from underneath, and a silver tooth hung from a chain around his neck. He smiled at Daniel, who saw the gap where the tooth should have been and felt a chill as his mind went off script, reaching out and pushing up against his soon-to-be attacker's.

Almost immediately Daniel felt them entangle.

The man-child was twelve when his "uncle" hit him with the hammer—broken pieces of teeth and gums and blood all over the cracked kitchen table and lino-leum floor. That night the man-child sat in a locked closet under a set of stairs, sucking on a wet towel and listening to the thumping and bumping until it was quiet. Then he forced the lock and slipped through the kitchen. They were in his mother's bedroom, wrapped in a sheet and the foul smell of their sex. The man-child raised the hammer, clean light from the hallway catching its heft. He saw the gleam of their eyes as they rumbled out of their sleep and opened their mouths but never screamed. And then the hammer fell and skulls cracked in the red moonlight and bone and brains leaked all over the man-child's bare feet. No one had ever heard the story because no one had ever told it. But Daniel knew it now, felt it pumping in his blood, a pulsing, living cord of tissue and flesh and feeling and memory, a flowing back and forth that Daniel wanted to cut off but couldn't. Cuz he'd entangled when he shouldn't have and now they were one.

"I'm sorry," Daniel said.

The man-child blinked and Daniel felt the weight of the gun hidden deep inside the man-child's leather coat. Daniel watched in his mind as the man-child pulled it free in a smooth, practiced fashion. The first bullet struck Daniel square in the throat, blood bubbling up into the back of his mouth and spilling over his chest. The second caught him in the shoulder, turning him as the final bullet ripped through his left cheek and roofed in his skull. Daniel fell forward, striking the ground with a dull thud and rolling onto his back so he was staring up at the white blue of the sky as his soul swirled down and away to whatever place went the souls of young boys who spent the coin of their lives foolishly and thoughtlessly and recklessly and reckoned the world would stand still as they fell when nothing could be further from the truth. Daniel saw all that in the wink of a moment as the mind of the man with the silver tooth yawned wider and Daniel peeked over the edge at the twisted ribbons of smoke blowing through the breach. Then he leaped, hanging on to the man-child's right arm before he ever had a chance to pull his gun, ripping at the man's coat, clawing at the weapon still tucked inside.

"Motherfucker." The man-child pivoted, Daniel clinging like a terrier, his weight peeling the leather coat back from the man's body and dislodging the gun. It flew through the air, still dark with fury as a brace of sirens sounded and three cop cars rolled into Latin School's back lot. The man-child with the tooth around his neck shook free of Daniel and felt for the gun against his ribs. He cursed when he realized it wasn't there and looked around wildly for it. Then he ran, quicker than anyone could ever have imagined, taking Death with him, leaving an ugly, rippling scar behind.

Daniel was still on his knees as the squad cars rolled up, chasing what remained of the mob across the bumpy field toward Avenue Louis Pasteur. Eddie and Ben were gone. Daniel had no idea where. He struggled to his feet and ran crookedly toward the steps and the side door Ben had been tasked to protect. He'd just reached the first step when he heard something he thought he knew—the soft sounds of a woman's struggle. In a stray panel of light Daniel could just make out a couple of backs, three backs, huddled on the far side of the Dumpster. They hadn't run like the others and the air rippled and danced around them. Daniel went up on his tiptoes, changing the angle enough to catch a glimpse of a red sneaker attached to a long leg. It was a girl's sneaker, Grace's sneaker, trapped beneath the hump-backed monster.

Daniel opened his mouth to scream, but heard only a high shriek, torn from his lips and borne away in the tumult. He began to run, taking one step, then a second. He felt his foot gouge the earth, pulling up clods of dirt and rocks. Daniel looked down as his legs narrowed, his feet, first one, then the other, curving into hard yellow talons. Feathers sprouted from his shoulders and traveled down his arms until they covered his fingers in fine, swirling ruffles. His bones hollowed and the breeze at his back coarsened, lifting him as he took a third step, then a fourth, and then he no longer touched the earth.

Daniel soared high overhead, flapping his wings in long, powerful strokes and peering down at the three sets of gray shoulders huddled over Grace. One turned and looked up, fleshed hood slipping off a bald head to reveal pulpy red eyes, a hooked beak, and the thick tongue of a vulture rattling in a hiss. Daniel angled back against the breeze and settled on a corner of Latin School's roof, almost directly above them. He could hear Grace's fear—thin music that pierced his skull to cracking and filled the air with its tremble. Daniel spread his wings again and dove, the cold slipstreaming over sinew and muscle. He clenched and unclenched his talons and sharpened his eyes as he dropped through the sky, hunting for a soft spot among the scavengers. Then he was back on the ground, back in his own skin, falling on Grace's attackers like hell's hammer with fists and teeth and spit and screams. They ran as one, overwhelmed by the fury without ever considering the size and strength, or lack thereof, of their foe. Daniel watched them go, nostrils laid back, sucking in air while one leg shook and there was nothing he could do about it. Grace was huddled tiny against the wall, fully clothed with her knees under her chin and her hands locked around her legs.

"They didn't do anything." She was looking straight ahead, voice stripped and tender and raw.

"I know."

"They didn't."

"It's okay, Grace."

"Don't tell me what's okay." She tried to get to her feet but stumbled and collapsed back against the wall. Daniel sat down beside her and touched her arm.

"You wanna talk to the cops or something?"

She shook her head. "They didn't do anything, Daniel."

"Grace . . ."

"They tried or they would have tried, but you stopped them." She leaned over and kissed him quickly on the cheek, touching a soft spot under his eye. "Tell Ben and the other guy I said thanks as well."

"Why don't we go inside and see the nurse . . ."

"I just wanna go home."

"All right."

"Maybe we can meet tonight. Nine o'clock at the fish tank?"

Daniel nodded. She gave him a hug and stood up, making no sound as she crept down the side of the building, holding on to the brick wall for balance, and then slipping through the back lot to the street.

He sat back and let the chemicals percolate in his blood. He was coming off it now, whatever "it" was, and fatigue was setting in. The moments, real and imagined, rampaged through his head, rippling in staccato bursts of color and sound. It all seemed slightly off-kilter, out of control. Daniel wondered about the meds he'd refused to take and dug his nails into his palms just to feel the bite. That was when he saw the beaded grip of the gun sticking out from under the Dumpster. He pulled it toward him with his foot and stretched his legs out, covering the gun with his thigh as the sirens whooped and someone on a megaphone told the crowds at the front of the school to disperse or they'd be arrested. Close by came the crackle of a walkie-talkie and the crunch of footsteps on cold gravel. The cops were circling back, putting together the pieces of the brawl. They'd want to talk to him for sure, but only if they found him.

Daniel picked up the gun, surprisingly snug in his palm, and stuffed it in his pocket. Then he crawled toward the door, duckwalking as he got closer to keep the Dumpster between himself and the cops. When he got close enough, he took a deep breath, paused for a second, and ran into the building. He expected to hear a cop yelling for him to stop, but there was nothing. Daniel went down to his locker and stashed the gun behind a text on Cicero's Catiline Orations. Then he wandered back to the school's main entrance. Kids filled the hallways, chattering excitedly about what had happened, the accounts growing wilder by the minute. Daniel hung on the edge of the conversation and listened. Eddie was the hero who'd saved Ben the bookworm. No one mentioned Grace. No one mentioned a gun. No one mentioned a student transforming into a bird of prey.

Daniel went into a bathroom and touched his face in the mirror. The images came ripe and unbidden. Claw and beak. His body morphing, lifting, soaring. He closed his eyes and tipped his head back as the headmaster's voice crackled over the intercom. Classes were canceled for the day; buses would be waiting outside. Daniel took his time washing his hands and walked slowly back to his locker. He pushed the gun he'd found down to the bottom of his bag and covered it up. Then he threw the bag over his shoulder and left by the same side door where he'd found Grace and fought his battle. The cops were still there, but they had bigger problems. It was just past eleven in the morning and a little more than a mile back to his new home.

He'd walk it. Unless he flew.

15

Tommy Dillon skimmed the surface of the Tobin Bridge at eighty miles an hour, flipping through stations, hopping and popping from blues to jazz to Elvis. He settled on Bowie's "Starman" and picked up the garage bill stuck in his console. Three hundred fifty bucks for what? Tommy pressed down on the accelerator. Piece of shit still had no pickup. He flew off the end of the bridge, sparks flying as he scraped bottom, and sipped from a paper cup filled with ice and Coke and a hit of fine, dark rum. Tommy called it taking the edge off.

He glanced down at the directions he'd printed on the inside of his wrist. Five-mile bomb down Route 1, then another mile or so once he got off. The Stones came on the radio. Tommy turned it up and started slaloming in and out of afternoon traffic, humming to himself as he hunted for gaps, then jumping into the breakdown lane and punching it. A piece-of-shit Vega tried to squeeze him into the guardrail. Tommy laid on the horn and flipped him off, laughing like a mother-fucker and loving it.

He peeled off the expressway in Revere, took a quick suck on the rum and Coke as he squeezed between two trucks, and pulled into a fenced-in parking lot behind an old cement factory. Fucking drama with this guy. Tommy could have met the prick in Faneuil Hall and it would have been just as good. He killed the engine and watched two men climb out of a puke-green Monte Carlo. The one Tommy knew was wrapped in a leather duster coat and wore biker boots with run-down heels. A Mexican was just behind him. Both stood with their backs to the sun and their legs spread, like it was the fucking OK Corral or something.

Not a problem.

Tommy made his way across the lot with a bow in his legs and a roll in his gait. John fucking Wayne, taking his John fucking Wayne time. The Mex was hard around the eyes, but nervous. He wore a brown corduroy jacket bunched at the shoulders and had a gun in his pocket.

"Tommy, you know Rafa?" The man in the duster

was nothing to Tommy. A means to an end. Another route through the sewer.

"Get rid of him," Tommy said.

The Mexican grinned, white teeth flashing, and mumbled something in Spanish.

"What'd he say?"

"He says he's seen you around. Says they call you *ardilla*. Means 'the little squirrel.'" The man in the duster thought that was funny as all fuck. Tommy pulled out his gun and whistled a slug by the ear of the Mex, who hugged the ground and looked like he might just piss himself.

"Hey, hey, hey." The man in the duster spread his hands. The Mex raised his eyes off the gravel, his piece in his fist. Maybe he was gonna shoot someone in the ankle.

"I ain't in the fucking mood," Tommy said, putting his gun away and bringing himself back to heel.

The man in the duster nodded at the Mex, who scrambled to his feet and walked backward to the Monte, never taking his eyes off Tommy as he climbed in the front seat.

"Why am I out here?"

"Fucking relax, Tommy. Jesus, it was a joke."

"I'm fine."

"Fine, my ass. What's the problem?"

"Nothin'. Cases piling up. Partner's nervous as a fucking cat. Yesterday we pulled your guy out of the harbor."

"Afraid I can't help you with that one."

"No shit. So why am I here?"

The man in the duster led Tommy back behind the Monte. Tommy toodled his fingers at the Mex as he went by, then stood back as the man in the duster cranked open the trunk. The inside was layered with fat bags of cocaine. Tommy moved closer, lip twitching, one hand resting on the rubber lining of the trunk, the other running smooth and light over his gun grip.

"You know I work Homicide?"

"Fuck Homicide. For you, this right here is forever money. Your wife, your kids. Game changer."

"Got the wrong guy."

"Do I?"

"If you think I'm gonna help you move this much product, absolutely."

The man in the duster slammed down the lid of the trunk, nearly catching Tommy's fingers. "Who said anything about moving product? I don't let users— sorry, former users—anywhere near that end. No offense, but it's bad for business."

"Then what do you want?"

"Small job, but it's gotta be done right. Everything goes well, you and I are done. And you get the taste."

"Why the fuck am I so lucky?"

"You have the skills for the job. Plus I'm getting out of the business and don't need any more cops in my Rolodex. Let's sit up front and talk. I think you're gonna like this."

They pulled the Mex out of the car and told him to take a walk. Where? Who the fuck knows cuz there was nowhere to walk. Still, the Mex went. Then the man in the duster sat behind the wheel of the Monte, Tommy beside him, listening as the man told him about the job. Tommy tried to keep it all in his head and wanted to take notes but knew that wasn't allowed. Mostly, though, he thought about the money. And when he wasn't thinking about the money, he was smiling and nodding at the man in the duster and imagining taking out his gun and decorating the inside of the car with the cocksucker's brains. Then he'd hunt down the Mex. *Ardilla, my fucking ass.*

Tommy never got another look at the product. When they finished, he shook hands and hopped in his car. This time he put the bubble on the roof and did a buck ten across the Tobin, amazed at all he had to do and wondering where he could get something to eat, while another part of his brain admired the sudden balls his car was showing. Fucking grease monkey might have actually done something after all.

Tommy buried the needle. Up ahead dusk was falling, and the city loomed.

16

Daniel ran loose-limbed along the path, footsteps soundless as he went. Evening traffic zipped past on his right, bullets of pure light reflected in long ripples across a glass canyon of buildings. He slipped under the BU Bridge and followed the bend of the Charles, the humped backs of old New England brownstones replacing sleek steel on the other side of Storrow Drive. Daniel slowed, then stopped in front of an apartment building three stories high and taking up two city lots. Someone had ripped out the building's guts and installed floor-to-ceiling windows, affording the occupants a sculpted view of downtown. He settled in a shelter of trees and stared up at the building's top floor. The fish tank was long and deep, an illuminated collection of blues and whites and pinks floating free in the night. Daniel slitted his eyes until he could just see his fish, slippery streaks of copper and silver cutting paths in their invisible prison. He sank into the pattern of color and swirl, sitting still against the tree, hearing her approach long before she arrived, footsteps caught between the thin scream of cars and the ceaseless murmur of the river. Daniel turned as she reached to touch his shoulder. Grace pulled her hand back, eyes painted in patches of light from the moving night.

"You scared me," she said.

"I told you I'd be here."

"Yes, but how did you know . . . Never mind."

"You wanna sit?"

She took a seat beside him on the bare ground. He could feel her warmth even though it was November and they were both bundled against the cold pushing in from the harbor.

"How are your fish?" She'd been here before. No one else had. Not even Harry.

"I think they're hungry."

"They sure are pretty. Like a painting."

They sat together, watching the fish do their fish thing.

"I'm sorry about this morning," Daniel said.

"I told you it was fine."

He snuck a look across. "Did you tell your parents?"

He'd never been to the walk-up in Chinatown where Grace lived. She'd explained once that her father didn't like "round eyes" and made a pair of circles with her fingers that she held up to her face. Daniel had laughed at the joke and they'd ignored the rest. It was Boston, after all, and that's just how the world was.

"They don't need to know," she said.

"Why not?"

"Nothing happened, Daniel."

"Okay."

"Did you tell your brother?"

"I haven't talked to him yet."

"Do you think other people saw? People from school, I mean?"

"I don't know. Ben won't say anything."

"No, Ben won't say anything."

"Eddie Spaulding won't either. He's actually a pretty good guy."

"If you say so. Was it on the news?"

"I doubt it."

"Good."

He reached over and covered her gloved hand with his. Their shoulders touched. "Hey."

She angled her face toward him and he could see peach fuzz lying against the smooth of her cheek. Her mind was running at a low hum, a perfect sphere spinning in a perfect circle just at the end of his reach. All he had to do was flick a finger and that perfect rotation would stutter, wobble for a moment, then resettle, except not the same now. He remembered what Simon had said about being careful. He was probably right, but what harm could it do, the two of them alone, here by the river?

"You should have worn a hat," he said.

She pushed at a lank piece of hair that hung over one eye, then shoved her hands back in her pockets, moving a fraction so their shoulders were no longer touching. "I'm all right."

He pulled off his Patriots stocking hat and put it on her head. She resisted at first, then let him adjust it until he could see Pat Patriot's face. They watched Daniel's fish some more. A gray squirrel with bright black eyes joined them for a while and left. Daniel knew she'd have to go soon as well.

"Are you hurt?" She peeled off a glove and reached out to touch a bruise and some scraping under his eye.

"I'm good. And don't call me scrappy."

"I won't." She took a closer look, probing gently with her forefinger.

"It's just a scratch," Daniel said, wincing a bit and wondering if she'd seen the gun, wondering if he should tell her about his hallucination during the brawl, wondering about dreams hung in flesh and a parade of pills bouncing under the wheels of a bus and on down the street.

"There's something I need to tell you," he said.

"You want your hat back?"

"Funny."

"It's not about today, is it?"

"No."

"Go ahead, then."

So he told her about Simon and his theories on entanglement. And how Daniel had used it on her in the record store. She put her hand over her mouth and laughed and he thought she'd never stop.

"You're saying you 'pushed' me? Is that the term you use?"

"Entangled, pushed. Yes."

"You pushed me in Music City?"

"Yes."

"You touched my mind and willed me to kiss you?"

"Yes, yes."

"So you're a mind reader?"

"No, it's not that."

"Mind control?"

Daniel shook his head. "It's more like we were two and then we were one. And, in that moment, things changed. Not necessarily cuz I planned it or anything. Just cuz that's how it was."

"I don't think so."

"Trust me."

"Daniel, I've been thinking about kissing you for a month and a half."

He popped his head back. "Seriously?"

"Sort of."

"That's just it. Everyone 'sort of' thinks about things, but you acted on it. Right in the moment."

"And that was because of you?"

"Could be."

"Okay, let's say I believe you, which I don't for even a second. Is this an apology?"

"More like a confession. I mean, it was just a kiss."

"Hmmm."

"What?" He edged closer, studying the curve of her face while an unconscious part of him thrilled at her nearness.

"Maybe there was something."

"Really? In the record store?"

"Maybe. I mean, I *had* thought about kissing you, just to see what it was like. I think we're better as friends, though. Don't you?"

Pain. Not as piercing as he'd imagined, but still. Daniel shoved it to one side for now. "Tell me what you felt."

"Well, it was like a click." Grace snapped her fingers.

"A click?"

"Something clicked and I just decided to plant one."

"That was it?"

"Yes, a click in my head and a warm pulse in my stomach, like I was going to do something fun and great and I shouldn't think about it because it felt so right and it might not always feel that way."

"All that in the click, huh?"

"And the warm feeling. Don't forget the warm feeling, Daniel. It was actually wonderful."

He sat back. "Wow."

"Wow is right. Fifty years from now, if I'm still alive, I'm pretty sure I'll remember it all, the record store and the kiss. A little touch of forever that blossomed right here." She pressed the spot over his heart. "So if you 'pushed,' whatever that means in your quantum physics world, then thank you." Grace leaned in as easy as that and kissed him again, dry and precious and fleeting on the lips. "Besides, maybe it was me who was pushing, maybe I'm pushing you right now. So there."

She stuck out her tongue and they laughed at the crazy talk that maybe neither thought was crazy at all. And then she took his hand and wrapped it in hers while the fish flew through the night in streaks of color and the cold river ran on behind them in a ceaseless current of conscience and memory.

"Tell me about your professor," she finally said.

Daniel felt the shift, something in his gut stirring and stretching, blinking itself awake. "What about him?"

"You don't think it's strange he talks to you about all this stuff?"

"It's part of his work as a physicist."

"And what are you? One of his lab rats?"

Daniel thought about his dreams, one living within the other. And Simon watching. "He's all right, Grace."

"He's changing you."

She was as wrong as she was right. There was a narrowing in Daniel's soul. At first he'd thought it was just part of growing up. But maybe it was something more. Maybe Simon was his watchman, lifting a spear in warning at an approaching storm. Or maybe the warning was meant for someone else. He touched the back of her hand.

"How are you getting home?"

"Green Line to Boylston. Then I walk."

"I should go with you."

"It's not even ten."

"You sure?"

"I'm fine, Daniel. I mean, what happened today was awful, but they didn't get anywhere and I'm tough and it's over. Okay?"

"Okay."

"What are you gonna do?"

"I don't know. Finish my run, I guess."

"Call me tomorrow. And don't run all night, crazy."

He watched her walk up the bare path to a footbridge that crossed over Storrow. She was halfway across when a squat, dark figure appeared behind her and quickly closed the gap. Daniel crept to his feet and began to run. He was about to yell when the dark figure paused, then retraced his steps across the footbridge and came down on Daniel's side, walking quickly in the opposite direction while Daniel stood in the shadows. When he looked up at the bridge again, Grace was gone.

Daniel thought about following, catching up with her, and riding the T back to Chinatown. But she'd hate that and he didn't want to ruin what had already happened. So he struck off in the opposite direction, jogging lightly along the path, keeping the river on his left and downtown just out of reach. He should have called Harry and told him about the fight at school. He would have wanted to come over and talk about it. Maybe they'd have gone on a run together, Harry beside him right now, matching him stride for stride.

Daniel picked up his pace as the wind turned, hard and black in his face. He thought some more about Harry, about the man following Grace and the brawl again. He thought about Grace behind the Dumpster, her lonely red sneaker sticking out and the feeling as Daniel sprouted feathers, grew claws, and took wing, all of it realer than real if only in his head. A foul odor walked off the turning river and he could taste that thing again, slick in his throat, alive and crawling blind in his belly. He knew what his doctor would say. PTSD, she'd call it. Post-traumatic stress disorder. Daniel preferred a simpler name. Terror. Free-floating and looking for a home.

He willed his heart to slow as he pounded along the path, shooting over another of the small footbridges spanning Storrow and dropping into a tangle of narrow streets that made up the Back Bay. A car nearly clipped him at a corner, the driver laying on the horn and rolling down his window to let loose a string of curses. Daniel kept going. Up ahead the Boston Common lay fallow, like a black, unplowed sea.

17

The Naked i was in full swing. In the front room, a dancer named Inga hung off a pole, Red Sox pasties on her nipples and zipper scars running underneath both breasts. No matter. They lined up at the low bar that wrapped around the stage and filled up the small tables, heavy eyes drinking in the show while they sipped their ten-dollar drinks and smoked their cigarettes and never said a word to each other, most barely aware of anything other than the scent of the woman above them and the swing of her hips. At one end of the bar, a bald man in a checked suit waved a bill between two fingers, hoping to catch Inga's attention. Beside him, his pal breathed into a paper bag between sips of his 7 and 7. Women drifted through the back of the lounge, working lurkers at the door—talking, laughing, flirting, touching, pushing them to buy a drink, then coaxing their fish into an alley outside where maybe there was a blowjob waiting, or maybe a pimp with a knife. Over the intercom the manager announced in his best Fenway Park voice that Desiree would be starting her show in the Pussy Galore in ten minutes. The Pussy Galore was the Naked i's back room. Not much bigger than a bathroom, it sometimes held fifty patrons, pressed up against one another and gazing at women even more past their sell-by dates than Inga. The guy with the paper bag lurched to his feet and headed toward the back bar. One of the lurkers grabbed his spot and ordered a drink.

Harry was sitting at a table near the door. The promise about staying in the car had lasted twenty minutes. Harry was surprised it took that long. A girl who knew him from his volunteer work brought him a club soda on the house. Zeus sat to one side, drinking a Bud that had cost him nine bucks. Neil Prescott had his back to Harry, eyes glued to the stage. He'd opted for a rum and Coke, a bargain at twelve-fifty. They'd started their night at the Harvard Club. Eaten dinner there, cardboard chicken and rubber rice, and drank three pitchers of beer. Zeus had done most of the drinking. Prescott seemed content to sip at the watered-down draft while Harry ordered a ginger ale. A couple of alums had stopped by to talk football. They'd gone on for a while and Harry thought the night might begin and end right there. But Zeus had his eye on the clock and told the alums they had people they needed to meet. That was partly true. There was a vague plan to meet other members of the team somewhere in the Zone. Exactly where and when remained a mystery, but the Zone wasn't that big and Zeus seemed certain everyone would somehow find one another.

It was just ten when they walked out of the club. A couple of women followed, asking where they were going, complaining that Zeus had promised to buy them a drink. Harry pulled his pals away and herded them down the block. *Stay together.* The photographer Toney's words rolled around in his head looking for something to bump up against. Zeus wasn't feeling any pain and wanted to take a stroll. They skirted past the Pilgrim Theater and then the Brompton Arms, a rent-by-the-hour hotel perched precariously at the corner of Washington and LaGrange streets. Women came out of the alleys, swarming like sucker fish to a herd of fat, slow sperm whales. Harry knew a lot of the faces, but none of them seemed to care. He was a potential john now and this was business. One of the girls slipped her arm around Prescott and pulled him down LaGrange. Another ran her hand up the inside of Zeus's leg and asked how big he was. Harry wasn't having it. The girls swore and one tried to kick him with the spike of her heel as he dragged his friends back toward Washington and the safety of the car. Prescott was driving and jumped in front. There was a cooler of beer beside him so Harry and Zeus got in the back.

"What the fuck, Harry?"

"Shut up."

"What did we come down here for? Neil, gimme a beer."

Prescott pulled a can of Schlitz out of the ice and handed it back. Zeus popped it and took a hit, all the while continuing to berate Harry for taking them off LaGrange. Harry ignored the noise. Zeus had been right this morning when he'd described the Zone. They were little more than tourists down here, staring out the window at the wildlife prowling past. Harry's job was to make sure no one got bit. Or dropped their pants in an alley no matter how much they had to drink.

"Where are the other guys?" Prescott said.

"No idea." Zeus took another hit on his beer, tapped Harry on the knee, and winked. "Hey, Neil. Check her out."

"Yo." Prescott knocked on the windshield at a black woman in a tight leather dress. She blew him a kiss. Prescott went off on how hot she was and what he'd do to her if he ever got a chance. Harry recognized the woman from his volunteer work and didn't have the heart to tell Prescott his "she" was a "he."

"Let's hang here for a bit," Zeus said. "If the rest of those guys are around, they'll come by."

Prescott thought that was a good idea and grabbed another beer out of the cooler. A couple more women appeared out of the smoke and the cold and the night. Zeus rolled down the back window halfway so one of them could lean in. Harry could smell her perfume but couldn't get a good look at her face. Zeus mumbled something. Prescott caught Harry's eye in the rearview mirror and mugged silently. There was another woman now, walking across the street with her eye on the car. Prescott cracked his window as she approached. Beside Harry, Zeus had pushed his window all the way down. Harry could see long fingers, nails painted orange, and a thin wrist flashing gold bracelets. Up front, the woman with an eye for Prescott had disappeared. Zeus shifted his weight, blocking Harry's view entirely as he talked in a low voice to the woman. Harry caught Prescott's eyes again in the rearview mirror and was about to suggest they go when there was a sudden movement beside him. He turned just in time to see the woman's silhouette as she disappeared down the block. Zeus was swearing and struggling with the handle on the door.

"She took my wallet. Fucking bitch took my wallet."

Harry grabbed at his friend. "Wait."

The sleeve of Zeus's coat ripped through Harry's fingers and the big tackle was gone, running hard after the woman. Prescott fumbled for his door handle. Harry gripped his shoulder.

"Stay with the car. You understand me?"

Prescott nodded, eyes wide and weak. Harry climbed out. Someone was watching from a doorway and pointed. The guy was drunk and cheered Harry like he was running the marathon. Half a block ahead, he could see Zeus turn down LaGrange. Harry took the same corner just as his friend ducked into an alley. Harry hesitated, then started back toward the car. He'd get Prescott and they'd go together. Easier that way. Safer. Someone called out. He turned and saw a woman standing in the middle of LaGrange. She was long and willowy and wrapped in a short leather coat. She started to raise her hand when the door to a club called Good Time Charlie's kicked open and a thick man stumbled out. He grabbed blindly at the woman, who stepped back, white light from inside the club catching her profile before the door slammed shut again. The woman slipped from the man's grip and ran into the same alley Zeus had gone down. Harry followed.

As he hit the mouth of the alley, he heard the dying

chatter of heels on asphalt, then nothing. Harry
called out for Zeus but got no answer. Blank windows
stretched up both sides of the passage, the occasional
lamp casting light here and there. A green door loomed
on his left. Harry tried it. Locked. He could make out
a Dumpster about halfway down one side and a string
of garbage cans down the other. Harry crept forward,
hissing for Zeus. He was about to start running again
when he caught a flicker of movement. The man was
crouched in a tight space between the Dumpster and
the wall. He came at Harry from behind, swinging a
blade that flashed in a yellow seam of light. Harry heard
himself yell and caught the man's elbow as the blade
swung. It sliced in just below Harry's rib cage, nicking
the corner of his intestines and starting a flow of blood
into his abdominal cavity. Harry felt the warm leak as
his legs turned to slush and the back of his head hit
the wall. Harry's pulse was hammering, mind racing,
wondering how, why, what. His attacker tripped and
stumbled forward, looming over Harry, who caught a
glimpse of gritted teeth and the shine of skin. A silver
tooth dangled from the man's neck. Then there was the
knife again, at the top of its arc, poised to swing.

Daniel plunged through the layered darkness of the
Boston Common. A necklace of streets surrounded it,

embroidering the edges in soft yellow while the golden dome of the State House hung steep and chaste overhead like some secular confessor god. Daniel accelerated up a hill, not knowing where he was headed but certain he was desperately behind. He ducked between a set of park benches and paused on the edge of a wide field.

Daniel could feel his heart beat in his blood, the flex and ripple in his legs even as his arms began to lengthen, fingers cracking and thickening into scaled pads of flesh, nails extending and hardening into yellow claws. Fur grew in ridges along his back, tawny orange with stripes of ebony running up his shoulders and around eyes that were sulfurous yellow with wet orbs of black in the very center. Daniel dropped to all fours and sprang forward, tearing up the earth as he powered across the field. He could smell the sourness of his breath and felt his teeth curve in his jaw, white whiskers bristling like wire in the November cold. He slowed, padding silently past Park Street Station—fully grown now, a Bengal tiger staring out at the passing cars and the fuzzy lights and the tender city.

Daniel began to move again, gliding past a kiddie pool and over another rise, night vision aglow, picking up the heat of a man bundled on a bench. There was the smell of liquor and cigarette smoke and stale popcorn. Daniel sped on, feeling the brush of spiked tops across his belly as he jumped an iron fence. He was in a graveyard, the ancient tombstones cut hard by moonlight, set down in ragged rows like a rotting set of teeth. Daniel wove between them, tail flicking. Two strides and he was back over the fence, racing the curve of a walking path, Boylston Street cresting just ahead. He paused for a moment, rubbing his flank against a tree, enjoying the scratch of the bark on his hide and the smell of the earth in his nose. Then he stepped out of the Boston Common and back onto the street, back into his own body.

Daniel had no memory of his run through the park, at least not on two feet, yet here he was. He looked down at his running shoes, Tigers of course, soaking wet and caked in mud. He took off his hat and shook the light sweat out of his hair. An image of Grace filled his head, followed by a black face with a silver tooth on a chain, swinging free off his neck as he reached for his gun. Harry rose up, Harry somewhere in the city, clutching at minutes, seconds, moments as they slipped through his fingers.

Daniel sprinted the rest of the way up Boylston to the intersection of Tremont. Half a block away, a squad car lit up its flashers and accelerated, the cry of its siren spiking his blood and freezing all thought. The squad

fishtailed around a van stopped at the light and disappeared down Tremont. Daniel followed, diving into
the fragrant, yellow heart of Chinatown, the Combat
Zone waiting just beyond.

Harry raised his arm as the blade fell, tearing at the
sleeve of his jacket before scraping off the brick behind him. He was on one knee and came up hard,
hammering a right under his attacker's ribs, driving him back against the iron spine of the Dumpster.
The black kid grunted and slumped halfway to the
ground, his knife clattering onto the hardtop. Harry
reached, but the kid was closer. He had the knife in
his left hand, swiping low this time, catching nothing
but air. The kid's eyes were moving and Harry could
see the clock ticking in his head.

"You got thirty seconds," Harry said. "After that the
cops are here and you're done."

The kid responded with another swipe of the knife,
wider now, wilder. A drunk stumbled against a garbage
can somewhere, the noise rattling through the maze of
concrete and brick.

"I'll tell them I didn't get a look," Harry said. "But
you got to go. Right fucking now."

The kid's eyes slalomed from side to side, weighing,
measuring, deciding. He slipped the knife into his

pocket and disappeared down the alley. Just like that, Harry was alone. He slumped back against the Dumpster, legs splayed, hand over his stomach, feeling his abdominal muscles twitch and the thin flow of blood between his fingers. Harry tipped his chin up and stared at the wall of faceless windows scaling up both sides of the alley. Jimmy Stewart and *Rear Window*. That's what it reminded him of. If Grace Kelly came walking down the alley, it might even be worth it. He chuckled and felt his eyes flutter. The cold was in his bones now as the adrenaline drained away. Shock wasn't far behind. He lifted his shirt and checked the wound, not more than an inch or so, angry and red. He could feel the blood leaking inside, but it was slowing, clotting, stopping. Harry would live. He was certain of that. And he'd keep his promise to the black kid. A soft scuff of shoes. Someone approaching. Didn't sound like Grace Kelly, but Harry wasn't complaining. Whoever it was stopped on the far side of the Dumpster.

"Over here." Harry's voice was that of an old man, not much more than a croak. Then the person stood over him, backlit by the glow from a streetlamp.

"I'm hurt," Harry said, and held out his hand. His savior crouched, withdrawing a long sinew of silver from under a coat. This time there was no doubt, the steel driving deep into Harry's belly, pinning him to the wall behind him. Once, twice, three times, the steel flashed. Then his attacker was gone and Harry lay flat on the pavement, blood bubbling out of the fresh holes with every pump of his heart. He turned his head, eyes clinging to each precious piece of life around him. He noticed the rough rub of the alley next to his cheek, the grit of dirt, and the crooked rubber wheel of the Dumpster six inches from his nose. J.J. ALBUS & SONS was stamped on the wheel's metal caster and Harry wondered what J.J. looked like, what manner of man he might be. One with glasses and a fine, even temperament, Harry guessed. His eyes reached for the far wall. He studied the strata of brick, taking apart each grain of sand that made up the mortar mix, puzzling over its composition and the men who worked with it one summer's day—months, years, decades ago. He saw a hot dog wrapper just beyond his reach and would have given what little was left of his life if there had been writing on it. A rat scuttled out from between two garbage cans and sat by his ear, whiskers twitching, eyes calculating. Harry moved two of his fingers in greeting. The rat lifted a paw, scratched its face, and scuttled off. Better things to do, no doubt.

Harry took a final look around, inhaling every particle of the alley, feeling the energy of "being" as it sparked and flickered and hummed all around him.

He could see clearly now the infrastructure that he'd always known without ever knowing, the cosmic glue, the light, the pure, effortless grace that bound and transformed and breathed life into inanimate lumps of clay we called "things"—people, buildings, cars, flowers, dogs, cats, rats and the garbage they picked through. He saw it all, entangled in a shifting, eternal, breathtaking pulse of light and dark, good and evil, birth and decay and birth again. And he knew, just as sure as he knew he was on the point of his own death, that Daniel was close by, that Daniel was coming, that they'd never really be apart again. Harry called out his brother's name as he closed his eyes and breathed his last, falling forward into the web of seamless light, into the warmth, enveloping, embracing, taking him home. A place he'd never been before. A place from which he'd never leave.

18

Faces floated past, painted eyes and curled lips, gums, teeth, and folds of flesh hanging loose from cheeks and under chins, all of it caught in harsh stripes of light. Daniel turned away, stumbling down one alley, then a second. In the close, sticky confines of the Combat Zone, he was forced to slow down. A door kicked open and a tide of human refuse flushed out, men, women, high heels and perfume, hard leather shoes and liquor, pushing him one way, pulling another. Someone asked if the kid was looking for a blowjob. Laughter. "Maybe a handy Andy. Denise, whaddaya say?" More laughter. Daniel was scraped up against the side of a building and left stranded as the tide drained off.

Terror blinked in his belly, opening its filmy eyes again, sinking its fangs into his liver. Daniel fell to his

knees and got sick, the vomit splashing up in his face
before being carried by a trickle of water to a small
grated drain and the sewer that ran rank beneath the
city. He stretched out flat on his stomach, cheek against
a rough cobble, and wondered what he was doing here,
if the docs were right after all, if he was losing his mind,
if he'd opened a door to something that would swallow
him whole. He thought about Harry as the thing inside
bit again, this time taking a chunk of his spine. Daniel
shivered and groaned and struggled to his knees.

Breadcrumbs of noise. Gruff voices giving directions, a high-pitched protest, someone cursing, the
whine of a walkie-talkie. A door opened to Daniel's
right, and a wrinkled Asian face ghosted into view.
Daniel tried to ask a question, but the door slammed
shut. The noise was getting louder, the voices closer. A
curtain moved in a window above him. A man leaned
out, forearms on the sill, and gawked at something in
the adjacent alley. He ducked from the window and
returned with a camera, snapping away at whatever
he'd spied below. Daniel got to his feet and took a final
corner so he was almost directly beneath the window. A
black man was kneeling beside a Dumpster. He turned
and fixed Daniel with a hollow stare.

"Who the fuck are you?" The black man was
dressed in a dark overcoat and had a gold badge hang-

ing shiny around his neck. "How the fuck did this kid get in here?"

There were more sounds, heavy footsteps pounding toward them. The man climbed to his feet and moved to greet the newcomers. As he did, Daniel got a glimpse of what he'd been bent over. And then Daniel screamed, high and dry like an animal caught in a trap, willing to trade a limb for his life. Or his brother's. The black man with the badge knew that scream, had heard it before, and dove. Too late. Daniel had Harry in his arms, still screaming, mingling tears with his brother's blood, thick and dark and warm as it frothed and flowed from the hidden wounds. Three cops had him now, too many hands tearing at him, dragging him off Harry and trapping him in a corner. The black man shoved his face in Daniel's and asked a bunch of questions, but Daniel didn't hear any of them. All he did was scream and scrape at the flesh on his arms and the flesh on his face. He screamed while they cuffed him, screamed while they dragged him down the alley, screamed while they muscled him through the crowd of pimps and hookers and johns and hustlers who'd massed behind the police tape to see what sort of entertainment the night held, screamed while they threw him in the back of the cruiser still covered in blood, screamed while they drove him away. Then it was quiet and the people on LaGrange Street talked among themselves, agreeing this was a fine show and when were they going to bring out the body.

In the alley a cold, black rain began to fall in earnest. Barkley and Tommy were huddled under an umbrella while a couple of forensics guys worked on the corpse. Barkley pulled Harry's Harvard ID out of his wallet and showed it to Tommy. They exchanged a look and told the forensics guys to go get coffee. Then Barkley crouched on his haunches and studied Harry's face, comparing it with the ID. Behind him Tommy was on the radio, calling for more backup and cursing their luck.

PART II

19

Barkley needed coffee. They had a pot, filters, and silver bags of the stuff stashed in a corner of the squad room, but he had neither the patience nor the palate for fresh-brewed. With a soft grunt he got up and walked down the hall to a vending machine not far from the front desk. He dropped in a quarter and selected COFFEE-BLACK. There was a whirring sound, then the good stuff began to hiss into a cardboard cup with a smiley face on it. He took the coffee back to his desk and settled before the typewriter. It was already loaded with a blank police report and four layers of colored carbons. Barkley had just typed 3:15 A.M. in the box where it said TIME when Tommy hit the door.

"Bark . . ."

"Typing, Tommy."

"It's the kid."

"You wanna do the typing, Tommy?"

"He's a problem. And no, I don't wanna do the typing."

Barkley looked up. "You get him clean?"

"He won't clean. Won't leave the fucking room."

"Where you got him?"

"Number one."

Tommy stepped aside as Barkley swept past and down the hall to holding room number one. Barkley stopped at the door and turned. "We heard anything from the press?"

Tommy shook his head. "How long you think before they turn up?"

"Hard to say. Prick from the *Herald* already had Fitzsimmons's name at the scene. He'll get here first. After that, it's the bigger prick from the *Globe*. And then the cameras."

"We gonna have to talk to 'em?" Tough guy that he was, Tommy hated the press. Pretty much shrank back into the skin of a ten-year-old anytime he got near a hot mike.

"Sure as shit they're gonna want my black face out there."

"Sorry, B."

"Ain't your fault. Now, listen, this kid here, he's gotta be gone before any of that starts."

"So we either arrest him or turn him loose."

"Arrest him? For what? You got an ID yet?"

"Nothing in his pockets. Actually, he's got no pockets. Looks like he was running."

"Did he give a name?"

"All the kid did was scream. Thank Christ he's stopped that."

Barkley pushed open the door. The kid was curled up in a corner, knees tucked under his chin, skinny arms wrapped around his shins. He wasn't wearing a shirt and his chest was smeared with Ivy League blood.

"You wanna take a seat?" Barkley turned one of the two chairs in the room toward the kid and sat in the other. Tommy leaned against the doorframe and folded his arms across his chest. The kid looked at both men, got up, and took the seat.

"You want something to eat?" Barkley said. "Something to drink? How about we take you into the bathroom and let you clean up?"

The kid shook his head.

Barkley had forgotten his coffee so he folded his hands on the tiny table wedged between them. The kid was gripping the shit out of both sides of his chair and rocking back and forth. His eyes were glued to the floor.

"What's your name, son?"

"Daniel."

Bingo. That wasn't so fucking hard.

"Daniel what?"

"Fitzsimmons."

The kid's last name crushed the room to the size of a closet. Barkley felt the familiar weight in his chest. Tommy shifted in his boots.

"My name's Barkley Jones. I'm a detective with the Boston PD." Barkley threw a thumb over his shoulder. "The other guy who's been helping you is my partner, Tommy Dillon. We're gonna need to ask you a few questions."

"Go ahead."

"Are you related to Harry Fitzsimmons?"

"He's my brother."

"I'm sorry, Daniel, but your brother's dead."

The kid rocked a little faster. "I already knew that."

"You sure you don't want some water or something? Go get him some water, Tommy." Barkley heard his partner leave and pulled the chair an inch closer. "Can we talk for a second, Daniel? Just me and you."

"Sure."

"Thank you." Barkley's voice was a clean river running over smooth stone. Most of the people he questioned called it hypnotic, soothing, comforting even. Whatever it was, it worked. People liked to talk to Barkley, unload their secrets, bare their souls.

"I'm sorry about Harry."

Nothing. That was all right. Barkley knew there was plenty bubbling underneath. So he'd talk. And he'd wait. Sorta like fishing.

"My partner tells me you were running."

"I was."

"You run a lot?"

The kid shrugged.

"How did you wind up in the alley, Daniel? Did you plan to meet Harry there?"

Why the fuck would you meet your brother in the middle of the night, in an alley in the Combat Zone, Daniel? Tell me that.

"Harry had no idea I was gonna be down in the Zone."

"But you knew he was gonna be there?"

Daniel shook his head. Barkley sat back. Cocksucker. Tommy came back in and set a Styrofoam cup of water on the table. Barkley waited until he returned to his spot by the door.

"Now, Daniel . . ."

"Who was he with?"

"We don't know . . ."

"Who was he with?" The kid rocked a little faster in the chair.

"A couple of his pals from the football team, best we can tell."

The kid stopped rocking and leaned in, eyes locked like fucking lasers on Barkley until a spot behind the detective's temple grew warm and started to throb. Barkley broke off, severing the connection with a subtle shift of his shoulders.

"Let's get back to the alley, Daniel. Why were you down there?"

"I told you. I went for a run."

"In the middle of the night?"

"I run at night all the time. I like it."

"You on a team?" Tommy's voice carried in a higher pitch that popped and pinged off the concrete walls.

"I run track for my high school. Sometimes, anyway."

"Where do you go to school?" Barkley said.

"Boston Latin."

Good, Barkley thought. *Good.* "You live with your parents?"

"They're dead. I live with Harry."

"How about relatives? Family in the area?"

"No one."

"Okay. We can get someone to take you home when we're through here."

"I'd like to go now."

"Tell you what. Help me with the alley and we're done."

"Maybe you should be thinking about finding the guy who killed my brother."

"Hey . . ." Tommy came off the wall. Barkley held out a hand.

"I hear you, son. Believe me, I fucking hear you. And if it was up to us, we'd drag the prick in here, give you a gun, and let you empty it in his skull. But it ain't up to us. And that ain't never gonna happen. And you're smart enough to know that, so I'm gonna ask again. How and why were you in the alley?"

"I told you. I was running along the river when I got a feeling Harry was in trouble. And I had to help him."

"A feeling?"

"Very strong."

"And you knew exactly where to go?"

"You wouldn't understand, but, yes, I did. I knew exactly where to go. At least until I got into the alleys. I lost it a little there and then I heard all the noise and I knew I was gonna turn a corner and find Harry, just like I found him." Daniel's eyes turned up again, yellow light glancing off the patterned black of his pupils. The pain that lived there sprang from love. Barkley knew that pain. It was the kind that fed on people's souls and had no use for tomorrow.

"You should get some sleep, son. And we've got a lot of paperwork to get through." Barkley scraped his chair against the floor as he stood. "Detective Dillon can arrange a lift home."

The kid didn't move.

"Daniel?"

"I'm guessing you don't want me talking to any reporters."

"Now that you mention it . . ."

"Not a problem. But you gotta do something for me."

Barkley sat back down. "And what would that be?"

The partners had identical desks, gunmetal gray, pushed together in a corner so they were sectioned off from the rest of the squad room. Barkley was tilted back in a swivel chair with his feet up. Tommy was drinking coffee from a thermos and eating a sandwich that had come wrapped in wax paper.

"Where did you get that?" Barkley said.

"Katie made it. Meatloaf with ketchup. You want a bite?"

Barkley held up a hand.

"Hungry as a motherfucker." Tommy chewed as he talked. "Ate around seven. Still starving."

"Where'd you go?"

"Fast food. Crap."

Barkley had been at his desk, filling out pain-in-the-ass paperwork when the call came in on the Fitzsimmons kid. Tommy had been doing his thing, beating the bushes on the guy they'd pulled out of the harbor.

"You get anything on the John Doe?" Barkley said.

"You mean Juan Doe. Didn't get shit. Something else came up, though."

Tommy's voice rippled across the empty squad room, stirring the chemicals in Barkley's brain. He looked up from the report he'd been reading. "We need to talk about it?"

"Got a dead kid from Harvard sitting in our laps. What do you think?"

"You sure?"

"It'll keep."

Barkley nodded and made a mental note to circle back to whatever it was that was bugging his partner. He flipped the report shut and eased his feet off the desk. "Okay, let's talk about our football player. What are we thinking?"

"Left word for people down the Zone. Should hear something soon."

"Yeah?"

"Why not? Probably some fucking street punk, sees Fitzsimmons wandering around in the alley. Figures he'll roll him."

"But Fitzsimmons fights back?"

"Exactly." Tommy took another bite of his sandwich and put it back on the wax paper he'd spread out on a corner of his desk. "You got a napkin?"

Barkley found a stack in a drawer with some Chinese take-out menus and tossed them over. Tommy wiped a lick of ketchup off his mouth. Barkley waited. Tommy wasn't as quick at putting things together, but when he did, it usually held up.

"So they fight?" Barkley said.

"Fitzsimmons is a football player. Young, tough. He's not gonna roll over even if he is an Ivy Leaguer. Maybe especially cuz he's an Ivy Leaguer. So, yeah, they fight. Fitzsimmons figures it's a fistfight. Takes a couple of swings, but our boy says 'Fuck that' and pulls out the knife."

"He's playing for keeps."

Tommy nodded. "Fitzsimmons probably never saw it. Blade in the gut, down he goes, and the guy books. My point is, whoever he is, he's a fucking punk, which means people are gonna be willing to give him up."

"And what if our guy's black?"

"What if he is?"

"Shitstorm, Tommy."

"We've handled worse. Either way, I'll get us a name by the end of the day. Tomorrow, at the latest. Just promise me one thing."

"No cameras in your face?"

"Fucking hey."

"Tell me about the Harvard guys."

"We already went over that."

"Tell me again."

Tommy sighed and pulled out a black leather notebook. They had stacks of the things, Tommy usually scribbling while Barkley conducted his interviews.

"Neil Prescott and Jesus Sanchez. Nickname Zeus. Both football players. Both say they were at the Naked i with Fitzsimmons. Came out of the club a little juiced, walked around a bit, then back to the car on Washington. Sanchez and Fitzsimmons are in the backseat."

"Prescott's up front with the cooler."

"Right. A girl comes by and starts chatting 'em up. At some point she reaches in and grabs Sanchez's wallet. Runs down LaGrange and Sanchez follows. According to him, it all happened real quick."

"Fitzsimmons is still in the back?"

"He tells Prescott to stay with the car, then goes after Sanchez. Prescott says it might have been ten, twenty seconds between Sanchez leaving and Fitzsimmons following."

"Okay," Barkley said. "Then what?"

"Sanchez says he ran after the girl. Thought he saw her take off down an alley and followed. Never knew Fitzsimmons was following him. Says he went down two or three more intersecting alleys . . . there's a shit-load of them back there . . . then found his way back down Washington to the car. Best we can figure, by then Fitzsimmons was already dead."

"How about the yelling?"

"Fuck, B, you did the interviews. You know all this shit."

"Just tell me."

Tommy flipped through the notebook some more, then tossed it on the desk and produced a second. "I haven't typed any of this up yet."

"That's okay."

"All right, here it is. Prescott says Fitzsimmons yelled at Sanchez when he got out of the car."

"When who got out?"

"Sanchez. Fitzsimmons yelled at him to stop. Then Fitzsimmons yelled again as he ran down the street."

"Prescott doesn't know what he said?"

"That's right. Says it might have been Sanchez's

name. He's not sure. Sanchez says he never heard a thing."

"How many beers did they have?"

"Sanchez says he had a few. Both of them say Fitzsimmons didn't drink."

"So he wasn't necessarily an easy mark in the alley?"

"The punk who did him wouldn't know that. Sees the kid wandering around. What else is he gonna think? My theory's still good, B."

"What do we got on the girl who pinched the wallet?"

"Caucasian. Sanchez says she had blond hair and might have been wearing heels. Not much, but we got people working it. They'll turn her up."

"Good." Barkley put his fingertips together and talked over the top of them. "What did you think of the little brother?"

"Felt sorry for the poor bastard."

They'd finished with Daniel Fitzsimmons just over an hour ago. His price for not speaking to reporters was a final visit to see his brother. Barkley wasn't a hundred percent on the request, but he didn't want the kid talking to the press either. So he made a couple of calls and told them to hold off on releasing the body to the morgue. Then they'd packed Daniel off to Boston City Hospital where he'd get to say his good-byes.

"Why was the kid in the alley?" Barkley said.

Tommy shrugged and flipped his notebook shut. He'd finished his sandwich and drained what was left of the thermos into a plastic cup. "Who knows? Maybe he just had a feeling like he said."

"You believe that?"

"You really don't get feelings? Intuition?"

"You're not gonna start on the fairy rings again?"

"Fuck you, Bark."

They shared a cop's smile, passed between partners who'd known each other too long and too well to have it any other way.

"Let me tell you a story," Tommy said.

"I was hoping."

"One night I'm off duty, drinking with some pals at the Tap."

"Southie's chapter of the KKK."

Tommy extended his middle finger and kept talking. "I have a few and decide I better not drive. So I leave my car parked in front of the bar and grab a ride home from one of my buddies. Katie makes me something to eat and I'm fucking comatose by ten. Right?"

"Right."

"So two thirty in the morning, I sit straight up in the

bed like someone greased the fucking Pesky pole and shoved it right up my ass. Katie jumps up with me—it's like we're sharing the same brain or something, except we're most definitely fucking not—and thinks I think someone's in the house. I'm swearing a blue streak. 'Fuck, fuck, fuck.' She's asking what's the matter and I tell her our car's been stolen. Tell her I left it parked in front of the bar and the fuckers just busted out a window, popped the ignition, and are joyriding around like a bunch of cocksuckers who need to get their roof caved. 'Fuck, fuck, fuck,' I say, and put on my socks and go downstairs into the kitchen. Katie follows me down and asks how I know the car's gone if I left it at the bar. I tell her I just do, but not to worry. Car's a piece of shit, go back to bed, we'll deal with it in the morning. She thinks I'm fucking Looney Tunes and goes back upstairs. I sit up in the kitchen, phone on the table in front of me. I sit there and I drink my coffee and I stare at the thing, not wondering *if* it will ring, just waiting for it. Fifteen minutes later, boom. It's a uniform calling from Station Six. Wants to know if I own a '65 Bonneville. Says they found the thing torched and dumped in a lot off Emerson. Windows busted out, ignition popped. Not a surprise to me. Not a bit. Cuz I knew. When I woke up, I just knew it was gone. How did I know? No idea. But I knew, Bark. Abso-fucking-lutely, I knew."

"So you're telling me you believe the kid?"

"What did I say yesterday? Not everything has to have a reasonable explanation, B. Some things just are."

"You wanna put that in our report?"

"The kid didn't kill his big brother, run off, and then come back to scream and wail over the body. That make more sense to you?"

"No."

"All right, then."

Barkley leaned his forearms on his desk and rolled the still mostly blank police report up and down in the typewriter. As usual, Tommy had a point. At the end of the day life was a blind free fall and no one could tell you when or where or how you were gonna hit the pavement. Just that at some point, sure as fuck, you'd hit it.

"Listen, I'm not saying you're wrong . . ."

"You can't buy in, B. You'd like to, but you just can't."

"I like facts, Tommy. Keeps me warm at night."

"Well, the fact is this kid was in the alley. And there's no getting around that."

"How about him wanting to see the body?"

Tommy shrugged. "It's fine. Besides, they said they'd watch him."

Barkley grumbled to himself, then checked a watch that wasn't on his wrist. "What time you got?"

"Just past five. Why?"

"Nothing. While we're waiting for one of your sources to call, why don't you do me a favor and dig in to some files."

"What do you want?"

"Daniel Fitzsimmons. And Harry. Police reports, newspaper clips, school records, whatever you can find. Just for the hell of it."

A door slammed somewhere and loud voices drifted back from the front of the station house. A skinny uniform named Guilfoyle stuck his head in.

"Yeah?" Barkley didn't like anyone from the outside hanging around when they discussed the guts of a case. That included cops he didn't know who worked the front desk.

"You guys caught the thing tonight in the Zone?"

"What is it?" Tommy said.

"There's a guy out front. Says he's a photographer. Lives right over the alley where the thing happened."

Barkley felt himself sit up in his chair. "What's he want?"

"Wants to talk to you guys. Says he got pictures of the killer. I'm not a detective or nothing, but I thought that might be something you'd be interested in."

Guilfoyle had a wiseass grin on his ugly face, but Barkley didn't give a fuck. He could have kissed him.

"Where'd you put him, Guilfoyle?"

"Down the hall in Room Three. Locked the door just in case the fucker changes his mind."

"So you take naked pictures for a living?"

"We're gonna do that, huh?"

Tommy Dillon smiled hard and toothy behind a blue screen of smoke. He'd wanted to take the lead on questioning the photographer. Unusual, but Barkley didn't mind. Best he could tell, it was all headed to the same place.

"I got a studio, top floor of the Brompton."

"You mean Hooker Central."

The photographer's name was Nick Toney. He was middle-aged, long and angular in that starving-artist, hippie-freak, I-might-be-banging-your-teenage-daughter sort of way some guys just had, even if most of them turned out to be harmless.

"Look, I take pictures of the girls, but it's art. 'Decisive moment' type stuff, you know?"

"Why don't you show us what you got?" Barkley said.

"I'm gonna, but why's this guy giving me a hard time?"

"No idea. You two know each other?"

"Only like I know every other fucking skeeze-ball

down there," Tommy said. "Giving fifteen-year-olds a skinful so they can take their picture, then get their dicks sucked."

"Hey . . ." Toney got up out of his chair. Guy didn't look like he was gonna start swinging, but he might just leave and Barkley couldn't have that.

"Whoa, whoa, whoa, Tommy. Sit down, Mr. Toney."

"I don't have to listen to this crap . . ."

"Give us a second, okay?"

Toney held up his hands but sat back down to his cigarette. Barkley and Tommy stepped into the hall.

"Guy's full of shit," Tommy said.

"You don't know that. What the fuck's eating you?"

"Nothing."

"We seen a million of these guys, Tommy."

"Yeah, but now I got the twins in school. I know that's bullshit . . ."

"It ain't bullshit."

"Every day, I kiss 'em good-bye and smile and watch 'em go off and think to myself it's a fucking sewer."

"The girls have lots of years, Tommy. And they got you and Katie. And they got me."

"I hear you. First fucking grade, right?"

"Wait till some poor bastard shows up for the prom."

Tommy laughed, the tension draining from his voice. "Come on, let's go in and I'll apologize."

Barkley shook his head. "Go home. Make your kids breakfast and grab some sleep. I'll take care of this."

"You sure?"

"Yeah."

"I'll pull some of them files before I go."

"Don't worry about it. I'm gonna crash on a cot in the back after I talk to this guy."

"What about the reporters?"

"I'll talk to 'em at some point. Why don't I swing by the house this afternoon? We can pick up the pieces then."

"Thanks, B."

"Tell Katie I said hey. And give those girls a kiss for me."

Barkley watched Tommy go down the hall and wondered again if it wasn't time to start looking for a new partner. Tommy was like a brother, but maybe that was the problem. He shook his head and walked back into the interrogation room. Toney took a final drag and crushed the remains of his cigarette into an ashtray.

"Your buddy head out?"

"He's been at it all night. Listen, I'm sorry . . ."

"Not a problem."

"Let's start over. You want some coffee? Something to eat?"

"I'm good."

"There's a bakery around the corner. Guy opens at five. Beautiful blueberry muffins. Still hot and everything."

"I'm good."

"All right." Barkley pulled out a chair and sat down again. "Tell me about your photography."

"What do you want to know?"

"Whatever you want to tell me."

Toney shrugged. "It's not like your pal said. No skin mags, nothing like that. I had an exhibit at the Museum of Fine Arts, for Chrissakes. I'll send you the pamphlet."

"Any girls from the street in the exhibit?"

"The girls *were* the exhibit. People love it. Living on the edge and all that stuff. That's why I have the studio down there. I live like they live. So they trust me. They open up."

"Yeah?"

"Lot of pain, Detective. Lot of pain."

"You got the photos, Mr. Toney?"

"Right here." Toney opened his jacket. He had a manila envelope tucked against the flat of his stomach. "Before I show them to you . . ."

"What is it?"

"I was listening to the radio on the way over here. Heard the name of the kid who got killed."

"Harry Fitzsimmons."

"Yeah. Football player from Harvard. That's all they gave out."

"What about him?"

"I knew him."

Barkley felt the skin under his left eye pucker. "How's that?"

"I knew him. Not well, but I actually saw the kid yesterday morning. Early. Him and his buddies were at a diner in Harvard Square."

"Small world."

"You think I didn't think that?"

"Relax, Mr. Toney. Stuff like this happens all the time."

"Yeah?"

"More than you imagine. You get any names?"

"Of what? His buddies?"

Barkley nodded.

"Neil Prescott was one kid. He's into cameras. I was helping him pick out some lenses. You know, make a buck or two."

Barkley wrote on a pad of paper—tight, coiled lines of cursive. "So you know Prescott?"

"Just through the cameras. How do you know him?"

"Have you spoken to Prescott?"

"When? Since this happened?" Toney shook his head.

"Okay, go ahead."

"The other kid he was with was named Sanchez. Zeus was the first name, I think. Something like that. They told me they might be headed down the Zone. Few beers, some laughs. Fuck me, I shoulda stopped 'em."

"Not your fault, Mr. Toney."

"Still feels like shit, you know?"

Barkley stopped writing and flipped the pad over. "Let's see the photos."

Toney pushed across the envelope. Barkley took out the photos and laid them down in a row on the table.

"Tell me what I'm looking at."

"I snapped these from my window."

"Overlooking the alley?"

"I heard some yelling and running so I looked down and seen the two of them. Black kid and a white kid."

"Definitely black?"

Toney touched one of the pictures. "You tell me."

"Go ahead."

"These two are circling each other. Looks like a fistfight. I got cameras everywhere in the place, so I grab one."

"You said it was a studio. You live there or something?"

"I got a pullout bed I make up in the back. As you can imagine, a lot of my work down there is at night."

"Sure, sure. So you see these two. You yell down, tell 'em to stop?"

"You know how many fights I see in that alley every week?"

Barkley shrugged like *What's a guy to do.* At the end of the day that was why people went to the Zone. To sit in the shadows and watch. "Go ahead, Mr. Toney."

"So I see them down there and I just pop off the shots. Bang, bang, bang."

There were five photos in all. The first two showed a white man with his back to the camera faced off against a black man. The pair were shoved up next to a Dumpster almost directly beneath Toney. In the third and fourth shots, the white man was on one knee, the black man swinging his arm down, a knife clearly visible in his right hand. In the last photo the white man's shoulders were turned toward the camera, one arm obscuring his face, the rest of his body lost in the thick back and shoulders of his attacker.

"Did you know it was Fitzsimmons?" Barkley said.

Toney shook his head. "I only saw what I saw through the viewfinder. Whole thing lasted less than ten seconds. As I snapped the last one, I did yell something."

"Why then?"

"Dunno. Guess I registered the knife. Anyway,

the black guy just took off running. I leaned out and saw the white kid was holding his side up against the Dumpster so I went into the hall and started yelling for help."

"And?"

"You can yell a long time in that building and never see a soul."

"You call the police?"

"My phone's out so I ran down two flights to a pay phone and called from there. By the time I got back to my apartment, there were people in the alley trying to help the kid, so I popped off some more shots. Then you guys showed up."

"Why didn't you come down when we were on scene?"

"I could talk to some cops or go in the darkroom and develop film. Which would you rather I did?"

"Fair enough." Barkley tapped the face of the black man, caught in a random bloom of light. "I assume you don't know this guy?"

"I'd only be guessing."

"Welcome to the world of police work, Mr. Toney."

"I think the pictures are enough, don't you?"

Barkley turned the photo over and stood up.

"You know I could have sold these for some coin to the *Herald*."

"I appreciate that. Give me five minutes and we'll get you a ride home." Barkley collected the photos and left the room. There was a young uniform standing in the hall outside.

"Couple newspaper guys are up front."

"What's your name?"

"Charlie. Charlie Herbert."

"Charlie, take this guy out the back and make sure the press doesn't get a sniff."

"Yes, sir."

Barkley scribbled out a few lines on a piece of paper and tucked it in the uniform's hand.

"What's this?"

"Name and address of the guy in that room. After you drop him off, I want you to call down to the phone company. See if his line's in service. If it's out, find out when and what's the problem. All right?"

"Yes, sir."

"Get going, Charlie. And remember, no press, especially the cameras."

Herbert went into the room. Barkley walked down to the can. He washed his hands and face and quick shined his shoes with a paper towel. Then he ran a hand over the top of his tight Afro and wiped the fatigue out of his eyes. Barkley adjusted the knot in his tie and gave himself a final look in the mirror. Shit. Sidney Poitier had nothing on him. Richard Roundtree, neither. He left the bathroom, swinging both arms loose and easy as he strode down the hall to meet the press.

20

Daniel sat on a bench in the basement of Boston City Hospital and stared at the entrance to the tunnel. He'd spent six months here as an eight-year-old and knew there was a passageway that burrowed under Albany Street, connecting Boston City to the morgue. Now he was staring down its mouth, gaping wide and stinking of urine. A woman approached, pushing a sheeted body on a gurney. She considered Daniel with the disconnected eyes of a prison guard before ducking into the tunnel and quickly sinking from sight. Daniel thought about Heracles and his trip to Hades, Cerberus and the river Styx. Was there something of Charon in the woman's flat-paneled gaze, the coin already in her pocket, slipped from under the tongue of the Bostonian lying perfectly still and perfectly dead under the woman's starched sheet? Daniel wondered why he wondered such things and figured he was in shock. Probably had been since the alley. And now he was here.

They'd given him a long-sleeved T-shirt at the police station. It was cheap and anonymous and itched his neck, but it covered up some of the blood and that was good. The attendant who'd set him on the bench and told him not to move appeared on the horizon. He carried a uniform appropriate to the setting and task—blue scrubs, gloves, even a mask. *Why the mask?* Daniel wondered, but slipped it around his neck, pulled on the scrubs, and followed the attendant to one of several doors cut at regular intervals down both sides of the hallway. The attendant opened it and stepped aside. Daniel had told the cops he wanted to go in alone, but they said that was impossible. The attendant would wait by the door. Daniel had fifteen minutes.

He circled the room, clinging to the plastered walls like he was afraid the floor might tilt and suck him into its center. Light arced from an overhead lamp, spitting shards that glanced off the steel legs and grooved runnels of the examining table. A plastic bucket of water and a sponge sat on a stool next to the table. Daniel moved toward it.

The air felt cold and stuck to his skin. He picked up the sponge and plunged it into the bucket, feeling it swell as it soaked up the warm water. Daniel washed his arms to the elbows, then his face and neck. He stripped to the waist and scrubbed his brother's blood off his chest, water streaming down the contours of his body and forming puddles at his feet. The attendant was watching but never moved from his post by the door. Daniel let himself look at Harry for the first time, face framed over the top of the sheet, feet out the other end, knobby lumps of flesh. Here was the prime of life, everything ahead and about to happen, decaying from the inside out. Daniel could feel it nest in his belly, smell it on his skin, cloying and impossible to scrape off no matter how many buckets of water they brought, no matter how many times he scrubbed.

He plunged the sponge into the bucket and squeezed it dry. Then he started. Daniel washed his brother's arms and hands first, running fingers along the small joints. He dabbed at Harry's face—eyelids, nose, cheeks, all cold to the touch, frosted in death. Daniel ran the sponge across Harry's stubbled scalp and watched the water sluice down his face and catch on his lips. They'd already processed the body for evidence and examined the wounds, photographed them, measured them, touched them. All that remained was the coroner and his tools—knives, saws, and rib cutters. They'd gut Harry, weigh whatever needed to be weighed, bag whatever needed to be bagged. And so on.

Daniel let the sponge fall from his hand and slumped to the floor, pressing his face up against the dark glass of his soul.

Two boys sit on a subway car, snaking somewhere beneath the tangled city. Daniel is just nine and wears a blue hospital bracelet around his left wrist. Harry is twelve and pulls out a folding knife to cut the bracelet. Daniel watches it fall to the floor of the streetcar. The driver calls out his stops in a voice that bleeds through a tinny speaker—Government Center, Park Street, Boylston, Arlington. People shuffle on; people shuffle off. Furrowed faces, Boston eyes, features carved from hard wax melting into soapy smiles when they see the two boys together. Daniel had emerged from his coma a week ago. That morning someone from the state arrived with a pile of paperwork and his ticket out. Harry insisted the brothers be allowed to take the T to the group home where they'd stay until something better came along. Harry's demand provoked a flurry of meetings, but the brothers didn't give a damn. In the end, they got their way.

The train rumbles out of Arlington and Harry looks down as Daniel looks up. He can see Harry thinking, even at that age, literally see his brother's thoughts as they whirl and hiss and sort and shape into words.

"I love you most," Harry says as the streetcar creaks around a curve and comes to a stop in the breathing darkness. Daniel smiles. It's the game their mother used to play on the T when she was wearing her high heels and her dress made of shiny silver scales, when she was cooked in a cake of makeup and rouge and lipstick, when she was dropping the boys off at the apartment of a woman they called their aunt but really wasn't. Mom always started. Daniel always went next. Now, his mom was gone. But the game runs on.

"No, I love you most," Daniel says.

"I love you most."

"I love you most." Daniel's voice feels small as sin and big as fear. He digs into his brother's shoulder as the overhead lights in the car flicker and they start to move again.

"I love you most, bud. I'll always love you most, and that's all there is to it." Harry draws him close and holds him, not giving a damn what anyone on the Green Line thinks cuz that's Harry.

"I love you most," Daniel mumbles.

"Nope, I love you . . ."

They rumble through Copley that way, then Auditorium, and, finally, Kenmore. The two boys get off *the streetcar, still playing their game, the "I love you"s more like a string of prayer beads now or a meditation, each boy lost in his thoughts, their thoughts the same while the ghost of their mother dodges their footsteps and touches their cheeks. And so it went. And so it goes.*

Daniel opened his eyes, the chemical air of the room dry at the back of his throat. The attendant was gone, nothing there but an empty chair and a wedge of yellow gleaming wicked beneath a crack in the door. Daniel knew where the attendant was—outside in the alley, in the early morning blush, enmeshed in a web of pulse and shadow, sharing a cigarette with a woman who worked in the hospital. The man was married, but Daniel could still feel his desire for her, hot and slick and blind and desperate. Daniel got to his feet and stood over Harry, hovering close enough that he could have felt a breath stirring on his brother's lips. Or maybe a word.

"You loved me most," Daniel said. "And we both know it." He climbed onto the table and curled up next to the sheeted body, drifting among the soft lights, words and memories sparking and dying in his head. When he finally left the room, he knew better than to look back. In the hallway he took a seat on the floor and hardly breathed, mumbling "I love you most" and wrapping himself in his new life, stitched as it was from the sins of the past.

The attendant returned from his smoke and they walked silently to the reception area, neither looking at the other. Daniel took off the scrubs and tossed them in a bin. Then he was on the flat sidewalk, head back, staring at the curved lines of the building outlined in a predawn light streamed with pinks and purples and rivers of black. The great aloneness was coming, a crushing wave that would only grow as he ran.

Daniel turned and started down the street. At the end of the block, two cops waited in a car.

21

They dropped him in the middle of Kenmore Square at a little after six. Two men and a woman were sleeping in the shelter of the bus station. One of the men was using his backpack as a pillow while the woman rested her head against his side. The other guy was bundled up in a camo jacket on a wooden bench, his nose pressed against a concrete pillar. Two more packs were stowed under the bench along with a guitar case and a tiny dog that looked like Toto. Daniel watched while an MBTA driver with a thick Italian face walked over and kicked one of the guys in the head. The guy rolled onto his back so his soft belly was exposed. The driver kicked him again, this time in the ribs, and left. The woman got busy organizing their things while Camo Jacket smoked a cigarette. Eventually, the trio cinched up their packs and picked their way through the square, Toto happily at their heels.

Daniel took his time climbing the stairs to his apartment. He sensed the space was empty even before he pushed in the door and lingered on the threshold, smelling the cold char of the fireplace, noticing the slant of morning light across the books on the shelves, listening to the pad of cat's feet on rubbed planks of wood.

He walked back to his room and sat on the bed. Daniel knew he should sleep and knew he wouldn't. In the tiny bathroom across the hall he showered, turning on the water as hot as it would go and standing under the spray and steam. He found a pair of scissors in the medicine cabinet and hacked at his hair until the floor around him was covered with curling piles of locks. Back in his room he changed into fresh clothes. The gun he'd found outside Latin School was still at the bottom of his book bag. He pulled it out and gripped it, pointing it at himself in the mirror. The gun knew death. Daniel could feel the knowing in his hand and it comforted him—something found even as everything else was lost. He stuffed the gun back underneath his books and returned to the front room, stretching out on the couch and closing his eyes. Harry lived in the space between thoughts, filling the void with grief that swelled and streamed like a heavy sea. When Daniel opened his eyes again, his face stared back at him from the ceiling, curling a lip before turning away.

He got up and cracked a window, then circled the room in a prowl, picking up various objects and putting them down. Simon's desk was its usual mess, which was why he almost missed the envelope set in the very center, *DANIEL* scrawled across the front in slanting lines of lead. He tore open the envelope and took out the single sheet inside.

ON THE ROOF IF YOU WANT TO TALK. SIMON

It took him ten minutes to find the staircase that twisted to the roof. Simon was sitting on a stool at the eastern edge of the building, staring out over the city with a sketch pad on his easel and colored pencils strewn at his feet like tiny licks of light. He was bundled up in a long coat and spoke without turning.

"A father has a dream. In it his wife is strangled by their infant son. The father has had these dreams his entire life and, one way or another, they always come true. So he becomes convinced this horrible thing will happen. One night while his wife is sleeping, the father leans into the crib with a hatchet and hacks off his son's hands at the wrists. The father goes to prison. The woman remarries and has another son, who strangles her one night in her sleep when she's deep into her seventies. Meanwhile, the father spends his life locked in a cell while the son he made a cripple visits him every Sunday and is the only person there when they wheel him out in a coffin."

"What's the point?"

"I know about Harry. I'm sorry."

"I was with the police all night."

Simon nodded but still didn't turn his head. Daniel took a seat on a wall that ran along the edge of the roof. From where he sat he couldn't see the sketch Simon had been working on and wondered if that was by design.

"He was killed in an alley in the Combat Zone. I wound up down there myself. I wasn't really sure how, but I knew where to go and knew what I'd find."

"I'm sure the police were curious about that."

"They asked some questions."

Simon slipped the sketch into a sewn leather case he kept by his feet and zipped it up. Then he swung around on his stool, the case laid across his lap. "Did you tell them about the gun?"

"What gun?"

Simon dismissed the response with a shrug.

"Have you been through my stuff?"

"Do you believe that?"

"No."

"Good. And, no, I haven't been through your belongings."

"You don't think I could have stopped what was going to happen to Harry?"

"I think that's what Harry would tell you."

"How do you know about the gun?"

"There are two major sources of energy in this world. Any idea what they are?"

Daniel shook his head.

"Love and hate. People think of them as feelings or emotions, but they're actually physical, tangible, measurable forces. In fact, they provide the foundation for everything they seem to oppose."

"Oppose?"

"Math, technology, logic, reason—they all live in the tension between these two. When you get into an entangled state . . . and you were in an entangled state when you found your brother, no doubt about that . . . when you're in that state, you're enmeshed in their paradox, trading on the physical energy of one or the other."

"I didn't feel hatred. I don't feel hatred."

"No? Why the gun?"

Daniel felt the lie he'd told like a dark rain in his chest.

"It's all right, Daniel. In fact, it's inevitable." Simon swept a long arm across the tatter of Boston's skyline. "The energy exists whether you understand its nature or not. It's what holds all this together—from the structure of the atom to the architecture of the universe, the blood that pumps in our veins and the infinity of a single kiss, everything you see, everything you don't, humming along faster than the speed of light, binding and pulling, usually at the same time. Some people cast it as a battle between good and evil, but those are moral, subjective measures. Relative only to each other."

"And you're talking about something that's absolute?"

"I'm talking about science. The reality is we're just beginning to see the first glimpses of how it all works."

"Which is how?"

Simon shrugged. "Imperfectly, like everything else in Nature. Sometimes hate is the answer. The need to separate and split things apart. The need to fight, to rage, to use that elemental bloodlust to accomplish one's goal. Sometimes it's love. Sometimes when we hate, we spin out a yarn of love somewhere else. And when we truly love, it nurtures hate. The truth is both can wound and both can kill. They just leave very different marks."

"Harry was pure love. At least for me."

"I believe you."

Daniel looked down into the guts of Kenmore Square, curled gray snakes of cars and buses clogging the streets, people on foot filling the gaps between.

"I used to do all my calculations, the higher math stuff, on white sheets of paper," Simon said. "Used a black pencil, strong, thick lead. Then one day I stopped."

"Using the pencil?"

"Doing the math. Harvard didn't like it, but fuck Harvard, right? Have you checked me out with them yet?"

"Should I?"

"You probably have better things to do."

"I was just thinking everything never seemed so random."

"The person who killed your brother will be delivered to you, Daniel. His life will be in your hands. That's what the gun is for."

"Did you know Harry was going to die?"

Simon considered him with a sadness that threatened to break him in two.

"What is it?" Daniel said.

"Do you like the girl?"

"What girl?"

Simon pointed. "The girl."

Grace was sitting on the steps of Music City, a hand shading her eyes, looking hard at the roof.

22

The mattress just wasn't made for two-fifty-plus pounds of detective. Barkley cursed and rolled onto his back, searching for a halfway comfortable spot. The mattress read his mind and shoved a metal spring up his spine. Message fucking received. He sat up and reached for his watch, nestled in his suit coat, which was folded in a neat bundle. It was just nine. He'd gotten two hours of solid sleep, not great but it would have to do.

Barkley stood and stretched, his reach filling the converted storage room from stem to stern. The first stories would be out by now. He could feel them circulating through Boston's bloodstream. He'd wanted to limit his presser to details about the victim. His boss was all about covering the department's collective ass, insisting specifics about Toney's photos be included so the city could see the Boston PD was on the fucking job. In the end, they'd compromised. Barkley didn't mention the pictures but did confirm they had a suspect—young, black, and in the wind. Now, the shitstorm.

Barkley walked into the squad room and plucked a newspaper off the nearest desk. The *Herald's* headline was an inch high, in bold, black type.

HARVARD FOOTBALL PLAYER SLAIN IN THE COMBAT ZONE
BLACK SUSPECT STILL AT LARGE

The department could try to downplay the racial angle all it wanted, but the press knew. And the public knew. In Boston, three years into the death march that had become forced busing, the Athens of America was bleeding, black and white and bigotry all over. Throw in Harvard and the stew of emotions that institution stirred up and the Fitzsimmons murder was big news. Letting a black detective run point on the investigation? Hell, that was just icing on the cake.

Barkley dropped the paper back onto the desk and went into the bathroom. He washed his hands and face, then got a cup of coffee from his machine. A couple of detectives gave him a shout as he made his way to his desk, but Barkley didn't play well with others. No wonder they paired him with Dillon. He'd told Tommy to go home, but Barkley knew that wasn't gonna happen. His partner was pure hunting dog. Barkley had given him a scent and Tommy was gonna scare up a couple of bones before he called it quits. So it was no big surprise when Barkley found a stack of files on his desk—background on Harry Fitzsimmons and the younger brother. A folder on top caught Barkley's eye. Tommy had taped a piece of paper to the front and scrawled on it in big fucking Tommy letters.

READ THIS ONE FIRST

Barkley took a sip of coffee and pulled across the file. It was an accident report from 1968. The name of the sole fatality was typed on the first page. Violet Anne Fitzsimmons, aged twenty-nine. The only witness, her eight-year-old son, Daniel Patrick. Barkley took another sip of coffee and cracked the file. A half hour later he picked up the phone and called out to the uniform who'd helped him with Toney. Charlie Herbert had dropped off the photographer at his place and was working on running down his phone records.

"Good. Do me a favor. Pull anything you can find on Violet Fitzsimmons. Lemme give you some details." Barkley talked to Herbert for another ten minutes, then hung up. An hour later he was hip deep in Violet's life, Herbert coming in and out with the occasional tidbit. And there were tidbits. Barkley pulled across the phone and dialed a number.

"McShane."

He smiled at her voice—the best kind of smile cuz it happened before he ever realized it. Catherine McShane was the county's medical examiner. A graduate of Holy Cross and Johns Hopkins medical school, the good Irish girl from Milton had returned home as the freshly minted ME a couple of years back. Barkley had worked with her on a handful of cases. He'd also asked her out for a drink and, surprisingly, she'd accepted. The drink had turned into dinner, then a stroll through a soft summer night to her flat in the Back Bay. He'd promised to call, meant to call. That was almost six months ago.

"Hey, Cat."

"Detective Jones. How can I help?"

Why hadn't he called this woman? The truth was he'd had a great time. Almost enough to forget he was big and black and scary as hell and she was straight masterpiece beautiful, face full of perfect lines and pleasing angles, the result of generations of money and careful breeding. It was easy to say that shouldn't matter, but this was Boston and the only black people

Barkley ever saw at a Celtics game were playing ball. Double down on that for Fenway Park and all points in between. Maybe that was why he'd bailed. Or maybe he was just like every other guy. Running scared.

"I owe you a call, Cat. I'm sorry."

"There's no need to apologize."

"Sure there is."

"You realize I could have picked up the phone?"

"Never thought of that."

"What a surprise. I like you, Bark. Like talking to you. I just don't want to date you. And it's got nothing to do with color."

"Did I say that?"

"You're not nearly as hard to read as you think. The truth is you're not ready to date anyone. Not now, at least."

"How do you figure?"

"I just do. If I'm wrong, so be it. But I'm not."

She'd pinned him like a butterfly to a mounting board. Ready for dissection. Barkley needed to do something quick before she pulled out the magnifying glass and tweezers.

"So you don't hate me?"

"Jesus Christ."

"What?"

"Are you listening? You're my friend. And that doesn't shake easy, at least not for me. Besides, you're gonna need all the help you can get."

"That bad, huh?"

"The radio just described you as the high-profile black detective investigating the stabbing death of a white football player from Harvard. Might as well make it easy on everyone and turn yourself in as his killer."

"Shit."

"Rolling downhill. And then some."

"How you doing with him?"

"Another couple of hours and I should have the basics. Toxicology's gonna be a while."

"Talk to me on this one first, all right?"

"You know how I operate. Your eyes only."

"Thanks, Cat."

"Not a problem. That it?"

Barkley ran a finger across the dog-eared pages of Violet Fitzsimmons's file. "I'm looking at an old case. Nineteen sixty-eight. Deceased's car jumped a seawall near a beach in Dorchester. Fire department found her in the front seat. Eight-year-old son was with her and survived."

"Deceased's name was Violet Fitzsimmons. Your victim's mother."

"How'd you know that?"

"What do you think, we're a bunch of idiots over here?"

"I've always thought of you as ghouls with long, sharp knives."

"Funny. We like to do a little background on our high-profile cases. When we ran Harry Fitzsimmons's name, the mom popped up. I assume the boy in the crash is Harry's younger brother?"

"Name's Daniel."

"I saw that in the report. So what's bothering you?"

"It says she went through the windshield. Suffered several blunt force injuries consistent with the crash, but none of them were fatal."

"So?"

"The cause of death was listed as asphyxiation. I also noticed she suffered a fractured hyoid bone."

"Where you headed, Detective?"

"When I see fractured hyoid, I think manual strangulation."

"Do you really?"

"I do."

"It can happen in other ways."

"Like a car crash?"

"Why not? Probably slammed her throat against the steering wheel."

"You ever seen that?"

"No, but that doesn't mean it couldn't happen."

"You saw the fingerprint?"

"I told you I reviewed the file."

Forensics had pulled a single bloody print off the hollow of Violet Fitzsimmons's neck, a fourteen-point match to eight-year-old Daniel's thumb.

"What do you think about that?" Barkley said.

"As I recall, the boy said something about trying to resuscitate his mom."

"By choking her?"

"He was eight, Bark. What does this have to do with your case?"

"It also says in the report they found him wandering away from the car covered in his mother's blood."

"He was in shock. He'd just crawled over her dead body to get out of the wreck."

"And the time he spent in the hospital?"

"I'm not an expert, but I'd guess some form of post-traumatic stress disorder."

"English, please."

"They're seeing a lot of it in soldiers coming back from 'Nam. The boy's mind couldn't take what had happened so he withdrew. You'd have to ask his doctors, but I've read about cases where people sat in a room and stared at the wall for the better part of a year."

"From what I understand, this kid slipped into a coma."

"Not unheard of, especially if he suffered physical trauma from the crash."

"So he couldn't have been faking it."

"Seriously?"

"Would he remember anything about the accident, aftermath?"

"Might not. That's the whole point. The mind is trying to protect itself from something it can't handle. What does any of this have to do with your murder?"

"Daniel's sixteen now and stumbled into the alley last night as we were working on his brother."

"Did he see the body?"

"Hell, yeah."

"Wow."

"I'm assuming that's not a good 'wow.'"

"Again, I'm no psychiatrist, but I'd guess that could trigger a lot of bad things."

Barkley was suddenly very happy he hadn't told Cat about letting Daniel visit his brother's body at Boston City. "What kind of things?"

"I don't know. Flashbacks, hyperarousal, withdrawal . . ."

"What the Christ is hyperarousal?"

"Inability to sleep or focus, irritability sometimes

escalating to irrational, self-destructive behavior, aggressiveness, violence, delusions. Can go a lot of different ways."

"All right. Thanks."

"You don't seriously believe this boy tried to strangle his mother?"

"Not really. It's just the pieces. I see them lying there in the file and can't help trying to fit 'em together."

"You want me to dig a little deeper on Daniel?"

"Can you do that?"

"Wasn't that your goal all along?"

"Mostly I was just hoping you'd take the call."

"I'll poke around and see if anyone remembers anything." Cat paused like she was writing something down. "Meantime, I've done my preliminary exam and there's one thing that's a little curious about your victim. I mean, there might be more, but there's one thing right off the bat that bothers me."

"Go ahead."

"The wounds. Did you notice anything?"

"Yeah. They were fatal."

"When we examined them, it was obvious he was attacked with two different weapons."

Barkley pulled his feet off his desk and sat up in his chair. "How do you know that?"

"Easy. There's a slash mark on the sleeve of his coat and what appears to be a related wound to the abdomen."

"Consistent with a knife attack?"

"Yes, but the abdomen wound was not fatal. What killed your football player were three puncture wounds. All driven in just under the rib cage, two exiting in the back."

"Shit."

"Yes. These wounds are small and square, tightly packed together."

"What are you saying?"

"There's no way they were made by a knife, certainly not the same knife that slashed him in the stomach. Whoever killed Harry Fitzsimmons got very close. And made no mistake."

"You're telling me this wasn't an alley fight?"

"I'm telling you this guy was gutted and put on a spit. Maybe that's what alley fights have come to these days, but you'd know better than I. I'll call you when I have more. And Bark?"

"Still here."

"If he's not already, make sure Daniel Fitzsimmons gets himself to a therapist."

Barkley hung up and thumbed through the file on the old car crash. There was one additional item he hadn't shared with Cat McShane, something he'd unearthed when they ran their check on Violet. She was a working girl, busted for solicitation and misdemeanor drug possession a half-dozen times. Maybe that was fucked up. Then again, one of her kids had gone to Harvard. The other was at Latin School. God bless her, Violet must have been doing something right. Barkley shoved the file in a drawer just as the phone rang. On the other end of the line was his captain. They'd IDed the black man in Nick Toney's photo. Surprise, fucking surprise, he had a record.

23

Daniel could feel Grace's pull as he walked through Kenmore Square. He kept his head down, eyes averted, gingerly but inevitably entering her orbit. And then he was there, crumbling into her arms on the steps of Music City, burying himself in the smell of her skin, stripping himself of himself.

"Let it out," she breathed, a whisper as ancient as the grief he felt, one that stirred the leaves of death and carried the seeds of something else, something women seemed to understand and embrace so much better and finer than men ever could. Maybe it was healing, maybe it was just acceptance. But Grace understood it. And so she comforted him and he could feel her edge, just a fraction, from young girl to young woman. And part of him marveled at such a thing even as the rest of him heaved in choking, shuddering gasps.

"How did you know?" he finally said. Did it matter how she knew? No, but the mind asked its questions to keep itself busy. Keep itself in the game.

"My dad heard it on the news."

"So you came over?"

"Was that okay?"

He nodded, wiping his nose on his sleeve and producing another spate of tears that filmed his cheeks and salted his lips. "Fuck." Daniel never swore, but he was tired and stretched and dangerously out of control and couldn't have that.

"Why didn't you come up?" He pointed vaguely toward his building.

"I don't know. Just figured I'd wait."

"Did you see us on the roof?"

"I thought it was you. You wanna walk?"

Moving seemed like a good idea so he nodded and they got up.

"What time is it?" he said.

She pointed to the clock on the insurance building. "Nine thirty-two."

Nine thirty-two. Harry had been dead how long? Daniel tried to do the sums, but the numbers wouldn't line up in his head. He wondered if they'd burned the body yet. "Let's walk to school."

"You sure?"

"You think people will know?"

"Probably." She reached out and touched the ragged line he'd chopped across his head. "You cut your hair."

"Yeah." He'd brought his book bag and slung it over his shoulder. "Come on. We can get there by third period."

They crossed the street and started up Brookline Avenue, over a bridge that spanned the Mass Pike. The Green Monster loomed on their left. Daniel noticed a baseball trapped at the base of the stiff, twisted netting and wondered if they'd leave it there all winter. And if they did, would it still be there in the spring? Maybe he'd come by every day and check. Maybe he'd be there when it fell.

"You sure you wanna go in?" Grace said.

He wasn't sure, but his feet seemed to have a mind of their own. And so he led the way as they slipped over the bridge and dipped down past Fenway.

"I was there last night," he said. "In the alley where it happened. Spent all night at the police station, then went down to see the body."

Grace didn't ask for more. She hadn't asked for what she'd gotten. Daniel continued, anyway, because it felt like it scrubbed at something inside.

"The police wanted to know how I got down where Harry was, but I couldn't explain it."

"You couldn't explain it cuz you didn't want to, or you couldn't explain it cuz you couldn't explain it?"

"The second one. I don't know how I got there, but I did. And I saw in my head what I was gonna find."

"You saw like a picture?"

"More like a color or a feeling. But I knew it was Harry. And I was hoping . . ."

"You thought you could save him?"

Daniel shook his head. "Don't think it works that way."

She skimmed him a fresh look and for the first time he saw that maybe, just maybe, she was a little afraid of him. They walked another block.

"You hungry?" Grace pointed to a Dunkin' Donuts on the corner of Brookline and Boylston. They went in and got a couple of plain crullers, sitting at a counter by the front window and staring out at traffic streaming through the intersection.

"He knew I loved him," Daniel said. "Harry knew that."

Grace made a small sound in her throat. Daniel felt her fingers brush his.

"Let's not talk about it anymore," he said.

"Okay."

His cruller had just come out of the deep fryer. There was a fine crunchy crust on the outside and it was warm and soft in the middle. He ate it slowly and, for the first time since the alley, allowed himself a respite, a moment where he enjoyed something of this world.

"Want mine?" Grace said.

Daniel shook his head and tugged a napkin from the dispenser.

"The guy you live with . . . the professor?"

"Simon."

"Are you gonna stay there?"

"For now, I guess. Why?"

Grace turned so their knees were touching. "What do you know about him?"

"I told you what I knew."

"I get feelings, too, Daniel."

"Everyone gets feelings."

"I mean something more, like what you described in the record store." She read the disbelief in his face. "Doesn't matter what you think."

"I didn't say anything."

"Have you ever thought maybe this professor is entangling *you*? Manipulating *you*?"

"Why would he do that?"

"Good question. Did you tell the police about the gun?"

Daniel felt his face grow hot and pink. "What gun?"

"The one you picked up outside of school yesterday. People see, Daniel. People know. Okay, people guess. *I* know." Her eyes moved to his book bag on the counter. "Is it in there?"

He put a hand on the bag and noticed the small muscles in his forearm as he moved his fingers.

She blew a puff of air from her perfect lips. "You know they have a suspect?"

"Who told you that?"

"My dad. I guess it's all over Chinatown."

"Do you have a name?"

"I don't. And if I did, I'd tell you to leave it to the police."

She was growing older even as he watched, body ripening, eyes deepening, her coltish movements becoming a study in poise and polish. He saw her standing at the back of a church, in a white dress with orange flowers in her hair and scent on her cheeks, a wedge of sun warming her face and turning it a dozen shades of golden. Her life flashed past in a series of flip cards—quiet nights on the couch, movies and popcorn as the snow piled up outside, summers and sun-brewed tea, puppies, children, cookouts, a husband, partner, friend. Love. Bubbling, endless, overflowing. And so it went to the end of her days. And then it was done and Grace moved on, one of ten thousand lives she'd lead and a special one at that. It was all as it should be, but only if he was part of none of it. Love and hate, pain and perfection, one tugged at the thread of the other and life unraveled.

"I never told you about my mom."

"What do you want to tell me?"

"She died in a car crash when I was a kid."

Grace didn't offer any condolences because he didn't need any. He needed to talk. So she took his hand and listened.

"We'd sit up in an apartment we had downtown. I was seven or eight and would lie in her bed, watching in the mirror as she put on makeup." Daniel remembered lifting his nose and the smell of her powder, sweetening the thick clouds of cigarette smoke. Coffee cups kissed with lipstick crowded together on the vanity as he ran up and down a short set of stairs, getting her this, bringing her that. A hiss of silk as she stood up in her slip, figure long in the mirror, and asked how she looked and he'd stare at her face and she'd smile in the glass and kiss him and tell him he was so perfect and don't ever change. Then she'd put on her dress and he'd zip it up and he'd thread a needle if she needed it because her eyes were no good for that and he'd watch as the rings and earrings came out and went on. When she was ready, she'd kiss him again on the cheek and tell him he'd be okay and if he wasn't he could go to the lady who lived downstairs or the Chinaman on the corner. Then she'd look at herself a final time in the mirror, that hint of something else always tugging at her lips, as if she was waiting, begging, for someone to tell her to stay. But no one ever did. And so she'd go.

"I'd watch her from the window, then sit up as the streetlights came on and wait for Harry. He wouldn't get home until late from football. We'd go down in the street and play catch." Laces spinning, perfect spirals in the night, a kiss of leather as the ball hit soft in his hands and he cradled it close to his body. Harry at the other end, smiling as Daniel threw the ball back, covering only half the distance and a wobble at that. They'd sit on the curb or a bench and talk while the sweat cooled on Daniel's neck. Sometimes, they talked about football. Sometimes, it was their mother. Sometimes, it was her "dates." Once Harry asked if Daniel remembered their dad. Daniel shook his head. He could feel his brother's angst rubbing and stretching and searching for a home and he never told their mother about those conversations. Not because Harry asked him to keep quiet, but just because Daniel knew. And now he told Grace because she was everything that was left.

"I'll help you, Daniel. But in my own way."

"What do you think I want to do?"

"Let's talk outside." She waited until they were back on the sidewalk before speaking again. "If I'm wrong, just tell me. You want to find Harry's killer. Right now. Today."

She'd spoken the words and he felt better, like it was real and normal and just the next thing.

"Yes, that's exactly what I want."

"But not the gun, Daniel."

"You don't think he's gonna have one?"

"Not the gun."

He pulled the heavy revolver from his bag and handed it to her. She turned it over quickly in her hands and shoved it in her coat pocket. Then they walked down Brookline Avenue in silence. Not perfect silence, but the words they said sounded wooden and hollow and meant nothing compared to what had already been said and left unsaid. Just before they hit Avenue Louis Pasteur, Daniel stopped and turned.

"It can't happen like this."

"Then how?"

"I don't know, but the gun's part of it."

She shook her head but took out the revolver. Whatever had been set in motion was running now, free and easy, and would be as it was meant to be, regardless of what they said or did or felt or didn't. So Daniel shoved the gun back in his bag and they walked the rest of the way down Avenue Louis Pasteur. As they hit the front steps of the school, Grace took his hand.

24

They went in a side door and down to the basement to wait for the end of the period. Eddie Spaulding was sitting on the floor in the hallway, eating a Hoodsie with a wooden spoon and reading CliffsNotes for Albert Camus's *The Stranger.* He fixed Grace with his golden gaze. She didn't give him a second look as they ducked into the cafeteria. A couple of women were setting up for lunch at a long steam table, carrying out pans heavy with Salisbury steak and industrial-strength mac and cheese, all of it arriving in clouds of white steam. Nearby a man with a face like an old bucket pushed a long-handled broom across the cement floor. Grace headed to the bathroom. Daniel sat on a bench at one of the narrow tables. The swinging doors to the cafeteria squeaked once and Spaulding walked in. He took a seat across from Daniel, propping up one sneaker and flexing his wrist as he spoke.

"I heard about your brother. I'm sorry."

Daniel ducked his eyes, hiding from his pain like any animal would. "Thanks."

"Great football player. Looked out for me when I was on jayvee."

"Sounds like Harry."

"He was a stand-up guy, Daniel. Real fucking deal."

Daniel was sure that meant a lot to Eddie Spaulding, but it didn't mean jack to him. He wanted his fucking brother back. Could Spaulding do that? No. And it didn't matter how many nice things people said.

"Ever tell you I lost a brother?" Spaulding's words were clipped and perfectly shaped. Daniel shook his head and waited for more.

"We live in Old Colony. Me and my mom."

Old Colony was a housing project in Southie. Daniel had never been there.

"Terry got hit by a drunk driver. I know the guy, but no one ever did nothing."

"How old was he?"

"My brother? Eleven and a half. I was ten."

Daniel thought about the almighty Eddie Spaulding, sitting in a one-bedroom box with his mom, both of them staring at a class photo of the dead kid who wasn't there and was always there. The man with the broom came down again to work their area. They let him sweep and didn't say another word until he'd left.

"You talk to the cops yet?" Eddie had cut his voice.

"Last night."

"The guy who killed Terry's still around. I know exactly where he lives."

"That must be tough."

"People in the projects still talk about it to this very fucking day. Wonder why I never went after the guy. Some of them think I'm a pussy. No one says it to my face, but I know that's what they think. Latin School, college boy. Didn't stick up for his dead brother. Pussy."

Daniel played with a seam on his book bag and felt the barrel of the gun through the fabric. "What do you think?"

"I think I want to get my mom the fuck out of the projects. My brother never gave a shit about school, but he wanted it for me. Told everyone I was gonna be starting for Harvard. He was gonna sit in the stands for Harvard-Yale. Not happening with my grades, but that's all right. Still gonna try the fuck out of whatever they put in front of me."

The zombie with the broom rotated through again. Eddie stood up. "You know they're looking for you?"

"Who's that?"

"Headmaster's office. Sent out word first thing this morning. Anyway, I gotta get."

"Thanks, Eddie."

Spaulding nodded. It was what you did if you were a certain kind of guy. You passed along what you knew to someone who was drowning. Maybe the other guy drowned anyway. Maybe you drowned together, but at least you tried. Grace came back from the bathroom just in time to see the star running back leave.

"What did he want?"

"Just being a friend."

"Really?"

"In his own Spaulding way. He's worried I might be out for blood as well."

"Are you?"

"I'm not gonna sit by, Grace. Not again."

"What does that mean?"

Daniel was about to respond when the cafeteria doors squeaked and Boston Latin School's headmaster stepped through. Daniel had never seen the great and powerful William Keating outside of the assembly hall and had a difficult time imagining him in a place as dingy and common as the school cafeteria. But there he was, blue three-piece suit, red tie, and black oxfords that shined like mirrors. Grace put a soft hand on the strap of Daniel's bag.

"Want me to take that?"

Daniel shrugged her off and stood up, his face etched in hard grooves of light.

They settled by a tall set of windows overlooking the front steps of Latin School. Daniel was in the middle of the loose triangle, Latin School's headmaster, William Keating, on his left, the president of Harvard University on his right.

"This is Lawrence Trent," Keating said.

"How are you, Daniel?" Trent wore a dark silk suit that made a hissing sound when he offered his hand.

"Fine, sir."

Keating got up, muttering to himself and looking for something on his desk. He returned to his chair with a sigh that whistled through his teeth. "I'm sorry, Daniel. So very, very sorry."

"Thank you, sir."

"Such a senseless tragedy. We didn't know if you'd be in today."

"I was with the police until early this morning but couldn't really sleep."

The word *police* caused Keating's shoulders to jump and Trent to blink. Harvard would be under the microscope for letting a bunch of its players loose in the Combat Zone. The fact that they were mostly white and entirely privileged while a lot of the girls on the street were black didn't help anyone, especially the guys from Cambridge.

"Have you given any thought to the funeral?" Trent said.

"There won't be any service. Harry will be cremated as soon as they finish with the body."

Keating's jaw dropped a full inch. Trent gave Daniel a lacerating smile.

"Do you think that's wise? There are many people at the university who would like to pay their respects."

"It's what my brother would have wanted. Besides, it's already done."

"Of course." Trent paused as if to gather momentum. "There are a few things about Harry we want to make sure get mentioned. First, of course, to you, and then to the public at large."

Daniel might be broken and bleeding and naked. Harry, beyond caring. All of that, however, needed to be weighed against how Harvard came out of this. And so Trent hammered on.

"Your brother was only on campus for a short time, yet he made an indelible impact on everyone he met. Harry was a brilliant student, a leader on and off the football field, and, most important, a young man of the utmost integrity, utmost character. He enriched everyone he touched and represented the very best of Harvard. We offer our condolences and join in your grief."

"Thanks."

"We want to remember Harry." Trent pulled a piece of paper from his pocket and fixed a set of reading glasses he kept on a cord to his treacherously long Beacon Hill nose. "And to that end, the Board of Fellows has decided to establish a full, four-year scholarship in your brother's name. It will be awarded each year to a graduate from the Boston Latin School. The recipient will be chosen by a committee of Harvard and Latin School alumni, chaired by the sitting president and headmaster of the schools, respectively. Criteria for the scholarship will be leadership, academic prowess, athletic ability, outstanding character, and service to the community. The scholarship will be fully endowed in perpetuity by the university and serve as a testament to the life and character of Harry Fitzsimmons." Trent folded up the paper and dropped the glasses to his chest. "We want this to be something special, Daniel. Awarded to an outstanding student from the city who might otherwise not have the means."

"That's great," Daniel said.

Trent lifted a patrician finger. "There's one more thing. We'd like to start the scholarship with your graduating class and we'd love for you to be the first recipient."

Daniel glanced at Keating, who had a smile slathered across his face like a smear of Irish butter. "Your academic record is outstanding, Daniel. Everyone here knows what kind of a person you are. And everything you've overcome. Frankly, we can't think of a better recipient."

Trent reached for Daniel's hand. "Daniel, I'm thrilled to offer you a place in our freshman class upon graduation from Latin School. I suspect you'll make a great Harvard man."

"Thanks," Daniel said, "but I'm not interested in going to Harvard. I mean, it's a wonderful school and all, but it's just not for me. Not with Harry having gone there and everything."

Trent smiled and nodded, still pumping Daniel's hand as if that might force-feed some sense into the boy. "Why don't you take some time and think about it?"

"I don't need to."

"Take it anyway. Please. We'll announce the scholarship next week. See where things go from there. William."

Both men rose from their chairs and walked out into the hallway for a private chat about the moron who'd just turned down a free ride to Harvard. Daniel stole a look across the flat expanse of the headmaster's desk. Behind it was an open door that led to a small, interior office. Daniel could see a row of pictures running down one wall and a man sitting in a chair just inside the door. Actually, he could see the man's cuffed pant leg and a brown shoe, heel tapping impatiently against the nub of carpet. Keating returned from seeing Trent out and sat down again.

"Well, Daniel."

"I know you want me to take the scholarship."

"Let's talk about it when things are a little more settled."

"Let's not. Tell Harvard I'll go to their press conference and sing their praises, but only if they award the thing to Eddie Spaulding."

"Spaulding?"

"That's it. He gets the first scholarship when he graduates at the end of the year and we never had this conversation. Now, why don't you go ahead and bring in the cop."

"Excuse me?"

"You have a cop stashed in the office next door. I recognize his shoe."

Keating narrowed his eyes and all the bonhomie was gone, if there had ever been any bonhomie in the first place. He ducked into the other room and returned with the black detective from the alley. The headmaster left without another word, closing the door behind him as he went. The cop took the seat Harvard's president had been keeping warm and smiled.

"Hey, Daniel. Remember me?"

"Detective Jones."

"Call me Barkley. That was a nice thing you did just now."

"Eddie will do a lot more with it than I ever could."

"I'll take your word on that. Thing is, I don't give a shit about Harvard or Eddie."

"No?"

The detective leaned forward, pressing his palms together and touching the tips of his fingers to his lips. "Let's talk about the gun."

He should have known better. Grace had told him as much. People see things. People know. And if people know, cops like Barkley know. It's how they make a living.

"Why didn't you tell me about it at the station?"

"About what?"

"Not gonna work, Daniel. Not gonna work at all. Have you been to bed?"

"I slept a little."

"There was a fight here yesterday. You were in the middle of it."

"What does that have to do with Harry?"

"Several people say they saw a gun. At one point you had your hands on it."

"I was in a fight, sure, but I didn't see any gun."

"Daniel . . ."

"I'm sure you've been in fights, Detective. It's crazy."

"There were at least two students hiding in the gym. They told the cops you knocked it out of the guy's hands."

"What guy?"

"Doesn't matter. You don't remember any of this?"

"I remember fighting a black kid. Had a silver tooth hanging around his neck."

Barkley took out a ballpoint pen and began to write in a notebook.

"He was bigger than me so I grabbed his arm. He threw me around like I was nothing. I remember being on the ground, this kid coming after me when the cops showed up. The kid ran and that was it."

"Was a girl attacked?"

"A friend of mine. A couple of other kids grabbed her, but she got away."

"What's her name?"

"I'd rather not say. What's any of this got to do with my brother?"

The detective stopped writing and looked up.

"She doesn't know anything. If she did, I'd tell you."

Barkley clicked the pen a couple of times with his thumb. "Would you?"

"Yes, I would."

"So you didn't see a gun?"

Daniel shook his head. Barkley's eyes flicked to the bag at Daniel's feet, then settled back on the boy.

"Why would I lie?" Daniel said.

"Maybe cuz you're thinking of doing something stupid."

"I'm not stupid, Detective."

"We have a suspect in Harry's death. We're looking for him right now."

A knocking came from pipes buried deep inside the walls, a scent creeping up from the building's ancient heating vents. It was the smell of dry powder, his mother's talced fingers reaching into the back of their old Buick and pulling his lungs from his chest, smiling and squeezing the pale pink sponges until all the air had bled out and Daniel was lying flat on the car seat, dead but alive, breathing yet unable to strike a breath while the detective sat in the front, feet up on the dash, and took notes. Daniel began to wheeze and cough like an old man, the sound harsh and rasping in his ears. Barkley reached over and patted him on the back.

"You all right?"

"I'm fine."

"You want me to get you some water or something?"

"What do you know about my mother, Detective?"

"I was just about to ask you the same thing."

25

She was standing on the corner of Washington and Essex, wearing a short yellow jacket with tassels, a tight blue skirt, and a floppy hat that hid one side of her face. A skinny Asian kid squatted on a box in front of her, working polish into her stiletto heels and buffing them to a high shine. The kid wore thin wool gloves with the fingers cut out and talked nonstop as he worked. The woman checked her makeup in a compact while keeping one eye on the street. Daniel slouched past, invisible to both of them.

Grace was waiting at the King of Pizza. It was a storefront shop set up in the heart of the Combat Zone with maybe the best slices in the city. Grace was parked at a counter by the front window, sipping a Coke.

"How did you know I'd come?" Daniel said.

"I didn't."

She'd taped a note to his locker telling him to meet her after he got done with Keating. She was right. Going into school today had been a bad idea. So he'd stuck the note in his pocket and headed out to meet her.

"You want something?" Grace pointed to a couple slices of pepperoni on a paper plate.

"Not hungry."

She pushed across a slice and Daniel took a bite.

"What did they want?" Grace plucked a pepperoni off the other slice, then picked it up and nibbled.

"They just wanted to talk about Harry. Make sure I was all right."

Outside the woman in the hat had finished getting her shoes shined and was talking to a tall man wrapped in a camel hair coat with a roll of dark fur around the neck. Daniel couldn't make out the words, but he could tell the woman was angry. She stood on the corner with her hip cocked and finger raised, waving it in the man's face then jabbing it in his chest. The man didn't seem to notice the woman until he did, catching her flush on the jaw with the back of his hand. She bounced off the side of a building that housed fifty-cent peep shows and would have fallen into the gutter, but the tall man caught her by the elbow, holding her up so he could plant a platform heel in the small of her back. The woman skidded on her hands and knees, snapping a stiletto and banging off the side of a parked car. The tall man followed her into the street, taking off his belt and wrapping it around his knuckles. A cab flashed past, swerving around the two of them and laying on the horn. The kid with the shine box materialized out of nowhere, slipping between man and woman, laughing and joking, forcing the man to make eye contact while the woman struggled to her feet and wobbled toward the King of Pizza. She stopped in front of the window and put on her shoe with the broken heel, then walked lopsided to the far end of the block. Across the street, the tall man had put his belt back on and was smoking a brown cigarette, one foot up on the shine box as the Asian kid worked his polish and talked his magic.

"We probably should've met somewhere else," Grace said.

"It's fine."

"Was it far from here?"

Daniel flicked a finger in the general direction of the alley where Harry had died some twelve hours earlier.

"Let's just go."

"I already saw the body, Grace. Can't be anything

worse." Daniel picked up the slice in both hands, then put it down again. Grace watched.

"You live close?" he said.

"Five minutes. My dad doesn't want me coming in here. He's always driving past. Checking."

"I don't blame him."

"The girls are actually really nice. Besides, no one bothers me."

Daniel considered the shine of her skin and clean lines of her face and thought, *Not yet.* She turned so their knees were touching.

"There's something I want to tell you."

"What's that?"

"If I tell you, you have to promise you won't do anything crazy."

"You mean with the gun?"

Her smile flickered like a lightbulb that was loose in its socket. Her eyes fastened on Daniel's book bag. "Is it still in there?"

"What do you want to tell me?"

"Harry's killer was a student from English. A guy named Walter Price. At least that's what I heard."

Walter Price. The name thrummed through his body and hummed hot in his brain. Daniel did his best to sound casual. "You know him?"

"My dad says he's a big black kid who hangs around down here. Says he's a drug dealer or a pimp, but someone else said he's just a wannabe. Anyway, the police are supposed to be looking for him."

"What does he look like?"

"I told you. Big, black. That's all I know."

"So you've never actually seen him?"

"My dad says I have, but I'm not sure. Everyone thinks it was a robbery, Daniel. Just a freak thing. I'm so sorry."

"Why did you tell me?"

"If the situation was reversed, what would you have done?"

"Told you."

"Exactly."

"But you're worried about the gun?"

"I'm not worried you'll use it."

"Then what?"

"Yesterday you were talking about energy."

"Simon was talking about energy."

"Well, I think he's right. Everything has an energy—people, places . . ."

"Even guns."

"Especially guns. If you want to find the guy who killed your brother, be there when the cops arrest him, tell him what you think, whatever, that's fine. I'll even help you. But lose the gun first."

"There was a cop in Keating's office today. He was asking about it as well."

"The gun's gonna kill you, Daniel. At least it could. That's what I'm trying to say."

A car pulled to the curb and laid on the horn. In the driver's seat was a square-faced Asian man with white teeth and a black buzz cut.

"Your dad?" Daniel said.

"Shit."

It was the first time he'd ever heard Grace curse and he knew he'd always remember it.

"I gotta go." She pulled him away from the window so her father couldn't see and took his face in her hands to kiss him. Not the sweet, storybook kiss from the record store. That was a lifetime ago, when they were still kids and anything was possible. This one was wet and sloppy and reeked of desperation, her mouth opening and tongue pushing through his teeth as she flattened him against a wall next to the ladies' room. Their time together was running thin and Grace felt it as much as he did. Maybe more. She nipped at his ear and whispered, "I'm so sorry." Then she ran out the door to the waiting car.

Her father glared at Daniel as the ancient Ford crawled across King of Pizza's plateglass window and was gone. Daniel rubbed his lips with the back of his hand and listened to his heart bump in his chest. He was suddenly ravenous and ordered another slice. He'd just gotten back to his seat when a tall man with curly brown hair and eyes the color of gravy slipped onto the stool beside him.

"You mind?"

Daniel shrugged and took a bite.

"Good slice, huh?"

Daniel remembered his warning to Grace. This was a place full of predators. And they didn't discriminate between male and female when it came to whom they preyed upon.

"Just leave me alone, okay?"

"What are you doing down here?"

Daniel grabbed his book bag and got up to go. The man reached out and gripped his forearm. Daniel tried to break free, but the man was surprisingly strong. Daniel thought about Simon, about men with layers.

"I wasn't gonna hurt you, kid. You know what, fuck it."

The man let Daniel go, turning on his stool and crossing one leg over the other. A small Italian with quick hands and a round face was behind the counter, throwing cheese on a pie. The man with the curly hair seemed to see him for the first time.

"Mr. Sal, how you doing?"

Mr. Sal looked up with four teeth and a full smile, nodding and talking while continuing to work on his pie. "Hey, Signor Nick. You wanna slice?"

"I'm good, thanks."

Daniel sat back down on his stool. After all, it was the middle of the afternoon and they were in a pizza shop.

"What do you want?"

The man turned, surprised at first but getting past it quickly. "You're looking for information on the college kid, the one that was killed last night."

"You heard us talking?"

"You and the girl? Sure, but I knew anyway."

"Yeah, right."

"I saw you last night. You came down the alley and ran right into it. Started screaming and the cops grabbed you."

Daniel let his mind spin through the images—black buildings with windows lit up like cats' eyes in the smoky darkness, the crunch of a cop's boot, Harry collapsed in a corner, face empty, gutted.

"Name's Nick Toney." The man held out his hand. His skin was cool and dry, the wrinkles of his palm fitting neatly into Daniel's.

"I know, you think I'm some kind of freak, but I'm not. Mr. Sal . . ." Toney looked back toward the counter. "Am I some kind of freak?"

Mr. Sal looked up again from his pie. "That's Mr. Nick. Good man. Caan."

"Thank you." Toney turned back to Daniel. "He thinks I look like James Caan. I don't see it either, but what the hell. You mind if I smoke?" Toney already had his cigarettes out and lit up, pulling a piece of tobacco off his tongue and studying it before flicking it away with the flat of his thumb.

"The man who was killed was my brother."

"Shit." Toney lapsed into silence, shaking his head and staring at the capped toe of his shoe while he drew on the cigarette and exhaled.

"My name's Daniel."

"Daniel. Okay, good. I'm sorry, Daniel. I made a mistake and I'm gonna go."

"You had something to tell me."

"Did I?" Toney let more smoke drift from his nose, then dropped the butt to the floor, twisting it into the yellowed linoleum. Daniel stared at the inner black of the man's left eye and thought about trying to go inside.

"My brother's dead, Mr. Toney, and nothing's gonna change that. If you have something to say, just say it."

Toney wet his lips. "You know a detective named Jones? Big black guy?"

"How do you know him?"

"Talked to him very early this morning."

"Why?"

"I'm a photographer. Got a studio on the top floor of the Brompton Arms. Looks right over the alley where you wound up last night."

Daniel summoned up the face he'd seen in the window above the alley. The man with the camera. "You took pictures of the murder."

"How'd you know that?"

"I saw you with the camera. Did you give them to the police?"

"Cops are looking for the guy right now, Daniel."

His name rolled off the photographer's tongue in a way that made the air prickle, but that was just the vibe you got in the Combat Zone when you were sixteen and swimming upstream, a gun in your bag and the idea of killing a man running like a rat through the maze in your head.

"Can I see them?"

"Probably not a great idea."

"Please."

Toney sighed and stared at the traffic on Washington,

looking for all the world like a man who wished he'd kept his mouth shut.

The studio had six windows, four looking out to the street, two staring straight down into the alley where Harry had died. Toney pulled the shades on all of them, flicking on a set of overhead lights and directing Daniel to a seat at a long worktable. He listened as Toney rummaged around in the back. Three lengths of wire were strung across the room. Attached to each were what looked like work prints. Finished photos hung on the walls. Almost all the shots were of women, most of them taken in the studio or at night on the street. Toney returned from the back with a couple more prints.

"Sorry for the mess." He pushed aside the remains of a Greek salad and a couple half-eaten chunks of gray meat.

"What kind of photos do you shoot?"

"I document lives. Girls, pimps, whatever catches my eye. Last night I was working with a fifteen-year-old girl. Runaway from Minnesota."

Toney pointed to a trio of pictures clipped to one of the wires. Daniel got up and took a look. The girl reminded him of Twiggy, except even skinnier and grimmer around the eyes. Honest, unflinching, a black-and-white study in the perfection of corruption.

"See this one." Toney had come up behind Daniel, plucking one of the few color shots off the wire and holding it under the light. The print shivered in his hand.

"Who is she?" Daniel said.

"Pretty, right?"

The woman was older, straight brown hair, hollow green eyes. Toney had caught her at a street corner in the morning, just as she turned and before she'd had time to armor up.

"Her name's Elena Benson. Haven't seen her in over a year. Happens a lot down here. Anyway, the reason I was looking out the window was because I thought she was down in the alley. Just a minute or two before your brother. I yelled at her, but she was close to La-Grange and couldn't hear me."

"What's her name?"

"I told you. Elena. Elena Benson. She wasn't there when Harry died, Daniel. I'm not sure she was ever there." Toney clipped the photo back on the wire. "Let's sit down."

Toney took a seat and placed one of the photos he'd brought out from the back facedown on the table.

"Before I show you anything, there's something you need to know."

"What's that?"

"I actually met your brother yesterday morning. Just a chance thing in Harvard Square. I can't say I knew him, but it still kind of shook me."

"Is that why I'm here?"

"I don't know. Maybe. I saw you sitting there with the girl and you looked like you'd had your guts kicked out . . ." Toney's voice trailed off to nothing.

"It's all right, Mr. Toney."

"What's all right?"

"You feel like you're part of what happened to Harry, maybe even a little responsible, but you're not."

Toney nodded and drummed his fingers on the table. Daniel's eyes were fixed on the blank back of the print. Toney rubbed a thumb along its border.

"I cropped it so you can only see the killer."

"Thank you."

Toney flipped over the photo. Harry's attacker was perfectly caught in a fracture of street light, staring directly up at the unblinking lens. If this was Walter Price, Daniel knew him. He'd fought with him outside of Latin School yesterday and had his gun stuffed at the bottom of his bag.

"You recognize him," Toney said.

"Why do you say that?"

"It's written all over. Don't worry. I ain't gonna tell no one."

"He's a student at Boston English. I go to Latin. It's right across the street so I've seen him around. Name's Walter Price."

Toney turned the photo around and gave it a hard look. "No shit?"

"You know him as well," Daniel said.

"I didn't have the name but, yeah, I've seen him down here from time to time."

"You know where he is."

Toney turned the photo facedown again and laid his hands flat over it. "I might know where he'd go if he was scared."

"Did you tell the police?"

"Nah."

"Why not?"

Toney shrugged. "Down here you depend on a lot of people for access. Part of the deal is I look the other way on some things. Otherwise, it's just no good."

"You gave them your photos."

"Maybe that's where the line is for me. Besides, I went down there at five in the morning. Made sure no one saw me coming or going."

"Give me the address, Mr. Toney."

"Go home, son. Bury your brother and let the cops handle it."

Daniel pointed his chin at the print. "Can I at least keep that?"

Toney kicked it across the table with a finger. "Go ahead, then."

Daniel unzipped his book bag and slid the picture inside. Then he pulled out Walter Price's revolver.

"Give me the address or I swear I'll put a bullet in your head."

After Toney got done laughing, he told Daniel to put the goddamn gun away. The photographer opened the shades to the front windows and cracked them each an inch. Then he got a couple of ice-cold bottles of Coke from a small fridge. As the city whispered in the street below and the sun worked its way across the sky, the two of them talked.

"I can't give you the exact address," Toney said.

"Why not?"

"Does the phrase 'lambs to the slaughter' mean anything to you?"

"You think I'm gonna go busting in there and start shooting?"

"I think you'll go busting in there and get yourself shot, but what's the difference? Truth is I don't have an exact address."

"I don't believe you."

"Tell someone who gives a fuck. Best I can do is put you on the same block. After that, you're gonna have to wait for the cops. Take it or leave it."

Daniel took it. After he'd left, Toney pulled the shades, turned off the lights, and sat in the dark, wondering like hell if he'd done the right thing.

26

Barkley pulled up in front of Tommy Dillon's apartment at a little after three. He unfolded his six-foot five-inch frame slowly from the front seat, well aware of the four kids arranged on the stoop across the street. Barkley let them get a good look at the piece on his hip as he walked past, listening for the trail of Irish whispers that followed like soft blessings all the way to his partner's front door.

Katie Dillon answered on the first knock, pulling him close for a hug and pressing her body against his. "God, that feels good." She leaned back a fraction to get a look at his face. "Come on in."

They walked into the living room. Barkley stopped near a table full of photos. Tommy with Katie. Katie with Tommy. Both of them with the twins.

"Tommy said you guys are on the Harvard thing."

"That's the rumor."

"It was on the news all morning, Bark. *You* were on the news all morning."

He picked up a photo of Katie playing hoops back in the day. "I hear you have a sweet jumper. Or should I say 'had.'"

She took the photo from him and put it back on the table. "I'm serious."

"So am I."

"Why's it always you two who catch these ones?"

"Which ones you talking about?"

"You know what I mean. White kid, black suspect."

"Black cop, white partner."

"It's just a boatload of stress, Bark. Tommy, me, the girls. All the way around. You know what I'm saying?"

"There's the big dog." Tommy came rolling down the hall, hair still wet from the shower. He tossed Barkley a can of Bud.

"Am I supposed to open this now?"

"I'll take it." Tommy gave him the other can he had in his hand and popped the first. A froth of foam bubbled out of the top. Tommy drank it off and plopped down in an easy chair. "Take a load off, brother."

Barkley sat across from Tommy on the couch. Katie took a seat between them.

"Smells good in here," Barkley said.

"Homemade spaghetti and meatballs." Tommy pointed to a crush of take-out bags in a wire basket by the door. "My wife says I need to eat better."

"She's right."

"This from a guy who eats beans out of a can."

"You got time for a plate?" Katie said.

Barkley held up a hand. "Grabbed something before I came over."

"Don't believe it," Tommy said. "He slept at the station. Breakfast was probably a Zagnut bar."

"Hey, you didn't go home like I told you."

"I was home by eight thirty, nine. Got five good hours, plus a little extra." Tommy grinned at Katie and yo-yoed his knees back and forth. Katie colored but didn't move from her chair.

"We got some things to run down, Tommy."

"K was just telling me. How'd we get a suspect?"

Barkley glanced at Katie, who got up neatly. "I've got sauce on the stove. Bark, we're still gonna set a date for dinner?"

"You got it."

"Thanks, babe." Tommy spoke without ever taking his eyes off Barkley. They waited until she'd left.

"The photographer."

"Toney?"

"He's got a studio looking right over the alley." Barkley pulled one of Toney's photos from his pocket. Tommy turned on a lamp and studied it under the light.

"Fucking hey."

"Dumbass luck."

"We catch all the shit when things go sideways. Don't be afraid to take a bow."

"Ever hear of a kid named Walter Price?"

Tommy shook his head and tapped the picture with his finger. "This him?"

"Looks like it. Student at English. Part-times as a hustler down the Zone. Got a sheet. Girls, dope, ragtime shit."

"Lemme guess. He's in the wind?"

Barkley nodded.

Tommy handed back the photo. "I'll have an address for us by the end of the day."

"That's what I want to hear."

"Just lemme say good-bye to the girls." Tommy got up, draining his beer and tossing the empty in the basket.

"Hold on a sec." Barkley waved his partner back to his chair. Tommy sat, one heel rapping a beat on the wooden floor. This was his thing, like letting a bloodhound off the leash. "Yeah?"

"Relax."

"I'm good."

"Fuck you're good. You look like you want to lift your leg and take a piss in the corner. How's Katie doing?"

"She's fine. Why?"

"Nothing. Let's talk about the file you left on Violet Fitzsimmons."

"Fucked up, right? Guy's mother dies in a car crash and then the kid himself gets offed."

"Did you read through the file?"

"Quick look."

"You know she was a hooker?"

Tommy popped his head back. "The mom?"

"Was raising both boys while she was working."

"Probably kept 'em for the welfare chit. Any dad listed on the kids' birth certificates?"

"Nope. The one we talked to last night was in the car with her when she crashed."

"No shit."

"Eight years old. They found him walking down the beach in a daze. Then he slips into some sort of coma."

"That was in the file?"

"Finding these things does you no good, Tommy. Not unless you read 'em."

"And if I did that, why in the fuck would we keep you around? Where's all this headed, B?"

"Don't know for sure. Just bugs me. I mean, what are the chances he's in the crash and then this happens? And why was he down in that alley?"

"Know what I think?"

"What's that?"

"Best thing we can do for that kid is find the cock-sucker who killed his brother."

"Yeah."

Tommy got up. "Let me say good-bye to the girls and we'll roll."

He disappeared down the hall. Barkley hadn't told him about Daniel's print, traced in blood and pulled off his mother's throat. Or about Barkley's trip to Latin School. He'd asked Daniel about the accident. And the print. Daniel said he couldn't remember a thing. Barkley hadn't bought it. And then there was the quiet way the kid looked at him, like he knew Barkley's heart and every mark life had left upon it.

He got up and walked into the kitchen. Katie was chopping garlic. Meatballs and sauce simmered in a pan.

"Smells good."

"You should stay."

"Can't."

"I know, you're all so goddamned busy." She swept the garlic into the pan and cracked a second clove with the flat of her knife.

"What's the problem, Katie?"

She glanced at the connecting door that led to the hallway.

"He's with the girls," Barkley said.

She walked around him and shut the door, putting her back up against it. "He's on that shit again."

"What? Blow?"

"I don't think he ever got off."

"My ass. He went through a six-month program."

"You know Tommy. All the Irish bullshit comes out when he needs it. He'd have those counselors eating out of his hand."

"What makes you think he's using?"

Katie pulled a baggie from her pocket. "How much is that?"

Barkley held the baggie up to a trickle of sunlight bleeding through a tiny window over the sink. "Quarter gram, maybe a half."

"I don't know what that is, Bark. I don't know what that is, but I can't have it in my house. Shit, I'm gonna start bawling, great."

There was a sound from somewhere. Katie cracked

the door, pushing the hair back from her face and yelling down the hall, "What are you looking for?"

"Never mind," Tommy said. "I got it. Tell Bark I'll be there in a minute."

She nudged the door shut and returned to the stove, wiping at her eyes with the heel of her hand and reaching up into a cabinet for a can of whole tomatoes. She was wearing a long-sleeved Celtics shirt that rode up to reveal an ugly purple welt running along her arm just above the elbow. Barkley touched her wrist and turned the arm gently.

"What's that?"

She tugged herself free.

"Is he fucking hitting you?"

Katie lifted her chin, Irish heat baked into cracked eyes, two red spots marking her cheeks. "You know better."

"Do I?"

"We were arguing and he grabbed me. I bruise easy. Makes it look a lot worse than it is." She reached to adjust a burner on the stove, brushing her hip against his thigh. He sensed the pulse of her blood sync with his and remembered the feel of her flesh, the way she moved above him, her amazing hips and the small sounds she made as he rocked inside her and filled her. It'd be three years Christmas. They'd separated, her and Tommy, both of them confiding in Barkley, both convinced it was so fucking done. Not that it should have mattered, not that it did matter. She showed up at Barkley's apartment one night. The snow was falling, first of the year, perfect and white, making everything blurry and soft in a city known for none of that. She didn't want to talk about Tommy. Just a Christmas drink with a friend. He never saw it coming. If he had, he'd have run like a hound from hell. Not that he regretted it. That was the best part and by far the worst. He couldn't ever have Katie Dillon for his own. They both knew it even as they lay together in his bed, with the moonlight tiptoeing through the window and the snow falling in great drifts across the roof-tops of Charlestown. And so every touch was a first, every kiss, their last. Hours slipped past in a moment and moments would have to last a lifetime. Six months later, she was back with Tommy. At his partner's insistence, Barkley met them for a drink at a bar near Fenway called Copperfield's. She hugged Barkley and said she was happy. But he could read her eyes and knew what was there and knew she was reading the same thing in his eyes. Meanwhile, Tommy watched both of them, tickled as all fuck cuz his life had been Scotch-taped back together and desperate to move on before anyone looked too close. And now this. The tiny-as-shit kitchen, her, Tommy in the back with the twins. The bag of dope.

"Who's he running with, Katie?"

"I dunno."

"Where's he getting his stuff?"

"That ain't hard. Walk a block in this neighborhood and you'll find someone who'll sell you pretty much whatever you can dream up."

"You scared?"

Katie shook her head. "I told you. Tommy would never hurt me. Not for real."

"The twins?"

"Exception to the rule." She reached behind her back and picked up a curved knife from the counter. "He'd cut me for those two. Wouldn't think twice about you, either."

Tread in the hall. Katie put down the knife and slipped her hands to Barkley's hips, sliding past and kicking the door open as Tommy turned the corner.

"Something smells good." He lifted his nose to the air. "You sure we ain't got time, boss?"

Barkley shook his head. Tommy had his service weapon clipped to his belt. He pulled his faded leather jacket off a hook and gave Katie a kiss, goosing her as they broke their clinch.

"See, Bark, girl can still move. Am I driving?"

"I'll drive."

"Be careful," Katie said, turning back to her stove. The two cops rumbled down the hall and left.

Barkley's car had a half-dozen eggs splattered across the side panel and windows. Tommy wanted to roust the little pricks. Barkley told him to climb in.

"I'll get the cocksuckers," Tommy said as Barkley turned on his wipers and squirted fluid across the windshield.

"Forget it. Where we headed?"

"Left at the end of the block."

Barkley started to roll. He figured they'd start in the Zone, but Tommy was taking them deeper into the neighborhood.

"You going local on this?"

Tommy shrugged. He was a million miles away now, playing with the silver-and-turquoise watch on his wrist, staring out the window as ciphers slipped past. Names, faces, connections only he could see. "Left here."

Barkley hung the left. "I talked to the ME this morning."

"What'd that bitch have to say?"

Tommy actually liked Cat, but talking that way about women made him feel like a big man. Barkley didn't give a damn. All he wanted was an address.

"She was going on about the wound patterns on Fitzsimmons. Said there were two different types. The first was nonlethal, in the belly. Made by a knife like the one in the picture. And then there were the wounds that killed him. Three of 'em, all deep puncture wounds."

"How deep?"

"Ran the kid right through."

"Not with the knife?"

"ME says no way."

Tommy let that sit for a minute. "Does it really matter? One knife, another knife. I mean, who gives a fuck? We got the photo. Let's just grab this guy and call it a day. Right here."

Barkley pulled up to a single-story wooden shack painted pure black for some godforsaken reason only someone from Southie would understand. A Schlitz sign hung off a rusted piece of pipe; green neon tubes spelled out THE IRISH TAP in the only working window. Barkley nodded toward the front door. "What are we gonna find in here?"

"People talk, B. Even in Southie, people love to fucking talk." Tommy popped his door and got out, then stuck his head back in. "Do me a favor."

"What's that?"

"When we get inside, order a beer and sit right in front. Fucking bartender will love it."

27

A couple of smoke hounds were set up at the far end of the bar, fluorescent skin, yellow teeth, eyes like two sets of pissholes in the snow. One of them hacked into his sleeve and spit into a paper cup while the other rounded his mouth into an "O" and popped out a parade of smoke rings that floated through layers of runny light toward the ceiling where they joined the rest of the ghosts drinking in the rafters. Tommy touched Barkley on the shoulder and nodded to a booth at the back of the place. Two women were staring out of the gloom like a pair of feral cats. Tommy headed their way with a cigarette angled between his teeth and a fresh bottle of Bud. Barkley watched his partner go, then settled on a stool directly behind the taps. The snow-capped barkeep had skinny legs, no ass, and the swollen belly they gave out as the door prize for a lifetime of drinking. He poured Barkley a thin draft and reached up to turn on a TV slotted over the register.

The Eyewitness News update led with Harry Fitzsimmons's murder. What else? Three guys played pinball beside a window boarded up with cardboard Schlitz cases. Closer to the TV another threesome looked to be fresh off the job—arms, neck, and hair splattered in smears of whitewash. Barkley had never met a painter who wasn't a drunk and was guessing this crew to be no different. The detective winced inwardly as his face popped up on the TV, assuring the city that the Boston PD was on the job and the unidentified assailant, a young black male, would be apprehended soon enough.

One of the painters, the thickest of the bunch, pointed at Barkley's face on the screen. "We lose one monkey, we send another one out to look for it. What the fuck?"

The painter had salt-and-pepper hair and a fox face that creased into a smile as he lifted a bottle of beer to his lips and slitted his eyes toward Barkley. His pal snickered nervously beside him while the third guy, by far the youngest of the crew, slinked off to the jukebox.

"What do you think, Willie?" Salt and Pepper yelled. "Hey, Willie, whaddaya think?"

The old bartender took his time walking back toward the painters, wiping the counter with a rag as he went. "Why don't you take your business down the street?"

"You barring me?"

"I didn't say that."

"Then what?"

The barkeep didn't need a scrape in his joint, especially not with a Boston cop. "You boys have had enough. Go home and get some dinner."

Salt and Pepper ignored him, draining a shot that was sitting on the bar, then heading over to the jukebox where the youngster was picking out some tunes. Barkley glanced toward the back. Tommy was huddled up with the women. Overhead the speakers cranked out the Stones' "Monkey Man"—Nicky Hopkins on piano, Keith on the slide. Salt and Pepper put his bottle of beer to his lips and offered up his best Jagger, lip-synching about a fleabit peanut monkey and again slipping his eyes toward the big, black Boston cop.

In an earlier life, Barkley would have already been picking bits of the guy's teeth out of his knuckles. Fucking maturity. Sometimes it really sucked. He threw down a five and got up to go. Didn't even get halfway to the front door.

"You know who this is?" Salt and Pepper grabbed his baby-faced drinking buddy by the back of the shirt like he was a fish he'd just pulled out of the surf at Castle Island.

"Afraid not." Barkley cracked a hard grin and kept moving toward the door.

"This here's Billy Randall."

Barkley knew the name. Six months ago, Randall had been standing next to the guy who'd attacked a black man with an American flag during an anti-busing rally at Government Center. A photographer from the *Herald* caught the moment. Two days later, it was national news.

"That ain't Randall," Barkley said, taking a step closer and brushing the gun on his hip with the tips of his fingers.

"He was there, though." Salt and Pepper shifted his story just as easy as that cuz that's how liars worked, especially when they were bigots. "Stood right behind Randall. Didn't you, Timmer?"

Timmer nodded and looked like he wanted nothing better than to crawl back to his barstool and be left the fuck alone. Barkley could have told Timmer what was gonna happen if he stayed in Southie. He'd always be the kid who was standing behind the kid who was standing next to the kid who went after the smoke with the American flag and got his face on the cover of the *Herald*, *Newsweek*, and who the fuck knows what else.

He'd never have to buy another beer in the neighborhood. And he'd never have a life beyond it.

"Sorry, boys, I don't have the time for your happy horseshit today. Now, go back to the bar and sit the fuck down before I lose my patience."

Barkley turned and headed for the door. His fingers had just brushed the curve of the knob when someone's head hit something hard and flat. Barkley knew it wasn't gonna be good and turned anyway. Tommy had been listening. Fuck, yeah, he'd been listening. And now he had Salt and Pepper pegged up against a wooden post that held up one end of the sorry-ass, saggy-ass bar. Tommy had a hand gripped around Salt and Pepper's fleshy throat. In the other hand, Tommy held a small, sharp blade that was pressed against Salt and Pepper's cheek.

"This one bothering you, B?"

"Forget it, Tommy."

Barkley's partner pressed the knife in, drawing a line of bright blood. "I don't *fucking* think so."

The three guys from the pinball machine came up behind Tommy. Two of them had bottles in their hands. The bartender pulled a billy club from underneath the taps. Barkley drew his gun.

"Tommy?" Barkley could see the crazy circling in his partner's eyes. "Not worth it, bud."

Tommy moved his knife from the cheek to just inside the left nostril. Salt and Pepper whimpered a little in the back of his throat. No one else moved.

"I go inch and a half and you never breathe out of this side again. Six months of rehab, plastic surgery, and you look like a fucking freak the rest of your life. Trust me, brother."

"Tommy."

"I know this guy, B. Fucking puke always running his mouth."

Maybe Tommy knew the guy. Maybe he knew his brother. Or his cousin. Or maybe Tommy bumped into him once at the grocery store. Didn't matter cuz no one manufactured rage like Tommy. He adjusted the knife.

"This here's an inch. You could live with this one. Still need surgery, but you could live with it. Might even help your looks. What do you think, Bark? Could you see this boy sucking some cock up the Brompton?" Tommy leaned close and dropped his voice. "That there's a *Boston* cop, motherfucker. And my partner. You know what that means?"

Salt and Pepper had lifted his chin as high as it would go. Anything to get away from Tommy's knife. "I understand."

"You understand what?"

"I understand, sir."

Barkley holstered his weapon and moved closer, kicking at a couple of plastic cups on the floor.

"Fucking cunts," Tommy said.

Barkley touched the knot of muscle that was his partner's shoulder. Tommy slowly withdrew the knife. Salt and Pepper came down off his tiptoes. The bartender dropped his club. Everyone exhaled. Quicker than the grin of a deformed freak show walking the streets of Southie with a scar that told everyone everything they needed to know, Tommy flicked the blade and laid open Salt and Pepper's nose. Blood geysered as the painter screamed and tried to hold his face together. Tommy snapped the knife shut and slid it back in his pocket. Barkley's gun was out again, covering their exit. Five minutes later, they were driving through a warren of side streets. Tommy had his elbow out the window, smoking a menthol cigarette and enjoying the cold air.

"No one's gonna say shit, B."

"Yeah?"

"Took a quarter inch. Half, tops. I call it the Chinatown cut." Tommy laughed at his joke and streamed smoke out the window.

"Not funny, Tommy."

"Seriously, two, three stitches, tiny little scar, no big deal. What the fuck, man's calling you a monkey. I'm supposed to sit there and take that?"

"We better not get a call."

"What did I tell ya? Ain't gonna be no call. Now, listen, I got a line on our boy."

Barkley bumped through an intersection just as the light went red. "Go ahead."

"Word is he's headed to the Bury."

"Who we getting this from?"

"Couple of broads I know buy from him."

"They sure?"

"They'd already heard rumors this guy was good for it."

"No shit."

"Price is a bottom-feeder. No one wants to help him. No one likes seeing the Harvard kid dead. Bad for business, bad all around."

"So you got an address?"

Tommy launched his cigarette butt with a flick of his finger and rolled up the window. "I told you he's headed to the Bury. One of the girls is gonna call with an address. Hang a louie."

Barkley took the left and two rights. They pulled up in front of Tommy's three-decker.

"Your source calling you at home?"

"Why not? You wanna come in and wait?"

"Nah, I gotta hit it. What time's the call coming in?"

"If it's happening tonight, it'll be in the next hour

or so. Otherwise, tomorrow. Where can I get hold of you?"

"Try the station. If I'm not there, leave a message."

Tommy started to get out of the car and stopped. "I know what Katie told you."

"How's that?"

"I know what she told you in the kitchen."

Barkley pulled the bag of coke from his pocket and dropped it on the dashboard. "Says she found it in the house."

"And what do you say?"

"What do I say? I say, 'What the fuck?'"

"That it?"

"You know how it works. One of us got a problem, we deal with it. No one else. Just us."

Tommy picked up the baggie, holding it between a thumb and forefinger. "I got a bunch more inside."

"Fucking great."

"Signed 'em out of Evidence last week. Cleared it with the captain and everything."

"Why don't I know?"

"Told him you did. Figured I'd catch you up later."

Barkley believed him. The story could be checked easy enough so what was the point in lying?

"Why you needing a bunch of blow, Tommy?"

"Sweetens the pot. Some of these lowlifes, you give 'em a toot and they're your best pal. Start talking and don't know when to stop."

"I never seen anyone cop to a homicide cuz he got fixed up with a couple lines of blow."

"Maybe it ain't about a homicide."

Barkley killed the engine and turned so he was facing his partner. "Let me guess. This is the other thing you wanted to talk about before."

Tommy nodded, eyes roaming around the car, searching for someplace safe to land. Barkley waited.

"Talking product, B. High-grade shit. Trunks full of it."

"And how'd you get hooked into that?"

"I'm an ex-junkie. I know this fucking world."

"Which is why you're the last person who should be working it."

Tommy offered up his best *Is what it fucking is* look. Barkley sighed and massaged his temple with the side of his thumb. "Who else knows about it?"

"No one knows shit. We clear the Harvard thing, then I need another week or so. After that, I bring you in and we decide what to do."

"We got options?"

"This is forever money, B." Tommy held up a hand.

"Listen first. I'm not saying you need to be bent or nothing like that. In fact, we make the fucking bust. But maybe we think about breaking off a piece. Just this once. Stash the money somewhere for a couple of years, then pack it in. Early retirement, place in Florida, California, big-ass boat, some fucking thing."

"Tommy, the Irish sailor."

Dillon laughed like hell. "Can't you see it? Listen, I don't wanna talk about this now. Not with the Harvard kid and everything. Just think about it. And if it's no, it's no. We move on. Not a problem. But think about it. Okay?"

What choice did he have? Tommy was Tommy was Tommy. Hopefully he didn't get himself killed in the process. And then there was the money. Barkley would be lying if he said he wasn't wondering how much money his partner thought qualified as "forever."

"How'd you know Katie told me about the baggie?"

"When I came back into the kitchen, there was something between the two of you. Mostly her, but you were acting a little funny. That's right, B, even you give it away, so fucking watch it." Tommy grinned that easy, crazy, spinning Tommy grin. "Just kidding. I was short a bag. She seen one I must have left out and grabbed it. All made sense then."

Barkley grunted and turned over the engine.

"We good?" Tommy said.

"Next time, fucking tell me. And tell your wife. She's worried sick."

"Will do. And we talk about the other thing later?"

"We'll talk."

Tommy got out of the car and stuck his head back in. "You don't wanna come in? Homemade spaghetti and meatballs."

"Rain check. And talk to your wife."

Tommy slammed the door and banged on the roof as the car pulled away. Barkley drove until he found the expressway and jumped on. The pint of Jack he kept in the glovie was out and sitting against his thigh. By the time he circled back to the station, he'd knocked back an inch and a half and Tommy had left his message. No address on Price tonight. Tomorrow, for sure. Probably just as well.

Cat McShane's preliminary autopsy report sat on the corner of his desk. Barkley tucked it under his arm and headed out again. There was a dive called Early's where no one knew he was a cop and no one cared he was black. He walked the five blocks and planted himself on a stool, the ghosts he was trying so hard to ignore settling all around. One of them grinned just like Tommy and thudded a sack full of coins on the bar.

"Forever money," he said.

Barkley toasted the phantom motherfucker with a water glass full of whiskey and drained it.

28

Cat McShane kept herself busy counting ceiling tiles. When she finished with those, she started on the slats in the venetian blinds. She was halfway down the second window when the door opened and Boston City Hospital's assistant superintendent walked in. Ruth Davis was thirty years older than Cat and everything about her seemed lovely. Straight spine, perfect posture, gray hair cut in fashionable layers, and a designer suit that hugged her exceedingly neat frame. Davis didn't say a word, keeping her shoulders square to Cat as she ran a finger along the edge of her desk, then found the wall and finally her chair. It was only after she was seated that Cat realized the woman was blind. Or as good as.

"Cataracts." Davis blinked a pair of milky whites from behind silver-rimmed glasses.

"How bad?"

"Left one's ninety percent gone. Other's a little better. They've tried a half-dozen procedures, but it's at the end now."

"I'm sorry."

"I can still see shapes, which is probably more than I deserve. Ruth Davis, by the way." The woman didn't offer her hand.

"Cat McShane."

"I've heard good things."

"Thanks."

"My fault for not arranging something sooner."

"Please, we're all busy."

"Yes, but we're both women. And there aren't a lot of us in Boston's medical community. At least not in jobs where we can make a difference."

She was right, of course. Cat knew her position as medical examiner came with a larger set of responsibilities. It was just that the whole thing was still new and she needed to get her own house in order before thinking about the bigger picture. Ruth Davis wasn't interested in excuses. Women from her generation typically weren't.

"My assistant says you wanted information on a case."

"Daniel Fitzsimmons."

Davis opened a drawer to her left and pulled out a file. "I usually have a member of my staff go through any paperwork and get me up to speed."

"Usually?"

"It wasn't necessary here." Davis nudged the file across the desk. It was thick enough, although perhaps not quite as thick as Cat expected.

"Were you one of Daniel's doctors?"

Davis shook her head. "I'm an internist. Was. They're putting me out to pasture at the end of the year, although really it happened a long time ago." She smiled vaguely. "I remember Daniel well enough. Just a slip of a thing. Looked so small in that big bed."

"Do you recall anything unusual about the case?"

"He was eight years old, had suffered some sort of head trauma as the result of the car accident, was initially conscious and lapsed into a coma on the way to the hospital."

"Who was his doctor?"

A small twitch ticked the corner of Davis's mouth. "George Peters. Head of neurology here for decades. One of the best."

"I assume he's no longer on staff?"

"Passed away five years ago. May I ask why all the interest?"

"Daniel's involved in a criminal case. He's not implicated, but he has been subjected to a certain amount of emotional trauma."

"Are you talking about his brother?"

"You knew Harry Fitzsimmons?"

"He was Daniel's only visitor during his time here. Three times a week he'd show up and sit at the foot of the bed. Stay for hours at a time. I heard about his death on the news. Such a waste."

"Yes."

"I guess I'm still not clear on how Daniel's time here might fit in?"

"I'm not sure either. The detective working the case is a friend and asked me to take a look."

"I see."

"Without revealing too much, I think the police are concerned the trauma of Harry's death might somehow provoke a reaction in Daniel. A little strange, I know."

"Lots of strange in the world. And lots of strange in Daniel's time here."

"How so?"

Davis peeled back her lips, revealing long teeth and a glimpse of the predator the woman must have once been. "My door's closed?"

Cat glanced behind her. "Yes."

"Good. There's no record of what I'm about to tell

you anywhere so don't bother looking. And don't bother asking anyone here about it. Agreed?"

"Sure."

"George Peters and I were close. Probably not hard to tell, right?"

"I saw a twitch."

"Really?"

"It was either hate or love. I tend to root for the latter."

"He was married, but I was still young enough up here." Davis tapped her temple with a skinny finger. "Bottom line is I didn't give a damn."

"And now?"

"Even less. If it's real, you'll never regret it. And will pay any price. But who wants to hear about an old lady's love life?"

"I don't mind."

"Yeah, right. George was a talent. He had an unerring instinct when it came to diagnosis and an extraordinary sense of compassion for his patients. Daniel's case troubled him like few others."

"How so?"

Davis raised her chin a fraction and Cat caught a brief glimpse of a pair of gray irises swimming furiously beneath the skim of white. "What you'll find in the file is a fairly standard recitation of Daniel's admission, an initial examination, and subsequent patient assessment."

"And?"

"George could never pinpoint the actual nature of Daniel's head injury. He ordered x-rays and conducted periodic brain scans during the entire time the boy was unconscious. If you look through the data, you'll find low-level brain activity typically associated with a coma."

"But?"

"Let's take a walk." Davis got up quickly, slipping into a black coat that hung on a hook behind her. She took four measured strides to the door and waited for Cat to open it. Then she touched Cat's sleeve and pointed to an elevator almost directly across the hall.

"Seventh floor."

Neither woman spoke as the elevator climbed. On the seventh floor, Ruth directed Cat to an empty room overlooking an alley. The bed had been stripped of its linens and the room smelled of dust and death.

"This was Daniel's room," Davis said. "You see the door on the far side of the bed? It leads to the roof."

"The roof?"

"I'll explain when we get there."

Cat took them through the door and up a run of rough metal steps. The roof was flat and covered in a dull sheen of tar that had cracked and webbed in a dozen different directions. Cat jammed her hands in the pockets of her trench coat. "Why are we up here, Ruth?"

"Walk me over to the edge."

Cat felt a twist in her gut but did as the woman asked. The facade of the building was ancient. Cat touched a brick with her foot and watched it crumble, loose chunks tumbling into the alley below. Davis's hand slipped to the small of Cat's back, grabbing at the belt on her coat.

"Watch it."

The old woman had a strong grip and it was all Cat could do to break free, nearly pitching herself over the edge in the process. She circled to her left, keeping Davis at arm's length.

"Nervous, Ms. McShane?"

"Should I be?"

"You're wondering what was missing from Daniel's file."

"If you want to tell me something, that's great. If not . . ."

"The brain scans. The real ones. They're not in there."

"Why?"

Davis raised one hand in front of her face and began

to surf it up and down. "Daniel's brain was fluctuating wildly the entire time he was here. High-level activity for a period of time, subsiding to levels you'd expect to find in someone who was comatose, then more spikes. George finally figured out the pattern. Three hours on, six off. Over and over and over again."

"What did Peters think?"

"This was 1968, remember."

"So what?"

"It was the first time I'd ever heard anyone use the term 'computer.' George explained how the machines processed information at amazing rates. Talked about 'work cycles' and 'batch processing.' Said that's what Daniel appeared to be doing. As you can probably tell, none of it made any sense to me."

"How was it Daniel remained unconscious if his brain was so active?"

"George never figured that out. He tried several times to rouse Daniel during the active cycles but got nowhere. Then one day we walked into the room and the boy was sitting up in bed, wide awake, looking for his breakfast."

"And Peters never included any of this in the boy's history?"

"He thought Daniel might be studied if the medical community got hold of the scans. Made out to be a freak show. My overall feeling was he was protecting Daniel. Can't be sure, but that would have been George."

"I assume no one ever told Daniel about the scans?"

"The boy hardly spoke. And when he did, he could only recall bits and pieces of the accident and, of course, nothing from his time in the coma. We left it that way."

"Thanks, Ruth. I'm not sure any of this is relevant to Harry's death, but I appreciate it." Cat touched the old woman at the elbow, turning her toward the door and the stairs feeding down into the building.

"I didn't say we were done."

"No?"

"Daniel woke up on the morning of March first, 1969. He was discharged four days later. The morning of March fifth. Harry picked him up."

"All right."

"Forty minutes after they left, a security guard found one of our attendants in the alley below. He jumped off this roof, from just about the spot where you're standing."

Cat couldn't help but peek again. The air between the buildings was swirling and dark and full of echoes. Ruth Davis's voice lived in her ear.

"The attendant's name was Lawrence Rosen. He'd

never actually been part of the team that worked on Daniel's case, but George had his suspicions."

"Are you saying this guy might have been bothering Daniel?"

"After Rosen's death, a couple of employees came to George and claimed Rosen used to visit Daniel at night. George had examined Daniel before his discharge. There was no obvious evidence of molestation or other physical contact, but the staff members were insistent. They said Rosen was obsessed with the boy."

"What about the morning Rosen jumped?"

"Best we could tell, Rosen was last seen on the seventh floor, near Daniel's room, roughly an hour before Daniel was discharged."

"Was Daniel in his room?"

"For about a half hour, yes."

"So the two could have been alone, in a room with a door that led to this roof?"

"Unlikely, but possible."

"Why unlikely?"

"There was a steady stream of people coming in and out that morning. Daniel had been here six months so there was a lot of do. A lot of folks involved."

"Did anyone see Rosen alive after Daniel was discharged?"

Davis shook her head. "The next time anyone saw

him, Rosen was dead in the alley. George was in charge of the hospital's inquiry and made sure the death was classified as a suicide. Then we forgot about the whole thing."

"Why tell me?"

"I don't know. I guess I thought if there was a chance Daniel was involved in another death . . ."

"The police don't think he killed Harry."

"I'm glad to hear it."

"Did you really think that was a possibility?"

"As I said, I hardly knew Daniel. A handful of conversations before he was discharged."

"And yet you seem afraid of him."

"Do I?"

"Do you think he killed Rosen?"

"Did he come up onto the roof with Rosen and push him off? No."

"Then what?"

"Have you ever met Daniel?"

"No."

"George thought he might possess the ability to influence people, affect their behavior. Perhaps even unwittingly."

"How?"

"I don't know. By talking to them, thinking about them. George was never clear."

"So you're saying Daniel walked your attendant off this roof without ever leaving his bed?"

"You don't believe it?"

"Of course not. Do you?"

"There was something there. Something heavy . . ."

"Heavy?"

"When Daniel looked at you, really focused, there was a heaviness inside your skull. I remember it quite distinctly, almost like you were falling asleep or being pulled into a rip current, one that was very fast and very deep." Davis tipped her face up again, raising blind eyes to a broken sky. "I'm sorry. It all sounds strange, I know."

"I appreciate your taking the time."

"Please remember I'll deny any of this to the police. Or anyone else, for that matter."

"Daniel's not a suspect."

"Good. I'm cold. Let's go downstairs and find some lunch."

Ruth Davis turned on her heel and walked directly to the door that led downstairs. Maybe she'd been able to see the whole time. Maybe she was familiar with the route. Maybe she was just guessing. Fifteen minutes later, the two women were being shown to a table at Maison Robert. Cat excused herself and found a pay phone. She dropped in some coins and dialed a number.

29

Barkley swiped at the phone, knocking the entire thing off his nightstand. Whoever had called was now talking a blue streak to the bedroom rug. Barkley uncoiled an arm, feeling along the floor until he found the receiver and lifted it to his ear.

"Yeah."

The talker had been replaced by a dial tone. Good riddance. Barkley replaced the receiver and felt around again until he located a box of Chinese take-out. He'd closed Early's, then gone to an all-night place in Cambridge called Aku Aku and gotten his regular, 13-A with extra pork strips and hot mustard. Barkley chewed on a cold egg roll as he trudged down the hallway. In the kitchen he found a couple trays of ice and dumped them into a sink full of water. Barkley buried his head in the basin, letting the cold burn his brain for a full minute before resurfacing like an orca, blowing water and groping for a towel. He sat at the kitchen table and dripped, consoling himself with the idea he didn't get drunk very often. All the alkies he'd ever known had told themselves that on their way to a lifetime of bad coffee in Styrofoam cups and AA meetings with a bunch of other miserable, dried-out motherfuckers counting their dubious blessings while inwardly jonesing for one more run at a hip flask full of the good old days. Barkley put on the kettle and made himself a cup of instant, letting the hot black liquid sear his throat and water his eyes.

The phone rang again. Jesus H. Christ. He picked up in the hall. It was Charlie Herbert. According to Ma Bell, the phone in Nick Toney's studio had been out for the past ten days. And yes, there was a pay phone in the hall two floors below. The photographer was telling the truth. Barkley wasn't surprised. He thanked Herbert and tried to hang up, but the uniform wasn't done. It was past noon and people at the station were wondering where Barkley and his partner might be. Barkley carefully explained they were working a murder and people should go fuck themselves. Herbert was going on about the captain and the media when Barkley cut the line, leaving the receiver off the hook.

He poured himself a second cup of coffee and settled in the living room with Cat McShane's autopsy report. Tucked inside the front cover was a photo of the puncture wounds that killed Harry Fitzsimmons. There were three of them on the left side of the football player's chest. A second photo showed a close-up of the two exit wounds in his back. Cat wasn't kidding. The kid had been put on a spit and gutted. Barkley took a sip of coffee. He kind of liked working hungover. Calmed his brain. Next he'd be wanting a slug of rum with his morning shower. Barkley gave the report a quick skim. The punctures that had killed Fitzsimmons entered his body at a slightly downward angle, indicating the killer was most likely standing over his victim. Barkley thought about that for a minute, the killer taking down Fitzsimmons with a knife to the belly, then pulling out a second weapon to finish him. Didn't make a ton of sense, but murders rarely did.

He read for another hour, scribbling thoughts in one of his black notebooks as he went. When he was done, he arranged the autopsy report and notebook on a table by the front door where they'd be easy to find. If anyone wanted to follow up, more power to them.

In the kitchen he sat at the table and stared at his boots and coat. He could hear the whispers coming from his fire escape and knew this would be the day.

He could see the anchor rods shearing, the mass of bars and bolts shivering and creaking in the breeze, then slowly pulling away from the building. He was falling now, no present, no future, the past sloughing off like old skin. It would happen today. His last ride. About fucking time, too.

He pulled on the boots and coat and stepped out, hearing the brittle metal groan and speak and sing its seduction. He found his spot on the windowsill and sat there, picking up his potting soil for the last time, sinking his thumb through the hard crust and finding soft earth below. Barkley pulled out his smokes and lit up. It was like his vision had been enhanced, allowing him to see all the seams in the grated floor, silent fractures in the iron, how the whole thing hung together, how it would all come apart. He was in Tommy's fairy ring now. And there was no getting out. Who would ever want to?

Barkley took a pull on his cigarette and blew out a fine blue haze. She moved through it like an ocean tide, taking no form he could later recall, sitting close enough so he could smell the powdered scent of jasmine. It was the woman from Hom's. Of course it was. She gestured for a cigarette and lit up, the red enamel of her ring winking and flashing as years slipped past and decades followed. Barkley realized he could see right through her and watched smoke run like a river down her throat and swirl in her chest. Then she exhaled, tendrils of pure light, crimson and yellow and orange and green, curling and blooming with flowers, wrapping around the bars of the fire escape, creeping up the side of the building and rushing toward the pavement below. The woman flicked her cigarette into the ether and glanced at Barkley with her liquid eyes. No concussion this time. No uncovering. She was simply here, sitting with him in the bottom of the hole he'd dug for himself, holding time as she held his hand, telling him it was every bit as real as unreal and that if he dared to believe, dared to let go, the soul he grieved for every moment of every day would be his and he'd be hers. They'd be nothing. And so much more. But only if. And then the woman was gone. And Barkley was alone again, in the cold on the fire escape, listening to the wind sing and the iron creak.

He stepped back through the window to find the hammer from that day twelve years ago sitting on the kitchen table. Alongside it were a half-dozen silver nails. Barkley would have sworn the hammer hadn't been there before, but who was present to listen? Who was present to grieve? So he took his time, driving fresh nails into old wood, feeling each bite and then testing to make sure the window in his pantry was pegged shut. Fuck the landlord. And fuck the fire hazard, too.

He took a long shower, scrubbing himself with soap and letting the scurf slick off his body and down the drain. He'd left his car downtown because of the drink, so it was the Orange Line today. The train arrived on a rush of warm wind and grease. He stood near the door, hanging on to a strap and turning his mind again to the case because what else was there now? Maybe Tommy had called in with an address for Walter Price. Barkley hoped so. Like any good homicide detective, he didn't want to dig any deeper than he had to. But there were things in the case that bothered him—small things, big things, things with roots. Barkley knew all about roots. And how they could strangle the life out of a man.

30

The flecked and formless beast stood in the doorway of a skin show, sloping slabs for shoulders and a bull neck, fleshed nose split in the middle and small, pink eyes needling down the block. She was leaning against a lamppost, tall and gawky, young, potent without knowing it. She wore a short jacket that shined. Under it, a sheer white dress with Daffy Duck and Tweety Bird printed all over in bright blossoms of color. The girl scuffed her shoe on the pavement and tossed her head. The wind shifted and the beast scented blood. He lifted a pinch of cigarette to his lips, then tossed the butt into the gutter and stepped out of the doorway. They talked for less than a minute, the girl pulling away once before settling, the man slipping a hand to the small of her back and gesturing for her to go first.

Barkley watched as they crossed the street and disappeared into the Brompton Arms. Like most things in the Combat Zone, the Brompton would be whatever you wanted it to be. A mouse of a man worked a small desk in the lobby, renting rooms on the first two floors by the half hour. The middle floors were let month to month, mostly to girls and pimps. The top floor was where the photographer Toney had his studio. Barkley got out of his car, hard shoes scratching as he followed the couple up the Brompton's short run of steps. He thought about going inside but settled for copying down the names on a row of doorbells set into a panel by the front door. Then he checked his watch and walked back to the street.

Next door to the Brompton, someone had shoehorned in a greasy Greek joint called Five Faces. Barkley ordered a Coke from a young woman with a lazy eye. He was the only customer in the place and watched while a smooth-skinned man with thin fingers and a bent nose worked a long knife over a shank of lamb.

"Gyros."

He grinned and offered a curling piece to Barkley, who took a pass. The counterman shrugged and popped the lamb in his mouth, then set about fixing chunks of broiled meat onto metal skewers. The place smelled like fried onions with more than a hint of decaying rat. Barkley figured they had one or two fat ones caught in a trap somewhere and was glad he'd passed on the food.

He took a booth by the window, sipping his soft drink and nursing a mild hangover while he flipped through a stack of photos. There'd been no word from Tommy. Barkley had called the house, but no one picked up. He'd thought about heading over but didn't see the point. His partner said he'd turn up an address; Barkley just needed to give him some leash. Besides, there were enough loose ends that needed tying up. He looked out the window as Neil Prescott got out of a cab. The kid from Harvard hustled across the street.

"Thanks for coming down."

"No problem." Prescott took a seat across from the detective. He was bundled up in a pearl gray topcoat with a cashmere scarf and a blue Oxford button-down underneath. Barkley didn't think he'd ever seen anyone who looked so young.

"You want a Coke? Something to eat?"

Prescott shook his head and kept his hands clasped tightly on the table. Barkley let him sit. He'd taken statements from Prescott and his buddy, Jesus Sanchez, on the night Harry Fitzsimmons was murdered. Barkley usually liked to do follow-ups at the station, but he wanted to get another look at the block and Prescott seemed okay with meeting here.

"Bother you being back?"

Prescott shrugged. Why should it bother him?

"Ever been down here before that night?"

"First and last."

"I bet." Barkley pulled out a notebook. "Mind if I take notes?"

"Go ahead."

Barkley turned to a fresh page and wrote down the time and date. "We wanted to meet with Sanchez as well, but I couldn't get hold of him."

"Zeus? He lives in Kirkland."

Barkley wrote down the name. "Is that a dorm?"

"We call them houses, but, yeah, same thing. I stopped in before I came down here, but he wasn't around."

"Any idea where he might be?"

Another shrug. "A couple of guys saw him around noon. Said he might have taken off."

"Taken off?"

"He was pretty shook up. We both were. Thanksgiving break's coming up, so he might have cut out early."

"You think he headed home?"

"Zeus is from Hyde Park. You could check. Knowing Zeus, he might have just gotten in his car and drove."

Barkley made a couple more notes. "Okay."

"He wouldn't have left if he thought you still needed him."

"Sure."

"Zeus was tight with Harry. A lot closer than me."

"How you doing with everything?"

"I'm fine. Well, as fine as . . . whatever. You know what, Detective, I'd just like to get this over with."

One buddy dead. Another, out of pocket. Barkley couldn't blame him.

"Harry lived with you?"

"I told you guys. He rented out the other bedroom. Couple blocks from campus."

"Did you know his little brother, Daniel?"

"Saw him once or twice. He was bunking in with Harry. I think he had a sleeping bag or something on the floor."

"Ever talk to him?"

"Like I said, Harry and I didn't hang out much. The night in the Zone was Zeus's idea. Said it was part of playing football at Harvard."

Barkley had already heard about the football players' ideas on team building and didn't really give a shit. "Daniel still living at the apartment?"

"He moved out last week. Harry wasn't happy about it, but I guess the kid found another place to stay."

"Any idea where he's living now?"

Prescott shook his head. Barkley scribbled a little more. "Okay if I send some officers over to look through Harry's stuff?"

"You won't find anything."

"Why do you say that?"

"Harry was a straight shooter. Didn't drink, smoke, chase women. He only went with us cuz Zeus pushed it."

"Part of the team-bonding thing?"

"He was big on that stuff. Probably why he took off after Zeus. Harry would have figured it was the right thing to do."

Barkley flipped his notebook shut. "Mind if we take a walk?"

"I heard on the radio you guys have a suspect?"

"We have someone we need to speak with."

"How so fast?"

Barkley shrugged. "People down here like to rat each other out. Keeps us in business."

The kid nodded like he knew, and Barkley let him pretend. "Ready?"

Darkness was dropping over the Combat Zone, the seedy blocks along Washington transformed into a valley of blinking sin. Barkley and Prescott walked together, past hard-core bookstores and strip-bar sleaze, rap booths that smelled like latex and jerk-off peep shows, triple-feature movies with titles like *Spiked Heels and Black Tights*, *The Depraved*, and *Flesh Gordon*. Barkley stopped outside the Pilgrim Theater. The front door creaked open, letting out a waft of boozy music and a thin black man who was a dead ringer for Diana Ross. He gave Barkley a glance before drifting across the street, where he leaned against a building and dug a spiked heel into the wall.

"That a guy?" Prescott said.

"Does it matter? Now, where, exactly, was your car parked?"

"Right about here."

"You sure?"

"I remember seeing the pizza joint." Prescott pointed in the general direction of King of Pizza.

"And the woman who grabbed your buddy's wallet?"

Prescott pointed. "Came from over there."

"Where exactly?"

"I don't know."

"You didn't get a good look at her?"

"No."

"But she walked right past you?"

"She must have. Look, there were a lot of people floating by, a lot of scenery, you know?"

"I understand. It would just help if we could find the girl."

"Zeus said she had blond hair. Came in quick, grabbed the wallet, and ran."

"Is that how you remember it?"

"All I know is there was a commotion, Zeus yelling and then he was gone. Harry told me to stay with the car and took off after him."

"I ask cuz usually the girls will stop and talk for a while. It's only if they see no one in the car is buying that one of them might try for a wallet."

"All I can tell you is what I saw."

"Sanchez. He's a running back?"

"I'm a running back. Zeus is an offensive lineman."

"Not too fast, huh?"

"Excuse me?"

"I was just thinking a football player should be able to run down a working girl. On top of everything else, she's probably in heels. Know what I'm saying?"

"Zeus isn't real quick. And if she was gonna lift a wallet, she probably wasn't wearing heels, right?"

Barkley winked and shot Prescott with his index finger. "Fucking Harvard education. Come on."

They walked back down Washington and stopped at the corner of LaGrange, a half block from the alley where Harry Fitzsimmons was killed.

"Sanchez and Harry ran down here?"

"Yeah."

"And the next time you saw them was when?"

"Not until Zeus came back down the street. Then we heard the yelling."

Barkley pointed his chin toward the alley. "Mind if we take a peek?"

"Why?"

"I just want to see the layout again. Helps me sometimes."

"I'd prefer not to. I mean, I will if you really think it's important . . ."

"Forget it. We've got more than enough for now." Barkley stuck out his hand and the two men shook.

"Can I ask you something?" Prescott said.

"Go ahead."

"No one ever told us how he died."

"Harry was stabbed."

"I know, but . . ."

"You wanna know if he suffered?"

"I guess, yeah."

Barkley shook his head and lied. "ME says it was quick."

Prescott nodded but didn't say anything.

"You need a lift?"

"I'm good."

"Had your fill of cops, huh?"

"Something like that."

"I don't blame you. Enjoy the break."

Barkley watched the Harvard kid walk off. Then he unsnapped the strap on his holster and started down LaGrange. Someone was tucked behind a collection of trash cans pushed up against the side of the Brompton Arms. Whoever it was had been watching and listening to every drop of his conversation with Prescott. Barkley cleared the cans and pivoted, pinning the eavesdropper up against the building.

"Fuck, man, that hurts."

"It's supposed to hurt." Barkley leaned against one of the cans until a ninety-pound Asian kid popped out the other side. He was wearing white painter's pants, a jean jacket, and high-top red Cons with one of the soles pulled away from the bottom so his sock was peeking through. Barkley waited until he stopped rolling and planted a shoe on his chest.

"You wanna tell me why you're so interested in police business?"

"Come on, man. Get off me. Police brutality, police brutality."

The cries were met with a collective yawn from the Zone. Barkley removed his foot and helped the kid up.

"What's your name?"

"Kenny Soo." The kid pointed to a wooden box, its contents spilled out across the narrow street. "You need a shine?"

"I need you to tell me why you're so interested in my conversations."

"I was here the night of the murder. Saw it all."

"You saw what?"

Kenny Soo's eyes danced. He thought he had Barkley hooked and maybe he did.

"I work the corner." Soo pointed vaguely. "See everyone come and go. Everyone."

"Tell me what you saw."

"Girls. They come out before the night shows start. Get their heels polished."

Barkley hadn't thought about that. Now that he did, it made sense. Soo dropped his eyes to Barkley's thirty-dollar Florsheims.

"I did them this morning," Barkley said.

"You need it bad, boss."

"Next time. Who else do you see out here?"

"Johns, pimps." Soo tapped his head with his finger. "Crazy people."

"Bet you see plenty of that."

"Plenty." A thin bruise ran along Soo's jawline, collecting in various shades of purple and yellow under his left eye and filling the white around the iris with bright red blood.

"Who beat you up, Kenny?"

"Asshole pimp. A girl I know gonna give him the drip."

"Good for you."

Soo smiled clean and white and Barkley thought he might very well grow up to be a vicious little fuck. Smart, too. Barkley pulled out his photos.

"You wanna help?"

Soo rubbed his thumb and forefinger together.

Barkley chuckled. "Come here." He found an empty doorway and laid out his pictures. Soo squatted with his elbows on his knees and his chin in his palms.

"Smoke?" Soo held out his hand, two fingers extended in a twitch. Barkley lit a cigarette and gave it to him. The kid smoked while he studied.

"You recognize anyone?"

Soo looked up, neon glitter reflecting off the sharp angles of his face. "How much?"

Barkley toed one of the photos. "Tell me what you know?"

"I was a block away when the murder happened." Soo pointed at the picture of Harry Fitzsimmons taken from Harvard's freshman face book.

"You saw him?"

"I'm on the street all day, boss. All night. Remember lots of faces."

"And you saw him?"

"He and his pals were in the Naked i."

"His pals?"

"These two." Kenny touched photos of Sanchez and Prescott. "Big man on campus, just another dick down here. Ha, ha. They were drunk, I think. Which one's dead?"

Barkley nudged Harry's photo. Kenny took a final suck on his cigarette and flicked the butt away, letting smoke drift from both nostrils. "Too bad." If Neil Prescott was a pup, this kid was fourteen going on forty.

"What else did you see?"

"Seen him." Soo tapped a mug shot of Walter Price, taken a year and a half ago when he was popped for possession. "He was out all night. Walking up and down. Talking to lots of girls."

"And you've seen him before?"

"Many times. Grade-A asshole. Number ten." Soo held up ten fingers.

"Where were you when the murder happened?"

"I told you. Block away. Two blocks away. Lot of yelling, police cars. I come running down."

Barkley noticed Soo's English went in and out, becoming a little more fractured as he got excited. Or maybe it was just a game he was playing. Barkley bent down and picked up the photo of Price. "So you didn't actually see this guy near the alley?"

"No."

"Did you see any of these other guys running down into the alley?"

"Too far. I only got there when the police showed up."

Barkley pulled out a twenty and slipped it into the hungry curl of Soo's palm. "Thanks, Kenny."

"That's it?"

"What else can you do for me?"

"Eyes and ears, boss. Eyes and ears."

Barkley pulled out another twenty and wrapped it around his business card. "All right. You see these guys, especially number-ten asshole, you give me a call."

"Yes, boss."

"Don't approach him. Just call."

"Yes, boss."

"Okay, Kenny. I gotta get going."

"What about him?" Soo nodded at the only photo left in Barkley's makeshift lineup. It was a shot of Daniel Fitzsimmons taken from his first year on Latin School's track team.

"You know him?"

"He here yesterday. I noticed cuz he was with beautiful Asian girl." Kenny rolled his eyes. "I think I love her."

"This kid was here? Where?"

"King of Pizza. Talked with the girl. Then he talked to Mr. Toney."

"Toney?"

"Photographer. Lives upstairs." Soo lifted his chin toward the back side of the Brompton.

"Fuck me."

Soo thought that was funny as shit. Barkley, not so much. He gave Kenny another twenty and watched him leave, the sole of his sneaker flapping against the pavement as he went. After that, LaGrange grew quiet. Barkley ducked into the alley where Harry Fitzsimmons had died, finding the exact spot and crouching so he was eye level with the bloodstains, dark smears on brick running crooked into each other and down across the pavement. He imagined the football player staring at the breathing holes in his chest, wondering how they got there, then scanning the alley, every inch of it precious while his life leaked away and Death came calling. A footstep cracked on LaGrange, the murmur of voices, then a woman's laugh that dissolved to a hum.

Barkley walked out to the street, stopping at the Brompton again to lean on Toney's buzzer. No answer.

He found a pay phone bolted to the side of a building on Washington and called Tommy, who didn't bother with a hello.

"Where are you?"

"Combat Zone. Why?"

"I'm getting us an address. Gotta be tonight or we might not get him at all."

"I'll pick you up at your place."

"What did you find in the Zone?"

"It'll keep. What time?"

"Swing by around ten."

Barkley hung up and dropped two more dimes. Cat McShane picked up on the first ring.

"It is alive."

"Funny. I got your report on the autopsy. Thanks."

"You don't sound happy."

"My partner's got a line on our suspect."

"And yet . . ."

"I don't know. Something's bothering me."

"Join the crowd. I went over to Boston City today. Talked to a doctor about Daniel Fitzsimmons."

"I'm listening."

Cat told him about Daniel's missing brain scans, her climb to the roof, and Lawrence Rosen's leap off it.

"You telling me you think Daniel Fitzsimmons was responsible for that?"

"No. Rosen committed suicide."

"So what's your point?"

"You asked me to look into Daniel's case. This is what I found."

"What if I told you Daniel was sitting in my skull right now, sitting there and watching my every thought?"

"I'd say you have an overactive imagination."

"He's been down the Combat Zone, Cat. Asking questions."

"Why?"

"Because he wants to find his brother's killer before we do. He wants to find him and he wants to kill him."

31

Franklin Park is five hundred acres of urban parkland spread across three of Boston's roughest neighborhoods—Jamaica Plain, Dorchester, and Roxbury. Daniel ducked into the park off Williams Street on the J.P. side. He knew the ground as well as anyone. He'd first run Franklin's cross-country course as a freshman, coming out of nowhere to win the city title over a leaf-blown course in late October. His strategy that day had been to lie back for the first mile then accelerate over a hill called Bear Cage. After that, it was a two-man race between him and an Asian kid from Boston Tech. Daniel put away the kid from Tech on a winding stretch of wooded trail called the Wilderness. Daniel was in the Wilderness again, trees sloping all around him in the moonlight. Franklin

Park was dangerous at three in the afternoon. Daniel assumed it was worse at night, even though he'd never met anyone stupid enough to find out.

He ran like a runner, easily, silkily, along the park's dim thread of a trail. He was dressed in black from head to foot with dark socks over his hands and black tape covering the white flashing on his Tigers. Daniel kept his hood pulled up over his head and could feel the weight of Walter Price's revolver strapped to the inside of his calf. He slipped off the trail about thirty yards in, accelerating as he went, blood surging, breath growing rank in the closeness of the woods. A warm current buzzed over his skin; bright bits of tinsel light flickered and flared at the edges of his vision. Daniel ducked to avoid a tree branch and felt his jawbone lengthen while his ears stood up and sharpened to points. A bristle of hair covered his cheeks and ran like a flame down his spine and along his flanks, his coat stiff and gray to the edge of blue, his eyes lasers of emerald and his tongue, thick and red and long and rich as it unrolled between a fanged set of teeth. Daniel dropped his muzzle, now fully formed, close to the ground, a lone wolf scenting the earth, making his map. The wind shifted and he could smell his own spoor and it comforted him. Another shift and there was something else to taste—ape, zebra, lion. The human part of Daniel's brain told him it was only the Franklin Park Zoo, even as hackles rose on his back and his jaws glistened with fresh ropes of saliva.

Daniel began to run again, measured strides cutting tight and fast through the woods. He stopped just inside the tree line, making a small circle then dropping to his belly, swinging his head from side to side as he crept forward, stopping at the edge of an open field. There was something else out there, some fresh scent in the night that wasn't coming from the zoo. Daniel buried his muzzle between his paws and covered himself in dirt, rolling around to get as much of the earth smell on himself as possible. Then he lay up against a bush and waited.

It took only a minute or so for the first to reveal himself, creeping along the tree line to Daniel's left. The hyena carried a ridge of orange fur along his humped back, haunches spotted in black, long curved snout sniffing at wisps of purple moonlight. Daniel sought out the second animal and quickly found him, a pair of burnt yellow eyes buried in a baseball field a hundred yards away. There was a third somewhere behind and to the right, but he wouldn't matter. Not if Daniel moved quickly.

The hyena to his left scratched at an ear, then raised his snout and gave a short coughing sound like a laugh.

His buddy in center field offered a low grunt in return. Daniel took off. The laugher was first to give chase, barrel of a body folding and unfolding in a *V* as he pumped his short legs and cut a swath close to the ground. Among the trees the calculation might have been otherwise, but Daniel was moving across open ground now, the smooth, long strides of a gray wolf easily outpacing his rival. On Daniel's right, however, it was a different story. The hyena closing from center field had an angle and knew how to use it. Daniel watched his back, a flexing whip of orange and black as the hyena moved to cut off Daniel and flush him back toward the woods. Daniel shifted imperceptibly, taking a straighter path then flaring out again, creating just enough space before turning to face his pursuer. The hyena was coming full bore, head down, muzzle streaming, claws extended. Blind. Daniel caught the animal clean, sinking teeth into a fleshy shoulder, scissoring his jaws and feeling the crunch of ligament and bone as the hyena went limp. Daniel immediately released, watching the hyena roll over so his spotted belly was exposed for a moment before he regained his feet and scurried off, tail tucked, limping into the darkness.

Daniel knew he only had moments and sped the rest of the way across the field toward vapor puffs of street light. He ducked into the trees, gliding silently among the bent oaks that bordered the perimeter of the park, listening as his pursuers called to one another in the night and turned this way and that, hot to pick up his trail. He stepped out of the park at Seaver Street and kept running, on two feet now, into the heart of Roxbury. At the corner he snuck a quick look back. Three kids were maybe a hundred yards up the block, standing in the middle of the street, staring down at him but not pursuing. They wore black jackets with slashes of orange on the sleeves and orange lettering across the front. Daniel took off at a run up Blue Hill Avenue.

When he finally stopped, he was in an alley. He slumped down between two trash barrels and pulled slowly at the socks he'd wrapped over his hands. One knuckle was smashed and his right pinkie finger was swollen and bloody. Daniel winced as he flexed the hand and noticed his sweatshirt was slashed at the shoulder as if someone had attacked him with a knife. He pulled off the shirt and T-shirt underneath, shivering and checking to see if he had any more injuries. Then he slipped the layers back on and stood up.

His hold on reality might be greasy, but Daniel knew he had to keep moving. Simon had made it clear he couldn't push into everyone's head. But if he did get entangled with someone—like he was with Walter Price—the connection seemed more or less permanent. It might wax and wane like a radio station that went in and out as you worked the dial, but it was always there if he just focused. And trusted. Daniel began to jog down the alley, picking up the pace as a police siren unwound and a pack of dogs answered, barking hard and angry against the night.

A mile later, he was sitting up against a chain-link fence and studying an arthritic three-decker. Price was somewhere inside. Daniel could feel his mind, fissured with heat, tongues of flame running fast and blue in the cracks. Fear? Hell, yeah. Price knew he was being hunted by half the cops in the city and knew it was just a matter of time. Remorse for killing Harry? Daniel couldn't find a drop. He loosened the gun he'd strapped to his ankle and noticed the shake in his hand. It was the terror of beginning, the finality of a first step. He'd made the decision to take another man's life. And now it was time.

Daniel climbed to his feet. The three-decker swayed above him, grinning like a skeleton in the night. He cut across the alley and up the back steps. One floor, two floors, three. The windows on the top were boarded up, the only door blown wide open. He stepped inside what had once been a kitchen. Crooked bars of light ran through the slats lighting up graffiti spray painted in wild slashes of black and green. Daniel followed one strand diagonally across a wall but couldn't make heads or tails of it. His foot knocked against something round. An empty bottle of Wild Irish Rose rolled in a small circle and stopped.

Daniel crept to the doorway and a narrow hallway that fed into the black belly of the apartment. He slumped to the floor and sought out Price's mind again, but there was nothing now. Snuffed. Daniel laid down the gun and flexed his hand, feeling the pain flare in his knuckles, down his fingers, and under his nails. He thought again about his run through the park. Part of him was terrified at whatever it was that was happening to him. The rest thought he might be seeing more than less, if only he'd trust it. On cue, a pair of eyes blinked to life at the far end of the hall. Then a second set. The scrabble of long claws on wood was followed by a whisper of air as something charged. Daniel reached for the gun but already knew he was too late. And then they fell upon him.

32

Barkley pulled to the corner and watched his partner climb in. Tommy had barely closed the door
before they were pushing away from the curb.

"What the fuck, B. Let me get in, for Chrissakes."

"You got an address for our boy?"

"Course I got an address."

Barkley crested a hill that ran down toward the
water. "He still in Roxbury?"

"Dudley Square. What's the matter?"

"Nothing." Barkley hit his blinker and took a right.

"I told you it might take a day or so. The captain on
our case?"

"We just need to make a collar."

"We will. Tonight."

"The kid's been down the Combat Zone."

"What kid?"

"Harry Fitzsimmons's brother, Daniel."

"How do you know that?"

"Someone saw him. Said he was talking to the photographer."

"How'd the kid find him?"

"Who the fuck knows? Hang around down there long enough and you meet every weirdo and asshole pervert in the world."

"I thought the photographer was all right."

"He is, but you know what I mean."

Carson Beach rolled past on the left. Barkley could just see the dark line of sand. Beyond it, waves curling white under the still moonlight.

"Relax," Tommy said. "So what if he talked to this guy. He's a fucking kid. Besides, the photographer . . . Toney's his name?"

Barkley nodded.

"Toney doesn't know where Price is."

"He's down the Zone. He could have heard something."

"And you think he'd tell the kid?"

"Maybe he thinks there'd be no harm in it."

"That's my point. What's a fucking kid gonna do?"

"I'm pretty sure he's got a gun, Tommy." Barkley

told his partner about his visit to Latin School and the handgun that had gone missing during the brawl.

"And the kid was involved in the fight?"

"The kid was involved in the fight. From what the headmaster told me, he could have easily grabbed the piece."

"Did you ask him?"

"Says he never saw a gun."

"And we don't believe him?"

"Here's my thought. Daniel's in the car when his mom dies. He's eight years old and can't do a fucking thing about it. But it eats at him. Maybe he doesn't know it eats at him, but it does. And then big brother's murdered. Butchered in an alley and again Daniel draws a front-row seat. This time, though, the kid's sixteen and not gonna let it pass. No fucking way."

"You think he's hunting Price?"

"We just need to get there first."

Tommy rubbed his lower lip and stared out the window. Barkley flicked on the radio. Gladys Knight was singing "Midnight Train to Georgia." There was something about Gladys that dug deep in his belly. Maybe it was three generations of Alabama slaves, people he'd never met, voices he somehow knew as well as his own, their blood in every note and every line of Gladys's music. Up ahead there was a dark tangle of traffic at K Circle. Barkley flicked on his siren and the cars parted. He accelerated, pounding over the expressway and down the oil-slicked roads of Dorchester, toward the smoke and lights of Roxbury.

Barkley was driving a low-slung, midnight-blue snarl of a Camaro. He pulled the car to the curb directly across from the address Tommy had given him. If Price was in there, they didn't have time for subtlety. Truth be told, it had never been their strong suit anyway.

The Camaro had barely rolled to a stop before Tommy tumbled out the door. He had his gun low by his side and ran in a crouch across the street. Barkley followed, .38 still on his hip as he flattened himself against the side of the three-decker. The place looked deserted, most of the windows boarded up with a couple of lights burning here and there. Tommy nodded at a set of stairs that accessed the three-decker's back porches. They'd agreed to start on the top floor, work room by room and stay together. Hopefully, Price was alone. And hopefully he didn't do anything stupid. Halfway up the second flight, Barkley's flashlight caught a smear of blood on the banister.

"The kid?" Tommy said.

"Could be." Barkley pulled his gun. "Go ahead."

On the third floor Tommy stepped through an open door into a kitchen. There were boards on the windows and curling trails of graffiti, exhales of glitter and smoke covering the walls from ceiling to floor. Tommy held his gun in two hands in front of his chest. Barkley had his piece in his right hand, the flash in his left.

"Easy now, bud."

Tommy nodded and took a half breath before ducking out of the kitchen and into a connecting hallway. Barkley leaned against the doorframe, stirring the darkness with his light. Tommy started to creep along one wall; Barkley hugged the other. A third of the way down, they found another door that opened to a staircase diving into the bowels of the building. Tommy wanted to take a look. Barkley nodded and watched as his partner disappeared. So much for sticking together.

Barkley clicked off his light and continued down the hall, aware of the old floorboards wincing under his tread and Gladys, back now, crooning low and smooth and sweet and wet in the deepest part of his brain where nothing lived but the stuff that spanned time and memory and never knew death. He came to the end of the corridor and an open space, cold with a current of something heavy that tugged at his legs, prickling the skin on his thighs and tickling his balls. He was tempted to click on his flash but knew Gladys would stop singing if he did and he wanted her in his head. His foot nudged up against the wooden bump of the threshold and he stepped across it. The wall to his left moved away from him, telling him the room was probably an oval. And big. Barkley could feel its depth and the height of the ceiling and wondered how and why they made a room so big in this neighborhood. Then he remembered Roxbury used to be a wealthy neighborhood, home to Boston's Jewish population thirty, forty years back. He thought of this even as another voice, the cop voice, told him he had a gun in his hand and should pay the fuck attention to what was or wasn't in the fucking room and a third voice told him Gladys had quit singing and that probably wasn't good.

He stopped near a window, boarded up tight so just tiny rivers of light leaked through. Tommy's lecture on instinct crawled out from under a rock in his brain and Barkley knew before he could know what was about to happen. Not the exact play-by-play, but he had the gist all right. Fuck, yeah, he had the gist. The detective backed up until he felt the crumble of plaster against his back and pointed his gun toward whatever was staring at him in the darkness. He made words in his mouth but no sound came out as whatever it was charged. He should have fired, could have fired, but something stayed his trigger finger. Then they were on him. Furnace breath, slit-back nostrils, and flashing teeth slick with saliva. The gun clattered from his fingers and skidded across the floor. After that, the only sound was the tearing of clothes and working of jaws as the two beasts fought silently over their prey.

33

Tommy Dillon was in a common stairwell that circled to the bottom of the building. He ignored the second- and first-floor apartments, heading straight for a door that led to the basement. Tommy didn't try to hide his approach, pounding down a broken set of steps and stepping around an old coal bin fixed under a boarded-up chute. Against one wall sat a coffin filled to the brim with car batteries and resting on a pair of runnerless rocking chairs. Beside it stood a six-foot cigar-store Indian wearing a Tribe cap. Tommy took a quick look at both and kept moving.

The tiny room bled out to a long passage covered in a chunky layer of dirt and trash. Tommy picked through the strata, trying to determine who'd been where and when. He found a McDonald's bag and fresh

burger wrappers stuffed into a crack in the wall. On
the ground nearby was a half-melted cup of ice. Bingo.
At the end of the corridor he leaned lightly against
a final door and listened. Like any cop who'd been
around awhile, he knew the layout of these old three-
deckers and knew the door probably led to the building's boiler room. And a dead end. He shouldered his
way in, smelling the rankness of stale water and scanning right to left with his weapon. Walter Price was
in the far corner, huddled against a hunk of scrap iron
that might have once been a furnace. Tommy could see
his hollow eyes, dancing in the dark like a couple of
question marks, and the blued steel of a gun, stretched
out and pointed square at the detective's chest.

"Drop it," Tommy said, and took a step forward.

"Someone cut their vocal cords." The boy sat between
the two beasts, one lying with his massive head in the
boy's lap, the other sitting upright, jaws open, tongue
hung like a fresh offering between a wet set of teeth.
Neither had taken their eyes off Barkley, sitting still as
a stone against the wall some ten feet away.

"You know what they are?" Barkley said.

"Big."

"They're called Presa Canarios, Daniel. Great dogs
if they're trained properly."

"And if they're not?"

"What do you think? Make pit bulls look like puppies. They just gonna stare at me the whole time?"

Daniel looked down at the dog's head in his lap and the dog looked back and Barkley saw worlds upon worlds spinning in the compass of the boy's gaze.

"They don't trust humans," he said.

"But they trust you?"

"I listen."

Daniel had placed Barkley's flashlight on the floor so it threw out a pale canopy of light between them. The detective's gun was close by the boy's side. Barkley moved to get up. He could see the Presas tense, smooth muscle quivering under tight coats of skin.

"Just because they didn't hurt you doesn't mean they won't," Daniel said.

Barkley sat again. The dogs collapsed back into their bones, listening to the hum of the boy's thoughts and watching the huge black man like he was their next meal.

"I can't stay here, Daniel. You know that."

"Walter Price didn't kill Harry."

The boy knew Price's name. Barkley wasn't surprised. "You're wrong."

"Whatever you think you see, you don't. And whatever you don't see can hurt you."

"What the Christ does that mean?"

Daniel pulled out a second gun he kept somewhere behind him and put it next to Barkley's.

"He's in the basement. The dogs led me there."

"But you didn't shoot him. Why's that?"

Daniel stroked a shelf of bone between the Presa's eyes. "You think I killed my mother."

Barkley felt a tingling somewhere deep in his skull. The dogs' ears stood up.

"Tell me about her, Daniel."

"Why do you care?"

"Maybe I'm playing a hunch."

The boy slid a small object across the floor. It spun as it skittered, a ring, red enamel, encrusted with diamonds in the shape of a rose. "She was wearing that when she died."

Barkley stared at the ring but didn't touch it.

"Pick it up, Detective."

"Where did you get that?"

"I told you. My mom was wearing it when she died. Pick it up."

Barkley shook his head. The boy's gaze narrowed and the Presas muscled up, one climbing to his feet, nostrils flared, breath bubbling low in his throat.

"I know about the fire escape, Detective. I've seen Jess fall."

"Fuck off, Daniel."

The other Presa was up now, straining to get at Barkley, held fast by an invisible chain fashioned by the boy. He flicked his finger and the dog charged, scuttling close and stopping an inch or two from the detective's face. Barkley could feel the Presa's hot exhaust on his neck and kept his eyes averted.

"You gonna let them tear me up, go ahead and get on with it."

Daniel lifted his chin as the dog retreated and Barkley felt his hand close over the ring. He was there, sitting in his kitchen on the top floor of the Roxbury tenement, windows flung open to the city, a summer breeze billowing sheer white curtains across the room in lovely, liquid streams. He could see Jess through the lacy mesh. She was at the stove, making pancakes and shimmying to a song Barkley couldn't hear but knew was Gladys cuz what else could it be. And then he saw who was helping with the batter. Long limbs, soft curls like her mom. She turned, warm and supple in the morning sun, and Barkley saw she had her dad's smile. And then he couldn't see anymore. Not because he couldn't. But because he couldn't. And so he released the ring and the boy was back, crouched close in the darkness.

"My mother says you're damaged. Says you need time to heal."

"Does she really?"

"Yes, but that's probably not gonna happen tonight." Daniel picked up the ring, putting Barkley's gun in its place. "You need to go."

"In a minute."

"Go. Your partner's in trouble." Daniel turned and left, one dog in the lead, the other following.

Barkley clipped the gun back on his hip, grabbed the flashlight, and climbed to his feet. Already what he'd seen was fading, the threads of a fever dream trailing off into the mist. Maybe it was for the best. Or maybe we tell ourselves what it is we need to hear.

He'd just reached the top of the stairs when he heard the first shot.

34

Daniel slipped down the alley. To his right was a fenced-in yard full of cold metal—engine blocks and steel frames, hunks of pipe and chains and random pieces of scrap, all of it painted in lashings of white and purple light. A howl of wind swept down off the roofs and the Presas froze. The one Daniel thought of as the leader leaped the high fence in one movement. The other followed before the first hit the ground. Daniel listened for some sound of their passage and heard nothing but the night. The Presas did their own bidding and that was as it was.

He started to walk again, coming to the place where the alley joined the street. A mustard-colored Caddy with a white vinyl roof swept around a bend, cruising past before stopping and backing up. A car full of black men in Boston got watched everywhere it went. Except in the Bury. Here they did the watching.

Daniel could hear the thump of a bass line as a window rolled down. He still had Walter Price's gun tucked under his sweatshirt. His hand drifted toward it as one of the Caddy's heavy doors rocked open. Then the Presas were back—the first vaulting a ragged row of bushes and circling Daniel before placing himself between the boy and the car; the other crossing in front of the Caddy and sitting in the street, just beyond the reach of the car's headlights. Daniel could hear voices arguing. A man leaned out of the rear window and pointed a gun at the dog in front of Daniel. The Presa stood up and waited, aware of death and unconcerned, brave as only a dog can be. The front door swung closed and the gun disappeared. Then the Caddy was gone, disappearing in a taste of oil and smoke.

Daniel knelt and put his forehead to the Presa's, feeling the simplicity of his needs, the nakedness of his wants, life shorn of artifice and full of all its raw, elemental power. It should have been terrifying, but Daniel craved it and celebrated it and tried to understand something he knew before he could ever remember and would never fully know again until he'd passed beyond all understanding.

He walked the rest of the way down the block, one

dog ahead, the other leaning up against him. Around the corner a second car waited, this one a silver BMW. Grace stepped from the passenger's side, and Daniel realized for once and forever that it wasn't going to be a teenage romance, no lovestruck, star-crossed, thunderbolt Romeo and Juliet deal. Wouldn't be a slow ripening either. They wouldn't find each other again and again—friends in high school, then dating in college, breaking up, realizing the mutual error of their ways and circling back to each other, this time for good. She'd never bear him children. They'd never grow old. Nope, this was it. Her stepping from the car and standing in an ugly stab of street light, urging him to hurry while the wind tugged and she pushed her hair back behind her ear. Him running, the dogs peeling away and disappearing as quickly as they'd appeared while he climbed into the car. Her never asking why, never asking how, never asking who, just turning and staring at him over the back of the seat as the years and decades and lifetimes flowed past and nothing ever changed as everything moved under-neath and around them and they played their part and spoke their lines over and over. He was sixteen, fall-ing in love and getting his heart broken all at once, for the first time and the last. And there was nothing to be done, save miss her for a million moments in the space of a breath and know he'd do anything for it. Again and again.

"You okay?"

Daniel glanced at the driver. "I'm fine, Ben. You didn't have to come."

Ben Jacob's intelligent eyes stared at Daniel from the rearview mirror. "What else did I have to do?" He'd grabbed his father's car and driven it into Roxbury in the ass end of a winter's night and Daniel would never be able to thank him enough. But Grace would. Daniel could see that, too, just as clearly as the other. For a second he fought it. Then the idea found its place in his heart and he loved both of them for what they were and where they were going, but mostly because they were here when no one else was. Ben put the car in gear.

"The police are in there." Daniel nodded and all three watched the three-decker as it slipped past.

"Did they arrest someone?" Ben said.

"I don't know. I think it's complicated." Daniel turned to Grace. "How did you know I was here?"

"I told you. I get feelings, too."

"We followed you," Ben said. "Lost you in Franklin Park, but Grace said to cruise Dudley Square. And here you are."

Grace put out her hand and Daniel placed Walter Price's revolver in it. She took a quick look. So did Ben as he drove. Then Grace stuck it in the glove compartment.

"The police are gonna be looking for that," Daniel said. "Maybe me as well."

"I don't think they'll be looking in the backseat of a BMW driven by a sixteen-year-old Jewish kid from the 'burbs." Ben's grin lit up the mirror.

"Probably not."

"All right, then. Keep your head down and lock the door. Grace, how the hell do I get out of here?"

35

Barkley hit the bottom of the stairs as the echo of another shot thumped off the walls. He thought about calling it in but just kept moving, through a small room and down a tight corridor. At the very end a door stood ajar. Barkley didn't hesitate. In the Bury hesitation only got you dead. He ducked low and shouldered through, the walnut grip of the Smith & Wesson slick and rough at the same time in his hand. Tommy Dillon was planted in the middle of the room, legs spread slightly, right arm extended as he fired a final time into the crumpled body of a young black man. Tommy dropped his arm to his side, service weapon hanging from his fingertips. Barkley moved in a slow circle, his gun not pointed at his partner but not holstered either. He waited until Tommy could see him before speaking.

"Hey, bud."

"I came in and he took the shot."

"How many did you fire?"

A small rise and drop in the shoulders. "Dunno. Five, maybe."

Meaning he had one left. Barkley took a step closer. "I'm gonna need to take the weapon."

Tommy looked down at the gun in his hand and tossed it near Barkley's feet. There was a second piece by the body. A .25-caliber Baby Browning. Looked like a toy. Barkley checked the magazine, then searched the pockets of the kid until he found a license. Walter Joseph Price. Nineteen years old and very much dead.

"We should call it in." Tommy's face played flat in the tinfoil light.

"Tell me what happened."

"Just did."

"Ain't gonna fly, bud."

"No?"

"Not unless I back it up. So tell it to me straight and make it the truth."

"You fucking serious, B? After all we done?"

"He fired once, Tommy. You put five in his chest. The last from about two feet away after the man was dead."

"You seen what he done to that kid."

"Tell me what happened."

"Just what I said. He fired. I put him down." Tommy was still wired, breath hissing through narrow slits in his nose. "Gimme his gun."

"Why?"

"Why you think? We pop off a few more rounds. Make it look like the fucking OK Corral. No one's gonna care, B. Gimme the piece." Tommy held out his hand as something stirred in the reptilian part of Barkley's brain and he knew this guy could kill him, right here in the fucking cellar. And it wouldn't even be a surprise. Outside there was noise in the alley. Someone had heard the shots. Tommy flicked his fingers impatiently.

"Give me the fucking gun, B. You call it in and deal with the locals."

Barkley handed over the service weapon and the Browning. Then he left the cellar. Somewhere in the distance, he could hear the winding scream of a siren. Closer, much closer, the pop, pop, pop of a pistol as Tommy Dillon staged his one-man shooting war.

PART III

36

G race sat in the curve of the doorway, staring at the black face of the apartment building, a lonesome rectangle of canary yellow floating in the middle of the second floor. It was the third night she'd been out there. The third night she'd watched Simon Lane pacing against the darkness. He paused in the eye of the window and Grace felt the pressure of his gaze. He couldn't possibly see her tucked up in the alcove that marked the entrance to Music City. Could he?

She shrank back against the rough cement and ran her fingertips over the architecture of his mind. The thing was a puzzle, a gleaming hall of mirrors riveted with narrow staircases, some leading up, some plunging down, one circling back on another, and everywhere she looked, Grace saw only herself. Was she truly inside his head, or he in hers? Was there a difference between the two?

Grace closed her eyes and lifted her chin, the better to drink in the morning air. She hadn't seen Daniel, hadn't spoken to him since the night in Roxbury more than a week ago. Still, she could feel his presence and knew he was sleeping somewhere inside the apartment. The idea soothed her. Calmed her. Grace's eyes flicked open. The window was empty, the front door to the building swinging wide on its hinges. Simon floated down the steps, gliding to a stop under a streetlight. She could see him clearly, wrapped in a long swath of coat with a red scarf and black watch cap tugged down over his face. He took out a pipe and knocked it on his heel. Then he filled and lit it, streaming a crest of smoke that circled his head as he looked directly at her. The clock on the insurance building clicked over to 5:07. He turned and walked away, sliding down Beacon Street, deeper into the oiled joints of the city. Grace stepped from her hiding place. He'd known about her all along. And now he was telling her to follow. It was the price she'd pay for Daniel's safety.

And so she went.

He moved incredibly fast, a gritty wind funneling him down Beacon, his thoughts reduced to a mumble in her head as she tried to keep up. He was twenty yards ahead when, without warning, he dipped into a side street. Grace sprinted to the corner and stared down an empty block sealed off at the end by a tumble of stone standing big-shouldered against a growing sky. The building looked like an old New England meeting-house or church, bounded by a black fence and flanked by iron-gray trees with sinuous branches that grew into the sides of the structure and overhung the roof.

Grace paused at the gate and listened. The silence ran wild in her blood, pounding at her temples and dilating the soft veins in her throat. The only marker on the building was a year, 1789, carved into a lintel set over the wooden door. Grace tugged at the door's handle. To her dismay and relief, the thing was locked.

She sat in a finger of street light, one step down from the top, and stared out at silken skeins—fear, desire, anxiety, confusion—flitting in and out of the trees, flying up into the branches and back across the courtyard. The smell of pipe smoke arrived on the ragged edge of a breeze, then a melody of thumps as something landed lightly behind her.

The big cat took his time, circling in and out of sight, drifting a silvered tail across Grace's cheek before coming up on the other side and angling close enough so she could hear the muzzled breathing that might have been a purr and might have been a growl.

The cat's face was cut close to the bone, one eye a dry, unblinking blue, the other bleached and blind to the world. Grace watched the cat's black and white whiskers tremor as he kneaded meaty paws, shoulder muscles tensing and bunching and working. The cat peeled back his lips, if cats had lips—Grace knew nothing about cats, except she knew after tonight she'd never have one—and showed his teeth, licking the side of her face with a coarse tongue. For the first time, Grace noticed the others—five, ten, twenty sets of eyes assembled from bits and pieces of darkness and arranged in receding circles around her, watching their leader as he jumped onto a stone railing and switched his tail. The word *subtle* came to mind, like the cat had decided to play with Grace before snapping her neck and feeding her to his friends. Then something whispered in the trees and the cat leaped without warning, bared claws hunting for anything soft, anything breathing, anything flesh, anything Grace.

She screamed and ducked, the cat flying past, tumbling and rolling down the steps in that elegant way cats always seem to fall. Somewhere at the end of a narrow tunnel was the gate and the street. Grace ran for it, felines coiling and closing on all sides, swiping and hissing as she fled. And then she was down the block and around the corner, sprinting through the empty city. Up ahead, Kenmore Square beckoned and teased and laughed at Grace's fears and Grace's foolishness. Behind her, pipe smoke eddied and swirled and she could taste it following in her wake.

37

The Public Gardens were mostly empty, Bostonians reduced to scuffs of gray as they hurried through the Arlington Street gate. Fat clouds scudded overhead, greased by a soft wind and sullen with the promise of winter rain. Barkley sipped his drink from the safety of a window seat in the bar at the Ritz. Cat McShane sat across from him, looking like she was in her own private Bogart movie as she toyed with the stem of the cherry atop her ginger ale. They'd given it to her in a tall glass loaded with crushed ice. Cat pointed her eyes at Barkley's tumbler, short, squat, and full of mind-numbing scotch.

"Are we going to eat, or is it that kind of thing?"

He'd bought meatballs and sauce in the North End. A bottle of Chianti. Cannolis from Bova's. Figured they'd have dinner at his place. Afterward, maybe a walk in the neighborhood. Forget about the day and live for the night. Just him and Cat. Then the hearing happened, and Barkley decided to drink his lunch instead.

"You go ahead and order," he said.

The DA's office had set up Tommy Dillon at a conference table ten feet away while one of their prosecutors ran out the dog, then the pony, then the dog again just for good measure. Afterward, there'd been a meeting in another room and then the official finding. Tommy was cleared of any wrongdoing in the shooting death of Walter Price. Pending some paperwork, he'd be back on the street by the end of the day.

"They read your report into the record," Barkley said.

Cat nodded as a waiter came over and dropped off a menu. "I did my job, Bark." He lifted a finger to speak, but Cat wasn't done. "Full autopsy, detailed wound descriptions, entry and exit angles. It's all there."

"You saw my statement?"

"Of course."

"And?"

"And what?"

"Come on, Cat."

"Come on nothing."

Barkley drained his drink and got a fresh one. Cat ordered half of a chicken salad sandwich and picked around the edges. Outside, the world exploded in cannon bursts of white as the sky broke into ripe, fleshy pieces and an unseasonably warm storm lashed against the windows.

"Between you and me . . ." Barkley said.

"Here we go . . ."

"Between you and me, what do you really think happened?"

"I know what happened. Anyone who looks at the file is going to know what happened."

"What happened?"

"There was a 'gun fight'"—Cat made quotation marks with her fingers—"between your partner and a young black man, now deceased. At close range, maybe ten, fifteen feet. The black man was hit five times, once in the shoulder, four closely grouped in the chest. The decedent somehow managed to squeeze off four shots before he died, and your partner, due undoubtedly to a second act of the Almighty, wasn't hit by any of them. Come on, Bark."

"Say it."

"Fine. Tommy Dillon executed that kid. Then he made it look like there was an exchange of gunfire. Maybe you helped him. Maybe you went along after the fact. I don't know. More important, no one cares."

"Why didn't you put any of that in your report?"

Cat laughed and suddenly looked older than she'd ever want. And just as suddenly Barkley's stomach turned sour with the whiskey and he hated the job more than ever for what it did to people.

"I'm not stupid, Bark." Cat pushed her plate of food away. "If the DA wants to put the pieces together, let him. But he won't and we both know it. Forget about this. Once the rain lets up, we'll go for a walk. Catch a movie or something. After, I can make us dinner at my place."

Barkley shook his head.

"I don't think any less of you, Bark. In fact, I think more of you."

"Great."

"Price was going to wind up dead one way or the other. Hung by his belt in a holding cell, shanked in the yard. I mean, was this any worse?"

"So I did the right thing?"

"You did the cop thing."

A flock of pigeons flew up in his head, blotting out their conversation, leaving behind nothing but Daniel Fitzsimmons, flanked on either side by his dogs, staring down at Barkley as he sat in a cold hole. Daniel had

374 · MICHAEL HARVEY

a shovel in his hands and began to backfill, the dirt hitting Barkley's skin and catching in his eyes and teeth.

"Bark?"

"Yeah."

"How's Dillon doing?"

"I'm sure he's fine."

Today was the first time he'd seen his partner since the night of the shooting. Tommy had been put on paid leave, the department requiring the two detectives not communicate until after the hearing. Well, they'd had their hearing. And now his partner was back.

"Chains, Cat."

"What?"

"That's what this job is. Chains with thick iron cuffs."

"Bark . . ."

"The chains don't seem like nothing at first. Hell, they're a badge of honor. But then they begin to weigh on you, every step you take they get heavier." He ordered another drink even though he hadn't finished the one in front of him. "You're in the job long enough, you're gonna get jammed up, slipped between the jaws of a vise, screwed in so goddamn tight you can't move, can't breathe. You can say it's never gonna happen to you and you'll believe it. Right up until it happens."

"Bark . . ."

"Seven years ago last month. You can look it up."

"Look up what?"

"Me and Tommy were on a case. Murder suspect we thought might be holed up in Columbia Point. Apartment's on the fourth floor and the elevator's out. So up the stairs we go. I'm in the lead, gun out. There's a noise somewhere above us. I look up the open stairwell just as someone tries to drop an AC unit on my head. Tommy pushes me and the fucking thing tears at the sleeve of my coat as it pisses by. No shit, it would have killed me."

"That's what partners do, B. That's why you guys look out for each other. All the way down the line."

"Someone taught you good, Cat. Who was that? Never mind, lemme finish. Tommy pushes me. Like I said, if he doesn't the fucking window unit probably takes me right over the railing and down three stories. Instead, I bounce off the wall and my gun accidentally discharges. The shot ricochets in the stairwell, catches a guy who's peeking out from behind a door a floor below us." Barkley pulled down the collar of his best dress shirt with two fingers. "Right under the collarbone. Goes straight through and explodes his heart. Dead before I can get to him. And it didn't take me long. The wife is there, baby in her arms, staring at me as her husband bleeds his good-byes from the mouth and I lay him down and the woman starts to scream. And now the baby is the one looking at me. But what's the difference, right? Then the old woman comes out."

"The old woman?"

"Dead guy's mother. Lives with them. Or they live with her. She comes out and picks up her son and cradles his head and carries him into the apartment. This guy was big, six feet plus, but she carries him like he's nothing. Tommy and I follow. There's all kinds of hell breaking loose. Chatter on the radio. We still have a suspect in the building. And it's Columbia Point. Half the projects gonna strap up and come gunning for us."

"What happened?"

"What always happens. We called for backup. Some cruisers rolled, some SWAT guys, and we got the fuck out of Dodge. Two weeks of shit followed, lootings, a half-dozen more shootings in the first couple days. They put my face out there as the shooter cuz I was black, but that didn't mean nothing. Far as the projects were concerned, I was blue. That's what mattered. Thing just boiled and raged and thrashed and killed until it died like it always does."

"So you owe Tommy?"

"More ways than one. I fucked up, Cat. The story I just told you was a lie. Not all of it. Just the important part, which, by the way, is the very best way to lie. Yeah, the window unit came down and, yeah, it almost took my head off. Tommy pushed me up against the wall, but my gun didn't accidentally discharge. I saw the fucker who dumped the unit on me peeking out at us from a doorway a couple floors up. So I took the shot. Stupid, right? Enclosed stairwell, no sign of a weapon, no imminent threat. Just some asshole playing games. But I'm shook, I'm scared, I'm pissed. Mostly the last. So I pop off the shot. Just one. It catches a railing, deflects down, and kills the guy one floor below just like I described. That's what really happened. And you know what it would have meant if I'd told that story?"

"I don't know, Bark."

"Like hell you don't know. Man one. Fifteen to twenty-five, minimum. But Tommy steps up. Tells me exactly what to say, exactly how to say it. You'd think I'd know, but your brain freezes when you're in the vise like that. At least mine did. So Tommy gives me the play-by-play and then he testifies at the hearing. All lies, just like me today. I walk and everything fades to background noise. We're back on the job the following week. I look at the guy and I love him. Cuz I owe him. And so right fucking there was the first link in the chain. The strongest link, the one that mattered. And today was the last."

"The last?"

"You want a drink, or am I doing this solo?"

"I think we should go." Cat started to get up.

"You know what else is bugging me?"

"The fact that I'm offering you my virtue and you're shrugging it off?"

"Harry Fitzsimmons's wounds. The two different types of wounds."

"They don't make sense."

"Bet your ass they don't make sense. Did you just offer me your virginity?"

"Is this 1958? Are you Richard Zimmerman from high school chemistry? Pay the bill and let's go."

The storm had blown out of the city as quickly as it had arrived, leaving the Public Garden little more than a carpet of mud. Still the walk was nice, with the weight of the trees overhead and the careful paths and rain washing everything clean. Barkley found a section from the *Globe* in a trash can and spread it out on a bench. Cat seemed dubious but sat down anyway.

"It's always quiet here."

"Yeah."

"Go ahead, Bark."

"Huh?"

"You wanted to ask about the wounds on Fitzsimmons."

"It's not just that. None of it makes sense."

"None of what?"

"The girl who grabbed the wallet. Where is she? Why didn't she stop at the car and talk to them longer before going for the leather? How was it that Walter Price was just waiting for Harry in the alley?"

"Every case has holes. I don't need to tell you that."

"The wounds. Why does Price use two different weapons? Why didn't Fitzsimmons fight back?"

"He did fight back. Price stabbed him. Hell, you've got a picture of it."

"I do."

Cat pulled a folder from her bag.

"What's that?"

"What you asked for." She dropped the folder in his lap. Barkley flipped it open. Inside was a photo of Violet Fitzsimmons, taken three months before she died. It was the woman he'd bumped into as she came out of Hom's Chinese restaurant in the South End, the woman who'd held his hand on the fire escape. Barkley drank in the liquid eyes and mobile mouth, the smooth, unlined face. Underneath the photo was a one-page inventory report from the car crash that killed her. Among Violet's personal possessions was a ring— red enamel encrusted with a dozen diamonds in the shape of a rose.

Barkley flipped the folder shut. Cat caught his eyes. "What is it?"

"Do you believe in God?"

She pursed her lips.

"Never mind."

"The 'god' I grew up with is too small to be real. At least for me."

"But there *is* something out there?"

She slipped a hand to his chest. "Or in here."

"Or both?"

"Or both. Why are you asking?"

"I believe in facts. Evidence. At least I always did."

"And now?"

"I think I might have been wrong. And I wonder what I'm gonna have to answer for."

Cat picked up the folder and considered the face of Violet Fitzsimmons. "Know what I think?"

"No idea."

"I think maybe you've seen a ghost."

"So you think I'm nuts."

"Hardly. Doing what I do, I've seen a few myself. And some of them can be quite wonderful."

Barkley grinned despite himself and felt the tension slip from his shoulders. Talking with Cat didn't change a thing, except everything. She let him pull her in, nuzzling her head against his shoulder and fitting her body to his, breathing softly and deeply and letting her eyes close. For a moment they were a couple and the world was full of possibility. Then a small man with a crooked face rolled out of the hanging mist, ringing a bell and setting up his sausage and peppers stand just inside the Arlington Street gate. He popped open a red umbrella and started roasting hunks of meat over a grill. Barkley chuckled lightly.

"Someone should tell that guy it's December."

Cat lifted her head and frowned.

"What?"

"Why do I think I'm gonna regret this?"

"What is it?"

"Evidence." She pointed to a row of metal rods the man had hanging on a piece of wire over the grill. "Right there."

"Where?"

"The skewers he's using for the meat. I mean, there's a million of these guys around the city, I understand that."

"But . . ."

"I'm betting any one of those would match up perfectly to Harry Fitzsimmons's wounds."

Somewhere a husband drank whiskey in a living room while a wife held ice to her face and fingered a knife in the kitchen drawer. A man picked through a pile of bills, listening to the landlord's tread a floor above and thinking about the cash she kept in a shoebox under the bed. A teenager stared at the top floor of a hotel, picturing his girl inside, hard at work on her old boyfriend. The seeds of homicide blew across the city of Boston, 24/7, finding fertile soil almost wherever they landed. For Barkley, however, there was only one. Until there wasn't. And a piece he was hoping he'd never find had just dropped into place.

"How certain are you?"

"I'd need to measure the wounds and compare them against anything you brought me, but I'm pretty confident. Yeah, the more I think about it, I'm sure."

"Did you drive?"

"Why?"

"We'll take my car."

They went less than a mile, parking a block away. Cat waited in the front seat with the doors locked as Barkley jogged down Washington Street, returning with two white paper bags, bottoms already soaked through with grease. The logo on one of the bags read FIVE FACES.

"I'm not gonna eat that," Cat said, pointing to the order of shish kebab Barkley held in his hand.

He used a napkin to pull off the hunks of sweaty

chicken and held up the naked metal skewer. "All I need you to do is measure."

Cat made a face. "I don't have a tape measure."

Barkley reached across to the glove compartment and took one out. From the backseat he dredged up a stack of files, rummaging until he found the one on Harry Fitzsimmons.

"You keep it in your car?"

"Bits and pieces. Your report's in here with details on the wounds."

Cat shook her head and covered her lap with a couple of napkins. She laid the skewer across them. "This won't be exact."

"Just ballpark it."

Cat stretched the tape measure.

"I owe you," Barkley said. "How about Jimmy's?"

Cat smirked, made a couple of measurements, and snapped the tape shut. "These would work."

"You sure?"

"I'm using a tape measure in the front seat of your car. No, I'm not sure. Why's that Asian kid staring at us?"

Barkley glanced across the street. Kenny Soo stood in the exhale of an alley. Barkley raised a hand. Soo waved him across.

"Cat . . ."

"I can walk back."

Barkley pulled out some bills. "Jump a cab."

"It's a ten-minute walk." She held up the skewer. "You want me to get a little more precise with this?"

"Can we keep it between us?"

She wrapped the thin piece of metal in one of the napkins and slipped it in her bag.

"You don't like this?" he said.

"I don't see the point. The guy who killed Harry Fitzsimmons is dead. Your partner shot him."

"The night of Fitzsimmons's murder Tommy was out on a case. We got the call on the body and arrived at the alley in separate cars. Tommy got there first."

"So what?"

"Tommy told me he ate fast food that night. The next day I was over to his place. There was takeout in the trash." Barkley held up the bag of Five Faces. "Fucking guy loves his shish kebab."

Cat McShane didn't have to lose bottom to know when the water was getting deep. "Call me, Bark. And I've never been to Jimmy's so don't think I won't hold you to it."

She leaned across and kissed him, running a nail across the stubble on his cheek before climbing out. Soo waved at her. Cat shook her head and waved back. Barkley watched in the rearview mirror until she turned the corner. Then he got out. Soo was sitting on the curb, smiling like a shit-eating motherfucker who thought for sure he was about to get paid.

38

Daniel found her picking through Led Zeppelin albums. "Really?"

Grace turned, hair tumbling about her shoulders like a dark waterfall of silk. "I can do some Led Zep."

"Yeah, right."

"How did you know I was here?"

"I woke up around eleven, looked out the window, and there you were, sitting on the steps, watching the rain fall."

"You think it's stopped for good?"

"Hard to say."

Grace held a copy of *Physical Graffiti*. Daniel took the album from her, scanned the back, and returned it to its spot in Music City's collection.

"What are you doing, Grace?"

"What are you doing? Besides sleeping all day?"

He'd gone off the grid after Roxbury. Grace and Ben had rung his doorbell, but Daniel wasn't in the mood.

"You ever coming back to school?" she said.

"I think I'm done."

"Smart, Daniel. Real smart."

"The police killed that guy."

"No kidding."

The *Globe* and *Herald* had both tried to track him down, looking for a reaction to the shooting death of Walter Price. The newspaper guys didn't get any further than anyone else. Unlike Grace, however, they gave up a lot easier.

"How's your roommate?"

"You've been out here most nights, you tell me."

Her face warmed at the edges and Daniel could smell something new on her skin.

"He walks your apartment, Daniel. Sometimes all night."

"I know."

"While you sleep."

"So what?"

"So it's weird." Grace picked up another album, this time *Houses of the Holy*, and pretended to give it a look before putting it back. She'd aged five years in a week and he thought there was something more physical, more knowing about her. The idea of Ben rose up in Daniel's mind. Him with her. Her with him, scraping long nails across his shoulders as she whispered his name.

"I know about Ben," Daniel said.

Her cheeks flushed and the air grew close. "It's not what you think."

"How about we go outside and sit?"

They left the record store, settling on the steps. It was Saturday and Kenmore Square felt sluggish, like it was still groggy from Thanksgiving and not quite ready for Christmas.

"I pushed him," Grace said, lifting her chin toward the blank windows of Daniel's apartment. "At least I tried."

"Simon?"

"I was sitting right here, staring up at the window, watching him pace. Guess I couldn't help myself."

"Do me a favor and leave it alone."

"Is that what you want?"

"I saw Walter Price that night in the cellar. Had a chance to shoot him myself."

"I knew you never would."

"He didn't kill Harry. Otherwise, I would have pulled the trigger."

"You can lie to yourself, Daniel, but that's all it is."

He knocked her knee with his and held her hand loosely, tracing a finger across the flutter at her wrist, watching the color wash from her face.

"We're gonna be fine," she said.

That was another lie, but only he knew for sure. So he let it pass and waited for her to tell him what she'd come to say.

"I followed your roommate."

"Did he see you?"

"I don't think so."

"Did he see you?"

"No. It was the middle of the night and I could barely keep up."

"Good. So where did he go?"

39

It had stormed off and on all afternoon, the sky grumbling in a drizzle of purples and blacks. The artistic soul, however, would not be denied. And so Zeus Sanchez watched from the window as a couple of men painted silhouettes of strippers on the side of the building. Sanchez followed the line of dancing women to an electric sign lying flat on the bed of a pickup. Three more men had set up a pulley and winch on the roof while a fourth ran a wire through two iron loops on the top of the sign and turned his thumb up. Sanchez read the block letters as the sign started to rise—KING ARTHUR'S MOTEL AND LOUNGE.

The Old Line Boarding House in Chelsea had been sold a few months back. Along with a new name, the owners were going to put in a bar and a couple of stripper poles downstairs. They'd keep the rooms upstairs, but now they'd rent them out by the hour. As far as he knew, Sanchez was the only guest left in the place. He hadn't paid for his room, never saw anyone else downstairs or in the hallway. There'd just been the key in an envelope, an address, and instructions. Three rings on the phone told him when it was time to eat. He'd troop downstairs and find his meal laid out on a table by the front door. When he was finished, he'd head back upstairs and stay there. If he didn't, they'd know and the deal would be off. At least that's what the instructions said and Sanchez had no reason to doubt it.

He walked over to the dresser and felt the weight of the envelope in his hand. He pulled out the cash and counted it, then counted again and put it away. He'd brought a transistor radio to keep up with the news. He wasn't sure if they knew about that and maybe he didn't give a fuck. He'd been scared at first, but things were changing. He was beginning to see the seams in their plan, cracks where before there'd been nothing. Was there risk? Sure. But he'd grown up immigrant poor and hungry as fuck. Plus he was a Harvard kid. Chances were he saw more than most.

The rain had returned in driving sheets. Sanchez was thinking about heading back to the window to watch the strippers as they washed off the side of the building when he heard a footfall. Three days and it was the first hint of another person in the place. Sanchez reached under the mattress and pulled out the Saturday night special he'd bought for twenty-five bucks with money from the envelope. He pointed the gun at the doorknob and watched it turn. Fucker wasn't knocking. And he had a key. Sanchez's finger tightened on the trigger as the door opened.

"You look like crap," Sanchez said, voice neutral and strong.

"Put it down."

"As soon as you tell me what's going on."

The visitor stepped inside. When you came right down to it, short of pulling the trigger, the kid from Harvard didn't really have a plan. So he dropped his gun hand as the visitor walked around the room, tugging down shades and acting like he owned the place, which he pretty much did. He sat down on the bed and the two began to talk. Actually, the visitor talked. Sanchez nodded a lot and listened.

40

Rain battered the windows, making a sharp sound before sliding off into infinity. Barkley paused at the top of the stairs, Kenny Soo on his shoulder. The detective put a finger to his lips. Soo was a statue even when he wasn't and shot Barkley a look that said *Let's get on with it.* Barkley led the way, easing across the hall to Nick Toney's studio. He gave the door a light knock, then tried the knob. Locked. Barkley motioned Soo back toward the stairwell and sized up the jamb for one of his size thirteens. Soo touched the detective's shoulder and shook his head. He crab walked around Barkley and crouched by the lock. From a pocket the little prick produced a leather case with a set of steel picks. Thirty seconds later, the door popped open. Soo was already inside. Barkley pulled his gun and followed.

They'd talked downstairs, sitting on the curb as trash blew down the street and the first drops of rain picked at their shoulders and hair. Soo had called the station three days earlier with some information. Barkley had been tied up with Tommy's hearing and never got the message. Now Soo wanted to pass along what he knew. And get paid.

"Kenny . . ." Barkley moved through the darkened photography studio toward a suite of rooms in the back. He found Soo in a small office with a cot in the corner. Soo was rummaging through a set of desk drawers.

"Stay here and shut up." Barkley threw Soo into a chair and checked out the other two rooms. One was a bathroom, complete with a claw-foot tub. The other looked like it might be Toney's darkroom. Barkley grabbed Soo on his way back to the main space. He sat Soo at a long table and flipped open the Fitzsimmons murder file.

"Let's go over what you told me again."

"Okay, boss." Soo sat with his hands folded like he was in third grade. Barkley couldn't figure out the kid and didn't really have the time. He pulled out Harvard's student photo of Zeus Sanchez. "This guy's name is Sanchez. Jesus Sanchez."

Soo nodded, eyes moving from the photo to Barkley and back again. "I told you downstairs. He's the guy."

"Go through it again, Kenny."

"Middle of the afternoon, three days ago." Soo held up two fingers. "He was in Five Faces."

Barkley's balls had tightened when Soo first mentioned Five Faces. Now the detective watched as Soo examined the photo a second time.

"I need you to make sure, Kenny."

"I'm sure. Pay me, motherfucker." Soo grinned and pushed the photo away. Barkley counted out three twenties.

"Pay as we go. Now, what else?"

"He was worried. Major-league worried. Sat in the shop for an hour before the other guy showed up."

"And you've never seen the other guy?"

Soo shook his head. Barkley pulled out a photo of Neil Prescott, as well as the picture of Daniel Fitzsimmons.

"Neither of these two?"

"Come on, man."

"He was a white guy, right?"

"Yeah, but older."

"And not Toney?"

"No way. I haven't seen Toney for a week."

"But Sanchez came up here? With the other guy?"

"I told you. They talked for a while in Five Faces, then they walked next door to the Brompton. I don't know if they came up here."

"Where else would they have gone?"

Soo made a pumping motion with his fist. "Boom boom. Lots of girls live here, boss."

"How long were they in the building?"

"Two hours, maybe."

"And you never saw Toney? Before or since?"

Soo glanced around the room. Outside, the weather couldn't make up its mind, bulleting against the glass one minute, then fading to nothing. "You think he's dead?"

Toney's studio had been emptied. No camera equipment, no photos, just a few strands of wire running the width of the place.

"I don't know, Kenny. You didn't see anyone moving shit out of here?"

"No."

"And you usually see Toney a lot?"

"Every day, in and out."

"Okay. I got some things I gotta do."

"Can I help?"

Barkley didn't want Soo around but figured it was

better to keep him close. "Sure. How about I deputize you?"

Barkley pulled on a pair of latex gloves and gave a pair to Soo. Then he got up and began to walk the perimeter. It took the rest of the afternoon and a good part of the evening, but he finally found what he was looking for in the bathroom. Soo had been on his shoulder the entire time, watching what Barkley watched, squatting where Barkley squatted. Now he studied the detective's face.

"What is it?"

Barkley was peering down into the tub. He reached in and ran a finger around the drain.

"Boss?"

"I think that's blood, Kenny."

"Think?"

"It's blood."

"Toney's dead?"

For the first time since they'd met, Soo sounded like a scared kid. Barkley led the way back to the main room.

"Sit down, Kenny."

Barkley made a show of going through the Fitz-simmons murder file a second time, pulling a thick stack of photos from the alley. He picked out five shots and spread them in front of Soo. "These are pictures we took of the crowd on the night of the murder." There were dozens of faces, smudges of color pinned back behind yellow police tape. "Sometimes a killer likes to get a look at his handiwork. So he comes back and watches."

Soo nodded but didn't take his eyes off the photos.

"Take your time." Barkley felt the building's prickly radiator heat laying down sweat and grime in the lines of his neck. "If you don't see the guy who was with Sanchez . . ."

"There he is."

Soo jabbed at one of the photos. Barkley had only been interested in one photo and only one person in it. Kenny Soo had nailed it.

"You sure?"

"He was with Sanchez in Five Faces. Ten out of ten."

Barkley studied the picture of Tommy Dillon, wrapped in a gray overcoat and peering over his shoulder at the camera. Then Barkley restacked the photos and put them back in the file. He locked the door on his way out and called into the station from a pay phone. He gave Toney's address to Charlie Herbert and told him to seal the room. Barkley didn't offer an explanation. Just seal the room and wait until he called. After he hung up, he gave Soo five more twenties and said there'd be another hondo coming if the kid did three things.

"Whatever, boss."

"First, keep your mouth shut."

Soo nodded.

"Second, stay out of Toney's place. Third, let me know if anyone else shows up looking to get in. Besides the cops, that is."

"And what if Toney shows up?"

"Toney ain't gonna be showing up, son. But if he does, you can give me a call."

Soo rubbed his fingers together. "More money?"

"Why not?"

41

Barkley unwrapped his sandwich and inhaled. Roast beef, sliced paper thin and piled high on a pillow-soft onion roll, a slice of white cheese, slightly melted, and slathers of barbecue sauce. Barkley ate half of it in one go and looked out the scarred windows of Buzzy's Roast Beef. He'd been driving around most of the night, figuring the angles, weighing the odds, writing his obituary in his head. All in all, it read better than he expected. A couple of college kids slipped out from behind the Red Line station, stumbling across the street and heading in the general direction of the Charles Street Jail. Buzzy's lived in the shadow of Boston's oldest lockup, providing an endless source of fun and amusement for a parade of drunks with a hankering for beef. Some sandwich shops gave their children crayons and paper to scribble on. Buzzy's offered its own life-size jail, replete with barbed wire, searchlights, and a twenty-foot-high brick wall.

Barkley watched as the drunken duo surveyed the outside of the jail, pacing first one way, then the other. Finally they found their spot and went to work, one guy giving the other ten fingers in an attempt to spider-man up and over the wall. Their efforts ended with the first kid folding back into the gutter and the would-be climber falling face-first onto the pavement. He bounced back up, both of them laughing and pushing and punching each other as they staggered the final few feet to Buzzy's.

Ah, the magic of booze.

The pair each ordered a roast beef sandwich and a knish from the guy behind the counter. Barkley took his food to the far end of the place where a pay phone hung on the wall. He crunched down on an onion ring, wiped the grease off his fingers, and dropped money into the phone. Cat McShane picked up on the third ring.

"Whoever this is, it had better be good."

"It's me."

"What time is it?"

"Almost four."

"Jesus Christ."

"I'm down at Buzzy's."

"Where?"

"Buzzy's. By the jail. I needed a sandwich."

"So you spend the night in the Combat Zone, then head over to Buzzy's and gorge. How very original."

"I'm working, Cat."

"And I'm sleeping. What do you want?"

"I need you to go over to the address we were at today."

"Five Faces? I told you, the skewers you gave me matched. There's not much more I can do."

"The hotel next door. Place called the Brompton Arms." Barkley gave her the address. "You'll find a cop on the top floor guarding a door. I told him to expect you. Go inside. There's a bathroom in the back."

"Is this someone's apartment?"

"It's a photography studio. Go into the bathroom and test the tub for blood."

"Your guy can do that. Just spray some Luminol around."

"I don't want him in there. No one but you."

Cat didn't respond.

"If you don't want to do it, I understand."

"I need to know more."

He told her about Kenny Soo and how he'd spotted

Zeus Sanchez at Five Faces with a stranger, how the two of them had paid a visit to the Brompton.

"And this studio belongs to someone connected to the Fitzsimmons murder?"

"The guy who took the snaps in the alley. A photographer named Nick Toney."

"What's the name of the student again?"

"Sanchez. Zeus Sanchez. He was the one who got his wallet clipped."

"So Harry Fitzsimmons went down the alley chasing him?"

"Yeah. We took a statement from Sanchez that night, then he dropped off the radar. The way things shook out, it didn't seem important."

"And now you have questions?"

"Soo was able to pick out the guy who was with Sanchez at Five Faces."

"And how did he do that?"

"I showed him a photo."

"Your partner."

"How'd you guess?"

"It's in your voice, Bark. Like a fucking bell."

"Why would Tommy be talking to Sanchez after the Price shooting? And why would they go up and see Toney?"

"You asking me?"

"Been driving around all night asking myself."

"Tommy Dillon has already murdered one kid, Bark. And you looked the other way. Now, you're worried it's not over. And you're worried you're gonna get sucked in even deeper."

"I think he killed Nick Toney."

"Christ."

"I want to make sure I know what I know."

"Then what?"

"You said it. This is a cop thing. And that's how it'll go down."

"Listen . . ."

"I understand, Cat. You don't owe me anything."

"Give me a number where I can call you."

He gave her the number of the pay phone.

"I'll ring back when I have something."

"How long?"

"An hour, two tops. Eat another sandwich and think about how much you're gonna owe me."

Cat hung up. Barkley picked at his onion rings and sipped at a Coke. The two drunks were outside again, throwing pieces of their sandwiches over the wall of the jail and into the yard. Ninety minutes later, Buzzy's was empty when the pay phone rang. The counterman gave Barkley a look like *It sure as shit isn't for me.* The detective picked up and listened. He left money on the counter and found his Camaro where he'd left it, parked illegally in front of the Beacon Hill Pub. A college kid was swaying back and forth as he pissed on one of Barkley's tires. He shooed the kid away and fired up the engine. The sky was just starting to lighten as he headed for the expressway.

42

Daniel woke up and walked into the kitchen. A cantaloupe was sitting on the counter, ripe and round and firm. He took up the knife that lay beside it and worked quickly, cutting first lengthwise, then across. He ate the fruit in large chunks, letting the flesh explode in his mouth and the juice run over his teeth, lips, and down his chin. When he was done, he picked up the knife again, holding it in his left hand as he started down the hallway. The doors to both of Simon's rooms stood wide open. That had never happened before and Daniel hesitated before going in. Simon's workroom looked much like it did in Daniel's dream. A long table, bare of even a scrap of paper, and a chair pushed in neatly as if the owner had washed his hands of the whole thing and wasn't planning on coming back. In the bedroom the mattress had been stripped and the only closet was empty. Daniel climbed the stairs to the roof. No easel, no colored pencils, no sign of Simon anywhere.

Daniel went back downstairs and sat behind the big desk in the main room. From the window, he could see an MBTA worker in one of the lanes of the bus station. The man nudged a cigarette from a pack and lit it, shaking his head at something while he shuffled his feet in the gray morning light. A bus rolled in and the station man stepped aside, acknowledging the driver with a jut of his chin. He had a newspaper stuck in his back pocket and pulled it out as he crossed the street, heading toward Charlie's Diner and breakfast—two eggs, toast, and home fries for a buck nineteen.

Daniel turned from the window. Grace had told him she'd followed Simon to a building that looked like a church. She hadn't wanted Daniel to go but knew he was beyond that now and would do what he would. So she'd avoided his eyes and given him the address, telling him to go in the early morning if he must go at all. It was just seven when he pulled on his coat and headed out.

An oculus was cut into the dome of the roof, fresh light spilling and pooling onto the floor, revealing every scrape in the stone, the wearing that comes from generations of feet shuffled one step at a time. Daniel walked the circle, careful not to touch its edge, content to live in the shadows that otherwise filled the space.

He knew he was being watched and waited while his eyes adjusted to the darkness. A gilded angel grinned from the rafters, studying with its Mona Lisa smile. Simon was sheltered in the alcove just below. Their eyes caught and Daniel saw a fighter plane scream, slashes of sun setting its wings ablaze as they tipped and dove. A tree bent over a river, white blossoms dropping from its branches while a circle of silent ripples fled outward. The two images twisted and bled until the wash from the plane and the chop across the water were one in Daniel's head.

Simon beckoned with two fingers. "This way."

He stayed just out of reach, salt on his tongue and in his words, leading Daniel to a room just off the main area. There was a desk with a lamp, a phone, an adding machine, and a spread of newspapers. A sleeping bag was rolled up in one corner and a fireplace was cut into the wall. Simon pulled two coffees from a plain white bag.

"It's black, but there's cream and sugar there." Simon took the top off his coffee, which turned out to be tea. He dunked the bag a couple of times and tossed it into a wastebasket as he settled behind the desk. Daniel sat in the only chair left.

"How are you feeling?" Simon said, blowing on his tea before trying it.

"What is this place?"

"Used to be a church. Puritan, Anglican, Catholic. Now, the Buddhists are giving it a go."

"You got a key or something?"

"I've got a key. They let me come in and think. Sometimes I sit in the sunlight."

Daniel pulled across his coffee but didn't take a sip. "I know you've been in the apartment at night."

"Yes."

"Why don't you come around during the day?"

"Why don't you come out at night?"

"Forget it."

From outside came the muffle of traffic. Simon set his tea on the desk and gave the cup a quarter turn. "In quantum physics there's a principle we call 'decoherence.' It says that the act of looking at or measuring particles in an entangled state will actually cause that state to collapse and cease to exist."

"So?"

"So to get around that, we take our measurements indirectly, with eyes averted, if you will."

"Is that what you've been doing with me?"

"In a sense. You needed space, Daniel. So I gave it to you."

"And now?"

"And now perhaps it's time to risk a more direct approach." Simon opened up a drawer and pulled out two files. One was red, the other green. He picked up the first and balanced it on the flat of his palm. "The autopsy report on your brother."

"And the other?"

"Your mother. Where would you like to start?"

Daniel picked up the green file. Simon stayed his hand. "Let me walk you through it."

Sometimes he referred to the file. Other times, he just sat back and talked and Daniel knew he'd been there, somewhere along the empty highway of beach, watching, studying, keeping score. Simon paused when he came to the part about how Daniel's mother died, why she died, the play-by-play of events that led to that moment. It was a tricky passage and Daniel wanted to take the corners at high speed.

"Who was in the car with her?"

"You mean who put you in the trunk?"

"How do you know so much?"

"I don't know any more than you."

"Afterward I was in a hospital."

Simon pulled out his pipe and took his time lighting it. "Boston City. You lapsed into a coma."

"There was a man there when I woke up. On the day I was discharged, he jumped off a roof."

"You wanted him dead. Just like part of you wanted your mother dead." Simon waited for a challenge that never came. He drew on the pipe and continued. "Coincidentally, they both died. And now, you're wondering if you . . . what's the term you use?"

"Pushed."

"Yes. If you pushed them. I already told you it doesn't work that way. The man jumped because he wanted to. All you did was applaud. As for your mother, you know what you know."

"I saw who was with her on the beach."

"Really?"

Daniel could sense the first bit of tightening around Simon's eyes.

"There are flashes. A glimpse of something as he slammed the trunk."

"What if I told you what happened to her was for the best?"

"I'd tell you to go fuck yourself."

Simon smiled, a sentient thing that stole over his face and was gone. He put down his pipe and picked up the autopsy report on Harry. "The police never told you about the different types of wounds your brother suffered?"

"No."

Simon tossed the file back on the desk. "You hungry?"

Daniel shook his head.

"Me neither." Simon opened up another, deeper drawer and pulled out a bag. It had a Five Faces logo on the side.

"I know that place," Daniel said.

Simon unwrapped an order of beef shish kebab. The meat looked cold and was thick with grease. He pulled the pieces off with his fingers, holding the skewer by one end.

"Open up the autopsy file, Daniel. Page seven, there's some highlighted language."

Daniel read while Simon talked. When he was done, he sat back and watched as Daniel's belly and bowels turned to water.

"You think that killed my brother?"

"One like it, yes."

"And you know who did it?"

"As I said, I know as much as you do."

"How did you get these reports?"

"I told you about computers, internetworking. It will

be commonplace in the future to do what I do. For now, it's not." Simon brushed his fingers across the spread of files. "Why do you think I'm sharing all this?"

"No idea."

"Why do you think you see the animals?"

"I became one myself."

"Yes, in the Boston Common. Then, in Franklin Park with the hyenas. And, of course, the first time, at Latin School. Why?"

"I don't know. Guess I'm hallucinating."

Simon turned up his nose at the notion.

"Then what?"

"The animals helped to crack your world open. Create the room necessary for change."

"What sort of change?"

Simon pressed his lips together, and the room seemed to dim. "Remember when I asked if you knew about 'deep time'?"

"Yes."

"It's a term more and more scientists are using to explain spans of time that otherwise seem incomprehensible. The earth, for example, is roughly four and a half billion years old. Does that mean anything to you?"

Daniel shrugged.

"Exactly. An impossible concept for most of us to grasp. But consider a metaphor." Simon snapped his fingers and a thin blue light flickered to life, a laser running in a line from the inside of his eye to the tip of his outstretched finger. "Are you still with me?"

Daniel would have gasped, except he knew if he did the light would disappear and, right now, that was the last thing he wanted. So he just nodded.

"Good. One of my colleagues has suggested we think about the earth's age as the equivalent of the old measure of the English yard—that is, the distance from the king's nose to the tip of his finger." Simon wiggled his outstretched index finger. "If we were to accept that premise, then the entirety of human history—the entirety, mind you—would be represented by the nail's edge on the very end of that finger. One tickle with a file and mankind is toast. Erased from all existence. That's how old the earth is . . . and how insignificant we are in the grand scheme of things." Simon dropped his arm and the blue light vanished.

"I get it," Daniel said, just to say something.

Simon shook his head. "You get nothing. What I've given you is an example of *horizontal* deep time. Interesting, sure, but on its best day little more than a tunnel into the past. What truly matters is something I like to call *vertical* deep time." He leaned closer so Daniel could see the swirl in his eyes. "As an object approaches the speed of light, time slows to a crawl.

If we could actually travel at the speed of light, time would stand still."

"But that's impossible."

"Is it? I suspect deep time doesn't just stretch back into history, Daniel. I believe it can also drill down into each passing moment, freezing reality and peeling it back, exposing all its dimensions and all its layers. Kind of like when you dream."

"Except you're not?"

"Except you're not."

"Is deep time tied into entanglement?"

Simon's smile was a flicker of curling flame. "Everything in the universe is connected, every person, every animal, every plant, everything, living or not. Not just spatially, but temporally. All things exist at the same time, all measures of yourself, all that's ever been and ever will be, flows continually like water from a spigot. And all at the speed of light. That's what we feel even if we don't understand. That's what we see even if we don't recognize."

Simon got up and walked over to the hearth, squatting to light a match. The fire blazed quickly, unnaturally, filling the room with its heat. He rubbed his hands together and took a seat against the opposite wall, pulling his knees tight to his chest as his face dissolved into shadow.

"It's the ghost in the mirror. The chill when you walk into an empty house. It's déjà vu, premonition, that tingle of 'clicking' with someone new as if you've known her all your life. People come up with all sorts of names, but what they're really seeing is a crack in the wall, a glimpse, a glimmer of the eternal we're all enmeshed in."

"Entangled."

"You're uniquely able to exist, persist in the great fields of connectivity. You can access them, navigate them. Maintain that space and actually live in it. It's a gift, Daniel. Nothing else."

"It didn't save my brother."

"Every man must one day stretch out his hand. Harry understood that."

"You talk like you knew him."

"I did. And I knew he had to die."

Daniel flinched, head turning as the fire in the hearth cracked like a gunshot. When he turned back, Simon was gone. On the floor where he'd been sitting was his leather case full of sketches. Daniel pulled out the top sketch, the one Simon had shown him on that first day at the apartment, except now it was finished. A piece of coastline—trees, a seawall, and a black road twisting down to a flat slab of beach. Daniel knew the place. And knew what it was he must do.

43

Barkley was parked on G Street, listening to the radio and watching all the crazy Irish fucks, asleep in their crazy Irish fuck beds. Except one. There was a light burning in Tommy Dillon's living room. Barkley was about to open the door when a set of headlights swept past. A station wagon trimmed in wood pulled up in front of the three-decker and a thick-legged woman got out. Katie Dillon met her on the porch. Katie was wrapped up in a robe and wore a pair of baby blue slippers. The other woman was bundled in a parka and kept it zipped to her throat. The two women seemed anxious, eyes sweeping the street as they talked. Serious talk between serious women. Women with a problem. Katie disappeared inside and returned a minute later, handing the other woman something and hugging her.

Barkley waited until the station wagon had turned the corner, then waited another couple of minutes, listening to Eddie Andelman talk about Norm Cook, the C's first-round draft pick, and how he sucked the big one. Barkley kicked out of the car and made his way across the street. The door opened before he could knock. Then he was inside, in the dark and the warmth, the scent of the house that was a home even with all the rest of it. She closed the door behind him and turned so he could see her face.

"He hit you."

Katie put a finger to her lips and led him down the hall to the bedroom.

"Where is he?"

"The girls are sleeping."

"Where is he?"

"I dunno."

"Let me see."

She let him turn her face into the light. The right side had ripened to a rich shade of plum and was already swollen, like someone had slipped a soft egg under the skin. Her left eye was partially shut, the white in the lower half clotted with blood.

"My neighbor's coming over."

Barkley let go of her chin. "I just saw her. In the wagon?"

Katie nodded. "Loretta Sweeney. She's gonna take the girls. Could you help get them into the car? I don't want them to see me . . ." She lifted her hands to her face and crumbled a bit at the edges.

"I'll get them."

There was a small knock.

"That's her," Katie said. "I told her to come around to the kitchen."

"Stay here."

"Just tell them it's a sleepover. Loretta will explain the rest."

Barkley went to the back door and let in the woman he'd seen in the wagon. If Loretta Sweeney was surprised to see a massive black man in the Dillons' kitchen at seven in the morning, she didn't let on.

"The kids?"

He led her down the hall and stood in the doorway as she gently woke first Molly, then Maggie. She left them in their pajamas, bundling them into heavy coats and sweeping them, stiff legged and still half asleep, down the hall. One of them, Barkley thought it was Maggie, finally seemed to realize what was going on when the door opened and the cold air hit her.

"Where's Mom?"

Loretta smoothed Maggie's hair with thick, blunt fingers and kissed the top of her head. "She and your daddy have to take care of some things this morning. So you're gonna stay with me. Okay?"

"What about school?"

"No school today. We'll sleep late, watch some TV. Maybe make cupcakes. What do you say?"

"Who's that?" Maggie pointed at Barkley, who squatted so he was eye level with the two girls.

"I work with your dad. You've seen me."

The twins nodded but didn't seem certain. Who could blame them?

"You go on now, okay? Your mom will pick you up this afternoon."

"Can we have cocoa?" That was Molly, finally coming around.

"Sure," Barkley said.

"And marshmallows?" Maggie was in on the game.

"Why not?"

"And cinnamon toast with butter?" Molly, again.

Barkley smiled and nodded, kissing each of the girls on the top of the head. And then they left, Loretta giving him a final, flat look before closing the door. Southie might be a closed book to the rest of the world, but they looked out for their own. And that wasn't something you could say about most places.

Barkley went back down the hall. Katie had been listening. She stepped into the bedroom and sat at a small table and mirror. She was barefoot now, dressed in a thin nightgown and not yet thirty, but Barkley could already see the gentle sag in her breasts, a hint of loose flesh under her arms. When she looked up at him in the mirror, her reflection was that of a woman who'd put in the miles, wrinkles carved around stiff eyes, a hardness at the corners of her mouth.

"I look a wreck."

"Like hell."

"I'm sorry, Bark. Fuck."

"Let's get a better look at your face."

He found a shallow pan and filled it. She fussed, but he made her sit still and soaked a washcloth in the warm, soapy water. Barkley didn't do a lot of gentle things and felt his pulse quicken and the spit in his mouth turn to dust as he dabbed at his partner's palm print tattooed in long red welts across the side of his wife's face. At first touch Katie winced and closed her eyes. His second touch caused her to shiver from the inside out. The third broke her wide open. Blood mingled with water, mingled with tears, mingled with life and ran down her face in a sticky, brave-as-fuck mess.

"It's okay, Katie."

It wasn't okay, would never be okay. She began to cry harder, quieter, fiercer, and Barkley could feel her strength, running generations deep and woman strong, stronger than him, stronger than her husband, stronger than any man could fathom.

"Tell me what happened."

She looked up, eyes fierce now, drenched in life for all its sadness and all its thankless bullshit.

"Tell me."

A tear rolled down one cheek. He caught it with a fingertip and she stroked the side of his hand, turning so he could feel the rub of her skin. She kissed his hand and took it in hers, hungry butterfly kisses along its length before slipping it slowly inside her nightgown so he could feel the fullness there and her nipple rise and grow hard.

"Katie . . ."

"Don't fucking talk."

"But . . ."

"No, Bark. Fuck, no." She pulled him down, pulled him close, opening her mouth as she kissed him, moving now, rising to her feet, pushing her body against his, pinning him against the wall, running her hands along his back, free inside his shirt. He heard himself moan lightly as she tugged at his belt, then slipped inside and gripped him, staring at him through her damaged eye as she began to stroke.

"K—"

"Shut up." She slid to her knees, never breaking eye

contact, and took him in her mouth. Then they were on the bed, her on the bottom, then somehow on top, her nightgown floating away as she began to move, leaning back so he could see the line of her body, feel the rhythm of her hips, the grind of her pelvis. Barkley rolled his eyes back in his head and let himself fill her, deep-rooted now, joined as one in mind and flesh, if only for this moment in time and this moment was everything that ever was and ever would be. And then the front door opened.

She never said a word, just slipped off him in one impossibly graceful movement, switching off the overhead so all that was left was a night-light by her feet and their breath stoking the darkness between them. Footsteps came from the front of the apartment, one, two, three. Whoever it was, and Barkley sure as fuck had a good idea who it might be, made his way to the kitchen, where he started to yell.

"Katie. Fucking Katie."

Tommy Dillon didn't sound drunk, but he didn't have to be. It was five steps from the kitchen to the bedroom. Maybe seven on a good day, which this clearly wasn't. Barkley was on his feet by the second stride. Katie had pushed the door shut and for the first time Barkley noticed the small latch—a dangling hook with an eye socket for when they wanted to keep the kids out. Tommy kept coming down the hall. Three strides, four. Katie was still naked, the curves of her body soft in the fuzzy glow coming from near her feet. She put a finger to her lips and slipped the hook on. Five strides, six. Tommy pulled at the knob.

"Fucking shit."

Barkley watched the hook bounce in the eyelet. Up, down. Up, down. If it stayed in place, maybe he wouldn't wind up shooting his partner. If it didn't . . . Barkley backed away from the door, eyes fixed on that goddamn hook as it danced. He'd gotten dressed somehow. Somehow pulled his gun and held it in his right hand. Katie motioned with her eyes toward a closet. Barkley ducked inside and closed the door until it was open just a crack. In one motion, the beautiful poetry of an all-state point guard maybe a half step past her prime, Katie slipped on her nightgown and called out to her husband, voice doused with the perfect amount of sleep.

"What the Christ do you want?"

Tommy's reply came from a bedroom down the hall. "Where are the girls?"

More footsteps, another wrench on the door and the heroic latch. "Katie, let me the fuck in. Now."

Still she took her time, pulling on her robe, cinching

it and running hands through her hair. "Jesus, I sent them over to Loretta's. Hold on."

"Why do you got the fucking door locked . . ."

"Quit pulling at the thing and I'll open it."

Tommy stopped tugging, and Katie slipped the latch free. Then he was in the room, shoulders and back filling Barkley's vision.

"Why did you lock the door?"

"Cuz I felt like it."

The blow came quick and flat, practiced and mean, the back of his hand slashing across the side of her cheek, lifting Katie onto the bed, where she banged off the headboard and wound up on her knees, hands in fists clutching the bedsheets.

"I'm sorry," Tommy said.

"Fuck you."

"I said I was sorry."

Fresh marks mingled with the not-so-old and there was a tickle of blood on her lip. Katie licked at it, then wiped at it with her hand. "You wanna know why I locked the door?"

"Katie . . ."

"You wanna know why I sent the kids away? You wanna let them see their mom like this? Is that what you fucking want, Tommy?"

He moved toward her.

"Touch me again and I swear you'll have to kill me."

Tommy stopped in his tracks. "K—"

"I fucking mean it."

He sank to the floor, elbows on his knees, head in his hands, curling up into less than nothing as he started to cry, wet, heaving, choking sobs dredged up from some place of pain that made Barkley wonder even more about his partner and how deep a hole he'd dug himself. Katie crawled off the bed, making small animal sounds in her throat as she settled close by her husband, taking his head in her lap and kissing the tears and salt off his face, stroking his cheeks and his temples, closing his eyes with her fingers and staring across the room at Barkley in the closet. For all his years in interrogation rooms, talking to every lowlife, psychotic motherfucker Boston had to offer, Barkley couldn't read a word of what was going on inside the woman's head. She lifted her husband's face and framed it in her strong, perfect hands. She kissed him and held him, all gentle now. He mumbled his apologies and tried to touch her cheek, but she wouldn't let him. She walked him back to the bed, undressing him as they went, and made love to him amid the warm wrinkles of the sheets Barkley had felt against his own skin. He watched and knew it was how it had to be because the relationship was a prison and an addiction and would always be for her no matter what might follow. And when it was done and Tommy had stopped crying and grown again from child to man, he told her he had to leave. And she didn't try to stop him, kissing him like it was the last time, in front of the dressing table where Barkley could watch in the reflection of the mirror if he chose, and then Tommy left, taking his gun with him. Katie sat quietly at the table as Barkley came out of the closet.

"If you're gonna follow him, you better get a move on." Her eyes were soulless, skyless windows, drained of everything now so all that was left was her. And she'd never been lovelier. Barkley turned to go.

"Bark."

He stopped, knowing better than to look back.

"You gonna kill him?"

"Why would I do that?"

"The girls need a dad, Bark."

He left the room, striding down the hall to the front door. He gambled Tommy was headed for the expressway and picked him up just as he hit the ramp. Barkley stayed four or five car lengths back. His partner was in the left lane, cooking at ninety miles plus. Wherever he was going, Tommy Dillon was in a hurry.

44

They jumped off the expressway in Chelsea, bumping along Williams Street, then Beacham. On one side was a span of railroad tracks. Along the other, a string of truck bays sitting behind high fences and covered in layers of Chelsea grit and Mystic River grime. Barkley tucked behind a delivery truck with a huge head of lettuce and a bunch of baby lettuces painted on its side. He rolled down the window, smelling the sharpness of garlic mingled with the root smell of turnip and wondered where Tommy was headed. They drove for another mile, then the road hooked left, curling past the main entrance to the New England Produce Center. Fifty yards beyond the gate, Tommy eased into a lot. Barkley kept going, slumping down in his seat as he passed a two-story building with a couple of eight-foot-high naked women painted in dancing whitewash along the building's face. It looked like someone had started to paint a third but gave up after half a head, one breast, and an elbow. Barkley drove another quarter mile and turned around, pulling into a gas station and parking so he had a view of the building and lot. Tommy was still behind the wheel, not moving, not doing a thing.

It was another half hour before he got out, hands stuffed in the pockets of his black leather jacket. Barkley looked for the gun on Tommy's hip, but it wasn't there. He hunched his shoulders as he walked, past the twitchy dancing girls and behind the building. Ten minutes later, he appeared on the other side and went back to his car, opening the passenger's-side door and getting in. A semi rolled past, this one featuring a row of smiling tomatoes that looked more like Mexican women than tomatoes, complete with rounded hips, straw hats, and plump red breasts. The semi slowed, then stopped, idling in the middle of the road and blocking Barkley's view. The driver hung there for a couple of minutes, pumping his air brakes a half-dozen times, then rolled again, heading straight for the gates of the produce center. Behind the semi, the front seat of Tommy's car was empty.

Barkley got out and jogged across Beacham, cutting

behind the building and coming up on the other side. He crouched beside a Dumpster fifty feet away and squinted against the glare of the sun, rising to his left and reflecting off the flat glass of the second-floor windows. A bank of clouds drifted overhead, cutting the glare for a moment, and Barkley blinked. The first set of windows at the back of the building looked empty. The second-floor window at the front corner, however, was a different story. Barkley could clearly make out the outline of a person sitting in a chair, staring down at the street below. There was something odd about the figure, the shift of the shoulders, the way the head nodded forward. Barkley threaded his way along the edge of the lot until he was almost directly across from the window. The solitary figure was a dark blotch, not moving as the sun peeked out again, bathing the scene in a shiv of morning light, revealing everything Barkley had thought, everything he'd feared.

He pulled his gun and began to run, past the window, around the corner, and through the front door. To his left was an old staircase winding up to the building's second floor. Barkley took the steps two at a time, bursting through a blue door at the top. The first thing he saw was the back of Tommy Dillon's jacket, faded leather wrapped around a torso rigged to the chair with a couple turns of rope.

"Tommy . . ."

Barkley holstered his gun and took three strides across the room, lifting the body's head and staring into the blank eyes of another dead kid from Harvard. Barkley cut Zeus Sanchez from the chair and laid him out on the floor, checking in vain for a pulse while taking note of the bluish tinge to his lips, damp hair, and absence of any visible wounds. He leaned forward to close the kid's eyes just as Tommy Dillon fired from a doorway. That would have been it, should have been it, Barkley's skull popped like one of the overripe melons sitting at the ass end of the truck bays across the street. But Barkley's lean had saved him, the bullet burying itself in a hunk of drywall an inch or so above the detective's head.

Tommy fired a second and third time, except Barkley was moving now, hugging the wall, giving his partner no angle as he closed the space between them. Tommy Dillon was nothing if not tough, and tough guys could never pass up a fistfight, even when they were giving away six inches plus and over a hundred pounds. So Barkley was ready when his partner charged, roaring like the crazy fuck he was, spitting another bullet and hitting nothing. Barkley caught Tommy's weight easily, tossing him like a sack of Vidalia onions. Tommy hit the wall, spine first, gun clattering across the floor.

Barkley kicked it away and waited as Tommy climbed to his feet. He lunged again, hands curled like hooks, hunting for Barkley's eyes. Barkley stepped to one side and loaded up with a short right, dropping his partner, who hit his head on a radiator and didn't move.

Barkley rubbed his knuckles and swore, picking up the gun and pocketing it. Then he stripped Tommy's leather jacket off Sanchez, grabbed him by the heels, and dragged him into the hall. In an adjoining bathroom was a tub with a puddle of water near the drain. Barkley returned to the front and cuffed Tommy to the chair. Barkley found a second chair and sat in it, watching Tommy not breathe, wondering whether he'd killed the fuck. All things considered, that might be for the best. Just then Tommy groaned and lifted his head. Barkley pointed the throwaway piece his partner had tried to shoot him with at his partner's nose and waited.

"You never could punch for shit," Tommy said.

"How's the head? I'm guessing you got a concussion."

"Like it matters."

Barkley shrugged. "How do you want it?"

"Clean. Fast. Don't wanna be no fucking vegetable, pissing on myself and drooling and all that shit."

"I got you."

"You'll make up something for Katie?"

Barkley nodded, breaking eye contact for the first time.

"I know you was boning her, Bark. Fuck, I knew all along."

"You were broken up."

"Exactly. Hell, I was proud of it, you wanna know the truth."

Barkley didn't wanna know the truth. At least not that kind. "Why Sanchez?"

"Where is he?"

Barkley rolled his eyes toward the hallway.

"He's no fucking saint, B. He set up Fitzsimmons. Whole thing was a setup."

"There was no girl grabbing Sanchez's wallet?"

"I sent one of 'em by to duck her head in the car. He was supposed to raise holy hell and then run down the street after her."

"Why?"

"Sanchez said Fitzsimmons would follow. All-for-one, stand-up guy and all that college crap. Big fucking game."

"But why?"

"They wanted Fitzsimmons in the alley."

"Who's they?"

"Can't go there, B. Might come back on Katie, the girls."

Barkley tried a different tack. "What did they have on Sanchez?"

"What do you think? He liked to gamble. Owed money to the wrong people. At first they were pushing him to shave points on a couple of Harvard games, but the kid never got off the fucking bench. Then this came up. Sanchez thought they just wanted to roll Fitzsimmons, grab his wallet or something."

"How about you?"

"You had it sniffed out from the jump. I never really got off nothing. Dope, booze, betting, all that shit. By the time I got halfway straight, the fuckers owned me, balls and all."

"Let me guess. Trunks full of blow and forever money."

"For Katie and the girls, B. You, too."

"All I gotta do is unlock the cuffs."

They both knew that wasn't gonna happen. Even if there'd been no bodies, Barkley wasn't ever gonna get rich skimming money off drug dealers. Would he have looked the other way if Tommy had broken off his piece? Maybe. But not now. Not with the bodies and all the rest.

"You hired Walter Price," Barkley said.

"Laid it out for him, chapter and fucking verse. Gave him the knife, for Chrissakes. Then he doesn't finish the job."

"So you did?"

Tommy smiled weakly. "I know what you're thinking. We weren't together that night, so I could have been down in the alley and done Fitzsimmons. Didn't happen that way."

"How did it happen?"

"Already told you, B. Not going there."

Barkley nodded in the general direction of the bathroom. "Why kill Sanchez?"

"Fucking guy went off the grid. When he finally surfaced, he wanted to meet. So I had him hole up here."

"He wanted to get paid."

"Worse. Conscience. He's torn up, talking about coming clean. I brought him some dinner. A burger and some fries."

"You put something in the food."

"He went night-night. Woke up at the bottom of the tub."

"And Price?"

"He was a dead man once he took the job."

A truck rumbled past, grinding its gears before accelerating and fading to nothing. Their time was coming to its end now and the air felt sodden and heavy.

"You gonna look after Katie? The girls?"

"You know I will."

Tommy pointed with his chin at his handcuffed wrists. "Take off the watch."

Barkley unclasped the silver-and-turquoise time-piece, weighing it in his hand.

"Pulled that off Juan Doe right after I popped him. Don't look at me like that. Guy was moving product like the rest of 'em. Got his hand caught in the cookie jar and paid the price." Tommy gave a half shrug. "Another one you can pull out of the cold pile."

"That it?"

"I got a file."

"What kind of file?"

"Bunch of stuff on the guy you shot over at Columbia Point."

"Were you gonna blackmail me, Tommy?"

"Insurance, B, that's all. It's in my locker at the bottom, under a pile of shit. Take it, keep it, burn it. Whatever."

"What else?"

"It's not about the Harvard kid. Not anymore."

"I know. It's about Daniel Fitzsimmons."

"You were always too smart for this job. Look after my family, B. And don't fuck this up."

Barkley raised the gun. "Open your mouth. I'll roof it and count to three. You won't feel a thing."

Tommy nodded and closed his eyes, mumbling soft crumbles of long-lost prayers and rocking lightly in the chair. Slowly his mouth yawned open, a string of saliva connecting an upper molar to a lower, all of it soon to be so much rubble. Barkley jammed the gun in deep. There was no shake in Tommy. Barkley gave the prick full marks for that.

"You ready?"

A nod.

"One, two . . ." Barkley pulled on the trigger and the back half of Tommy Dillon's head exploded, whatever was left of his consciousness sliding down the far wall in a slick mess of tissue and bone. Barkley uncuffed his partner's wrists and got up carefully, checking his shoes and clothes for splatter, then standing over the body and taking note of the details. Not that it mattered. The report was already written in his head. Cat wouldn't buy a word, but she'd go along because she was part of it now and that's what people did.

He walked to the door and stopped, taking a final look at Tommy, slumped back in the chair, not a fuck-

ing care in the world. Barkley felt a sudden softening inside, old soil being turned over, something new
pushing up from underneath. It scared him and shook
him and he turned away, shielding himself with the
curve of his shoulder as he reached for the doorknob.
Outside the hallway was empty; a cruel breeze blew up
the stairs.

45

No one said a word on the drive in. Grace sat in front next to Ben. Daniel sat in the back. There was separation between them now, a parting that was as real as it was inevitable. Ben turned on the radio. Grace's gaze found Daniel's as Aerosmith hammered a couple of lines from "Last Child." They pulled into a gas station just off Neponset Avenue. The station had a steady stream of morning traffic at the pumps and a small convenience store next door where folks could get their coffee and the paper. Grace got out almost before the car stopped, swinging a small green pack across her shoulders. Daniel touched Ben's sleeve and caught his eyes before climbing out.

"In another life," Ben said. Daniel nodded and picked up a gym bag. Grace was already walking.

It was a half mile to the underpass with the whistle of the expressway above it, another quarter mile along a road made of black cinders and bordered by a low seawall winding down to the beach. They didn't talk, each content to match the other's stride and let the concussion wash over as a car or truck zipped past. Daniel ducked into the underpass first, leading Grace through the dark passage to a small hut on the other side. M.D.C. used it in the summer to store gear for the nonexistent lifeguards who patrolled the beach.

The hut was locked up tight, but one of the windows was busted out. Daniel shimmied through and opened the door. A second door cut into the opposite wall fed back to the road and down to the beach. They sat on the floor, with the smell of the ocean all around them. Grace opened her pack and took out some bread, a rind of cheese, and an apple. She sliced the apple with a small knife and cut off a piece of cheese, laying it all on a white towel with a blue stripe down the side. They drank water and ate, neither really wanting to start. When they were done eating, Grace folded up the towel and put all the food away. Then she bent her legs and wrapped her arms around her shins, setting her chin on her knees and staring across at him.

"What?" Daniel said.

"What's in there?" Her eyes moved to the gym bag.

"A gift." He pulled the bag over and opened it. Inside were three of Simon's sketches, rolled up one into the other. He'd left behind seven altogether. The first had brought Daniel here—a perfect rendering of the road and beach that ran just past the hut in which they were sitting. The other six laid out the life of Grace Nguyen, decade by decade. One was a colored pencil sketch of a football game, Grace huddled against Ben, the wind staining her cheeks as the crowd rose and roared around them; next, a chalk pastel of her wedding day, she and Ben cradled in a cocoon of flowers and light; an ink drawing, loose-limbed, of a family around a picnic table, splatters of ice cream and frosting, the sun ripening as they smiled in their youth and celebrated their son's fifth birthday; back to pencil, this time thicker lead, stronger strokes, catching the sweep of leaves across a college campus as Grace walked with a young woman who was her echo, the only difference the lines around Grace's eyes and threads of gray in her hair; the fifth was acrylic on paper, a dirt and pebble road spiraling into dusk, a cottage at the end of the path with a single light burning in a window; and the last, just a few elegant lines on vellum, Grace, old, willowy, a shadow walking alone through a graveyard.

"Simon did them," Daniel said, and pushed the sketches toward her. He'd only brought the first three.

The others he'd burned, except for the map. That he'd left for another.

"It's your life," he said. "Or at least part of it . . ."

Her eyes flared in the dim light of the hut. "How many?"

Daniel held up two fingers. "A boy and girl. They'll be strong and they'll be good."

She nodded.

"You'll live long and full with him because he's true and he loves you."

"That's what the drawings tell you?"

"Yes."

"And you believe that?"

It was an impossible question with the cruelest of answers. So Daniel said nothing at all.

She moved closer, inching imperceptibly along the floor then stopping as if she'd hit a wall. "Tell me about this place."

A seagull soared in his head, black eye blinking like the shutter on a camera. Click. A stretch of hard-packed sand. Click. The moving, shifting sea. Click. Daniel's mother, openmouthed for eternity as the front wheel of her upturned car spun slowly.

"This was where my mom died. Flipped her car over the wall outside and down onto the beach. I was with her."

"In the car?"

For a moment he thought he might tell her what he'd never told anyone, about being locked in the trunk of a 1958 Buick, listening as his mother was slowly strangled. Then he looked into Grace's open face and knew that was a conversation that could never be. "The doctors said I should have died. Sometimes I wish I had."

"I don't."

"Good."

"So why are we here?"

"I'm here because I have no choice. You're here for the sketches." He nodded at the drawings. "Take them and go."

"I'll go when I'm ready." Defiance packaged in a sad, sweet, braver-than-hell smile.

"Thank you."

"For what?"

After the accident, Daniel's world consisted of him and Harry. It was a mute existence. Muffled in stone. And then Grace came along.

"Just thank you."

"You think you know how our story ends, Daniel, but maybe you're wrong."

"Maybe."

"Who are you meeting?"

"I'm not sure."

"Let me come with. Together we can . . ."

He reached across and touched a finger to her lips. She kissed it and pressed his palm against the silk of her skin. He remembered their first kiss inside Music City. That was magic and neither of them wanted to ruin everything they had. Not so close to the end. So she got to her feet, tucking a small object in his hand, then packing up the sketches and making her way to the door that led back to the underpass, Ben Jacob, and the rest of her life.

Daniel stayed where he was, listening to the thump of the ocean and the dying hum in his head. He stood up and walked to the door opposite the one Grace had taken, twisting the knob just as the sky cracked, veins of fire sparking and running wild under a purple skin of sky. He stepped out into a freshening wind and watched a squadron of gray birds with white undersides wheel toward the storm that was slashing a path across the harbor. Daniel started to walk, slowly at first, down the black road toward the beach. In his hand was the object Grace had given him—a small, silver tape recorder. Daniel pressed RECORD and slipped it in his pocket.

46

Barkley drove through what was once Chelsea's rag shop district. Three years ago it had burned to the stumps, leaving behind cold piles of rubble and choking layers of ash that whipped and swirled across a graveyard of forgotten blocks. The city had begun its rebuild. Like most things in Chelsea, however, it was gonna take a while. Barkley pulled into a lot and watched a half-dozen cats scatter, taking up residence in the grinning husk of a building where they whisked their tails and licked their paws and watched Barkley's every move. Fair enough.

He pushed back the Camaro's bucket seat and summoned his freshly dead partner. It was the flat pint of Jack, however, that answered. He popped the glovie and pulled it out, catching a whiff of himself in the rearview mirror as the bottle lifted and the whiskey tickled his lower lip. Maybe it was how all cops were after a while. Bottles and secrets stashed everywhere, cheap insurance against a colleague or cold comfort when the dead swam up, asking their questions with their dull eyes and freezer-burn smiles. Why should he be any different?

Barkley cranked down the window and dumped the liquor, tossing the bottle into a field already winking with broken bits of glass. The Fitzsimmons file sat on the floor of the car. He picked it up. His notes on Daniel were clipped to a drawing of the alley where the body was found. The boy had given them Harry's Cambridge apartment as his address, but the two cops who'd driven him to Boston City had dropped him off at an apartment in Kenmore Square. The address was scribbled in pencil on the second page of Barkley's notes. 528 COMMONWEALTH AVE. He copied it down and wondered if anyone had heard the shot that took Tommy Dillon's life. They'd call Katie first thing. She'd play the role of grieving cop widow to a T. Then it would be his turn.

He slouched down low in the seat. The softening he'd felt standing over Tommy's body was still there, except now it had become a yielding, a great breaking up inside. The mottled ice that had encased his soul for so long was cracking, an uncharted river feeding up from somewhere, bubbling to the surface in gushes of warm, white water. Barkley had killed his partner because he'd loved him. That was the truth of it and it filled him to overflow, healing him even as he grieved.

He risked another look in the rearview mirror. She was there, weighing with her quicksilver eyes. He couldn't help but grin and Violet Fitzsimmons grinned back, lips frozen in a half curl, eyes flashing one last time before hardening into a pair of pale blue stones. Barkley whipped his head around, quick as that, only to discover the seat empty. If she'd been there, and she had, she was gone now, flown into his heart, mingled in his blood, one with his spirit. He didn't understand why, couldn't fathom how, but he didn't need to. Like his dead partner said—some things just were.

Barkley cranked the seat forward and started up the car, feeling the steering wheel alive under his hands as he weaved through the tangle of cats and rolled onto the blacktop, nose pointed toward downtown and Kenmore Square.

He pulled up in front of the Rathskeller and slipped a police placard on the dashboard. The two cops who'd driven Daniel said there was only one apartment above the bar. Barkley pushed a buzzer at the top of the steps and got no answer. The door was open so he went inside and walked up a second flight to the front door of the apartment. He knocked once, heavy and hard, then took a step back and put his boot in it, splintering the jamb as the door kicked in.

The place looked deserted. Barkley walked over to a desk by the window and did a quick check of the drawers. Nothing. Toward the rear of the apartment he found a hallway that led to a small bedroom. This was where Daniel had slept. There was no sign of him, no clothes or other belongings, not a stray wrinkle in the sheets because there were no sheets. Still, Barkley knew this was the boy's room. And he'd been here not too long ago.

At the other end of the hall was a pair of doors. The first opened to a room with a large drafting table facing a window. The second door led to another bedroom. Placed neatly on the bed was a pencil sketch. Barkley picked it up and knew two things immediately. Whoever left the drawing had wanted it found. And whoever it was, he'd probably already killed the boy.

47

The rock picked up speed as it fell through time and space, soaking up the blood of an English battlefield, men on horses and in the mud, gutted on steel pikes and trampled underfoot, screaming and biting and raging as each whirled down to his death; a plain at Somme, thousands in trenches, the unburied rotting in the long graves they'd dug for themselves as the smell of gunpowder and mustard gas hung and twitched in the air; black smoke and soot from the chimneys of Auschwitz, Dachau, and Buchenwald. The faces of Holodomor and Armenia. Backward the rock spun, even as it spun forward—Genghis Khan taking a million heads a day; more blood, winding rivers dark and clotted on the sandy floor of the Colosseum; a string of crosses on a hill; Cain striking down Abel while a mother birthed a child. All hung in the balance as the rock turned ever faster, forward now, closer, hurtling through the cathedral of the heavens. Hitler, Stalin, Pol Pot, Amin. A book depository in Dallas, a balcony in Memphis, a hotel kitchen in Los Angeles.

Daniel raised his eyes and saw the rock dropping through the massing thunderheads. It turned once more and landed at his feet. He picked it up. Cold to the touch, it carried no judgment, no memory. Just ahead the wind lifted off the water, parting the storm and revealing a man standing with his back to Daniel, shoulders angled, clad in a long duster coat that hugged his body in slick folds. Daniel walked forward, rain slicing, peeling off his old skin, leaving him naked as a newborn. And then the man turned.

"I'm surprised you picked this place," Nick Toney said.

"I didn't pick anything."

"I followed you and the other two in the car. But I already knew where you were headed." Toney shifted his weight, slipping his hands into the pockets of his coat as the wind skirted the shoreline and the storm circled back out into the harbor. "It's good you didn't bring the girl."

"She's gone."

"I'd give you my word I won't harm her, but what's the point? Better if you just look for yourself."

Daniel frowned.

"You like to look inside people's skulls. Go ahead. See if I intend to kill her."

Daniel licked his lips, tasting pennies at the back of his throat. "You killed my mother."

"My wife."

"You killed my brother."

"My son."

"And now you're here to kill me."

Hungry smile. "We're the only family we have left."

Daniel lifted the rock in his hand and felt his father's mind swing open, sweeping him back into the trunk of the Buick and slamming the lid, fusing the three of them—father, mother, and son—in an endless loop of shame and fear and death. Daniel knew it had always been so and wondered why he'd ever thought it could be different.

"I only met your brother twice," Toney said. "The first time was on the day your mother died. She said she never told him who his dad was, but I didn't believe a word of it. Anyway, I stopped by her place and we made plans for that night. Harry was in the next room, eleven or twelve but already like a little adult, the way he watched me, keeping fucking score. She said she was gonna drop him off with a friend, but the friend didn't want to take you. So your mom said she'd figure something out. Course she didn't and there you were sleeping in the backseat of the car when I showed up that night. But it was Harry who bugged me. What the fuck did he hear? What the fuck did he know? It was like a little bird pecking away inside my skull, fucking pebble in my shoe. Still, it didn't have to be that way."

"Shut up."

"Next time I saw him was on the day he died, at the diner in Harvard Square. Sure as shit there was that jump in his eye. He didn't realize it yet, but he would. I could already see that." Toney grinned. "That's right, Daniel. I can look inside people's heads just like you. Where the fuck you think you got it from?"

"It's called entanglement."

"Call it whatever you want. I could see he'd recognized me at some level and it was just a matter of time before he pieced it together. Once he figured out I was who I was, it was a short step to putting me with her that night. Not a chance I could take."

"So you set up the alley?"

"I hired someone. He hired the black kid who fucked it up."

"And you finished it?"

"Had to. When the cops search my place, they'll find just enough of my blood to write me off as dead. The guy I hired will take the fall for all of it."

"Why did you let me live?"

"You were what? Seven? Eight? Too young to remember shit. Besides, you never saw me in your mom's apartment. Never got a look at me when you went in the trunk."

"How about later?"

"You were tough climbing out of that fucking car. Hell, I was proud of you. Then when I finally met you, I figured you might actually go kill the black kid for me. Seemed fitting. Me killing your brother, you helping clean up the mess. So I gave you a nudge. Fed you the address in the Bury and waited."

"Maybe I'm not the killer you thought I was."

"You're worse."

Daniel felt his fingers tighten and the rock start to hum in his hand. His father could feel it, too.

"Your mother was a cunt, Daniel. Great piece of ass, but once she got her hooks in, pure fucking cunt." Toney cocked his head. "You feeling it yet? Want to have a go at the old man? Here, let me help." He dropped to his knees in the wet sand and made furrows with his fingers. Then he put the slurry to his nose and inhaled, closing his eyes and tipping his face to the sky. "Go ahead, son. Close the circle."

Daniel raised the rock over his head and became one with it. Perfect symmetry, perfect balance. Then he brought it down to his side and dropped it on the beach.

One eye popped open. "No, huh?" Toney climbed to his feet and picked up the rock, weighing it in his hand before hurling it into the surf, where the sea sucked it under. Daniel felt his father's DNA wrapped inside his, and wrapped inside that, rotting at the core of himself, the memory of his mother and all he'd wished he could have done for her, for Harry. He turned off the recorder in his pocket.

"Don't put my body in the water."

His father pulled a pistol from under his coat, black and huge and gleaming with grease in the winking eye of the storm. He touched it to Daniel's forehead as Daniel sank to his knees and closed his eyes, waiting for the flat bang that would mark his passage under the archway we all must pass through on our way to whatever waited beyond. When it came, Daniel felt nothing, except the release of his soul and the meaty thump of flesh against earth. He opened his eyes to see his father staring back at him, loose-jawed, dark blood pooling and soaking into the hungry sand from the back of a blown-out skull. Simon stepped around Daniel, picking up Toney's gun and taking a quick look at his handiwork. Then he came back, crouching between the body and Daniel, touching his cheek.

"You all right?"

Daniel nodded. Simon helped him to his feet and they walked a few yards, sitting on the edge of the seawall that marked the beginning of the road that led up to the hut. Daniel felt a shiver in the air and stared at his father's body, still sprawled where it fell. "I wanted to kill him, but it wasn't in me."

"You had the rock in your hand and chose to drop it. You knelt and pressed your head to the muzzle. That changes everything."

"He's still dead."

"And you think it's murder?"

"That's what the police will tell you."

"Reality has its own plasticity, Daniel. Warm, alive, capable of being molded and shaped."

"This isn't one of your sketches. And a bullet to the head isn't some string of numbers on a blackboard."

Simon pulled out Toney's gun and another, carrying both down to the water and throwing them in. He walked back slowly, taking a seat across from Daniel, positioning himself so he was blocking any view of the body. "What is it you'd like to know?"

"Nothing. Just leave me alone."

Simon picked up a stick and began to draw in the sand. "Remember I told you about entanglement, that it works temporally as well as spatially, that all measures of yourself exist at the same time, in the same space."

Daniel fixed on the swell of the sea and the waves, one after another, covering everything that came before.

"This planet will quickly become a smaller place, the gap between the few that have and the billions that don't growing wider and wider. Hatred will see its opportunity, stoking the fires while religion takes hold, evil, black, divisive religion, the worst kind, carried like a virus on the back of the technology we've spoken about.

"Our leaders will be leaderless, old wounds of race reopening and bleeding all over again. Money and greed will hold sway, everyone grabbing what they can as the politics of hatred spur us forward through an ever-telescoping window of time. Until finally it all falls apart, the center collapsing and the rest with it."

Simon tossed the stick away. Daniel glanced down at a tangle of lines that looked like two towers.

"I'm more or less a messenger," Simon said. "A harbinger of what's to be. Or what might be."

"And me?"

"You're connective tissue, a way for many to be one. But only if you're free."

"Free from what?"

"You lived her death, Daniel. Right here on this beach. You looked in her eyes and stroked her face and sobbed and prayed and watched your mother choke on her own blood. And then you walked away, mourning as only a child can mourn, but knowing also, in the quietest rooms of your soul, that you were rid of her. Rid of the shame you'd felt for how she lived. Rid of her pain and her suffering. Her anxiety and her touch. Her needs, her limitations, her shackles, her sores, her all-consuming fears. And even deeper, in a room you never visit, a room you might not even know exists, you were happy. No more watching as 'dates' came and went, no more listening while you lay in your bed. No more trying, desperately trying, to make it all smooth, to fix what was so unfair, so far beyond the reach of a child. And when the darkness came after the crash, you welcomed that. And when you awoke, it was just you and Harry."

"Harry's dead."

"You said it yourself. Your brother was that rarest of things, pure love. His heart beats within you now. As does your mother's." Simon pointed a finger back toward the unseen body. "There's only ever been two choices, Daniel. Bury yourself deeper or dig your way out."

"How? By killing him?"

"By deciding not to."

"He was my father."

"And mine as well." Simon winked and in that wink Daniel saw himself, twenty years in the future, fifty years in the past, a hundred years forward and another hundred back and he knew he didn't understand, but knew he didn't need to. The circle never explained itself. It just was.

Simon wiped the sand smooth with his foot. He was wearing a pair of Tiger racing flats, identical to Daniel's right down to the yellow laces, but battered and torn from decades of use.

"Bad sneakers?" Daniel said.

"But great for a run." Simon grinned and opened his palm. Daniel traced the creases there. His own. Flesh and blood. Bone and sinew. Real and not. Then he watched as Simon went softly, stepping carefully in the footprints he'd already made. A gray wave crested, blowing a spray of salt and brine across Daniel's vision as it crashed ashore. When he wiped his eyes, the beach was empty, sea and sky woven into a seamless, stillborn haze. A gull cried, dipping its wings as it skimmed the edge of the water before flicking away.

High up on the ridge, a car with a blue bubble on its roof rolled into view. A black man got out and slammed the door, the sound echoing in the well where water met land. Daniel watched as the detective named Barkley made his way down the road of cinders to where Daniel sat. The detective stopped at the body, crouching over it in much the same way he'd crouched over Harry in the alley, like a predator picking over the bones of his latest meal. Daniel crept forward as Barkley turned.

"Stay there, son." The detective had a radio in his hand and was calling for an ambulance. Daniel shuffled to his left, suddenly anxious for a last look at his father. Nick Toney was sitting up, shaking his head and rubbing his neck. No splintered skull, no blood, no corpse. Toney was alive. Groggy, but very much alive. Daniel slumped to the sand as Barkley's radio crackled and the sun split a mass of thunderheads, bathing the three of them in a slant of eternal, eclipsing light.

48

Mike Ripp drew on his cigarette and exhaled, smoke boiling up into the circle of a fan that beat overhead. "Walk me through the beach again."

Barkley grimaced. They'd been at it most of the day. Cat McShane had come in for the last half hour. Otherwise, just Barkley and the assistant DA for Suffolk County. No one else wanted any part of the sad tale they were cooking up. Who the fuck could blame 'em?

"I went through it three times, Ripper. You got all the statements. Nothing's gonna change."

"Once I sign off, it's my ass, too. Correct?"

Barkley nodded.

"All right, then. Give it to me again. Just the bare bones." Ripp was like that. Nice guy, but a survivor. Smart, tough, with a keen understanding of the slushy

world and shitbag people homicide investigators dealt
with on a daily basis. Ripp would work with you on the
facts. But if things went south and it was you or him,
you'd best believe it was gonna be you.

"I got out of the car and saw the two of them on the
beach."

"Daniel Fitzsimmons and the guy we're calling his
father?"

Barkley nodded. "Daniel was sitting on the seawall. Toney was lying on his side. I marked it all up
on one of the maps." Barkley pointed vaguely toward a
wreck of files strewn across the conference table. Ripp
didn't give a fuck about Barkley's drawings and kept
his hound-dog, smoke-filled prosecutor's eyes fixed on
the detective.

"Toney wasn't moving when you first saw him?"

"Not until I got closer."

"How close?"

"Had the gun out and was maybe ten feet away when
he first moved. I holstered my piece, checked his vitals,
and helped him to a sitting position."

"Where was the boy?"

"Behind me. Starts to come closer and I tell him to
stay where he is. He sees Toney and passes out."

"Passes out?"

"Falls to his knees, then down for the count. Backup

comes in and goes to work on him. I cuff Toney and we stick them both in ambulances."

"Why cuff Toney?"

"At that point I had reason to suspect him in at least two murders. Turns out I was right."

Ripp took another drag and crushed out his cigarette, blinking against the smoke and carefully pushing away the full ashtray like he wanted nothing to do with it and how the fuck did it get there in the first place.

"Beach doesn't matter," Barkley said. "We got the confession."

"Famous last words, fucko. Give me the boy's story again."

"He insisted Toney was dead."

"Didn't he see him alive? Ten fucking feet away?"

"That's why he fainted. Swore he watched Toney get popped in the head."

"And the boy claims the gun was fired by this mysterious Simon?"

"Simon Lane. Daniel says he rented a room from him. Claims Simon was down on the beach and shot Toney at point-blank range."

"Because Toney was gonna shoot Daniel?"

"That's what the boy said, yes."

"And we found no guns anywhere, on anybody?"

Barkley shook his head.

"Nor did we find any Simon?"

"Had both ends of the beach blocked off, as well as the road. If anyone was there, we would have picked him up."

Ripp leaned back, ham hands locked behind his head, heft of his belly testing the springs in his chair. "Maybe he went for a swim? Maybe we should be looking for him at the bottom of the harbor? What do ya think?" The assistant DA chuckled, a luxuriously smoky sound that jiggled his cheeks and punched a hole in the balloon that was Barkley's carefully constructed tale. "Sorry, Bark. If I don't laugh at some of this shit, I might as well take a gun and blow my own fucking brains out."

Cat McShane cleared her throat. "I think someone should offer some context for the boy."

Ripp raised an eyebrow. "You an expert in this area?"

"No, but I am a doctor. And I've talked at length to the mental health professionals who interviewed Daniel. You have their reports. They're all in agreement."

"I'm listening."

"The boy saw his mother killed when he was a child.

Years later he sees his brother murdered. He's admitted to not taking his meds and, as a result, suffered a series of hallucinations."

"You mean his stories about the animals?" Ripp said.

"Yes. He's experienced a number of breaks with reality over the past month or so, culminating with what he thinks he saw on the beach. As far as he's concerned, that *is* his reality."

"And you think I think he's lying?"

"I just want to provide some context."

"Thank you, Doctor." Ripp glanced at Barkley.

"There's no record of a Simon Lane ever teaching at Harvard," the detective said. "And the room Daniel claims to have rented from him has been vacant for more than a year. We think the kid must have been squatting in there. Brought in some furniture, whole fucking nine yards."

"So, what you're telling me, what you're both telling me, is there's no way, six months from now, after we put this thing to bed and my name's all over it, there's no fucking way asshole Simon Lane is gonna pop up with some fucked-up story about who knows what?"

"I don't see it, Mike."

Ripp glanced at Cat.

"He lives in Daniel's head. Nowhere else."

The prosecutor grunted and rubbed his lower lip

with his thumb. Barkley had seen him do the same thing in the courtroom, usually as a signal to the jury that he was about to shift gears.

"Let's say I accept your version for the moment. Explain to me what did happen to Toney. EMTs found a small puncture wound on his neck. Fast-acting barbiturate in his system. Are we saying the kid did that?"

"We searched his person," Barkley said. "Searched the beach. No evidence of a syringe, needle. Nothing."

"He was seeing a doctor every other week. Not a stretch to think he might have lifted something."

"Like I said, we found nothing on the beach."

"What does Toney say?"

"He and Daniel were talking. And then the world went black. Says Daniel's hands were empty."

"Why does Toney say he was down there?"

"Just wanted to talk to his son."

"And now?"

"Doesn't want anything to do with the kid. Says he's haunted."

"Haunted?"

"That's what he says."

"Fucking beautiful." Ripp did a little dance in his chair, using his feet to pull himself closer to the table, then picking up a set of papers and weighing them in his hand. "Asshole confessed to killing Violet Fitzsimmons in '68, as well as his son, Harry. Correct?"

"He had no choice."

"Because of the tape recorder Daniel had in his pocket?"

"It cuts in and out, but there's plenty there. And everything Toney said on the tape fits with the case we were developing."

"You and your partner?"

"Yes."

Ripp dropped the confession back onto the table. "Let's talk about that for a minute."

This was what the meeting was really about. The dead cop in the room and how it was gonna play.

"You and Dillon suspected Toney of running a drug operation out of the Combat Zone?"

"We didn't have all the pieces, but that was the idea."

"And Dillon was working on one of Toney's alleged accomplices. The other Harvard kid, Sanchez."

"Tommy tracked Sanchez to Chelsea while I went after Toney."

"That's how you two divvied up the case?"

"Tommy had the address in Chelsea. Must have walked in on them drowning Sanchez."

"Them?"

"We believe Sanchez was getting cold feet and thinking about going to the police. Toney sent someone over to kill him."

"Toney admit that?"

"He's not gonna cop to anything that's not on the tape. What we know for sure is there was a shoot-out and Tommy got hit."

"Five times?" Ripp held up five accusing fingers and glanced at Cat for confirmation.

"Three in the chest. One in the arm, one in the head. It's all in my report."

"Yeah, well, that's a hell of a good thing, Doc, since no one from my office actually got a look at Dillon's body."

"My mistake," Barkley said. "Tommy's wife wanted the body cremated. I thought we had everything we needed and gave the go-ahead."

"Seems like your partner should be in line for some kind of medal."

"You want to recommend that, Mike?"

"I want to be up in Vermont, in some fucking lodge, skiing all day and sitting by the fire at night, getting shitty on good booze and thinking about all the assholes down here, stuck in meetings discussing fucked-up cases like this one with lying sack-of-shit detectives. But that's not you, right, Bark?"

"Tommy had two little girls. We'd like to make sure they get taken care of."

"So give 'em the benny package and fuck the medal is what you're saying."

"Fuck it all, Counselor. Or not. Your call."

Ripp wrinkled his nose at all the bad smells they'd laid out on the table and flipped a hand like he was sweeping out the trash. "Toney takes the fall on the two. Put the rest of it to bed."

Barkley and Cat got up as one, heads down, eyes averted, anxious for the deed to be done and it all to be gone. Ripp, however, wasn't finished.

"One more thing, Detective. Daniel Fitzsimmons."

"What about him?"

"You left out a few details he offered up on Simon Lane."

"Most of that was just psychobabble . . ."

"Simon Lane wasn't just a guy he rented a room from. According to Daniel, Lane was, is, some future version of himself."

"Not exactly a future version," Cat said. "Daniel believes it all runs simultaneously."

"I don't know what the fuck that means, Doc, and, more important, I don't care. The bottom line is this kid thinks Lane's real and that he and Lane are actually the same fucking person. Correct?"

"Correct," Barkley said.

"So the kid's soft as puppy shit."

Barkley opened his mouth to respond when Cat jumped in. "He just needs to stay on his meds. Along with the counseling."

Ripp pulled out a loose sheet of paper. "You ever think about that name, Doc?"

"Excuse me?"

"Simon Lane." Ripp scribbled off a couple of lines and turned the sheet around so Cat could read it.

S-I-M-O-N L-A-N-E

F-I-T-Z-S-I-M-M-O-N-S D-A-N-I-E-L

"It's an anagram for Daniel Fitzsimmons," Ripp said. "Last name becomes first, first becomes last."

"Actually, it's an imperfect anagram, Counselor. Several letters missing in both names."

"So you think it's a coincidence?"

Cat shrugged and pushed the paper across to Barkley, who glanced at it and kicked it back to Ripp.

"What do you want, Mike?"

"Only one question that matters."

"Yeah?"

"Do we need to worry about him?"

49

He could feel their weight in the empty apartment—cops, detectives, evidence techs, all fingers and flashbulbs, notebooks and eye rolls, dusting, measuring, conjecturing. They'd all been looking for some trace of Simon Lane. And finding nothing. Daniel cracked a window and took a seat at the desk. They'd removed every stick of furniture in the apartment except the desk. Barkley told him it was just too big to get through the door. No one could figure out how it had gotten there in the first place. Daniel brushed his hand across the handle on one of the drawers. It was smeared with fingerprint powder and he felt the silk rub between his fingertips. The man who owned the apartment was named Stephen Maas. He was eighty-eight, lived in California, and had never heard of

Simon Lane. As far as Maas was concerned, the flat was empty. Had been empty for a year and a half. How about Harvard? No professor named Simon Lane. No student. Not even a onetime visitor on a sign-in sheet. Ghosts. Crickets. The wind in the trees. Or so the police said.

Daniel wandered down the hall to his old room and sat cross-legged on the floor. At the end of the day, what could they really charge him with? Being delusional? Maybe. But he hadn't committed any real crime. And even if he had, Barkley knew better. Daniel felt the bottle of pills in his pocket. All new meds. All new doctors. These ones kept track. Appointments, three times a week. Monthly physicals. Blood work. They'd watch him. Keep his brain on a nice, low simmer. Maybe he'd take up drawing. Wouldn't that be fun? Someone smiled in the corner of the room, long teeth and gums, gone as quickly as Daniel could turn his head. No matter.

He walked out to the main room and sat again at the desk. Barkley had given him an hour alone. They were probably watching through the windows. Of course they were. He thought about Grace. She'd sworn up and down to the police that Simon Lane existed, except she'd never actually met him. Closest she came was a silhouette in a window, a shadow smoking a pipe on a street corner. And what was that? What was anything?

Daniel pulled the pills from his pocket and shook out a couple, swallowing them dry as his eyes watered and his head fuzzed. He'd keep his distance from Grace. Like any respectable madman would. All in all, he was lucky to have the time he'd had. Friendships. Memories. He'd parcel them out like crumbs in the hungry days and years and decades ahead. He and Simon, alive inside his skull if nowhere else.

Daniel closed his eyes and got down to business. His mind was a river, running wild and fast, swelling against the crumbling banks of reality. Daniel dove into the flow, down into the cracks and seams where nothing lived but noise so loud it was quiet. He searched until he found the door and a passageway, wide and dry and rising. Daniel walked until he climbed, a set of stone steps cut into a wall and a second door that opened to the apartment and the same room where he sat. Simon lived in the iron grip of a shadow, the smile Daniel had glimpsed in his bedroom now attached to its owner. Simon beckoned and Daniel drifted closer. The smell of berries was strong, Simon's tobacco pouch open on the desk and oozing fragrance. He pulled out a pinch with one hand, fingers of the other disappearing down the side of the desk and reappearing with his precious pipe. Simon filled it carefully, tamping down the bowl then striking a wooden match as flesh burned and reality stripped itself to its bones before collapsing in a pile of ash.

Daniel opened his eyes. He was standing now, in the same spot where Simon had stood. Daniel's hand rested on the same edge, his fingers crawling of their own accord across the same two feet of desk before slipping down the side. Daniel felt a seam in the wood. He should have been astonished but wasn't. The seam led to a small depression. Daniel sensed the tension of a spring underneath and pressed. A flat ledge flipped open. On it was the pipe. Daniel picked it up and put it to his nose, tasting berries again on his tongue. He turned the pipe upside down and found the Dunhill markings and the number "4" Simon had shown him on that first day.

Daniel sat down, hands moving over the pipe as he pondered. Barkley had questioned him closely about the puncture mark they'd found on Nick Toney's neck. At one point, they'd even searched him. Daniel had nothing for them except the story of the gun that never existed, a murder that never happened, and a dead man who was his father and still very much alive. The pipe separated in his hands, stem twisting free of the bowl and a small slip of parchment sliding out. Daniel felt his heart in his fingertips, forty-five beats a minute, as he unrolled the tinder-dry paper. Three tiny darts, razor-sharp and gleaming silver, dropped into the palm of his hand. He slid one into the hollowed-out stem, put the stem to his lips and blew. The dart popped out on a burp of air, streaking across five feet and burying itself in the wall. Daniel couldn't help but grin and pulled the dart, putting it, along with the other two, back in the stem and reassembling the pipe. Maybe Simon had left the Dunhill for Daniel. Maybe Daniel had left it for himself. Maybe it was a distinction without a difference. Two beings entangled, one with the other, collapsing time, collapsing space, collapsing reality until they were one. Hadn't that been the point all along?

Daniel stuck the pipe in his pocket as Aerosmith's "Walk This Way" strutted in off the street. He let the music wash over him and felt the sun fragile on his face. A breeze tickled the back of his neck. It was the cat, fur shimmering a hundred shades of silver as he leaped through a timeless throw of light and landed neatly in the middle of the room. Daniel made a small motion with his hand and the cat orbited closer, marking out a slow, wide circle before jumping onto the desk and wrapping himself in a tight ball. Daniel ran his fingers across the animal's knotted flank and listened to his purr as the light outside flickered and failed. Then Daniel laid his head down and the two slept as one. When he awoke, it was night and the fireplace was lit. Harry sat on the floor nearby.

"I love you most," he said.

Daniel shook his head. "I love you most."

Harry shrugged and they both laughed. Daniel got up and took a seat beside his older brother. They talked as the stars chased themselves across the sky and the moon doused itself in the sun. And their conversation knew no beginning and had no end.

Notes and Acknowledgments

I f you're a nonscientist like me and would like to learn more about the world of quantum mechanics, Brian Greene's *The Elegant Universe* is a great place to start. For the evolving relationship between quantum physics and spirituality, I would suggest *The Universe in a Single Atom* by the Dalai Lama; *The Divine Dance* by Franciscan priest and spiritual leader Richard Rohr; and *The Quantum and the Lotus*, a conversation between Matthieu Ricard, a molecular biologist and Buddhist monk, and Trinh Thuan, an astrophysicist at Caltech. For a deeper dive, treat yourself to anything by Pema Chödrön, Eckhart Tolle, Thomas Merton, and any number of books by Father Rohr, who also runs the Center for Action and Contemplation in Albuquerque, New Mexico. All of these writers provided critical background and context for this novel. All are profound thinkers and essential voices in this most uncertain of times.

And then there's Daniel's shape-shifting. My favorite Latin poet was (and is) Ovid. My favorite poem? A tie between *The Iliad* and *Metamorphoses*. If you haven't read the latter, pick it up. It's fun and funny. Timeless and timely. It's a study in the human psyche—how we hide from the world, and particularly from ourselves.

The murder of Harry Fitzsimmons, while entirely an account of fiction, was inspired, in part, by the 1976 murder of Andy Puopolo in Boston's Combat Zone. I won't go into all the details of the actual crime, but Andy's tragic passing had a big impact on the city and still resonates to this day. At the time of his death, I was a student at Boston Latin School, where Andy had graduated four years earlier. I didn't know Andy, but I remember the pall it cast over the school. For many of us, Andy represented the future in all its infinite possibility. He was also a sudden reminder of how fragile life can be and how everything can (and does) change in a moment. As I said, Harry's death is pure fiction. None of the details or characters in the novel are drawn from or based on anything in real life. At the end of the day, however, I'd like to think there's a little bit of Andy in Harry. A little bit of the eternal nature of hope, the pristine wonder of youth, and the immutable power of love. If we can reflect on those simple principles and make them part of our DNA, that's probably a pretty good thing.

Thanks to my editor, Zach Wagman, and everyone at Ecco for believing in this book. Thanks to my agent, David Gernert, and to Garnett Kilberg Cohen for her early read and wonderful editorial eye. Thanks to all the independent booksellers who are responsible for getting my novels, as well as those of other writers, into the hands of countless readers. And, of course, thanks to you, the reader. As always, it's a privilege and an honor.

Thanks, finally, to my family and friends, and especially to my wife, Mary Frances. Love you.

About the Author

Michael Harvey is the author of seven previous novels, including *Brighton* and *The Chicago Way*. He's also a journalist and documentarian whose work has won multiple news Emmys, two Primetime Emmy nominations, and an Academy Award nomination. Raised in Boston, he now lives in Chicago.